# THEIR LOST DAUGHTERS

A gripping crime thriller with a huge twist

# JOY ELLIS

Published 2017 by Joffe Books, London.

www.joffebooks.com

© Joy Ellis

ISBN- 978-1-912106-55-4

I was so close to giving up. So, thank you, Jasper, for believing in me and for giving me the opportunity to do what I love.

And thank you, Anne. Your amazing paragraph-pruning and word-weeding skills turn an overgrown flower bed into a thing of beauty!

# CHAPTER ONE

For a second Jackman lay still. Then his eyes flew open and he grabbed his mobile phone from the bedside table. 'Rowan Jackman.'

'It's Sergeant Danny Page here, Inspector. Sorry for the early call, but we've just received a report of a body on the beach over at Dawnsmere.'

Jackman gritted his teeth. His present investigation involved a missing teenager. 'A body, Sergeant?'

There was the slightest pause. 'Yes, sir, and I'm afraid it *is* a young woman, although that's all we know until someone can get out there. I've got two cars responding, but I'm assuming you would like to deal with this?'

Jackman was already out of bed. 'I'm on my way, Sergeant. Would you please alert DS Evans for me and ask her to meet me at the scene? And you'd better get the pathologist and some SOCOs down there as well.'

'Consider it done, sir.'

His shower could wait. Jackman threw open his wardrobe and grabbed a pair of chinos, a warm shirt and a thick sweater. The coast was bitterly cold at this time of the year, especially just before dawn. He pulled them on, found a pair of hiking socks and ran down the wooden staircase and into the hall. He chose walking boots from the rack by the door, checked that he had his warrant card, mobile and wallet all safe in his pocket, and took his old Barbour wax jacket from the hook and pulled it on.

He locked the door to his converted mill-house and ran across the drive to where his car was parked beneath a covered gazebo. He rarely used his garage, preferring the option of a quick getaway. Like now.

\* \* \*

First light was a weak, watery and dismal affair, but today the chilly grey dawn was probably more appropriate than one of Mother Nature's more dazzling displays. Jackman gazed around. For a moment or two he tried not to look at the very thing he had come there for.

It would have been generous to call it a beach. Dawnsmere was a bleak spot, a narrow strip of sand and dunes sandwiched between the wild marsh and the cold, uninviting waters of the Wash. But even so, it had a strange beauty, even if that beauty was lonely and austere. The thing that always struck Jackman about these long stretches of fenland coastline was the absence of almost any indication of humanity. There were no colourful beach huts, no deckchairs, no cafés and no amusements, just the landscape and the sea. Right now, if you chose to ignore the presence of the police and their sad find, it looked almost primeval. Gathering himself, Jackman silently ordered his inner philosopher to retreat to a safe distance, and called upon the seasoned policeman to step forward and take charge.

The dead girl lay on her side, her bloated face half buried in the wet, muddy sand. Her clothes clung to her in rags and her feet were bare. Jackman stared at the slender narrow ankles and saw scratches and cuts etched deep into the pale skin. He looked closer and frowned. There were bruises too, lots of them.

He tried not to get ahead of himself. Foul play was always his first thought, but submersion in water could cause massive injuries to the body. He knew only too well that the tides could buffet a frail human against rocks and debris, inflicting all manner of trauma. Jackman reached into his jacket pocket and removed a photograph. The picture showed a slim youngster with shoulder-length light brown hair. A girl with laughing green eyes, a narrow, delicate nose and a wide toothy smile. He stared back down at the lifeless tangle of clothes and unnaturally white flesh and shook his head. It could be Shauna Kelly, but it would take more than a happy snap to identify her. He drew in a long sigh. Their missing girl had no tattoos, scars or other identifying marks, so they would have to resort to dental records, unless one of the distraught parents insisted on seeing her. Frankly, Jackman would walk over hot coals to prevent that happening.

He looked at the body, trying to make some kind of positive connection with the smiling girl in the photo, but apart from similar length hair, there was nothing.

'Wicked waste. Poor little kid.' A uniformed officer was standing a little way away, viciously stabbing the toe of his boot over and over into the wet sand.

Jackman recognised the man as being one of the mess-room jokers, a right laugh-a-minute maestro under normal conditions.

He looked at Jackman and hung his head. 'Sorry, sir. Got three girls of my own.'

Jackman threw him an understanding smile, followed by a lifeline. 'Do me a favour, Constable? Go and see whether DS Evans has arrived yet.'

The constable nodded, straightened up and loped away from the scene.

Left alone with the girl, Jackman wondered, not for the first time, how they coped with so much death. Dead adults were bad enough, babies were beyond devastating, and children tore his heart out, but teenagers affected him in a different way altogether. There seemed to be so much loss attached to juveniles. They had *nearly* made it. *Almost* become what they were intended to be. All that potential was suddenly gone, their untapped talents wiped out in the blink of an eye and their young dreams stolen forever.

The light breeze off the sea rippled the shallow puddles of water that surrounded the girl, making her sodden clothes move slightly. Just for a moment, in the poor light, she seemed to be alive.

Jackman shivered, and then voices echoed across the narrow dune-edged beach and dragged him away from his sombre thoughts.

DS Marie Evans was hurrying towards him, accompanied by the county's forensic pathologist, Professor Rory Wilkinson. Jackman was glad that the man himself had turned out this morning and not delegated the task to another. Wilkinson was an oddball, but much better than his predecessor. Jackman had always struggled with Arthur Jacobs. He knew that the old pathologist was competent, and indeed very clever, but Jackman found him cold and spiritless, and working with him was hard going. Rory Wilkinson was at the other end of the spectrum, and once Jackman had seen past the high camp humour, he realised that Saltern-le-Fen was very lucky to have him.

Not that there would be much in the way of banter today.

Marie arrived a few steps ahead of the pathologist. She must have left home as swiftly as he had, but her motorcycle leathers concealed the evidence. She looked wide awake. He supposed that riding a big Suzuki V-Strom 650cc bike in the cold of the early morning would probably do that.

'Is it her?' she breathed.

He shrugged. 'Take a look for yourself. I'm not sure.' He turned to Wilkinson and nodded a greeting. 'Glad you're the one to turn out this morning, Rory. By the look of it, I'm really going to need your help and expertise.'

'Oh, but you *always* need my help, Inspector. And you might be happy that I'm freezing my bollocks off on the edge of the North Sea at five in the morning, but I'm not so sure. My fluffy duvet is still calling out to me.'

Rory stepped towards the dead girl and dropped the act immediately. 'The jungle drums tell me that she may belong to one of our people?'

Jackman noticed the softness to his tone. 'It could be. We have been looking for a runaway for the last three days. Shauna Kelly, fourteen-year-old daughter of Liz Kelly, a civilian who works in the control room.'

'The age is probably similar,' murmured the pathologist, kneeling down and gently inspecting his new charge. 'But I'll have to get her back to the morgue before I can tell you anything constructive.' He stood up and pushed his wire-rimmed glasses further up onto the bridge of his nose.

'And I'm afraid I have to warn you that it is not easy with these particular cases. Sometimes it's almost impossible to determine the manner of death from a post-mortem. Maybe the lungs and the sinuses will turn up something, but our best bet will be a complete toxicological analysis. So don't rush me, okay? I promise to do my best and I'm fully aware it's high priority.' He beckoned to a SOCO who was waiting tentatively near the dunes.

'Time to shine, my friend. I want photographs and a very careful examination.' He turned back to Jackman. 'We'll get her shipped out ASAP. It's the best I can do. And I hate to say this, but right now I know little more than you. The poor kid is dead, and it didn't happen in the last few hours. She's been in the water for quite a while.' He drew in a whistling breath and stared hard at Jackman. 'Sorry, but I'm passing the buck back to you, DI Jackman.

You need to discover the circumstances behind this girl's death, and then we'll try to tie it in with my findings.'

'I need to know who she is before I can do that,' said Jackman grimly.

'Well, there are two simple ways that you can either confirm or eliminate Shauna Kelly. Bring in the next of kin to identify her, or failing that, wait for the dental records report.' He gave them a rather sad smile. 'And I'm pretty sure which of the two options you guys will go for.' He picked up his bag.

'And now, as I have no wish to hear what I'm sure will be a simply divine dawn chorus, I'm going to get back and make arrangements for this poor girl.'

Jackman and Marie watched him stride back up the beach.

'What they call an acquired taste, I believe.' Marie grinned.

'I've acquired it already. He's good. In fact, he's one of the best I've come across.'

'Agreed.'

They walked to a quiet spot further up the beach, a little way away from the blue lights and the gathering uniforms. Jackman sat on a low stone wall that edged the dunes.

'What do you know about the tides along this stretch, Marie?' Jackman asked.

She sucked on her bottom lip. 'Not much, but I know a man who does. Jack Archer, a real web-foot if ever there was one. He lived way out on the marsh for most of his life. His dad and granddad were eel-catchers. Now he's in an old people's place just outside your village. Social Services moved him off the marsh when he took ill and there was no one to look after him. He knows these fens better than anyone.'

'Go see him, Marie. Tell him the exact spot where the girl washed up, and ask him if he could give us an idea of what part of the coast she went in from. If he knows the area that well, he might be able to help us.'

'Okay. He's in his eighties, but I reckon he'll still be an early riser. I'll grab a shower, then go round and see him as soon as it's properly light.'

Jackman took in the sight of the liquid gold sun breaking through the grey marbled sky and reflecting across the quicksilver waters of the Wash. 'Look at that,' he said softly. 'This place is something else, isn't it? If it weren't for that poor kid lying on the beach, it would be magical.'

'It's still magical,' said Marie softly. 'And let's consider it a blessing that we have her back from the deep, *whoever* she is.'

Jackman took one last glance back to the beach and was glad to see that the girl was no longer visible. A group of police and scene-of-crime officers were working around her now. Soon she would be lifted up from the cold, wet sand and taken back to Rory's mortuary, where hopefully she would see fit to give up her secrets to the one man who was able to hear.

# CHAPTER TWO

Jackman was up to his neck in reports when Marie got back from seeing Jack Archer. 'Waste of time?' he queried, noting her unusually serious expression.

'No, far from it. He's a great old guy. Really helpful.' Marie placed two coffees on his desk, and pushed the office door closed.

'So why the mardy face?'

'Oh nothing, sir. It's just the thought of that lovely young girl dying in that manner.'

Jackman closed the file that he was working on and pointed to a chair. 'Sit.' He helped himself to one of the coffees and a handful of sugar sachets. As he tore open the tiny packets and shook them into his drink, he looked at her thoughtfully. Marie was a handsome woman. She was tall with long, rich brunette hair and an upright stance that still turned heads at forty-six years old. She had an Amazonian quality that she used to full advantage with both villains and coppers alike. The consensus of opinion in the mess room was "Don't mess with Super Mario!" Jackman knew a different side of Marie, compassionate and gentle, but very, very astute. He trusted her opinions and her judgements. Their upbringing and backgrounds could not be more different, but they shared a deep love for their chosen career, and although they reached their conclusions by different paths, they usually agreed in the end.

'Why has this one hit you so hard, my friend? You've seen more than your fair share of deaths.'

Marie shrugged. 'My very first case was a drowning. Another youngster, not much different to the lass this morning. We never managed to identify her.' She pushed her hair back over her shoulder and reached for her coffee. 'I always felt we let her and her family down. We never traced them and no one came forward, but she must have a family somewhere. It seemed so awful that she was never taken home to rest.'

'We can't help them all, Marie. We do our best, but sometimes the odds are stacked against us.'

'Do you think that girl was Shauna Kelly?'

'My gut feeling says yes. But I don't want to go down that route until we get those dental records back.'

Marie nodded and sipped her coffee. 'No matter who she is, we have to find out exactly what happened to her, and if it was no accident . . .' She left the sentence unfinished.

'Oh yes. But tell me what your ancient local had to say about those tides.'

Marie placed a dog-eared map of the coastline on his desk and smoothed it out. 'Jack Archer thinks that the girl went into the water around this area here.' She tapped the map. 'Allenby Creek. The tides, the currents and the recent light winds all make this the most likely spot, unless she fell from a boat. We just have to hope that isn't the case.'

'Allenby Creek? That's a remote spot, isn't it?'

Marie stared at the map. 'It's on the borders of our patch and Harlan Marsh. And yes, that area is all farmland and wild salt-marsh.'

'Come to think of it, I remember it from when I was a kid. There used to be one accessible beach there. It was close to the old seal sanctuary at Hurn Point.'

'Mmm . . .' Marie's slender finger moved slowly along the coast. 'Ah yes, I see where you mean. Shall I ask uniform to go check it out for us?'

'I'd rather we went ourselves.' Jackman gnawed on his bottom lip. 'But no, you're right. I need to get these reports sorted before the end of the day and uniform are more than capable of dealing with it.' He lifted his desk phone. 'I'll see if the duty sergeant could get a crew over there to take a look around, maybe ask some questions of the locals.' A few moments later he replaced the receiver. 'Sorted.'

'Sir?' The door opened and the tousled head of DC Charlie Button, the youngest member of their team, pushed through the gap. 'Sorry to interrupt, but Superintendent Crooke would like to see both of you in her office.'

Jackman thanked the young detective and swallowed the rest of his coffee. 'Oh dear, *both* of us. That sounds ominous.'

Marie stood up. 'Let's get it over with, and pray that it has nothing to do with budgets, spending cuts, performance or targets.'

'Or all four at once.' Jackman smiled ruefully. 'It *has* been known.'

\* \* \*

Superintendent Ruth Crooke was a narrow-lipped woman who looked permanently pissed off, probably because she usually was. It took a lot to stir any emotion other than a negative one in the super, and when she summoned you, it was advisable to jump to it.

Marie took the stairs two at a time to keep up with Jackman. She didn't look forward to entering the "Lioness's Den," but she had worked with the superintendent for long enough to know that if you could get past the hard, controlling exterior and the acerbic tongue, there was a damned good policewoman underneath, and that was what really counted.

Marie walked in behind Jackman and bestowed on the super her very best radiant smile. It failed to bring even the slightest movement to those tight, thin lips.

Superintendent Ruth Crooke gestured irritably to the only two chairs available in the room and launched into a lengthy complaint about whoever she'd just been speaking to.

'I've had some damned financial analyst bleating down my ear for the last ten minutes and I swear he's never set foot in a police station in his whole life. Every initiative he came up with was bloody crap.' She flung a notebook across her desk and leaned back in her chair. 'Not that I think he'll be phoning back. I told him exactly why his money-saving theories should be flushed down the pan.'

'I don't know how you do it, ma'am,' said Jackman. 'Your job would have my brains turning into minestrone in five minutes flat.'

She shrugged. 'Well, someone has to. And what I do, I do rather well. At least you guys have someone fighting your corner. For instance, last time I looked, you still had radios, Kevlar vests, and cars, or has something changed since I last went downstairs?'

Jackman smiled. Marie knew that although he didn't like the boss much, he had a grudging admiration for anyone who could juggle budgets and targets.

'No, we're still communicating, protected and mobile. And thank heavens, because I don't think we'd do too well trying to police these fens on bicycles.' He sat back and gazed across the oversized shiny desk.

Ruth Crooke shook her head. 'Anyway, as talking to you two about anything other than criminal activity is a

complete waste of my valuable time, I'll save my breath.'
She pushed a thick folder across the table towards them.

Marie saw the name on it and a shiver went through her.

Kenya Black.

'We have some pressure on us. It's a cold case I know, but the mother has decided to resurrect her campaign. She's trying to get the press to run with it again, but big style this time. She is attracting interest from some famous faces and using social media to really stir things up.' She gave a little shrug. 'Can't blame the poor soul, of course, but we won't look good if we are doing sweet FA, so upstairs want it put to bed, permanently. It was never closed, and although I know that you are dealing with Shauna Kelly's disappearance, I specifically want your team to take this one, and I want you to make it your number one priority.'

Jackman sat bolt upright in his chair. 'My God. It must be seven or eight years since Kenya disappeared, and you are making it high priority?'

Everyone in the area knew about the disappearance of the little girl, but as neither Jackman nor Marie had been directly involved in the case, the finer details were hazy.

Jackman frowned. 'I know it was put on the back burner, but it is still an ongoing investigation. Surely one of the other teams went over the whole thing less than three months ago?'

'They did, but science and forensics move forward every day.'

Marie racked her brain for information. Emblazoned across her mind was a photograph that the media latched on to at the time. A child with white-blonde hair sitting on a beanbag with her pet dog. She wore jeans and a yellow hooded sweatshirt with a teddy bear motif on it. Her small fingers were clinging to the animal's fur. She was the epitome of angelic. This heart-wrencher had instigated the biggest public-supported hunt that the Fens had ever known.

Marie frowned. Memories were coming back like flashes from a newsreel. 'Someone thought they saw her, didn't they? With another child, playing close to the seal reserve out at Hurn Point?'

'And a week later one of her trainers was found washed up on the beach three miles up the coast from the sighting, which gave credence to the man's report.' The super's face was stony.

'And it was assumed that she'd been swept out to sea.' Marie remembered the tabloid headline: *Was it Murder, or just a Terrible Accident?*

'That's the long and the short of it. The parents were well off, but no ransom demand ever came, no more evidence was found, and there were no more reported sightings — well, none other than the usual crank ones. And after a while it was decided that she had most probably drowned and we were forced to scale down the investigation.'

'But now you want us to give it priority again?' asked Jackman.

'We want you to start at the beginning and go through it with fresh eyes *and* a considerably enhanced budget should you need it.' The superintendent looked at Jackman with an unnerving intensity. 'I want this case closed, for good. And although we don't always see eye to eye, I have to admit that your team has something about it. I don't know what it is, but if anyone can find out what happened to that little girl and get this wretched case sewn up, I believe it's you.'

Jackman took up the file and stared at it.

Marie felt a strange sensation course through her. Excitement was not quite the right word, it was more like trepidation. No one who had worked the original investigation had bought into the accident theory, but after years of fruitless digging it had been taken out of their hands. So, maybe it *was* time for a new team to try to provide her grieving family with some sort of closure.

Jackman stood up. 'We'll give it our very best shot, ma'am, you can depend on that. But Shauna Kelly has to come first right now. And if that girl who drowned is her, I'm not going to compromise these early days of the enquiry. She belongs to one of our own, and although I wouldn't treat it differently to any other death, we do feel deeply for her mother.'

'Of course, I'd expect no less. And if you need help, ask, okay?' Ruth Crooke stared at them. 'But don't procrastinate over the cold case either. There is a lot at stake with this. When I said the powers that be want it dealt with swiftly, I meant it, understood?'

The interview was over.

Marie's instincts shouted that this investigation was going to be far from simple.

They walked towards the lifts.

'Kenya Black.' Jackman almost whispered the name. 'I never saw that coming.'

'Me neither,' replied Marie.

'How do you feel about taking this on?' asked Jackman.

'Well, of course we should. The super's right. The family needs answers, and maybe new eyes will see something different.'

'That's not what I asked.' Jackman levelled his eyes at hers. 'How do *you* feel about it?'

They slowed their pace. 'If I'm honest, and I have no idea why I feel this way, I'm quite troubled by the thought of tackling this investigation.'

As they entered the lift, Jackman nodded. 'Me too. From the moment I saw that file with that name on it, my stomach has been doing somersaults.' He drew in a long shaky breath. 'But you are right, it's time that dreadful case was closed, so we'd better get our heads together and sort it, don't you think?'

In the silence as the lift descended, Marie had a strong sense of foreboding.

# CHAPTER THREE

Jackman and Marie went directly into his office and closed the door.

Jackman sat down heavily in his old leather captain's chair and swung round to face Marie. 'I need to get my head around this before we tell the team. I'm not sure how we are going to juggle it all. It's going to take quite a bit of strategic planning.'

Marie puffed out her cheeks. 'Well, the super seemed absolutely determined that we be the ones to tackle the case, even if we are already working the Shauna Kelly investigation.'

'Mmm, she was almost complimentary about the team, wasn't she?'

'But thinking about it, there really is only us, isn't there? Our counterparts are up to their ears in tying up that big fraud case and getting it ready for the CPS. They certainly couldn't tackle something on this scale. And DI Andy Feltham's team are way understaffed due to illness and accident.'

Jackman made to answer but was interrupted by a knock at the door.

DC Max Cohen entered, carrying a large sealed envelope. 'Sorry, boss, but I think you'll want to see this. It's from the pathologist, marked urgent.'

'Thanks, Max. We'll be out in a moment, so perhaps you'd get hold of Charlie. We'll meet you in the CID room in ten for a briefing, okay?'

As the door closed, Jackman stared at the manila envelope in front of him. His name was written across the front in Rory Wilkinson's version of Gothic script. An awful lot rested on what this brief report would tell them, not least the fact that he might have to break it to one of his own staff that her daughter was dead. From the moment he had seen the girl on the beach, Jackman's gut feeling was that she hadn't fallen, and she hadn't jumped.

He frowned and tore open the envelope.

The dental records confirmed that the drowned girl was Shauna Kelly. Without a word, he passed the sheet to Marie.

Marie sighed. 'I so hoped . . .'

'I guess we know what our next step is.'

'A very sad visit to Liz Kelly. We'll do it together, shall we? We've both known Liz for quite a time, and I'm sure she'll appreciate it coming from people she's familiar with.'

Jackman nodded. 'I wish we had more to tell her.'

'Whatever we say today will be lost on her. The only words she'll hear are the ones telling her that her child is dead.'

Jackman stood up. 'You go tell Max and Charlie about this, and I'll notify the super.' He grimaced. 'And then we'll go and break the news to Liz.'

'And Kenya Black? Shall I tell the others?'

'No. Let's get something rolling regarding Shauna. Kenya Black has been gone a very long time, so a few more days won't make any difference, whereas we need to really move on Shauna's investigation while there may be evidence to gather and people's memories are still fresh.'

'Wilco, sir.' Marie strode outside to find the others, and Jackman made his second visit in twenty minutes to the superintendent's office.

Ruth Crooke looked almost haggard. 'So what do we actually know about Shauna?'

'We have no idea what happened to her yet, ma'am. Rory Wilkinson is treating it as a priority, so we just have to hope that something shows up in the post-mortem that will determine whether foul play was involved.' He pushed a hand through his thick, light brown hair. 'Apparently Shauna was always a handful, but not a bad kid. Six months ago her father left home, and things got worse. She started drinking, and Liz told me that she has had trouble keeping her away from some of the wilder kids in town.'

'And the night she went missing?'

'Max and Charlie have located her three times on CCTV, all around the town-centre area. The last sighting was of her laughing with a man, close to the Lincoln Arms public house on Brewer Street.'

'Drunk?'

'Not paralytic, but probably tipsy.' Jackman thought back to the footage Max had shown him. 'One thing stood out though. From the way she was acting, we are all certain that she knew the man. The image of him is poor, but Max has enhanced it as much as he can, and uniform are taking it out on the streets for us.'

'Not much to go on.'

'It's better than nothing, ma'am. We could get lucky.'

'Let's hope. Now, to help out I've got you another detective. DC Rosie McElderry from DI Feltham's team is at a loose end, so for the duration of this enquiry, she's all yours.'

'Thank you, ma'am. I like Rosie, she has the makings of a very good detective.'

'Look closer, she's already a very good detective.'

Jackman grinned. 'Point taken.' He pushed back his chair. 'I'd better go, ma'am, I need to tell Liz Kelly before the grapevine does it for me.'

Ruth looked at him and he saw sympathy in her eyes. 'Get her the best family liaison officer that we have, Rowan. I'll notify them further up the chain and she'll be offered every help, but . . . that poor woman.'

'I know. And I can't say I'm looking forward to this.'

'I'm sure you're not. It's the worst part of this job, and no mistake.' She gave him a rare smile. 'But you'll do it properly, I know that.'

Jackman hoped she was right.

* * *

It was after two p.m. by the time Jackman gathered the team together for a full briefing. His meeting with Liz Kelly had been extremely harrowing. The sound of the woman's anguished cry still rang in his ears.

He was under no illusion about the Kenya Black case. He knew he had been handed a poisoned chalice. That case had a reputation, a bad one. It didn't help that one of the detectives on the original investigation had topped himself over it. Jackman gritted his teeth and swore silently that whatever happened, he'd never let any of his colleagues get to that state, or anywhere near it.

He watched his small team move around the large incident room. They had no idea what he was going to say, but they had picked up on his tension. Jackman knew that this investigation, if successful, could affect all their futures in a big way. The disappearance of Kenya Black was referred to as one of the great unsolved crimes of the decade. To be part of the team that finally brought the truth to light could be a career maker, and even he felt a rush of nervous enthusiasm. But first he had to update them on Shauna Kelly.

'Before we get down to it, I'd like to welcome DC Rosie McElderry to the team. She's lending a hand as we will be running two investigations.' He nodded towards a young fair-haired woman who sat little apart from the others. Rosie had an elfin face with fine-boned features and greenish-blue eyes. She looked much younger than her twenty-four years, but Jackman knew that she had a quick brain and a knack for picking up discrepancies in statements. She was also in possession of an extremely good memory.

The young detective raised a hand and smiled at them. 'Happy to help.'

Jackman leaned back against the wall. 'Now, as I just said we are going to be working two cases in tandem. The first, as you will all know by now, is that of the death of Shauna Kelly. Before we can make too much headway with this we will need the forensic reports, and the prelim should be with us by tomorrow morning. If it is foul play, then we have a murder enquiry. To get one step ahead, I want you to keep working on finding the identity of the man that Shauna was seen talking to on the CCTV, and also go back to all of her friends and contemporaries. Someone must know something about Shauna, something that led up to her either going missing, or being abducted.' He took a breath. 'And the second case is something that you youngsters will have to do a lot of homework on, because,' he paused, 'we are about to take a closer look at the Kenya Black enquiry.'

There was a collective intake of breath.

'Blimey! That's a turn up for the books!' Max's cockney accent came to the fore.

'Yes,' said Jackman. 'And to be honest, even Marie and I will need to do some in-depth reading on this case, as neither of us were around at the time. So, Marie, where are we at?'

'Well, I've already called the Evidence Storage Facility. They are releasing the evidence containers later this afternoon. I reckon we'll need a forklift to get all the boxes over here.'

'I'll want some items sent directly to the forensic lab. I've already alerted Professor Wilkinson about it.'

Rory Wilkinson was usually based in Greenborough, but for the time being he had decided to work at the County Hospital mortuary on the outskirts of Saltern town. He had immediately offered to help. His willingness didn't surprise Jackman. The entire country had been mesmerized by the search for little Kenya Black.

'I haven't had time yet to go over everything, but a swift glance gives me the distinct impression that the last review of this case was something of a balls-up.' Jackman thumbed through a sheaf of reports.

Marie nodded. 'Quite possibly, sir. That last review took place at the time when we were being overhauled. Civilians were being brought in for a lot of jobs that some thought should have been done by coppers. Plus, that case has been dragged out of mothballs more times than I've had hot dinners. Maybe their hearts weren't in it.'

'Probably not. But that is not going to happen this time. We are going to find out what happened to that little girl if we have to spend every damned penny of the super's generous budget. We *will* find Kenya, or at least discover exactly what occurred.'

'DI Jackman?' A uniformed officer entered the room and handed Jackman a memo. 'The man you are looking for from the CCTV has been identified by PC Kevin Stoner. He believes the man works in the area where the girl was last seen.'

Jackman summarised the memo: 'His name is Asher Leyton. He's not actually known to us, but it seems he has been warned a couple of times for curb-crawling.'

'Which doesn't bode well, does it?' said Marie.

No, Jackman thought, it doesn't. Sometimes the next step up from hassling women on the street was taking them away.

'Have they got an address for him, sir?'

'Granary Court on Norfolk Street. The garden flat.'

'Posh pad for a pervert. Granary Court is one of the most expensive locations in Saltern.' Max sounded almost envious.

'I think we should go and have a word with Mr Asher Leyton, don't you?' Jackman looked at Marie.

Marie took a set of keys from her pocket. 'No time like the present. There's a fleet car downstairs.'

* * *

The door to the garden flat was opened by a petite young woman with long, wavy blonde hair and perfectly made-up eyes. She wore skinny jeans with a cream cowl-neck top and a wide studded leather belt. Marie decided she had the look of a WAG about her.

'Asher?' She stared at their official identification cards and the eyes became even larger. 'Oh, dear, Detective Inspector, I'm afraid he's not here.'

'When do you expect him back, miss?' asked Marie.

The girl smiled, treating them to a display of top quality orthodontic work. 'Not until late, I'm afraid. He's working until around ten o'clock.'

Dazzled by the teeth, Jackman tried not to squint. 'And you are?' he asked.

'Lynda. Lynda Cowley. I'm Asher's fiancée.' Her smile faded. 'He's alright, isn't he? I mean he's not been in an accident or anything?'

Jackman gave her a reassuring smile. 'No, it's nothing like that, Miss Cowley. We just need a word with him. Maybe you could tell us where he works, or give us his mobile phone number?'

The girl still looked worried. 'He works for a company on George Street — Hanson and Co., but he won't be there. He's at a meeting this afternoon and then going on to a client dinner tonight. Of course I'll give you his number, but he switches his mobile off when he's busy.'

'Do you know where this dinner is taking place?' Marie was feeling slightly twitchy about his being so conveniently out of contact.

The girl shook her head slowly, and the long blonde hair swung gently from side to side like a TV advert for shampoo. 'He didn't say.'

Client dinner, my arse, thought Marie, recalling Asher Leyton's penchant for a little late night curb-crawling. She handed the girl her card. 'Well, please give him this. Get him to ring us the moment he returns, Miss Cowley, no matter how late, okay?'

'Or failing that, get him to ring us first thing in the morning, as a matter of some urgency,' added Jackman.

'Can I tell him what it's about, Inspector? I know he'll worry if I tell him the police want to talk to him.'

I'm sure he will, Marie thought. 'We need to speak to anyone who might have been on Brewer Street a few evenings ago, that's all.'

'Brewer Street is directly opposite George Street, where Asher works, isn't it?'

Jackman nodded.

Lynda Cowley looked somewhat relieved. 'I'll give him your message.'

As they walked back to the car, Marie said, 'Just how gullible do you think one person can be?'

'About as gullible as that, I should say.' Jackman shook his head. 'Poor kid.'

'She only looked about sixteen. How old do you think she really is?'

'Probably closer to twenty, maybe even older. I think she's another Rosie, looks much younger than she really is.'

Marie frowned. 'Is it worth a trip around to Hanson and Co.?'

'I get the feeling he won't be there, and Lynda was right, I've just checked the mobile number that she gave us for him, and it is switched off.' Jackman mused. 'We'd make better use of our time by returning to the station and putting wheels into motion. There's one heck of a lot to do.'

'Will he contact us, I wonder?' Marie clicked the remote on the car keys.

'We can but hope. And if he doesn't, in the words of Arnie Schwarzenegger, "I'll be back!"'

# CHAPTER FOUR

Hours later, as darkness enveloped the fen, two youngsters, unsteady in their high heels, tottered along the pavements of Harlan Marsh town.

'Are you sure this is the place?' Jasmine drew her thin top closer to her skinny body, and shivered.

'This is it,' said Chloe. 'I followed Paul here last week. I watched him go in.'

The two girls looked dubiously at the rusting wrought-iron fencing that surrounded the concrete steps, and the peeling paintwork on the old door down in the shadows of the basement area.

'Well, nothing is happening tonight, that's for sure. Let's go home, Chloe. This place is a dump, it gives me the creeps.' Jasmine had been unenthusiastic about gate-crashing the party from the outset.

Chloe frowned. 'But I sneaked a look at his mobile. There was a new message saying that it was on tonight. And I *know* this is where my brother came before.'

'Maybe it was cancelled at the last minute.' Jasmine shifted from foot to foot. It had been a stupid idea anyway. So what if there was free booze? She didn't even like the taste of alcohol, and if her dad found out, he would go ape-shit and probably ground her for the rest of the year.

'Can I help you young ladies?'

The voice was friendly enough. Jasmine turned around to see an older man smiling at them. He had a short, fashionable haircut, trendy clothes and was carrying a large case of wine bottles.

'You the geezer who runs the parties?' asked Chloe.

The man narrowed his eyes. 'What parties?'

Chloe jabbed a finger towards the case of wine. 'So you are going to drink that lot all on your own, are you?'

'Smart kid.' He grinned at her and placed the heavy box on the ground. 'So, are you two club members?'

Jasmine felt a stab of anxiety, and wished again that they'd never left home.

'Course we are,' said Chloe, trying to look bored. 'Why else would we be here? And my mobile phone message definitely said it was on, so . . . ?'

The man shook his head. 'But you never received the venue change. Ah, well, I'm sorry about that. Must have been some sort of mix up.'

'Oh great!' Chloe snorted. 'So if it's not here, where is it? We don't want to spend all night on the frigging pavement.'

The man looked from one girl to the other. 'Funny, I've never seen either of you before, and I've got a pretty good memory for faces.'

Jasmine took hold of Chloe's arm. 'Come on, Chlo, just leave it.'

'No way!' Chloe pushed Jasmine away and placed her hands on her hips. 'These guys have cocked up, end of. Just because we're new, it doesn't mean we should miss out on a party. Does it, Granddad?'

The man, who couldn't have been more than thirty, tilted his head and stared at them for a moment. 'How old are you?' he asked.

'I'm seventeen,' said Chloe quickly. 'And she's sixteen, if it's any of your business.'

'ID?'

An odd look of interest, or maybe amusement, passed across the man's face when Chloe told him they had left them at home. Jasmine began to shiver again. She hated it when Chloe lied about their age. She knew they looked much older than fourteen, but this was beginning to get uncomfortable. 'Sorry, but I'm going, Chlo. You do what you want.' She turned to walk away.

'Okay, okay.' The man shook his head and grinned at them. 'You win. The venue is in Carters Way tonight. There's an old warehouse, it's about halfway down on the left-hand side, there's a side door and . . .' He stopped and gave a little sigh. 'Oh, wait here, I've got another of these crates to collect and then I'm going down there myself. I'll take you if you like, by way of an apology for the muddle with the text.'

'It's the least you can do,' said Chloe.

Jasmine threw her friend a horrified look as the man walked a few doors down and disappeared into a rather shabby house. 'You can't get into his car alone, Chloe! Don't be totally stupid! We never do that, never!'

'Then come with me. It'll be fun. We've practically got him eating out of our hands. Lighten up, Jasmine, for God's sake. My brother thinks these parties are the coolest thing ever! Really wicked! Free drink *all* night, music, dancing, snogging, anything you want.' She lowered her voice. 'And I mean anything. He didn't know I was listening, but I heard Paul telling his spotty mate Darren, that he actually *did it* with his girlfriend! Can you believe that?'

Jasmine didn't even want to think about it. The thought of Paul and his skanky girlfriend jammed up against a wall made her feel ill. Doing it, as Chloe had put it, should be special. Jasmine wanted flowers, candles and a big soft bed for her first time, not some dingy basement surrounded by piss-heads.

'I'll go on my own, Jas, honest I will.'

'You can't. What if your brother turns up? He'll kill you if he finds you there. *And* he'll know you've been snooping through his mobile.'

'He won't, he's gone to a concert in Sheffield.' Chloe looked along the deserted street as a door closed further down. 'Please, Jas? Just let's see what it's like. If you don't like it, we'll go home, I promise.' She watched the approaching man. 'And *he's* harmless, you can tell by just looking at him.'

Two minutes later, Jasmine reluctantly followed Chloe into the back of the car. She knew she was making a seriously big mistake, but there was no way she could have watched her best friend drive away alone.

\* \* \*

It was close to nine when Marie finally got home. She was tired, but pleased with the amount of work they had managed to do. They all knew that it was going to be full on from the moment they set foot in the station the next day, so it made sense to get the groundwork done.

Marie opened the fridge and selected a light M&S ready meal for her supper, and to go with it, a glass of chilled rosé wine. She was just about to pop her food into the microwave when the phone rang.

'Marie?'

She smiled to herself. Why did her mother always sound so surprised when she answered? 'As I live alone and to my knowledge, the cat hasn't yet mastered answering the phone, yes, Mum, it's me.'

A tinkle of laughter drifted down the phone. 'Just checking, sweetheart.'

Marie loved the soft Welsh lilt to her mother's voice. It had soothed her as a child, and in times of trouble it still did. 'How are you, Mum?'

'More to the point, how are you? You've been on my mind all day, Marie. Have you got a big investigation going on?'

They didn't call her mum, Rhiannon Roberts, the "Welsh Witch" for nothing. 'Funny you should say that. We are just embarking on what could be a very worrying one indeed.'

'Well, you know where I am if you want to offload.'

Marie sipped her wine. 'Who else would I do that to? So stand by, you could be in demand over the next few weeks.'

'It sounds big.'

'Massive — no, even bigger than that, and high profile too, so keep an eye on the papers. You might just see your daughter's name in print.'

'I promise not to believe a word they say.' Her mum laughed again, and Marie felt a stab of longing. She wished that her mother was not so far away, in the wilds of Wales.

'When are you coming up next? The spare room is always made up ready.'

'I'll come if you really need me, you know I will.'

Marie understood. Her mother had other people who needed her too. Rhia ran a kind of retreat-cum-hostel, cum food bank, cum drop-in centre for anyone and everyone who needed help. She also helped out at the local school and delivered prescriptions to disabled villagers for the doctor's surgery. In short, she was an angel disguised in knitted cardigans, long flowing skirts and Doc Martens. Her mum was a one-off, and Marie adored her. When Marie's husband, Bill, had been killed in a motorcycle crash, Rhia had kept her going. Her mother had pulled her through, and now Marie believed she was a stronger woman for it.

They spoke for a few minutes longer, then Marie promised to ring her mother the following night.

'Be careful, Marie. I sense that you will be under a lot of strain over the coming weeks. Eat well and try to sleep as much as you can. Tired workers don't function well, and that could be dangerous.'

'You sound like Jackman, that's one of his favourites.'

'Then he is a sensible man. Listen to him. And, Marie? If you do need me, I'll be there. You know that, don't you?'

'Of course I do. Love you. Sleep tight.'

'Don't let the bedbugs bite.'

Marie replaced the phone in its holder. Her mother had a sixth sense where her daughter was concerned. The young Marie could not tell a lie or try to cover anything up, because her mother always knew. And if things were worrying her, no matter where she was, nine times out of ten her mother would ring.

She put her meal into the microwave, thinking that it was a bit like having a guardian angel watching over her. And in her line of business, that was no bad thing to have.

*  *  *

It took Jackman longer to get back to Mill Corner than it took Marie to get home. His village of Cartoft was a drive of fifteen minutes or so from Saltern-le-Fen station. He locked his car and walked across to the mill-house, balancing several folders and a box file in his arms. The smell of something delicious cooking met him at the door. He dropped his paperwork on the kitchen table and found the note left by Mrs Maynard.

*Mr Jackman, I've left you a hotpot simmering on the stove, and Mr M. said the lavender wagon will be here tomorrow, but he'll see to it. Hetty.*

Jackman smiled and wondered what he would do without the old couple who "looked after" him.

Before he did anything, he wrote a cheque for the drainage company who would be emptying the septic tank — Len's "lavender wagon." Cartoft was not on mains drainage so every two or three years they had the dubious pleasure of the emptying ceremony. Jackman grinned to himself. Yet another reason to be grateful for the Maynards.

He helped himself to a large bowl of the beef stew, turned on the radio and sat down at the old pine table. He glanced at the pile of reports and decided that his homework could wait until he had eaten.

For the next fifteen minutes Jackman listened to Classic FM and enjoyed his supper, until the magnetic attraction of the Kenya Black files became too much for him. He rinsed his bowl and placed it in the dishwasher, then returned to the table and opened the reports.

They made depressing reading. It was clear that Kenya's mother, Grace Black, had worked tirelessly to keep her daughter's unexplained disappearance in the public eye for as long as possible. Every time interest faded she found a way to rekindle the flame, but almost a decade on, no new information had come to light. Jackman knew they had a daunting task ahead of them, but it was a battle that he was determined to win. Grace Black deserved to have someone fighting beside her and his team, along with an enhanced budget and new advances in technology, might be able to give the distraught mother hope — or closure. Jackman shivered. He could only guess at the anguish Grace Black suffered, not knowing if her child were dead or alive. Wondering whether, if she was dead, had she suffered? And if she was alive, what sort of life was she living? The dark imaginings that must haunt her waking hours and sleepless nights were hard to even begin to contemplate.

Jackman abruptly stood up and walked across the kitchen to where the coffee pot lived. He put the kettle on the stove, and spooned rich, dark Kenyan coffee into the percolator. He needed a strong caffeine hit if he were to read more of this heart-breaking stuff. Tomorrow, he would visit Grace and tell her that he was going to move heaven and earth to find out what had happened to her beautiful daughter.

Just as he had said to Liz Kelly earlier that day:

*'Liz, we'll find out what happened to Shauna, and if someone is to blame, then we'll bring them to justice. You have my word that we will not rest until we can give you answers.'* Liz had not replied. He had not expected her to. The poor woman was in a private hell and no words could ease the raw pain of the news that he had had to deliver.

'What a shitty world we live in,' he murmured to the singing kettle. Then he thought of his team, all of them dedicated, determined to help make things better.

'No, the world's not all shit. There are just some seriously shitty people in it,' he said to himself.

# CHAPTER FIVE

Marie rode away from her village early next morning, marvelling at the sky-scape before her. The low farmland still held on to a carpet of diaphanous mist, and the sky above it was a heavy gunmetal grey, scattered with dispersing night clouds. Above this, appeared a wide rift in the iron sky. A dazzling strip of the brightest flame orange tore the greyness apart, and the scarlet orb of the sun began to rise.

Already, her reservations about taking on the Kenya Black enquiry had melted away. Today forensics should give them more on Shauna Kelly, and then they could plan a course of action. She was actually looking forward to her visit with Mister Curb-Crawler, and she also wanted to take a look at the area where Shauna had apparently gone into the water.

She approached the road junction into the town and waited as a tractor towing a trailer full of bright green broccoli lumbered past. As she sat there, she silently prayed that Shauna's death had been a tragic accident, and that it wasn't the precursor of things to come.

By the time she eased the big motorbike into her parking space at the station, a hint of the tension of the night before had seeped back into her mind.

* * *

Jackman had barely set foot in the CID room when he heard his name called out.

The gravelly voice belonged to the superintendent's office manager. 'Sorry, sir, but can you go upstairs? Immediately.'

When he reached the super's office, Ruth Crooke was waiting in the corridor.

'Listen,' she said urgently. 'I know you are not going to like what my visitor has to say, but I'm asking you to run with it, okay? And just remember, your present cases involve a *missing* girl and a *dead* girl. Hold that thought.' She then turned and without waiting for a reply, pushed her door open and marched in.

Standing by the window was a tall ramrod of a man wearing a chief superintendent's uniform. Jackman recognised him instantly. Cade worked out of one of the neighbouring divisions, and had the reputation of being a slimy bastard that it was best not to cross if you valued your career prospects.

'This is Detective Inspector Rowan Jackman, James.'

The super gave a tight smile.

'Chief Superintendent Cade here has a problem over in the Harlan Marshes area. A young woman has gone missing and both of their CID teams are tied up on another serious crime. He needs our help. Well, *yours* to be precise.'

Jackman wasn't too sure what he was supposed to say. Just yesterday, he had been given a high priority, get-us-out-of-the–shit-before-it-hits-the-fan job, something to work alongside the death of Shauna Kelly. Now he was being asked to forget about that and save another station's bacon because of *their* workload?

Words failed him. Then he drew himself up and said, 'Sorry, ma'am, but as you know, my caseload is not exactly light either. You will have to give it to another team. Even DI Feltham has enough staff to cope with that.'

Cade interrupted. 'Ah, but I'd really appreciate it if *you* could spare me just a little of your precious time, DI Jackman?' he said with a reptilian hiss.

Jackman looked at the super for help. 'Ma'am? My priority case?'

'I'm going to suggest that you get your team to put the wheels into motion on that. There's a lot of preparation they can be getting on with.'

'And Shauna Kelly?'

'The same. You are still waiting for forensic confirmation as to whether it is a tragic accident or something else, aren't you? So, let your team keep working on the basic prep. Meanwhile, you and DS Evans go over to Harlan Marsh and make some enquiries.'

'It may be nothing, Jackman.' Cade smiled. 'The girl does have previous for running away, in which case you will be back before you know it. *But* while I am certain that is the case, she *is* the daughter of a local businessman, and a generous benefactor to the police charities, so I promised him that I'd send him our best officers, if you catch my drift?'

He did. Ten-to-one this "benefactor" was a golfing buddy with a funny handshake, someone who took a locked case with him when he went out for the evening.

His teeth jammed together in anger, but he bit back his reply when he saw the super's expression. It was clear and concise.

*Just you dare, Jackman!*

'Thank you, Rowan. I knew I could count on you.' Ruth dismissed him with a flick of her head and a glance towards the door.

'My pleasure, I'm sure.' And Jackman made his escape.

The first person he met as he stepped off the last stair was Marie. It was all he could do to hold back until they reached his office.

Safe inside, he let rip. 'I don't believe it! We have more work than we've ever had and the super wants us wet-nursing Harlan Marsh! What a damned cheek! Wasting *our* time because they have *serious ongoing cases*. Whatever it is, I bet our canteen staff could handle it quicker and more efficiently.'

Out of the corner of his eye, he caught sight of Marie, almost shaking with suppressed laughter at his outburst.

'And it's no laughing matter! They have no right playing the Lodge brother's card when the missing kid has probably just bunked off to Sheffield for the weekend to see some boyband.'

He ranted on for several minutes before the futility of it hit him. They had no option but to comply, so best to get it over with as fast as possible. At least it was only a twenty-minute drive away.

He sat down, his anger burnt off like morning dew in the sun. It had suddenly dawned on him that Harlan Marsh was only a few miles from where Kenya Black had supposedly been sighted for that last time. It was also very close to Allenby Creek. Maybe he and Marie should take a detour on their way back, and have a look at the place for themselves.

Jackman cleared his mind and took a deep breath. Yes, this unwanted trip could turn out to be a blessing in disguise. And there was always the chance that another young girl really had gone missing. He might be angry with Cade, but he wasn't stupid enough to ignore the possible connections.

'Better now?' Marie asked with a grin.

'Much better, thank you. Okay, so go tell Max, Charlie and Rosie what is happening and get them to press on. The evidence boxes will be here later this afternoon. Get them to find a home for everything, get it into some kind of order and begin setting up the investigation log. Any spare moments, they can read all they can about the original case, but tell them *not*, and I emphasise that, *not* to be influenced by anything other than proven fact. They should take no one else's suppositions for granted. Okay?'

He handed Marie copies of the file the super had given him the day before. 'To read and digest. We will be going back to day one when we start. We will treat the disappearance of Kenya Black as if it were a new case.' He threw her a grim smile. 'It won't be easy, but I have faith that our team will find the truth regarding that little girl.'

Marie took the folders. 'Me too. By the way, who is it that has seen fit to demand our services?'

'Chief Superintendent Cade. He seems to think that we are the only officers in the entire force that can help him.'

'Cade? James Cade?'

Jackman nodded. 'Not a pleasant man, as I understand it.' He looked at Marie and saw that she looked suddenly pale, almost haggard.

'What's wrong?'

'I don't want to have anything to do with that man, sir. Could you take one of the others with you?'

Jackman sat back and stared at his sergeant. Never, in all the years they had worked together, had she reacted in this way. 'What's the problem, Marie?'

'Don't take this the wrong way, but it's kind of personal and really not something I want to talk about right now.' She looked horribly uncomfortable, then seemed to pull herself together.

'Oh well, although I'd rather have a lumbar puncture than have to walk into the same room as Cade, there *could* be a connection with Shauna if they have a girl missing. So forget what I just said. I'll go and organise the troops and I'll be ready when you are.'

As she slipped through the door, Jackman wondered why she had so neatly avoided explaining her dislike of

Cade. He shrugged. He'd find out at some point. He gathered up his coat and car keys and was about to leave when the phone rang.

It was the desk sergeant. 'Mr Asher Leyton phoned in, sir. He says you want to speak to him and he'll be at home all morning. He'd mislaid your number so he rang the front desk.'

'Okay, thanks. I'll deal with it.' Jackman had not expected to hear from Leyton. He would have put money on having to chase the man down.

Jackman muttered a curse to himself. Just as things were hotting up, they had to take a trip to the most miserable and remote spot on the planet. It was a small backwater town surrounded by acres of flat arable farmland, dykes, ditches and marsh. Harlan Marsh was considered the bottom of the pile when it came to postings.

He walked out into the CID room and gestured to Marie.

'Ready!' she called back.

'Oh, Max, if the pathologist's report on Shauna Kelly comes through, ring me immediately.'

Max gave a thumbs-up. 'Will do, boss.'

\* \* \*

Jackman had decided that they should make a swift call on Asher Leyton on their way out to Harlan Marsh. He told Marie that he didn't want the man to get cold feet and do a runner.

Asher Leyton led Jackman and Marie down a wide hallway and into a huge open-plan lounge. It was modern, tasteful, and reeked of money. Marie noted that his fiancée was not there.

'Lynda told me that you called, DI Jackman. I'm sorry to have caused you two trips.' He indicated for them to take a seat on an oversized ivory leather couch, while he sat in a matching leather recliner. 'How can I help?'

Marie looked at him with interest. He wasn't exactly what she had expected. Asher Leyton was in his mid to late twenties. He was of medium build, with thick wavy fair hair and had a rather old-fashioned appearance. Wearing beige cord trousers and a tweed check waistcoat, even his clothes looked dated. Some new retro trend she'd missed out on?

'Mr Leyton, we have reason to believe that you were on Brewer Street, three nights ago. Can you tell us if that's true?' asked Jackman.

'Most likely, Inspector. I work flexi-hours and I walk down Brewer Street to get home.' He looked at him calmly. 'Why? What happened?'

Marie reached into her pocket and took out a photograph of Shauna Kelly. 'Did you see or speak to this girl, sir?'

Asher took the picture, and immediately smiled. 'I certainly did.' He handed back the photo. 'In fact, I've spoken to her a couple of times recently.'

Jackman's eyes narrowed. 'And why would that be?'

Asher Leyton's smile faded from his face. 'Has something happened to her? Is that why you're here?'

'Do you know her by name, sir?' asked Jackman quietly.

'It's something like Shona? Or Sheena? I can't remember exactly.' He ran long, narrow fingers nervously through his hair.

'How do you know her, Mr Leyton?' Jackman's voice was getting colder by the minute.

'I don't *know* her. I've just talked to her on a few occasions, that's all.' The man almost squirmed in his chair.

'And why would a man of your age be talking to a fourteen-year-old girl that he doesn't know?'

'Fourteen? Oh my God, but she looked . . . she said . . . you've got the wrong end of the stick, really you have.' Asher Leyton swallowed. 'I saw her one evening on

39

Brewer Street. She was alone, standing on the edge of the pavement, and for a moment I thought she might be a, a . . .'

'Prostitute?' filled in Marie. 'You'd know about those, wouldn't you, Mr Leyton?'

The man's face suffused with colour. 'I've never been in trouble with anything like that! Check your records! You won't find me on them. I have no convictions!'

'We've already checked, Mr Leyton, but our patrol officers have had a quiet word with you in the past, haven't they?' Marie said calmly.

'Oh Lord. But I explained all about that at the time. Those girls worry me. I talk to them, try to help them, that's all. I'm a clean-living, honest, working man. I'm engaged to the most beauti—'

He stopped mid-sentence, and his red face paled. 'Please tell me you haven't mentioned this to Lynda?'

'Your secret is safe with us, sir — unless there is anything we should know about you and Shauna Kelly?' Marie stared coolly at him.

Asher Leyton exhaled. 'But there's nothing to tell. I only spoke to her because a car splashed her as it went past. She jumped back and swore at the driver, and I asked her if she was alright. She then swore at me, until I picked up the handbag she'd dropped, and offered her my handkerchief to dry herself.'

'Quite the knight in shining armour,' said Jackman.

Asher ignored the comment. 'She told me she was waiting for friends and was on her way to a party. And that's all.' He shrugged. 'I saw her a few days later and she smiled, so I asked her if she'd enjoyed her party. She said it was different, but no more. I assumed it had been a washout. I only saw her once after that, a few days ago. She said she was going partying again.' He looked from Marie to Jackman. 'Has something happened to her?'

'I'm afraid Shauna is dead, Mr Leyton.'

Asher's mouth dropped open in surprise. Marie was pretty sure it wasn't faked. If it was, he was damned good.

'Dead?'

'I'm afraid so. Perhaps you can now appreciate why we are so interested in her recent movements.'

Asher nodded dumbly, and Marie thought he might cry. After a moment or two he said, 'Poor little kid. She was really sweet.' When he looked up his eyes were moist. 'How did she die?'

'I'm afraid we can't say until certain formalities have been completed, sir.' Jackman's tone was softer and more compassionate. 'And that is really all you know about her? Just a few passing words in the street?'

'You have my word, Inspector. And I swear to God that I never knew she was only fourteen.' He hung his head. 'In this sad day and age, I wouldn't have dreamed of speaking to a girl that young without being introduced.'

Jackman nodded to Marie, and they both stood up. 'I'll give you my card in case you think of anything else. Now you have my direct number, Mr Leyton.'

Leyton walked them to the door and as they left, he said, 'About that other matter? If she heard about what happened and got the wrong idea, my fiancée would be devastated.'

'As I said, sir, that's not our affair. We are only interested in Shauna's last movements.' Marie levelled her gaze at the rather odd young man. 'Just give those "chance meetings" some careful thought, would you? Anything she said to you may be of use to us, okay?'

Marie glimpsed the face of a very troubled soul as Asher closed the door.

* * *

They had just got back to the car when Max phoned. 'Rory Wilkinson rang, sir, he needs to talk to you. Could you give him a bell?'

Jackman thanked him, then dialled the pathologist's number.

'Ah, Detective Inspector, sorry to interrupt your day. Although I'm far from through with my findings on this girl, I thought you should know that I ran a few initial tests.' He paused, then said, 'Toxicology has shown that she had both alcohol and drugs in her system.'

'Oh shit,' murmured Jackman. 'What kind of drugs?'

'Foxy methoxy, if you know what I'm saying?'

Jackman knew very well. He'd seen all the highs, lows, comedowns and agonising aftermaths of most street drugs by now.

'It's a club drug, a tryptamine psychedelic.'

Rory gave a little chuckle. 'I'm impressed! Not many detectives can quote that with such ease.'

'I remember it because I helped to scrape a little kid off a concrete playground after he had taken one of those and "flown" off the school roof.' Jackman said.

'Oh dear, I'm sorry about that. I can see it would etch the word rather firmly into your memory.' He paused. 'I suspected something might be amiss because of the injuries to her feet — the soles to be precise. I'm sure you are aware that when a person drowns, the body assumes a facedown position, hence the awful facial injuries we sometimes see. I expected the girl to be badly battered, but on examination I also found abrasions and lacerations that are not typical of underwater trauma.'

'To her feet?' asked Jackman, beginning to frown.

'Mmm, and on taking samples from the wounds, we discovered that the materials embedded in her flesh are not from the seabed. I suggest she ran barefoot over some pretty uneven ground before she went into the water.'

'Chased?'

'You'd need a witness to tell you the answer to that one.'

'I cannot believe that Shauna Kelly willingly took Foxy,' murmured Jackman.

'But you said yourself that the mother was having trouble keeping her away from some of the wilder kids.'

'Yes, but a few experimental drinks are what you'd almost expect with a teenager whose father has recently done a runner. Her mother said her daughter was never off her head on alcohol, and she swore that Shauna had never taken drugs — in fact she was quite anti.'

'Respectfully, Inspector, they *all* say that to their parents,' said Rory gently.

'Of course, but Liz works as a volunteer at the drop-in centre on Church Street. She would have spotted any signs of drug use a mile off.' Jackman drew in a breath. 'If Shauna had drugs in her system, I'll be willing to bet that she didn't know she'd taken them.'

'Sadly, that is more than possible. That, or peer pressure. Oh yes, and one last thing. Just a small thing, but there were no signs of any plant material, or anything else from the seabed in her hands.'

'Sorry, Rory, I'm not quite with you on that one.'

'The struggle to survive, Inspector. A drowning human grabs at anything to try to save themselves. It is usually proof that they were alive when they went into the water, although there is more to it than that. I think it's indicative that Shauna was either not fully conscious, or totally spaced out. Not a pleasant thought, I know, but I thought I should update you on that rather than leave it until the full report is ready.'

'I appreciate it. Thank you.' Jackman hung the phone up and stared at it. Shauna Kelly had been rebelling against her dad leaving, but she hadn't gone completely off the rails and according to the rest of the family, the girl still loved her mother. They had always been close, and there was no hint that she blamed Liz for the father buggering off.

It didn't make sense, and from her expression as she listened to the conversation on loudspeaker, Marie was just as baffled.

'Shauna wasn't like that, I'd stake my life on it.'

'I agree. Liz is not your average mum. She has been trained to look for all the giveaway signs in a teenager. She would know, I'm certain of it.'

'So she was drugged?' Marie shook her head.

'That's my theory.'

'And here we are, chasing around after bloody Harlan Marsh! This stinks!' Marie was almost shouting.

'Don't forget, their case also involves a missing girl. We *do* need to check this out in case they are connected. Let's just go and get it over with.' He looked sideways at her, 'I don't think I've ever seen you so riled up over something.' He paused. 'Or is it some*one*?'

Marie narrowed her eyes. 'As you said, let's just get it over with, shall we?'

Jackman put the car into gear and said nothing further.

* * *

Not far away from Asher Leyton's fancy abode, someone else was equally as troubled.

Her small home was far from elegant, but it was clean and tidy and usually it felt warm and safe to Jasmine. But not today.

Jasmine lay on the sofa, her duvet drawn tightly around her thin body. She was alone at last, although it had taken some time to convince her mother that she should go to work. Jasmine's mother, who worried about absolutely everything, had finally accepted her excuse that it was just a really bad time of the month. After making Jasmine a warm drink and a hot water bottle, she had hurried off to her job as a bookkeeper at the food factory.

Jasmine stared at the blank television screen and tried to decide what she should do. She wasn't ill, there was nothing wrong with her at all. She just couldn't face school and more to the point, she couldn't face her best friend, Chloe.

Her thoughts kept going back to the party. Jasmine gave a little snort of disgust. It had been like no party she'd ever been to. She shivered and pulled the duvet higher up under her chin. The place had been horrible. It had been dark and dirty, it stank of sweat and booze, and the worst thing of all was the fact that Chloe seemed to be having the time of her life.

A tear slipped slowly from Jasmine's eye. How could she? They had been friends since they were in nappies, and now, well . . . She grimaced. A picture flashed up in front of her. Chloe dancing with a boy she didn't even know. Chloe lifting up her skinny T-shirt top and thrusting her naked breast towards the gyrating boy's open mouth.

Jasmine felt as sick now as she had then. She sipped the drink that her mother had made her and tried to forget all the other things she had seen.

Worse things, far worse.

She placed the mug back on the table and nibbled anxiously on her bottom lip.

She should tell her father, she *knew* she should. But how could she? He'd kill her if he thought she'd been to such a dreadful place.

More tears began to fall. It should be easy. She wasn't a bad girl, she should simply do what she knew to be right. And she might well have done, if it hadn't been for the man with the horrible eyes. He had known immediately that they had gate-crashed. And then he had taken her to one side, and coldly and calmly told her what he would do if she ever breathed a word about the parties.

Jasmine knew he wasn't joking. She shivered again. That should have been okay, considering that she never wanted to go back as long as she lived, but he hadn't threatened *her*, had he? The terrible things he had said he would do . . . were to Chloe.

Jasmine began to sob. Because Chloe wanted to go back. The man had put her number on his special list, and stupid, stupid Chloe could hardly wait for the text telling her where the next party would be.

# CHAPTER SIX

'You know, I've been around these parts for decades now, but I've probably only ever been out to Harlan Marsh once or twice,' said Marie, gazing out of the window across the great expanses of flat, cabbage-covered fields.

'It's not the sort of place you go, is it?'

The bleak never-ending farmland stretched on until it met the river, then the marsh and then the sea. There was no town at the end of the road. No pretty village awaited them with quaint antique shops and cosy tearooms. And on a day like this, as the drizzling rain draped its chilly fingers around them, it was just mud all the way to the Wash.

Marie smiled to herself, because it wasn't always like this. It was in many ways a magical landscape, ancient and wild, alternating through the changing seasons between strange and inhospitable, and achingly beautiful. Marie loved the great wide ribbons of waterways, straight and shining as quicksilver, home to swans, kingfishers and water voles. And the panoramic light shows at sunrise or sunset would melt the coldest heart.

Marie remembered walking the field pads, as the locals called footpaths, with her father's spaniel racing ahead of her. The dog would run into the "litter" fields and bark as skylarks rose up ahead of him. Even as she sat in the car, Marie could still smell the meadow plants, the ragged robin, meadowsweet and clover, all cut as a hay crop for the animals. At times like this she missed her dad. Her parents had split up when she was very young, but she had benefited from having two loving homes, one here with her dad, and one in the Welsh mountains with her mum. Her parents had been wonderful, doing all they could to keep their daughter happy and well-balanced. The fact was, her parents had loved each other deeply — they just couldn't live together. Their decision to part had worked well. They remained lifelong friends, until her dad died of a heart attack some fifteen years ago.

'Fancy a detour?' Jackman slowed down as they approached a crossroads. He stared at the signpost, then pulled over. 'We are about five minutes away from the spot where your Mr Archer thinks that Shauna went into the water. If we go later we'll lose the light.'

Marie nodded and her pleasant thoughts about her father evaporated. 'Sure. Since I'm *so* looking forward to seeing Cade again, any diversion is a good one as far as I'm concerned.'

Jackman turned into the side road and they drove on.

'Over there.' Marie indicated a faded sign, half obscured by straggly bushes. 'I think that's a sign for Hurn Point, Allenby Creek, and the seal sanctuary.'

Jackman eased the car around a sharp bend. In front of them they saw an apology for a car park. Ahead were the sea-bank, the marshes, and a decrepit wooden hut with a weather-beaten painting of a seal on the wall.

They got out of the car into a damp miasma of salty drizzle.

'Lovely,' murmured Marie, turning up her jacket collar against the wind. 'Just lovely.'

Avoiding puddles of sandy mud, they walked to the old hut.

The first thing they saw was a warning sign for an MOD bombing range. The RAF still used great stretches of the Wash for target practice and Jackman and Marie both understood the red flag warning system. Below that was a dog-eared notice informing them that there was no longer any access to the seal sanctuary and that the public should take the coast road to the "new" visitors' centre.

'Dreary place,' muttered Marie.

'That it is.' Jackman moved forward. 'This spot has never been popular. The stretch of marsh between the car park and the beach has a reputation for being dangerous at high tide, which generally puts off all but the brave or the foolhardy.'

'So how on earth did Shauna finish up here?' asked Marie, gazing around at the deserted landscape.

'Most likely driven here by someone who knew just how deserted it is.' Jackman pointed towards the dunes. 'There are a few dwellings over that way, and another scattering further along the coast, but apart from those, it's just dune, marsh and sea.'

They trudged across the sand-flats, between dense clumps of sea buckthorn and areas of reeds fringing shallow pools. Then Marie stopped. She knew that old Jack Archer had been right. This was the place where Shauna Kelly went into the water.

Jackman was still walking slightly ahead of her, unaware that she had stopped in her tracks. 'Now we're here, I remember coming here with my parents when I was a little boy. Although it was very different back then. They say this coastline reinvents itself every year. Sand blows in from the offshore sandbanks and forms dunes. The whole place has changed beyond belief.' He pushed his hands deeper into his pockets. 'It looks so wild now, but I seem to recall it was quite pretty back then.' He stopped and looked around. 'Marie?'

Marie stood staring out across the grey waters of the Wash, then squatted down on her haunches and gently ran her fingers through the damp sand. 'She was here. I know it.'

Jackman shivered and looked around him. 'You're probably right. It is the perfect spot to bring a body, or to kill someone.'

'Let's go up the edge of the dunes, towards that rundown beach hut, and see if there are any houses that have a good view of this strip of beach.'

They perched side by side on a tiny stretch of crumbly stone wall, and looked across the desolate sands.

'Uniform have been out here and they had nothing to report. The few people that they did get to speak to didn't see or hear a thing.' Jackman kicked at a small pile of pebbles, sending them scattering across the path.

'When we've sorted this thing out at Harlan Marsh, I'd like to come back and talk to them myself,' said Marie.

'Me too. We'll pick a different time of day and see if we can catch some more residents.' He stood up. 'But right now, I'm afraid we have an appointment to keep.'

Marie pulled a face and sighed loudly. 'Okay. Let's get it over with, shall we?'

\* \* \*

'The chief's in a meeting, DI Jackman. He'll see you when he's through.' The Harlan Marsh desk officer looked more bored than apologetic. 'He's told one of our men to bring you up to speed and he's allocated you an office to use.'

Jackman frowned. 'Such a wonderful welcome. And please don't get carried away with the accommodation, Constable. We aren't moving in — or I sincerely hope we aren't.' He glanced at Marie. Her face was a mixture of emotions. He wasn't sure why, but she looked like she wanted to escape.

'I'll take you to your office, sir, and then I'll tell Pritchard you are here.'

The office, if you could call it that, was a small, obviously hastily cleared out cupboard of a room. Not that it worried Jackman, he had no intentions of staying.

'No place like home,' muttered Marie, peering out of the small, grimy window. 'How lovely — a room with a view.'

'We have two chairs, a desk, a phone and a computer terminal, what more do you want?' Jackman looked over her shoulder at the crumbling red brick wall of a derelict warehouse on the opposite side of an alley. They were stuck at the back of an old Victorian heap of a building. Their own nick was beginning to look more like the Ritz with every passing second.

'What do you know about Harlan Marsh?' Marie asked.

'It's a miserable little town, but it covers a huge area. I worked here for a few weeks not long after I moved up to CID, and it was the most unfriendly nick I've ever been in.'

'So when they call this division the plug-hole of the marsh, they mean it.'

'That's the polite version. Still, if all I've heard about Chief Superintendent Cade is correct, maybe they deserve him.'

Marie's face creased into a mask of contempt, and she spat out vehemently, '*No one* deserves Cade. That bastard's a really nasty piece of work.'

'I'm not sure that you should be speaking about a senior officer like that, Marie.'

Jackman tried to get over the shock of hearing his sergeant blast off in that way. 'Although, off the record, I have to agree. Most likely his officers are only such miserable sods because they have to work under him. At least we can go home when we've sorted this. They are stuck with him.' He glanced across at her and said, 'I didn't know that you'd had dealings with Cade before?'

Marie pulled a face. 'It was a while ago.'

Jackman raised his eyebrows. If that was the case, it must have been pretty serious to still bother her so deeply. 'What happened?'

It was like drawing teeth. Marie sighed. 'When Cade was a DI, he shafted a colleague of mine. Blighted her career and she never managed to make the grade after it. So, as you can imagine, I have no love for him.'

Jackman had never heard her badmouth another officer before. The aggression in her voice was about as normal for Marie as a fish climbing a tree. In his book this meant some sort of emotional involvement. 'So were you close? You and this colleague?'

At first he thought Marie wasn't going to answer, then she said quietly, 'She was my first crewmate, a great girl and so full of potential, until she turned down that slimeball's advances.' She shrugged. 'It wouldn't happen now. Cade wouldn't have dared, for fear of a sexual harassment charge, but back then a young policewoman didn't stand a chance against a senior officer like him.'

Jackman desperately wanted to delve deeper, but decided that now was not the time. He nodded and took it no further. Not that he'd leave it alone for too long. Marie had obviously never forgotten her old crewmate, and the anger she had felt had never dissipated. There was a story there that he was very interested to know — when the time was right.

A knock at the door dispelled his thoughts.

'I'm your liaison officer, sir, PC Gary Pritchard. And I'm very pleased to meet you.' An older man entered the tiny room and held out his hand.

As they shook hands, Jackman's eyes narrowed. 'Have we met before, Constable?'

'I was seconded to your area to help out on the Red House Farm murder, sir. I'm surprised you remember me.'

'I do. I always remember good coppers, and you were polite, helpful and remarkably efficient, considering that you were working way out of your comfort zone and for a different division.'

Jackman saw that Pritchard was blushing.

'Glad to have been a help, sir,' he murmured to his boots. 'That was a nasty case, that one. All those deaths under one roof.'

'Still, we eventually caught the intruder who killed them. Thank God.' Jackman frowned. 'That was the second of three terrible investigations in this area.'

'Yes, sir. Years before, Harlan Marsh had the Mulberry shootings, when Simeon Mulberry shot his wife and then himself, right in front of his children. Then you had the massacre of the farm workers at Red House Farm, and then there was that tragedy at Dovegate Lane.' He shook his head. 'What a world we live in.'

'Well, let's hope this case is a simple one. Come on in, PC Pritchard, although I can hardly say make yourself at home.'

The constable looked apologetic. 'Not exactly roomy, is it? This old place is pretty well ready for the wrecker's ball. They keep promising new premises, but then they say the budget won't stretch that far.' He bit his lip and growled. 'Even so, this is taking the proverbial. Shall I try to organise something a bit better?'

'No, we'll cope. Hopefully this is just a flying visit. Go find another chair, *if* you can fit it in, and fill us in.'

Gary Pritchard left, returning shortly dragging a chair, and in his other hand balancing a tray holding three polystyrene cups of coffee, a heap of sugar packets and some creamers. 'I hope you both drink coffee. If you don't you are unlucky, the tea here tastes like something left behind after the tide's gone out.'

Jackman smiled. 'Coffee's great, thank you. So, Constable, why are we here?'

'Well, actually it's your own fault.' Gary gave a cheeky grin. 'Chief Superintendent Cade read the county stats regarding your recent arrest rate. When a Masonic friend of his hit a problem, he promised him he'd get the best team in the area onto it. And here you are!'

'Oh, great! And are you really rushed off your feet with a serious investigation?' asked Jackman.

'We are up to our necks, sir, but then we don't have the staff that your division has. And what seems serious to us out here in the sticks is probably not as bad as the things you deal with.'

'Okay, you'd better give us the background.'

Gary sat down, stirred his coffee and frowned. 'The girl, Toni Clarkson, is sixteen and a right little tearaway. It seems that her father, Neil Clarkson and his wife Ellen, have spoilt her to the point of ruining a kid who's bright, if somewhat unruly.'

'Has she run away before?' asked Marie.

'This is the fourth or fifth time. That is why there is no missing persons alert, even though she's vulnerable because of her age. We could go public, but Daddy is shit-scared that we'll find her crashed out, drunk as a skunk, in some squat and make him look a total fool.'

Jackman's forehead had become a mass of creases. 'So good old Chief Cade, his chum in high places, has roped us in to sort it out for him?'

'As quickly and as quietly as possible, sir.'

'Well, we'll see about that, Constable,' snapped Jackman. 'I'm not renowned for my diplomatic fairy feet. We'll do what needs doing, and in whatever manner *I* see fit.'

Gary nodded and gave a satisfied smile. 'Oh, good.'

'Nice to know we already have an ally in the camp. So what happened this time, Constable?' asked Marie, taking out her notebook.

'Yesterday Toni had a row with her mother over something quite trivial, but it escalated into a huge dust-up. Dad stuck his oar in and grounded her. Toni, as you'd expect, didn't take it well, and when night fell she bunked off out of the bedroom window.'

'Where do they live?' Jackman asked.

'Cameron Court, the only posh address in the whole town. They have a ground floor apartment. It's a gated community, and has around a dozen townhouses as well as the main Court itself. That's three storeys of executive flats. Cost a mint.'

'Has she been seen since?'

'She and two mates were caught on CCTV sitting on the steps of the war memorial. They were drinking from a bottle concealed in a bag. The time was logged at 10.27 p.m.'

'And after that?' Marie was scribbling rapidly.

'Nothing. We recognised the other two girls and had a quiet word with them. They said she got stroppy when they refused to gatecrash the local nightclub with her. After a row she called her friends a pair of losers and said she was going "Somewhere where she would be welcome and there was plenty of booze." That's the last time she was seen.'

'And did they know where she meant?'

Gary shook his head. 'They had no idea at all. Then we were pulled off, for fear of attracting too much attention. At that point it was assumed that Dad still believed she was just sulking and hanging out at some friend's place.'

'I wonder if he's as certain about that in the cold light of day,' muttered Jackman.

Marie snapped her book shut. 'Maybe we should go find out?' She looked across at Gary, 'Will you be our local tour guide, Constable?'

The man rubbed at his close-cut greying beard with surprisingly slender fingers and beamed. 'Oh yes, Sergeant. Best job I've been given since there was break-in at the brewery. As long as we can take your car, that is. The duty car is off the road and we are precious short of wheels.'

'No problem.' Jackman was about to say more, but stopped abruptly.

A tall, ramrod of a man in an immaculate uniform stood in the doorway, silently surveying them.

'Oh, good morning, sir.' Gary straightened up. Jackman noticed that his smile had disappeared.

'DI Jackman, Sergeant . . . this is Chief Superintendent Cade.'

'We've already met.' Jackman's tone was cool.

'Good of you to come so quickly, DI Jackman.' The words seeped from the man's thin lips and Jackman felt a hint of revulsion tug at his gut.

Cade smiled coldly. 'I do realise that this is probably nothing, but her father is *such* a generous supporter of our police charities . . . well, what could I do?'

'We fully understand the situation,' said Jackman sourly. 'And whereas we will do all we can to assist you, we do have pressing cases of our own running, and we are anxious to get back to them.' He paused, then added a clipped, 'sir.'

'Naturally. I wouldn't expect such a *talented* team to be lounging around doing nothing.' Cade raised his eyebrows. 'So, as time is obviously of the essence, I'll let you get on. And thank you, Rowan. I knew I could count on you.'

Jackman was bitterly offended at this use of his first name. The only person who called him Rowan was Ruth Crooke. By using it, Cade implied that they were buddies, and Jackman wouldn't choose him for a friend if he were the last man left in Lincolnshire. Plus, he had totally ignored Marie!

As Cade moved away from the door, Jackman murmured, 'Oh, our pleasure, I'm sure,' then added, 'I don't think.' He stared at Marie. 'Well, he really loves you, doesn't he?'

'I'd have it no other way,' growled Marie.

* * *

Marie drove, while Jackman fired questions at Gary.

'You know this girl, Gary. In your opinion, do we have cause for concern?'

'Funnily enough, sir, for some reason I *am* worried. Maybe I'm just being a bit oversensitive, but it doesn't *feel* right.'

'How come?'

'Well, when they told us to back off, I decided to have a quick word with her mother about Toni's previous escapades.'

'And?'

'Even though on each occasion she had had the most dreadful set-to with her parents, her escapes were all carefully planned.' He paused to give Marie some directions. 'She had taken the time to pack a bag, and get herself to a cash machine before she left. Once she even took her passport. That wasn't the case this time.' His voice was sombre.

'So she hadn't intended to run away?' chipped in Marie.

'She's a clever girl and quite calculating. I reckon if she'd been doing a runner she would have prepared better.'

Jackman nodded. 'So by going out of the window she was just defying her father's curfew? Just off for a night out, sticking two fingers up at her parents?'

'Exactly. I'm certain that's how it was.'

As they passed through the gates of Cameron Court, Jackman felt inclined to agree with him. For the first time, he felt a frisson of real fear for Toni Clarkson.

# CHAPTER SEVEN

Neil Clarkson turned out to be nothing like Chief Superintendent Cade. Neil and Ellen Clarkson's concern about their wayward daughter's disappearance was undoubtedly genuine. They admitted their faults, blamed themselves for pandering to her and apologised repeatedly in case they were wasting police time.

'We lost a child, Inspector Jackman, killed in a road accident. He was only four.' Clarkson ran his hand through his thick iron-grey hair. 'It's wrong, I know, but Ellen and I have totally overcompensated with Toni.'

His wife gave a sad smile. 'And look where it's got us. We love her with all our hearts, but she's turning into a nightmare.' Ellen Clarkson was too thin, and looked like someone who didn't sleep enough.

'We are not dealing with it particularly well,' added her husband wearily.

Jackman felt for them. He had no children of his own, but he often looked after his seven-year-old nephew, Robert. There were times when he was certain the boy must be an alien, a being from a planet that bore no resemblance to the one he lived on, but he loved him.

They took the names of friends, and places Toni frequented. Jackman was mostly interested in a recently ditched boyfriend called Ethan Barley. Hurt, rejected or angry, he may have been looking for payback.

'What sort of boy is Ethan Barley?' he asked.

'He's the son of the vicar of Fendyke Village, a student, and a bit of a rebel. We met him once and weren't very impressed.' Clarkson looked at his wife.

Ellen nodded. 'Not our cup of tea. I got the impression that he was born at the wrong time. He was very passionate about causes.'

'We commented at the time that he should have been leading the miners' strike, or distributing copies of Che Guevara's manual on guerrilla warfare.' Neil Clarkson shrugged. 'Not that he was a thug or anything like that. He clearly came from a decent home and his manners were surprisingly good for such a driven young man.'

Marie asked about Toni. Was she easily led? Impressionable? Her parents both laughed at that one. Apparently Toni would argue about anything, including the weather, let alone be persuaded to do something she didn't want to.

Jackman was just about to bring the meeting to a close when his phone rang. He made an excuse and went to the hallway to answer it.

'Sir? It's Rosie here. I'm in the A&E department of Saltern General Hospital. I thought you should know that a teenage girl has been admitted, and she's in quite a bad way.'

'Rosie? How come you're at the hospital? And what makes you think it's our missing girl?'

'I overheard a call come in about a youngster found wandering around on the outskirts of one of the fen villages. She had no ID on her and she was well out of it. Then I remembered what the sarge told me, about you checking out another missing girl from the Harlan Marsh area. I decided to come down and take a look for myself.

Can you give me a description of the girl you are looking for?'

Jackman glanced at his notebook. 'Brunette, shoulder-length hair, slim, brown eyes, and wearing a yellow skinny T-shirt and boot-cut jeans.'

'Then I think you should get over here ASAP.'

'I'm with her parents right now.' Jackman bit his lip. 'You say she's in a state. Can you clarify that, before I frighten the life out of her family?'

'Battered and bruised. Possible broken ribs. Nothing immediately life-threatening, although she's pretty unstable. The medics are working on the supposition that she's taken, or been given, a drug of some kind.'

Jackman thought of Shauna. 'What? A hallucinogen, or a Rohypnol-type drug?'

'They don't know yet, it's too early to say, although thankfully there are no signs of sexual interference.'

'That's one blessing. Now, Rosie, are you sure enough about the description to allow me to bring the parents to the hospital?'

'It's close enough, sir. I'm almost certain. The clothes, the hair colour and her build all seem to tally, but please don't get their hopes up, just in case I've found a lookalike.'

Back in the lounge, Jackman carefully rephrased what DC Rosie McElderry had just told him. 'Now this may have nothing to do with Toni, but I do need one or both of you to come with us. And please forgive us if this turns out to be another girl, and not your daughter.'

Husband and wife both jumped to their feet. 'We'll take our own car, Inspector Jackman. We'll follow you.' Marie travelled with them.

Gary with Jackman discussed the case as they sped towards the hospital.

'Looks like the lass finally came up against someone tougher and nastier than she expected,' mused Gary. 'You can only push your luck so far before it runs out.' He glanced worriedly at Jackman. 'There's something else you should know, sir. For the past year, we've been trying to trace an underground drinking club. Sounds innocuous, but it's far from that. Someone is supplying underage youngsters with alcohol and God knows what else. It seems that the kids get in free and get free drinks as long as they party themselves silly, and socialise with the paying members.'

A wave of nausea hit Jackman. 'Socialise?'

Gary's face drew into a dark frown. 'Mmm, we're not sure exactly what form that takes, and no one is prepared to talk about it. Whoever runs it is damned clever. They've been one jump ahead of us for months.'

'So why can't you locate the venue?'

'That's the clever part, sir. It moves around. We suspect that members are sent a text with a time and location just a few hours before it kicks off, a bit like the old acid-house parties?' Gary shook his head. 'We've been close, but so far we've discovered zilch. And hell, wouldn't I like to get my hands on the men behind it!'

Jackman slowed down for a red light. 'Gary, at the moment we are investigating a drowning. A fourteen-year-old, with both alcohol and Foxy Methoxy in her bloodstream. We suspect she was taken to a deserted beach and dumped. The fact that she drowned must have been an added bonus for whoever drugged her. Any chance there is a connection?'

Gary nodded. 'I'd say so. If this new girl turns out to be Toni Clarkson, and she has a date-rape drug in her system, that could be connected too.'

'Then we've got to find this club and get inside it.'

'Easier said than done.'

Jackman accelerated towards the town. 'No offence, but we have better resources than you, Gary. I'm willing to bet we can crack this. What would you say if I managed to swing a temporary transfer? Get you on our team for a while?'

'I'd welcome it, Inspector Jackman, really I would.' Gary sat back and took a deep breath. 'Actually things have been pretty shitty over the last year. I lost my sister a few months back, and although the guys at the station are not a bad bunch, the atmosphere and the working environment is bad. I've been thinking about a change of scenery, but I need that club to be closed down and our kids safe from their clutches before I consider my next move.'

'Then I'll put some wheels in motion. I think Saltern-le-Fen Division could do with a man like you, PC Pritchard.'

Gary gave a broad smile.

They drove the rest of the way in silence. Jackman feared that this was turning into something far nastier than he had ever imagined.

\* \* \*

They found Rosie waiting for them in the hospital foyer. After a brief introduction she rushed them through to where the teenager was being treated. A doctor greeted them and they waited anxiously while he made sure that she was ready to be seen.

'She's still very confused, and we are concerned because we have no idea what she has taken.'

The doctor looked about twelve. His shirt was untucked and he appeared exhausted.

'Toni doesn't take drugs,' said Ellen Clarkson in a very small cracked voice.

And neither had Shauna. Jackman wondered how many times he'd heard that empty statement. The parents were always the last to find out.

'That's as maybe,' said the doctor gently, 'but there *are* drugs in her system, and some pretty powerful ones from the symptoms she is presenting.' He turned towards the door of the examination room. 'Let's just see if you recognise her first, shall we?'

They stood back as the Clarksons tentatively approached the trolley on which the agitated girl lay.

Jackman realised that he was holding his breath. Then he heard a low cry from the mother.

'Darling! My God! Whatever has happened to you?'

'Bingo,' whispered Rosie. 'Game over!'

Jackman didn't answer. Something wasn't right about all this.

Marie and the others moved away, talking animatedly, but he remained looking through the observation window.

The young woman was still hallucinating. One moment she seemed almost comatose, and the next she was throwing herself around, fighting, screaming at anyone who went near her. Her eyes were wide, her pupils contracted to little more than pinpricks. She obviously did not recognise her parents. For that reason, and to spare them further upset, a nurse quickly led them out and took them to a nearby relatives' room.

'May I go in?' Jackman asked the doctor.

'Sure. But keep well back. We've already had a syringe of sedative aimed like a dart at the far wall!'

'I just want to observe her.' He looked at the trolley and a large plastic bag beneath it. 'Her clothes have been bagged for forensics?' he asked.

'Yes, they are all there. Although the shoes are separate. They were covered in thick mud.'

As Toni yelled and cursed, Jackman stared at the clear plastic bag holding her footwear.

'She was alone when she was found?'

The doctor looked across at him. 'Yes.'

Alarm bells rang in his head.

Toni's bare feet thrashed and kicked out at the nurse closest to her. Her feet were narrow, very slim with long toes, but clearly no more than a size five. Jackman looked again at the plastic bag and the pair of mud-covered, chunky wide trainers.

'These are not her shoes,' he said softly. 'Why is she wearing someone else's shoes?'

The doctor blinked. 'Pass. Although she does keep calling out for someone called Emily. Maybe it's connected.'

As if on cue, Toni screamed the name several times and whimpered, "Where are you taking her?" Then she began shivering violently and curled into the foetal position.

An icy trickle of fear coursed down Jackman's spine.

They'd found Toni, and thank God she was alive, but who the hell was Emily?

Jackman left the room, took Toni's father to one side and asked him if he knew of a friend called Emily. The man looked blankly at him, then shook his head and returned to his distraught wife.

Jackman's mind was spinning. What did Toni mean by *"where are you taking her?"* Did they have another girl to find? He swallowed hard. He believed that they did, and considering what had happened to Shauna Kelly, whoever Emily was, she was in grave danger.

# CHAPTER EIGHT

They could do little more until Toni was able to talk. Gary offered to stay with her at the hospital, while Jackman and Marie drove back to Saltern.

Jackman said very little during the journey. Marie knew that his mind would be working overtime. They had no choice but to take seriously Toni's anxiety for this Emily, even though she was still high as a kite.

'Neither the parents nor Gary Pritchard can place a youngster called Emily in Harlan Marsh, and Gary's been working that patch long enough to know most of the little yobs and tearaways around there. Which makes this one devil of a situation. I'm not sure where the hell to start.' Jackman sounded tired.

Marie slowed down as they approached a roundabout. 'All we can do is start running the usual checks, hoping that this mysterious girl is known to us in some way.'

Jackman nodded. 'My first job will be to wire Max up to his beloved computer and let him do his stuff.'

Marie agreed. Max was by far the smartest of the team when it came to IT. She pulled up in front of the station security gates and swiped her card through the machine. 'Let's hope we have more luck than Harlan Marsh, because if we hit a brick wall too, I guess we'll have to go back there and take to the streets.'

'I have an awful feeling that's exactly what we'll be doing.' Jackman got out of the car and slammed the door. 'Oh well, nothing for it. We'd better get started on some basic checks.'

* * *

Max came up with over twenty girls with the name Emily. Mostly teenagers, they were either missing persons or petty criminals that had crept onto police files via a variety of misdemeanours. A barrage of phone calls to private homes, prisons and young offenders' institutions eliminated all but three names. One of them had died of an overdose and the other two were long-term mispers with no connection to the area.

Marie ended her last call and pulled a face. She really didn't fancy traipsing the streets of Harlan Marsh, but they needed more information and that was most likely where they'd find it.

Jackman called out from his office door. 'Marie, finish up there! We're going back to the hospital. Gary Pritchard has just rung and Toni's more or less ready to speak to us. I've told him to stay with her and not to let her talk to anyone else, not even her parents, until we get there.'

Marie pulled on her jacket and felt around in her pockets for the car keys. If Toni could say something specific about Emily, it would save them a whole load of shoe-leather.

They arrived at the hospital in seven minutes, and in another two they were standing looking down at Toni Clarkson's bruised and tear-stained face.

'Toni, this is DI Jackman and his sergeant, Marie Evans. Like I said, they are here to help you.' Gary sounded warm and reassuring, like a favourite uncle. He'd clearly used the time before their arrival to try to gain the girl's confidence.

Marie looked at Toni and saw a touch of belligerence in her eyes.

Jackman drew up a chair close to the bed and placed himself on a level with the girl, so as not to intimidate her. He assured her that she was not in any trouble, and all they wanted to do was find whoever had hurt her and punish them.

The belligerence in Toni's eyes slowly disappeared, and only fear remained. 'I don't know anything,' she whimpered.

'Well, let's start when you left your friends at the war memorial, shall we?' asked Jackman softly.

Toni's eyes darted around the room. She swallowed several times, but said nothing.

'You told your friends you were going somewhere where you'd be welcome.'

Toni drew in on herself, and despite the almost unbearable heat of the room, she began to shiver.

'Did you go to that place, Toni?' Jackman asked.

Marie knew that if she did exist, with every second things were looking blacker for Emily. 'And were you welcome?' she added softly. 'Were you given alcohol?'

Toni gave a long, shaky sigh and nodded miserably. 'There's always free booze if you want it.'

'And where is the place?'

'As if I'm going to tell you lot!' Her defiance returned. 'They'll kill me if I grass them up, and anyway . . . It's not that straightforward.' She wiped a tear from her cheek and winced as she touched the bruised bone.

'But I'll tell you this, there were people there that I'd never seen before.' She drew the bedclothes tighter to her and rocked backwards and forward. 'They said they were going on to another party.'

'And you went with them?' Jackman looked at the girl. She nodded again.

'In a car?'

'Yes.'

'What kind? Was it a 4x4?' Jackman asked.

'No, just an ordinary car.'

'Were you alone?'

'I thought some of the others were going, but when I got into the car, it was just me with one of the men.'

'It's okay, Toni. You're safe now.' Jackman's voice was gentle. 'We won't let anything else happen to you. But do you know where you went? Did you recognise the place where the party was held?'

'There was no party.' Her voice was heavy, flat. 'And I don't know where I was taken. We drove for ages, way out onto the fen somewhere. The place stank of rotting cabbage. It made me want to throw up.'

'Was it a farm?' asked Marie. 'Or some sort of farm building, maybe?'

The girl shook her head. 'I dunno. I don't think so. It was old and really creepy.' She frowned. 'But I could hear music, so I wasn't scared. We went down into a sort of cellar. It had oil lamps and candles and the seats were old boxes with blankets thrown over them. There were wine bottles everywhere. I thought it was pretty cool to start with . . .'

But not later, Marie thought angrily, seeing the welts on her face and watching as she clasped her midriff to protect her cracked ribs.

'How many people were there with you, Toni?' Jackman asked.

'To start with, just me and the bloke who drove me there. He said we were early, and the others would be along soon. He gave me a glass of red wine.'

'And you drank it?'

'Free wine?' Toni rolled her eyes at Jackman as if he'd just said something quite insane. 'Uh, yeah.'

'Can you describe the man, Toni?'

'Kind of old, bit like you I guess. But he had a great haircut, and trendy clothes.'

'Tall? Short?' Jackman was smiling slightly at being described as old.

Toni looked at him. 'Your height, but he had a hotter body. More muscles.'

Marie was trying hard not to grin. 'What about his clothes?'

'Faded jeans, but expensive. Blue T-shirt and trainers, and a grey zip-up jacket with a hood. Yeah, he was trendy for an old guy.'

'Listen, Toni,' Jackman said. 'Would you recognise him again?'

She shrugged, then gasped and put a hand to her broken rib. 'Maybe. He was kind of ordinary looking, and a bit shy, although he smiled a lot. Oh, and he smelled good,' she added.

Jackman threw a puzzled look in Marie's direction. Whatever this man had done to her, thought Marie, talking about him didn't seem to upset Toni. And he didn't come over as some sinister psycho either.

'Was he the one who hurt you?'

Toni shook her head. 'Oh no, not him. When the others arrived, he left. I didn't see him again.'

'The others?'

Toni tensed, and swallowed hard. 'I . . .' She paused, her young brow wrinkled in confusion. 'Things got weird. I can't remember any more.'

Marie's heart sank. The damned drug must have been in the wine. Just as they were getting to the crux of the matter, Toni was slipping off the radar.

'Can you recall how many people were there?'

'I don't know. Not many.'

Jackman was regarding the girl thoughtfully. Then he gave Marie a look that said they'd pussy-footed around for long enough. His expression changed. 'Toni, when you were brought in you spoke about someone called Emily. Do you remember her? Was she there with you?'

A look of terror stamped itself on Toni's face.

69

'Toni, who is Emily, and exactly what happened to her?'

A gurgle escaped from the teenager's throat, and then a loud, low moan. Marie hoped it wouldn't bring the medical staff running.

Jackman leant closer to the bed. 'Listen, Toni! She may be in grave danger. You have to tell us anything you can remember. Please!'

Tears began to flood down over the livid bruises. 'I told you, it all got weird. It's like a bad dream. Everything's all jumbled up together.' Toni sobbed. 'Someone was singing, and then someone was shaking me and asking me stupid questions.'

'What questions?'

'Like when was I born.'

The age of consent. Marie gritted her teeth. The bastard was checking whether she was underage. 'You mean the year you were born?'

'No. The whole thing. The day, the month *and* the year.' Wordlessly, Gary held out a tissue to her and Toni took it and wiped her nose. 'He did the same to Emily.' The tears welled up again.

'Then I was out in the fields! I was so scared. I felt sick. Emily had gone, and I was lost. I wanted my mum and dad. I wanted to go home.'

'Who is Emily, Toni? You *have* to tell us.' Jackman was almost shouting. Marie gave a sharp cough that meant, "Don't blow it now."

'I think my patient has had enough for now, Inspector.' The young doctor was standing in the doorway and he was no longer smiling.

Jackman nodded brusquely, smiled tightly at Toni, and they reluctantly left the room.

'I'll hang on here, sir,' said Gary, 'until you can organise some uniforms to come and take over from me.' He gave them a conspiratorial wink. 'But there's no rush.

I'll do my best to get another word with her when she's calmed down.'

Jackman drove back to the station, giving Marie time to read through her notes. Two things bothered her. 'What was all that about *exactly* when she was born? I mean, if they were checking her age with sex in mind, she's sixteen, so . . .' she shrugged. 'So why ditch her and take the other lass?'

Jackman shook his head. 'Maybe they *wanted* underage girls, and Emily may be younger than Toni. Or perhaps Toni was hallucinating by that time? Then again, if someone was looking for a particular girl, then he'd need an exact birth date.' He pulled a face. 'Nothing really makes much sense, does it?'

'And another thing, what the hell did she mean by saying that the club she went to "wasn't that straightforward?"'

'Well, I think I can answer that.' Jackman muttered a curse and accelerated past a slow-moving vehicle. 'The Harlan Marsh officers have been chasing a venue that constantly changes location.'

Marie sat and listened with growing distaste as Jackman told her about the drinking club. 'Sounds like a pretty nasty set-up, sir.'

'It does. And because the venue moves about, it has been difficult to nail them. Every time they get close, it moves off again.'

'I see, so that's what Toni meant. Maybe she'll feel like telling us a bit more when the seriousness of what happened finally hits home. It might even be something of a turning point for her.'

Jackman raised an eyebrow. 'Let's hope so. I think it's scared her senseless.'

'Oh well, let's hope Gary gets a lucky break with the kid. He's a good man, isn't he?'

Jackman nodded. 'He's not that old, but he reminds me of the old-style proper coppers.'

'Exactly,' said Marie. 'Give me that any day rather than the lads who go in with one finger on the CS gas canister.'

'And that leads me neatly to another point, Marie. If you agree, I'm going to be asking the super if we can have Gary temporarily transferred to our team. What do you think?'

Marie nodded. 'Excellent idea, sir. His local knowledge could help.'

'Good, then let's get back and I'll get that sorted.'

It was dusk by the time they got back to the incident room, but Max, Charlie and Rosie were still heads down at their computers.

Jackman grinned at them. 'Okay, you guys. Get home, get some rest, then get back early tomorrow.'

Rosie looked up. 'I'm happy to give it another hour, sir.'

Marie smiled at her. How come a mature woman, sharp as a butcher's knife, managed to look like an eighteen-year-old school prefect?

Jackman shook his head. 'Thanks, but no. You get away. Take the opportunity to rest while you can.'

Rosie gathered up her coat and bag. 'Okay. See you tomorrow.' She glanced across to Max, hunched over his keyboard. 'Are you coming?'

Max leaned back, stretched his arms above his head, and groaned. 'I guess. This search is going nowhere anyway.' He stood up. 'Hang on for me, flower, and I'll walk down to the car park with you.'

Jackman watched them go, then went off to see if the office manager had left him any messages before he too went home. Marie was left to think over what had happened in the last few hours.

She was certain of one thing at least. There *was* an Emily.

But where was she?

* * *

72

Jackman was just hanging up the phone when Marie walked into his office. 'That was Gary. Toni has calmed down considerably, and when her parents went for a coffee they had "a bit of a natter," as he put it.'

Marie smiled, glad that they'd chanced upon PC Pritchard. 'And?'

'First, she confirmed that Shauna Kelly was at one of the parties. They weren't friends but Toni knew her by sight. And Emily does exist. They'd never met before that night, and because of the drink and the drugs, her description of the girl was vague. Long, dark hair and beautiful eyes was the best Toni could come up with. Apparently the man who was molesting them got very excited when Emily told him her date of birth, and soon after that she was dragged away. Then Toni only has vague memories of being manhandled into a car and dumped miles from anywhere.'

'Well, at least we know we're not chasing shadows.'

'That we do. The uniforms are there with Toni now. Gary's going to hitch a lift back to Harlan Marsh with a mate of his who is a porter in A&E. He said he'll stay with Toni until his friend's shift finishes.' Jackman leaned back in his chair and Marie saw how weariness had darkened his eyes.

'The main thing is that now we know Emily is real. And it looks like she's been abducted.'

A shiver rippled across Marie's shoulder blades. When you'd seen what supposedly civilised people were capable of, it was almost impossible to stop your imagination settling on the very worst scenarios.

Jackman abruptly stood up. 'I know it goes against the grain to walk out when there is a girl missing, but we have uniform both on the streets and checking out any "old and creepy" properties, as Toni put it. Let's go get some rest.'

Marie nodded. He was right. It went against the grain, but they were going to need to keep their wits about them, and you couldn't do that on no sleep.

* * *

Asher Leyton pushed back his office chair and stretched. He had intended to work on for another hour or two, but he was having trouble concentrating. He kept seeing the face of that kid on Brewer Street. She was dead, and it was bothering him deeply.

He picked up his Parker Duo fold pen from the polished desk, tucked it into his jacket pocket and stood up. He should go home. It would be nice to surprise Lynda. Maybe he'd take her to supper at Lorenzo's. She'd like that. She liked the finer things in life. And he knew that was why she had got engaged to him, and why she had agreed to live with him before they were married.

When he was with Lynda he was the perfect gentleman. He acted honourably, and with old-world decorum. Just what she expected and wanted.

Asher closed his eyes and groaned. It was killing him. He had needs, and right now they were threatening to overpower him. He adored Lynda, worshipped her. He wanted her. But he knew that the only way he could keep her was to respect her puritanical, Victorian-era wishes, no matter how painful they were to him. She might appear to be a chic, modern young woman, but her deeply religious parents had instilled in her an inflexible, old-fashioned morality.

With another, deeper groan, he drew his wallet from his desk drawer and checked its contents. Plenty for what he needed. With a satisfied little grunt, he pushed the wallet into his pocket and made for the door.

He'd take Lynda to supper, buy her champagne and escort her home, just like the perfect gentleman. But before he even laid eyes on her flawless porcelain skin and shimmering soft hair, he would have to keep another very different appointment.

## CHAPTER NINE

Before they left the station to visit Toni's ex, Ethan Barley, Jackman and Marie took some time to make a list of derelict or abandoned places for uniform to check out for them.

'There's the old pumping station at Quintin Eaudkye, and what about that big old place on the Roman Bank?' Jackman stared at the growing list.

'Windrush? The old sanatorium?' Marie grinned. 'I know that old dump quite well. I spent a week there when I was a probationer. The owners rented it out to us for a training course, search and rescue and fire safety stuff. It had been an army billet in the Second World War, and then it was a TB sanatorium. Really creepy, but interesting. The course was dead boring so I spent quite a bit of time tracing its chequered history.'

'Sounds like you could have done guided tours in the summer months.'

'Probably should have.' Marie looked at the clock. 'Time to go. We have a vicar and his offspring to meet.'

\* \* \*

The name Fendyke Vicarage conjured up an image of chocolate box prettiness. In fact, it was a 1940s four-bedroom house, built in the grounds of the church to accommodate the vicar and his family. Its successive occupants had made no effort to make it more homely. And if the house was unexpected, then the vicar himself was even more of a surprise.

The man that answered the door was around six foot tall, and as broad as he was high. His full beard conjured up salty seadog rather than vicar. Jackman wondered about his sermons.

'Come in, come in.' He stood back and they squeezed in between his bulk and the doorframe.

He led the way down a long hallway and into a large, airy lounge. Busy floral-patterned curtains did battle with a colourful carpet.

On a modern leather sofa, which looked incongruous amid the flower prints, lounged a black Labrador, a white cat and a spotty youth.

All three looked up as they entered. Jackman had difficulty deciding whose expression was the most disdainful.

'Nicholas, call your brother down, please.' The vicar turned to the detectives. 'I thought I'd better have both my sons available for you to talk to.' He raised a bushy eyebrow. 'Whatever the reason for your visit, it's bound to concern at least one or possibly both of them.'

The teenager slouched off, and shouted 'Ethan!' from the bottom of the stairs.

Jackman smiled at the vicar. 'They aren't in trouble, sir. We just need some help with our enquiries regarding a missing teenager.'

Reverend Barley indicated two armchairs, and heaved the reluctant dog from the couch. As he lowered himself down, the sofa springs gave out a squeal of protest.

'Ah, this is Ethan, my eldest boy, and Nicholas, the baby of the family.'

The 'baby' flopped back down at the far end of the couch and glowered at them from beneath a lank fringe.

Ethan dutifully stuck out a hand, then dragged a giant leather beanbag towards the fireplace and casually draped himself over it. He was thin and narrow-faced, with dark hair. He wore black-rimmed designer glasses and jeans slung so low that they appeared to be defying gravity.

Marie gave them an abridged version of Toni's ordeal, and asked if either of them knew a girl called Shauna Kelly, or a girl called Emily with long, dark hair.

Jackman watched them keenly. Nicholas's face remained blank, but at the mention of Toni's name, Ethan took in a sharp breath.

'Is Toni going to be okay?' asked the boy.

'We hope so. She was very lucky to have escaped with only relatively minor injuries,' said Jackman.

The vicar spoke in a low growl. 'Best day's work you ever did, boy, breaking up with that girl. She's trouble. I always said so, didn't I?'

'It's hardly her fault if some bastard spiked her drink.'

'Language, Ethan!'

'Do you have a better word for someone who does that kind of thing?'

Jackman couldn't think of any, but decided not to join in the family argument.

'And Shauna, or Emily?' asked Marie.

'Nah,' mumbled the younger boy.

They looked at Ethan.

'Not Shauna, but a week or so ago a student friend of mine tried chatting up a girl called Emily in a pub in Harlan Marsh.' He shrugged. 'Might not be the same Emily of course.'

'Do you know what she looked like?'

Ethan shook his head. 'I never saw her, but my friend said she was a stunner. He was gutted when she told him to get lost.'

Marie took down the boy's name and number.

'We'll see if he recalls anything that might help us. Now, can you tell me if you've ever heard about an illegal, underage drinking club? One that regularly changes its venue?'

The vicar leaned forward. 'Whoa there! My lads wouldn't go near that sort of place.'

'I'm sure they wouldn't,' Marie said. 'But they might have heard rumours about it, mightn't they?'

The vicar sat back again. 'I suppose so. Boys?'

Ethan shook his head. 'I've never heard of it, but I'd guess Toni Clarkson could help you. She was always on about some place where you could get legless for free. Not my kind of scene.' He bit his lip. 'And, if you must know, that was one reason why we broke up.'

'Good thing she dumped you. Cheap tart,' muttered Nicholas. But Jackman had seen his expression. Nicholas knew more about the drinking club than he was letting on.

'And you, Nicholas? Anything filtered your way?'

'Nah.' He shifted slightly in his seat. 'Dunno what you're on about.'

Jackman did not believe him, and he knew Marie didn't either, but neither of them commented. It would be better to get the boy on his own. 'And finally, Reverend Barley, would you know who holds a key for the old chapel out on the Fen Road?'

Jackman glanced quickly at the two boys. Ethan maintained an indifferent expression, but Nicholas gave a small start that he hastened to cover up.

'Well, *I* do actually. Why do you ask?' The vicar looked bemused.

'We are checking all deserted and unsafe buildings,' said Jackman. 'Because of the missing girl. Could we please trouble you to either unlock it for us, or let us have the key temporarily?'

'Of course. I'll get it for you now.' He eased himself up, and the sofa squeaked again, probably with relief.

He came back and handed Jackman a metal keyring with a tattered card label attached to it. 'I wouldn't like to say how long it is since the door was opened, DI Jackman.

I think it must have been last autumn when we had all those high winds. The bell tower collapsed and we checked inside for other damage. Since then it's remained shut up.'

Jackman wasn't so sure about that. He nodded and took the keys.

The vicar glanced at the mantle clock. 'I'd come with you, but I have an appointment with one of my parishioners in fifteen minutes.'

'No problem, sir. We'll bring them straight back.' Marie looked around and smiled. 'Maybe one of your lads would like to come down there with us?'

'No way.' Nicholas rose from his couch with unprecedented speed and headed for the door. 'Stuff to do.'

Ethan placed a hand behind one ear. 'Oh yeah. I can hear the plaintive cry of an abandoned PlayStation.'

'Get stuffed!'

'I'll go with you.' Ethan didn't sound exactly enthusiastic, but he *had* volunteered.

'Good boy,' said the vicar. 'Do you have children, DI Jackman?'

'No, although my brother has boys and, when I can, I spend time with them.'

The vicar shook his head. 'Well, they are a blessing and a curse. I somehow suspect that Nicholas will not be following in his brother and sister's footsteps to university.'

'I doubt he'll even make it to the Job Centre,' added Ethan grimly.

The reverend sighed. 'We mustn't give up on him, son. Maybe he'll surprise us all one day.'

By the look of his younger son, the only surprise Reverend Barley was likely to get would be an unpleasant one.

As Jackman drove back towards the chapel he glanced in the rear view mirror at Ethan. He was not the kind of boy he had expected, considering Neil and Ellen

Clarkson's rather scathing opinion of him. Above all, even disregarding their age difference, Jackman could not picture him with the belligerent, lippy young Toni.

'So what are you studying?' Jackman asked, smiling into the mirror.

'Politics and International Relations. I'm doing a degree at Nottingham.'

'Are you going to specialise?'

'I'm planning on doing Globalisation in my third year.'

'Interesting. Did I hear your father mention that your sister is also at uni?'

Ethan's narrow face broke into a smile. 'Oh yes. Daybreak is the brains of the family.'

'Daybreak?' Marie queried.

'Her name's Dawn, but she hates it. She calls herself, Danni. Daybreak's my version of her real name. She's at Oxford studying Theology. Dad is over the moon. If it weren't for Nick, he'd really believe he'd been thrice blessed.'

'You *do* know that your brother knows about this drinking club?' said Marie casually.

'What? Nick? You're kidding!' Ethan laughed. 'Nick would need satnav to find his own belly button. He's thick as sh—, as two short planks. He'd never be clever enough to keep quiet about something like that.'

'I wouldn't be so sure,' said Marie. 'He reacted when we mentioned it. He almost slid down the back of the couch.'

'I can't believe that.'

Jackman gave a shrug. 'We'll see, shall we? Forgive me for saying this, but what on earth did you see in Toni Clarkson? You two seem poles apart.'

Ethan took a deep breath. 'Don't be deceived by Toni, Inspector. She's far cleverer than she lets on. What did I see in her? Well, I loved the way she kept true to herself, despite her family's wealth. I loved the way she

80

kicked against the system. I saw a free spirit, and I think I may know her better than she knows herself.'

Jackman turned into the lane leading to the chapel.

'She'll calm down as she grows up.' Ethan spoke more like her mentor than a former boyfriend. 'You might not believe it, but Toni can be really sweet when you get her away from her friends.'

Jackman pulled up and switched off the engine. In the sudden quiet Ethan said, 'She had a close call, didn't she?'

'Yes, Ethan, she did.' Jackman's expression was grave. 'About as close as it gets. We believe she narrowly escaped being abducted.'

'Is she allowed visitors?'

'She may be going home this afternoon, so ring first, but yes, I think it would do her good to see a friendly face.'

They got out of the car and walked up to the entrance. Jackman had decided to check the main chapel before they went into the cellar.

Ethan brushed plaster dust from his skinny jeans. 'What a dump!'

'Have you been in here before?' Marie asked.

'I was at home when the storm hit. I came down with my father and a few of the parishioners to check for damage.'

'Did Nicholas go with you?'

The boy frowned. 'Come to think of it, he did, which was pretty weird. He doesn't usually help with anything.'

They scoured the old building for some ten minutes, finding nothing but dusty broken masonry and pigeon droppings.

'Okay, let's check the cellar, shall we?'

'There's a cellar?' asked Ethan. 'On these silty fens? I never knew that.'

Marie nodded. 'Well, I suppose it's a crypt really. There's a door round the back.'

They watched his face, but saw only mild surprise. It intensified when he watched them lift aside matted nettles and brambles to expose the steps down to the door.

'Bloody hell!' He glanced at Marie and shook his head in disbelief. 'I bet my father doesn't know about this. What do you think is down there?'

'Let's find out, shall we?' Jackman decided that the boy actually looked genuinely stunned by their discovery.

Marie tried the smallest of the three keys into the lock. The old door swung open more smoothly than it ought to have done, and they stepped inside.

The crypt was a large open area. It had a stone floor, a low ceiling, and the remnants of one mega party.

Ethan let out a low whistle.

Marie glanced at Jackman. 'I think we just found one of the venues for that drinking club.'

Jackman gazed around the crypt. Bottles, cans, plastic glasses, cigarette packets and dog-ends, and dozens of spent candles were strewn across the floor.

'This is gross.' Ethan's navy and white Converse boot kicked at a used condom. 'This was a place of worship.'

Jackman noted the disgust on his face. Ethan might be a student radical, but his father's influence was clearly still there.

'So was Medmenham Abbey,' said Jackman, 'And look what the Hellfire Club used that for.'

'It's still gross.'

'It is. Now, I wonder *how* the partygoers got hold of the key for this place?' Marie directed a shrewd glance and a raised eyebrow towards Ethan.

Ethan Barley stared back, wide eyed. 'Nick? Oh no, surely you can't think—?'

'I do, actually.'

Jackman was picking his way through crushed lager cans and discarded crisp packets. He called back, 'Sorry, Ethan, but I'm with Marie on this. I think your brother is more savvy than you give him credit for.'

Ethan turned pale. 'My father will kill him if he finds out.'

'I hope you mean that figuratively.'

The boy said nothing.

'I am afraid that we are going to need these keys,' said Marie, dangling the ring on her index finger. 'We need to seal this place up, and get a SOCO down here.'

'Forensics?' Ethan's eyes grew wider.

'This may have been the place that Toni and Emily were brought to.' Marie said gently.

He stared at the floor. 'If you find evidence that my brother has something to do with this, he'll be in serious trouble, won't he?'

'Up to his sticky-out ears, I'm afraid.' Marie pushed her hands deep into her pockets. 'Unless, of course, you could get him to talk to us. We'd be a lot more lenient with him then.'

'And, Ethan, we need to know if there has been another key cut,' Jackman added. 'Do you think you could find out for us? Meanwhile we'll say nothing about suspecting that Nicholas may be involved.'

'I need some air.'

Ethan walked slowly back through the door and up the steps. Shoulders hunched, he went over to a low wall that edged the churchyard, and sat down heavily.

Jackman went over and sat down beside him. 'We could be wrong. But we *have* to find out what's going on, you realise that, don't you, Ethan?'

Ethan nodded. 'I'll help — for my family's sake, and for Toni and the other girl.' He looked at Jackman. 'Is this Emily in serious danger?'

'What do you think, Ethan? According to Toni she was drugged and dragged away, God knows where. She hasn't been seen since. It doesn't get much more dangerous than that.'

The boy bit his lip and stared at the ground. 'I'll do all I can with Nicholas.'

Marie walked over to them. 'I'll call this in, sir, and get uniform down here. Then we'll get Ethan home.'

Back at the vicarage, Jackman gave the boy his card. 'Any time, day or night, okay?'

Ethan nodded and pocketed it. 'I hope you find her.'

Jackman glanced at Marie as they pulled away. 'He's not a bad kid, but his brother gives me the creeps. No mention of a mother.'

'I'm guessing she's dead,' Marie said flatly. 'I saw some photographs in the lounge, all rather old. No new ones.'

'Mmm, I rather thought the same.'

'Maybe that's why Nicholas is so . . .' Marie shrugged. 'Hard to find a word to describe him, isn't it?'

'I can think of a few, but none are repeatable.' Jackman grinned at her, and then the smile faded. 'This whole thing is getting complicated, Marie, and I keep thinking about the fact that we are supposed to be finding time to reopen the Kenya Black case.' He sighed. 'We need to get to the bottom of these clubs fast. If we can close them down and collar the men behind them, we stand a good chance of halting the abductions.'

'And finding our missing girl.' Marie nodded, almost to herself. 'Well, at least we now have a starting point. The chapel was definitely a venue. We will certainly find forensic evidence there, so . . .' She smiled at him. 'It's a positive thing, sir. We are moving forward at last.'

Jackman was glad of Marie's confident approach, but hoped that they would not encounter yet another obstacle.

Or worse still, another missing girl.

# CHAPTER TEN

Max stretched and pushed back his chair. 'Hot chocolate?' he called across to where Rosie sat at her computer.

She looked up and smiled. 'I'd kill for one, as they say.'

Max walked out to the vending machine, and glanced back at her. Rosie was still staring at the monitor, idly twisting her hair into a tight corkscrew. He smiled. He'd often noticed her doing that when she concentrated.

As he sorted out some change, he wondered why he'd always taken Rosie for granted. They were on different teams but had worked in the same office for years, so why hadn't he found out more about her. He knew she was one of three girls, all in the police force, and all in different divisions, and that she had a flat over a flower shop in the High Street. End of. She was supposed to be his colleague, maybe even his friend. Should he ask her to go for a drink with him?

Max pushed the coins hard into the machine. They had a missing girl to find, and he needed to keep his mind firmly on that. This was no time for idle daydreams.

\* \* \*

PCs Andy English and Kevin Stoner sat in their squad car and appraised the scene before them.

Windrush was a massive old Gothic Victorian property, sitting in overgrown parkland that rose up on a hill that bordered the marsh. It must have been quite something in its heyday, but those times were definitely over.

'Oh my,' murmured Andy. 'We'll need a fortnight to check this dump thoroughly.'

Kevin didn't answer. He was still trying to take in the scale of the old mansion. The main house was more or less intact, but someone was apparently demolishing some of the outbuildings. Piles of rubble and stacks of old timber were heaped along the edge of the lawn, and Kevin could see a plume of grey smoke rising from around the back.

'Well, someone is here.' He pointed to the smoke. 'Let's go have a word.'

Andy nodded. The two policemen stepped out onto the weed-covered gravel drive and slammed the car doors. They made their way towards a flight of stone steps that led up to the main entrance.

A JCB stood at the foot of the steps. They both heard a soft ticking sound as they passed it.

Andy nodded at it. 'Engine's cooling down. You're right about someone being around.'

'What are they doing with this place?' murmured Kevin.

'No idea. I haven't been out this way for years.'

Kevin pushed open one of two big front doors and they stepped into a huge foyer. 'Fenland Constabulary!' he called out. 'Anyone home?' His voice echoed across the cracked marble floor, up the empty staircase.

'Must be outside.' Together they walked around to the side of the house.

On what was left of an expanse of concrete patio was a battered metal skip with a thick plank of wood resting against the lower edge. As they approached it, they saw a mountain of a man, his fat hands gripping the rubber handles of a loaded builder's wheelbarrow, stride effortlessly up the plank. With a roar, he heaved upward and sent the weighty contents crashing down into the dented old container. With a deft twist, he turned the cement-caked barrow and marched down.

Sweat dripped from a brow that creased into a scowl of disapproval when his eyes fell on the two policemen.

Kevin fought to retain his normal calm expression as he gazed at the ugliest man he had ever seen. 'Er, good afternoon, sir. Are you the owner here?'

Every inch of the man's huge frame flashed a warning signal.

'No.' The frown deepened and he added, 'There's nothing here for you. This is private property.'

'Sorry, sir, but we have a young woman missing.' Kevin tried to look taller and tougher than he actually was, but gave up quickly. 'We are checking all the unoccupied buildings in the area, and we'd like the owner's permission to have a look around.'

Something darted across the giant's face. Andy found his expression hard to read, but the mention of the girl had clearly affected him in some way.

'Oh, well, that's different.' He didn't smile at them, but his anger seemed to abate somewhat. 'A girl, you say? Well, I've been out here from dawn to dusk for the past month and I've seen no one.'

'It's a big place, sir. She could have sneaked in, or been brought here, and you'd not necessarily have noticed. We do need to have a look, I'm afraid.'

'Yes, of course, uh, I don't suppose the owner, Mr Broome, would object.' He brushed dirt from his meaty hands and wiped them down his trouser legs. 'But I'll have to come with you. This place is not safe. And some of it is locked. I'll need to get the keys. Oh, and you'll need hard hats too. Health and safety, and all that crap.'

'Thank you, sir,' said Andy politely. 'And you are . . . ?'

The man took his time. 'Micah. I'm Micah Lee, Mr Broome's caretaker. He don't come here too often, so I keeps an eye on things for him.'

'And you are doing a lot of work too,' added Kevin, looking at the site that Micah was in the process of clearing. 'What are the plans for this place?'

'It's a big project, a dream really. But you'd better ask Mr Broome about that. I'll give you his card when we go into my office.' He sniffed loudly. 'Now, come with me and we'll get those hats.'

An hour later, their shoes scuffed and their uniforms dirty, the two policemen decided that enough was enough.

'No one has been here, have they?' grumbled Kevin.

'They'd be barking if they did,' added Andy, rubbing plaster dust from his trouser leg. 'This place is a death trap.'

Kevin looked at Micah. 'Sorry to have disturbed you, Mr Lee. Good luck with the project.' He grimaced. 'Because I reckon you are going to need it.'

'Oh it'll happen, you'll see, Officer. It will take time, but Mr Broome will get his dream one day.'

Kevin opened the car door and sank gratefully down into the driver's seat. 'I hope so, sir.' He turned on the ignition, waved, and then drove down the wide driveway as swiftly as he could.

'Bloody hell! That was one ugly son-of-a-bitch, wasn't it?'

'Hagrid meets the Incredible Hulk.' Andy swallowed. 'I'm going to have nightmares thinking about that face, and did you see the calluses on his hands?'

'I did, and I certainly wouldn't want to meet him in an alley on a dark night.'

Andy stared down at the tatty dog-eared card that he held in his hand. 'Shall I give this Broome bloke a bell?'

Kevin slowed down at the gatehouse then pulled out into the deserted lane. 'Not much point. I get the feeling that the big guy will probably have already contacted him about our visit.' As he accelerated away from the desolate old property, he frowned. 'But I will make sure the boss knows about this place. I can't say that I'm really happy about it, are you?'

Andy let out a whistle, 'Want me to be honest? I've never felt so spooked by a place since I was a cub scout and someone shut me in the churchyard at dusk.' He rubbed his hands together. 'Shit-scared, my friend, that's how I felt. Shit-scared.'

* * *

Back at the station, Jackman went to check for any messages from forensics. Clive, his office manager, flashed a cheery grin and began to root around in the masses of untidy paperwork on his desk. He located the correct memo sheet in seconds, something that always amazed Jackman.

'One of the SOCOs rang us from the scene, boss. She reckoned there were enough bodily fluids floating around in there to crash their computer's DNA file, but unfortunately the tests take time. It will be over a week before we get the results.'

'Sod it! How about prints?'

'A shedload. She'll stick them on the database as soon as she gets back to the lab. If there's any matches they'll come up straight away.'

'That sounds a bit more promising. Keep me posted, will you?'

Jackman went back to his office, where Marie joined him. 'Marie? I suppose you don't know if we've ever bumped into young Nicholas Barley before — in an official capacity.'

'He's had his collar felt a few times,' said Marie. 'Unfortunately it was nothing bad enough to warrant taking his dabs.'

'No matter. We'll take them anyway.'

'I'll get that sorted,' said Marie. 'By the way, can I run something past you, sir?'

'Fire away.'

'Do you think Toni Clarkson would be up to going to the old chapel, to see if she can remember if that was where the so-called party was held?'

Jackman nodded. 'I think she's got the nerve, don't you?'

'Yes, I do. Shall I go over to the hospital and ask her?'

Jackman shook his head. 'No offence, but why not ring Harlan Marsh nick and get Gary Pritchard to do it. He seems to have a way with that kid.'

'Good point. I'll contact him. And I'll ring that friend of Ethan's too.'

Jackman walked back out to the CID room and saw Rosie, Max and Charlie all gloomily staring at computer printouts. 'I guess from your faces that we've nothing more on Emily?'

Rosie looked up. 'Sorry, boss. We are running out of options to explore.'

'I'm beginning to wonder if that drug messed with Toni's head. We could be hunting a hallucination.' Max pulled a face.

'We can't rule that out, but the kid is remembering more every time we speak to her. I'm sure Emily exists. Sorry, guys, just keep looking.'

Marie joined them. 'Ethan's friend isn't answering his mobile, so I've left a message on voicemail. Let's hope he gets back to us.'

'And Gary?'

'He's on his way to the hospital now, and he was certain that he could get her to visit the chapel.'

'Excellent. We'll meet him there, and then go back to the chapel with Toni. If she recognises that cellar, it will tell us something definite. And we'll ask her if she can remember any more about Emily.' Jackman straightened up. 'Right, time to move. Rosie, you check our own records and see if we have anything logged here in Saltern-le-Fen about illicit parties or drinking clubs. Keep me updated on anything you unearth, and Max, you and Charlie keep digging regarding mispers, and listen out for this call from Ethan Barley's friend. Get as much as you can from him about the Emily he chatted up in the pub, okay?'

Max nodded. 'Wilco.'

'Then go to it. We *have* to find out what happened to Toni Clarkson, and particularly whether we have another missing girl. We need something to corroborate Toni's story about the beautiful Emily with the long dark hair.'

\* \* \*

Jackman tossed Marie his keys. 'You drive. My phone's ringing.'

He pulled his mobile from his pocket and walked around to the passenger door.

'DI Jackman? I'm sorry, but I need to understand something.'

It took him a moment to realise it was Ethan Barley. 'Sure, Ethan, fire away.'

'Can you assure me that it really would help my brother if he spoke to you? I mean, it's not some kind of trick on your part, is it? I know a bit about entrapment and shit like that. It does happen, so don't tell me otherwise.'

'I wouldn't lie to you, Ethan. That sort of thing does go on, but not with my team, okay? If Nicholas knows something, and he comes to us freely, it will go well for him. Likewise, if he knows something and hides it from me, I'll hit him harder than a speeding lorry. Is that clear?'

The line went quiet for a long time. Finally, Ethan said, 'Then I think he needs to talk to you.'

'If he needs a bit of persuasion, Ethan, you can tell him we have lifted an awful lot of fingerprints from that cellar. If his are there, on a bottle maybe, and he denies knowing about the party . . . I guess your father won't be too pleased to see his younger son in handcuffs.'

'I'll bring him down.' Ethan sounded scared.

'In two hours, okay? I'll meet you at the front desk.'

'Yeah. Oh, and forget the girl my friend chatted up, I've just heard from him and she was a blonde with spiky hair.'

The line went dead.

'Well, thanks to a little arm twisting from big brother, young Nicholas is about to pay us a visit.'

Marie smiled. 'Perfect. Could save us a lot of legwork.'

'And if Toni recognises the crypt, then everything could fall into place pretty quickly.'

But Jackman sounded more confident than he felt.

* * *

Marie managed to persuade the Clarksons to wait in their car while she and Jackman showed Toni the chapel. She would probably be much more willing to talk if her parents weren't hovering in the background.

Toni held onto Marie's arm as she led her along the gravel path, and Marie felt her growing more and more tense with every step.

She patted the girl's hand. 'You've nothing to fear, Toni. Just tell us whether or not you recognise the cellar, and then we'll get you out of there straightaway.'

'I *hate* not being able to remember everything. It's so scary. I mean, those freaky perverts could have done anything!' Toni winced and touched her side with her free hand.

'But they didn't, Toni, hold on to that.' Marie stopped, took the girl by the shoulders and looked into her eyes.

'It's bad enough that they hurt you, but they never sexually assaulted you, okay?'

Toni nodded, and mumbled, 'Yeah, I suppose.'

They walked to the top of the steps and looked down. 'Okay, let's get this over with.' Toni stepped down, touching the wall tentatively with her fingertips as if she were reading Braille.

Gary was waiting at the bottom, and he held out his hand to her.

'Good lass. Well done,' he said. 'Just a quick look round, and then we'll get you on your way home, okay?'

Toni stood at the entrance to the crypt and stared about her. She wrinkled her nose as the smell hit her.

'No, this wasn't it. This smells even worse than cabbages, it stinks like piss.'

'Are you sure, Toni?' Jackman had been so certain that this was the place.

'Yes, this is bigger, and well, it looks like part of an old church. That place I was in,' she gave an involuntary shiver, 'it was a proper cellar, you know? Like there was old stuff around. Boxes and cases, that sort of thing.'

'Do you see anything here that reminds you of where you were taken?' asked Gary.

The girl walked further in, then stopped and looked around her.

'There were bottles with candles stuck in them, like those.' She pointed to a stone shelf lined with empty wine bottles with candle stubs in their necks. She walked towards them and picked one up.

'Emily showed me this label! She thought it was funny, and we laughed at it.'

'Put it down, please, Toni,' said Marie. 'We may need to check the prints on it. Are you saying you were offered the same type of wine?'

Toni nodded furiously. 'I wouldn't forget that name, would I?'

They leaned over her shoulder and saw the label. *Old Tart.*

'There was one called *Old Git.* We laughed at that too.'

Jackman shrugged. 'People buy the label not the wine, I suppose.'

93

'Actually they are deceptively good wines, sir. One's a Sauvignon blanc and Terret, the other's a Grenache/Syrah,' Gary said.

'I had no idea you were a connoisseur. Are they hard to find?'

'No, sir. A lot of the supermarkets stock them.'

'They would, wouldn't they?' Jackman muttered.

'Can I go home now? This minging place is making me want to hoop up.'

Marie put an arm around Toni's slender shoulder and smiled at her. 'Of course. I feel exactly the same. Thank you, Toni, you've really helped us.'

'Have you found Emily yet?'

Marie's smile faded. 'Not yet. But when you've settled in at home, we really need to talk to you some more about her.'

'Sure. Although I don't know what else I can tell you. It's all so fuzzy.'

Marie tried to sound positive. 'Hey, you just remembered laughing over the wine labels, I'm sure other things will start to come back to you.'

'Maybe.' Toni glanced towards the doorway, where her father now stood, anxiously shifting from foot to foot.

'I hope so. Emily was really nice.'

\* \* \*

Gary and Toni drove away. Jackman needed to call the station so Marie slid in behind the steering wheel, started the engine and waited while he strode around trying to find a signal. She yawned, tapped her fingers on the wheel, and then eased the car round to face the road. When she looked up again, Jackman was hurrying across the grass towards her.

'Rosie has found two incidents reported in the last few months where youngsters attended underground parties and finished up the worse for wear.'

'Right. They were local?'

'Local kids, but the venues were out of town. That's all she knows. She's still digging. Right now, we need to go interview the Barley boys, so put your foot down, Marie. I can't wait to hear what baby brother has to tell us.'

# CHAPTER ELEVEN

Whatever Ethan said to Nicholas, it had a profound effect. The boy was spewing out information like a broken tap.

'I thought it was cool to start with. Make a load of wonga for getting a shitty key copied? I mean, who wouldn't? It wasn't till later that I got scared,' Nicholas said.

'Shame you didn't think it through first, dickhead,' murmured his brother. 'What did you think they were going to do down there? Hold prayer meetings and plan World Peace?'

'I didn't care what they did! The place is a craphole anyway.'

'So what was the story they gave you, Nicholas?' asked Jackman.

'They had crates and crates of booze and were happy to share it with us if we kids just hung out with them. No strings.'

Jackman's gut twisted into a small, painful knot. 'And what sorts of activities were involved in this *hanging out*?'

Nicholas shrugged. 'Just drinking, dancing together. Bit of a feel and a snog.' He bit his lip. 'Though I think some of them went further.'

'We saw the condoms, thank you.'

'Well, I didn't know that was going to happen, did I? The old guys, well, they just looked, didn't they? I mean, they never touched us or anything like that. They just sat in the shadows and watched us.' Nicholas stared down at the table. 'Some of the kids wanted to give them their money's worth. Kind of shock them, show them what they could do.' He turned his acne-spattered face towards them.

'It was the drink, wasn't it? Most of them were hammered by that time.' His eyes returned to the table. 'I split when I saw one of the men had a camcorder in one hand and his di—' he grimaced and pointed to his crotch. 'If you catch my drift?'

'Sorry, Nicholas, but we need to be clear on this, one of the older men was touching himself as he watched the youngsters?'

Nicholas nodded. 'Wanker.'

'You realise we have to stop this, don't you? Before one of these kids gets . . . God knows what could happen to them.'

'Yeah, but there were no names used.' He sighed. 'I'll tell you all I know if you can keep it from Dad.'

Jackman saw the consternation on Nicholas's face. The good reverend must have something of a temper, he thought. The lad was terrified. 'Tell us all you know, and I'll keep most of it from your father. And I'll make sure he knows you helped us.'

'Just tell them, arsehole! And thank your lucky stars you are getting let off so easily,' hissed Ethan.

Twenty minutes later, they let the boys go. They had descriptions, locations and best of all, Nicholas described the exact spot in the cellar where the "main man" had sat. Any DNA evidence found in that immediate area could be traced to him.

Jackman closed the interview room door, and exhaled loudly. 'I can't wait to tie this up with what Gary Pritchard has already got. We can't waste a moment in getting these perverts into the custody suite.'

Marie nodded. 'Bastards! Just the thought of those slimeballs watching young kids makes me want to heave.'

Jackman thought of his nephew. 'I know exactly what you mean.'

Two uniformed officers were walking hurriedly towards them.

'Sir? Could we have a word, please?'

Jackman nodded and said to Marie, 'Go check on the others, would you?' He turned back to them. 'Sure, lads, but make it snappy.'

'We were asked to check out a place called Windrush for you, sir,' said the older of the two.

It was PC Andy English, a good copper who'd worked with Jackman on numerous occasions. 'Yes, so did you find anything?'

'Not exactly, sir,' said the younger officer, PC Kevin Stoner.

Jackman looked at him with interest. PC Kevin Stoner was a bright young copper, and Jackman had recommended him for the CID examinations. However, Stoner had decided that as he had a really good crewmate, he would do a few more years in uniform.

'The thing is, sir,' continued Andy, 'we spent a lot of time there, and when we left we wrote it off as a no-no, but now we're not so sure. We think it warrants a second look, but with a lot more feet on the ground.'

'What's worrying you, Andy?'

Andy adjusted his heavy equipment belt and frowned. 'Hard to put a finger on it, sir, but I reckon it's the bloke that showed us round, more than anything.'

'We think he directed us to where we needed to go a bit too carefully, sir,' added Kevin. 'I'm certain we saw just what he wanted us to see and no more.'

'Who is he?'

'His name is Micah Lee, and he looks like the kind of man you wouldn't want to upset.'

Andy sniffed. 'I'm pretty good at reading people, sir, and that man was hairspring taut. He was well angry when we showed up unannounced, but then he put up a good show. Nice as pie, but underneath . . . boiling, he was, sir. Absolutely boiling.'

'And he's the owner of Windrush?'

'No, he's the caretaker. It's owned by a man named Benedict Broome. Lee wouldn't say what was going on there, but he opened up a bit as we walked around, and he told us that Broome has massive plans for the place. Micah Lee seems to be working his socks off down there. And, hell, Windrush is one scary dump.'

'And dangerous,' added Kevin. 'It needs bulldozing and starting again.'

'What are these great plans?'

'Broome wants to turn Windrush into a retreat, somewhere for people to go and get away from life for a while. A remote spot where they would eat well, sleep well and relax. Lee was going on about water gardens, covered courtyards for silent contemplation, a garden of tranquillity, reading rooms, music rooms, quiet rooms, you name it. You'd have thought Broome had millions to spend.'

'Maybe he does.'

Kevin laughed. 'Well, he's not spending too much on labour! You didn't see Micah Lee, sir! He's out there on his own with an old digger, a bloody great shovel and a barrow, no sign of any other workmen or helpers. It looked like he was doing it alone.'

'It was odd, sir,' agreed Andy. 'But you could see that some major clearing work had been done.' He frowned. 'I wouldn't mind seeing the plans and the planning permission reports.'

'Then get them, Constable, as soon as possible, and bring them straight to me. Meanwhile,' he took the scruffy card that Kevin Stoner offered him, 'I'll have a word with this Benedict Broome, and perhaps we'll pay Windrush another visit.'

Jackman watched as the two constables hurried down the corridor, and felt a chill of apprehension. Over the years, Jackman had learned never to ignore these feelings of unease. It could prove costly.

He walked slowly back towards the lifts, deciding that Marie's Windrush guided tour might come in useful after all.

\* \* \*

Jackman walked into the CID room and beckoned to Marie. 'I've been thinking.'

Marie grinned at him. 'Dangerous.'

'Probably. But the fact that we have had no time to even look at the Kenya Black case is really starting to worry me, especially if her mother is planning a major media campaign in the near future.'

'You're going to clone us?'

'I don't think I could cope with two Charlie Buttons, could you?'

'Bless him. He does try.' Her smile faded. 'So what do you have in mind regarding Kenya Black?'

'I think we should ring the mother, Grace Black, and go and see her — right now, if she's in.' He ran a hand through his hair. 'I'm going to throw myself on her mercy, tell her that we are reopening the case, but that there are other girls missing. I'm going to try to get her to see our problem, and promise to give our full attention to Kenya the moment we have a breakthrough on our present case.'

Marie thought for a moment. 'I think you're right. If we at least make contact, it will give her something to hold on to, *and* keep the super off our backs.'

'Then I'll get Clive to telephone her.' He lowered his voice. 'We have to tread very warily with Grace Black. From what I've read in the files, she has never given up on finding her daughter. And as you've probably heard, she never misses any opportunity to criticise the police. And frankly, I don't blame her.'

Marie nodded. 'I've read the reports too, sir. We need to do everything by the book where Grace Black is concerned.'

'Right. So what are the others up to while we're away?'

'Don't worry about them, they are all gainfully employed, including Gary Pritchard. He's down in the dark room with Charlie, staring at the CCTV screens.'

'Ah, Nicholas Barley's info.'

'Yes, they are looking for Nick and the guy who was the parties' main man.'

'Excellent,' said Jackman. 'Then I'll see what we can arrange for this visit.'

\* \* \*

Grace Black had said that she would be at home for another two hours, so Jackman and Marie left immediately.

They were shown into a large lounge that looked more like a city trader's office than a comfortable living area. Cardboard document boxes were stacked along one wall, and reams of printouts, letters, desk diaries, and newspaper cuttings littered every surface. Video and CD cases, all with spidery writing on the spines, were balanced in untidy towers beside the television. Marie spotted a computer, a laptop, and at least three telephones.

Marie knew that Grace was in her early forties. She had a thin, wiry body, piercing brown eyes and short dark hair, cropped, Marie assumed, for ease of care. From her rather creased appearance, it looked as though Grace Black spent little time on herself.

They were not given a drink, merely an impatient command to sit, not an easy task amid the clutter.

Marie carefully removed a copy of the Yellow Pages and a local phone book from a hard-backed chair, and perched herself uncomfortably on the edge. Jackman eased his tall frame in between a heap of box-files and an open gym bag full of dirty rugby kit.

'Throw that on the floor. It's only there so I don't forget to sort it out before tomorrow night.' She made an irritated huffing sound. 'Not enough hours in the bloody day.'

Jackman smiled. 'We won't keep you long, Mrs Black, but there is something that we would like you to know.' He launched into his semi-prepared speech, and then waited.

Marie waited too. They were both expecting an angry tirade but to their surprise, she remained silent. Then she said, very softly, 'I've heard all this before, you know.'

'Not from me, you haven't,' said Jackman, sincerely. 'We have one case to tie up first, and then, I promise you, we will not let this go again until we have found out what happened to your daughter.'

'I want to believe you, but—'

'You can. You have my word.'

'Frankly, I don't think you are in a position to give it. If the powers that be pull the plug on you, you'll do what all the others did and give up, making the same old excuses. And believe me, I've heard them all. Manpower, budget, priorities, you name it.'

'This time it's different, Mrs Black. I have their assurance that I can stay with this case until its conclusion. And I will use every tool and every officer available to me.'

'Forgive my scepticism, but this sounds as if your top brass need this nasty little mess swept away. They've probably got wind of the fact that I intend to start making serious waves again. They don't really care about me or my family's grief, DI Jackman. I'm just an embarrassment and an inconvenience and they want to shut me up.'

Marie felt that she was probably right. 'Does it actually matter about their reasons or their politics, Mrs Black? The main thing is that the case is going to be re-investigated from the very beginning, *and* they've chosen the best detective in the whole of the region to deal with it.'

She tried not to look at Jackman. 'Plus, if DI Jackman gives you his word, then accept it. If anyone can find out what happened to your little girl, he's right here.'

Grace was silent for a moment or two.

'My! Maybe things *will* be different this time.'

'Then can we rely on your support?' Jackman asked quickly. 'Even if it means dragging up all the old pain again?'

'Do you think it ever went away?' Grace replied.

'No, I'm sure it didn't. But I will want to go over every report, every statement, every move of every person involved — times, dates and what they had for breakfast. We might ask questions that seem irrelevant or very painful, but I'll want answers to all of them. Can you cope with that?'

Grace Black straightened her spine, and pulled her shoulders back. Her whole demeanour altered. 'Yes! Yes, I can, and what's left of my family will too. Just how long will this other case take? The one you have to tie up first.'

Marie wished Grace hadn't asked that question. They were making such good progress.

'You should know that it's a missing person case, Mrs Black,' said Jackman. 'Not a child, but a teenage girl, and under the circumstances I'm sure you will bear with us for a short time. Initially there were three missing girls, but we have found two already. One is safely back with her family, but the other, sadly . . . she is back with her family but not the way we hoped. I'm sure we will be able to find the third girl very soon. We do have leads that we are following.'

Grace shook her head sadly. 'Then I wish you all the luck in the world, for the missing girl and her family's sake, and for ours too.'

Jackman stood up. Marie felt an overwhelming urge to run from the room. There were just too many children torn from their homes, too many daughters lost to their mothers, too many heartbroken families looking for answers.

As they moved towards the door, Jackman paused and said, 'We do appreciate your time, Mrs Black. You'll be hearing from us just as soon as possible.'

Grace Black stood and tilted her head to one side. Marie was reminded of a bird. Then she gave them a sad smile and said, 'Do you know? For once, I believe I will.'

## CHAPTER TWELVE

Charlie Button, Max Cohen and Gary Pritchard sat in the flickering darkness of the monitor room, their eyes trained on the CCTV footage that flashed across the screens.

'I hope you three are working and not hiding down here eating Big Macs and fries.'

Jackman flopped into a spare chair and Marie looked over Max's shoulder at the monitor.

'No such luck,' said Max, eyes on his screen. 'We are still looking for Nick Barley's meeting with the leader of the Sicko Society.'

'Well, while you look, I have a bit of good news for PC Pritchard here.'

Gary paused the footage and swung around to face him. 'Sir?'

'As from ten minutes ago, you are on our team.'

Gary face creased into a smile. 'That's great, sir! I just hope I can be of help.'

'I'm sure you will, Constable. Now are you happy to commute, or can we organise somewhere temporary for you in Saltern?'

'He can have my guest room, boss.' Marie turned to Gary. 'If you want it?'

'That would be perfect, as long as I'm not putting you out, Sarge?'

Marie smiled. 'No problem. It'll be good to have someone else around, other than the cat.' And she meant it. Since her husband's death, she had preferred to be on her own, but having only old memories for company was sometimes depressing. She liked Gary and believed that he was lonely, and that it also stemmed from tragic loss.

'That's settled then,' said Jackman.

Gary was grinning from ear to ear. 'When I get home tonight I'll sort out a few things and get some clothes together. I can move in tomorrow, if that's okay? It'll be much better to be on hand if I'm needed.'

'My thoughts precisely,' said Marie. 'Although perhaps I should fill you in on some of my eccentric habits before you commit yourself to becoming my lodger.'

Gary raised an eyebrow. 'Sounds intriguing, but I'll take my chances, Sarge. When you've lived out on Harlan Marsh you've seen it all. That place has characters that make eccentric look normal!'

Marie laughed. 'Well, I don't think I'm that bad!'

'Don't you believe it,' said Max. '*I've* heard the rumours in the mess room.'

Marie cuffed him across the back of the head, suddenly feeling very pleased with her new domestic arrangement. She'd been on her own for too long.

'Sarge! Boss!' Gary stopped his machine and ran it back a few frames. 'Got them!'

Marie stared at two dark figures, both staying well back in the shadows, while young Nick Barley, blissfully unaware, stood right in front of the security camera.

'Damn! They could be anyone,' she cursed.

'Hang fire, Sarge. The one on the left turns in a minute. Look, just there.' Gary pointed to the screen.

'That taller one, he's familiar. I think we know him,' murmured Jackman.

'Maybe, but . . .' Marie squinted as she tried to make out any recognisable features.

'The quality is crap. Even if he were the biggest villain in town, we'd never get an ID from that.'

'I'll get some stills printed off. Maybe they'll show something more.' Gary went to talk to the IT operator and returned in a few minutes with a batch of printouts.

Jackman sighed. 'These are no better. Max? Can you clean them up, make them clearer?

'No, sir. I can tell that the IT operator has done his best with them. Young Barley's face is clear as crystal, as you can see. But the head honcho and his side-kick keep close to the buildings and in deep shadow.'

'If they're local, they probably know the exact positioning of the cameras,' Jackman muttered. 'Is this all we have?'

'We just need to check out the last of the meeting places that Nicholas Barley told us about.' Charlie threw them a tired smile. 'You never know, we *may* get lucky.'

'Okay. You guys were here at the crack of dawn, so finish those and get home. There's little more we can do now.'

'Are you getting away too, sir?' Marie noted the dark patches beneath Jackman's eyes.

'I need to talk to this Benedict Broome guy first, and then I thought I'd go see Toni Clarkson at her home, and try to find something, *anything,* that might give us a clearer idea of the identity of Emily.'

'I'll go with you,' said Marie.

'No, you finish up here, and then for God's sake take the opportunity to get some rest. I get the feeling that things are about to hot up.' He stabbed a finger at the grainy photographs. 'It's all about these sick bloody parties, isn't it? Nick Barley helped to organise one of the venues, Toni went willingly to one, Emily too, and Asher Leyton told us that Shauna Kelly said she had been to a weird party and was going to another. We *have* to find a way to stop them before more kids disappear, or get killed!'

Marie thought about Emily. Time might be running out for her, wherever she was. *Who*ever she was. 'If only we could get someone inside one of these parties,' she murmured.

'You find me a venue, and I'll get in.' Rosie McElderry stood in the doorway, a determined look in her eyes.

'The problem is *finding* the next venue,' said Gary flatly. 'Don't forget, we've been one step behind these guys for months and we're no nearer catching them.'

'But you didn't have Nick Barley, did you?' Rosie looked down at the photographs of the boy. 'As long as no one knows that he's helping us, he could be our way in.'

Jackman puffed out his cheeks. 'He told us he did a runner when he found out he was dealing with a load of pervs. He may not find it easy to get in again.'

'Maybe not, but I'm willing to bet he knows some of the kids that do go,' Rosie said doggedly. 'At least let's talk to him.'

Max frowned. 'Well, if we do manage to get a location and a time, why don't we just raid the place? Avoid any risk to Rosie and lock the bastards up, job done!'

Rosie smiled. 'So sweet of you to care. But think it through, Max. It may not *be* job-done if a vanload of flatfoots charges in. What if the bosses aren't there? I doubt the organisers attend every rave. Or what if they leg it and we lose them? I'm one hundred per cent certain they have an escape route worked out. *And* the place could be full of minors. It's too iffy. We need more intelligence before we can hit them.'

'Rosie is right,' said Jackman quietly. 'We do need to infiltrate one of these damned parties.'

'Maybe I can help you, sir.'

Marie saw a tall figure standing behind Rosie. A stony-faced Danny Page, the desk sergeant, stepped into the dimly lit monitor room. 'Sorry to butt in, but I think you ought to hear what a new witness has to say about your parties.'

Jackman stood up. 'Someone has finally come forward?'

'After a fashion.' He ushered a blonde teenage girl into the room. 'Detective Inspector Jackman, meet my daughter, Jasmine. I think you'll find she has quite a lot to tell you.'

* * *

Half an hour later Sergeant Page, arm around her shoulder, escorted his daughter from the station. Jackman and the others discussed their next move.

'So, all we need is Jasmine's friend Chloe's mobile phone, and as soon as the text comes through, we'll have the location of the next venue. We're in' We've got her address. Shall Max and I go pick it up, sir?' Rosie sounded excited.

Jackman nodded. 'Yes. From what Jasmine heard, there are sometimes several parties a week, which could make the next one anytime, tonight even!' He looked at Rosie. 'Go! And I don't have to tell you how to handle Chloe and her brother, do I? There are lives at stake. You can scare the shit out of them for all I care, just make sure they co-operate *and* keep their mouths shut, okay?'

Jackman and Marie walked back upstairs, leaving Gary and Charlie to check the last of the CCTV films.

'I guess you'd better hang on now until Rosie and Max get back. I want us all to be in close proximity to that party, wherever it is, if our flower is going in undercover.'

'I'm not sure I'm happy about her doing this alone,' said Marie.

'Well, sorry to say this, but I hardly think any of the rest of us would pass for teenagers anymore.'

'Why not send Max in with her?' asked Marie. 'He seemed pretty worried about her taking this on.'

'Max isn't very good at getting down and dirty.' Jackman gave a little laugh. 'Remember the last time we tried to rough him up a bit? He still looked as if he'd walked off the cover of GQ. He's a trendy young man alright, but certainly not the kind to attend a party of this nature. He'd stand out like a sore thumb. And anyway, I think Rosie will attract less attention if she plays this one solo.'

'What about a wire?' asked Marie.

'Don't worry. I wouldn't let her do it without one. We need to know what's going on every step of the way. She'll be fine, Marie. You know Rosie. This is all part of the job, it's what we do. She's a tough cookie when she needs to be, and she can take care of herself, so stop fretting.' He glanced at his watch. 'I'm going to ring Benedict Broome. And I'm still hoping to visit Toni Clarkson, but I guess that rather depends on whether one of our nasty parties will be taking place. Perhaps you'd see if PC Andy English has had any luck with Broome's planning permission?'

Jackman went into the office, picked up the tattered card that Kevin Stoner had given him and dialled the number.

Benedict Broome answered in a deep voice, the words clearly enunciated.

Jackman introduced himself, and briefly told him of the missing girl and the earlier visit to his property on Roman Creek.

'Mr Lee did tell me,' said Broome, with a slight hint of amusement in his voice. 'I hope his rather overwhelming appearance didn't upset your officers? And I hope that he was accommodating. Sometimes he can be a little overprotective of the old place.'

'My men did mention his size, sir, but I can assure you that he was obliging enough to show them around.' He went on to say that considering the size of Windrush, they would need to make an extended search, and asked his permission to go ahead.

'Of course you must, Detective Inspector. I'll notify Mr Lee immediately, and tell him you have my full permission.'

After a few words of thanks, Jackman hung up. The man had been charming, and his concern for the missing girl had sounded genuine. Jackman stared at the phone. So why did he feel so uneasy?

With a light tap at the door, Marie entered. 'Andy's off duty, but he left you this.'

Jackman took the memo and read it aloud:

> *'Sir, regarding planning permission for Benedict Broome's project at Windrush. Will know more after I've spoken to a senior council official tomorrow, but I suspect things are not straightforward. I'm* <u>*certain*</u> *it warrants taking another look. PC Andy English.'*

Something in Jackman wanted to jump up, grab a van full of uniforms, and chase out to Windrush immediately. They would need to search the place under their terms, not those of the giant caretaker, Mr Micah Lee.

'I'm sorry to say it's too late to move on this today. There aren't enough hours of daylight left. We'll go tomorrow. Why don't you go downstairs and see how much support uniform can offer us? We'll need a pretty big team for a place that size.'

Marie nodded. 'I'll see what I can organise.' In the doorway she hesitated. 'You will let me know as soon as Rosie and Max get back, won't you?'

'Of course I will,' he said.

He watched his sergeant walk out. He fully understood her concerns. Young women were the common denominator in this investigation, and Rosie was a very pretty young woman, who looked much younger

111

than her years. But she was also an experienced and very capable police officer. There was no doubt in his mind that she was perfect for the job. Even if it was risky.

# CHAPTER THIRTEEN

After Marie had liaised with uniform regarding a full-scale search of Windrush, she walked back into the office to get her jacket and keys. Jackman sat on the edge of her desk, deep in thought.

'Thought you were going to visit Toni Clarkson?'

'I am, but I've been thinking. Would you come with me?'

'Of course, but why the change of heart?'

'Her father. If I go alone there'll be little chance of talking to her without him sitting in on the conversation, and that's not what I want. If you are there too, we should be able to get her alone.'

'I agree. She'll talk much more easily if her parents aren't there.' She looked at him. 'Any news from Rosie?'

'It's on tonight at ten thirty. Max rang me just before you walked in.'

'Where?' asked Marie, feeling her throat constrict.

'Apparently they don't divulge the location until half an hour before it kicks off. I'm not sure what Rosie and Max said to them, but although Chloe is well pissed off, her brother Luke is singing like a bird. Max reckons he's got the wind up about something that happened there a week or so ago, plus he has confirmed that Shauna Kelly was one of the partygoers. *And* he's very keen to help us.' Jackman gave her a tight smile. 'He's told Rosie that she can use his name to get in.'

'She trusts him?'

'Luke has been going for a while now. Not to every party, but quite a few of them. He is considered "safe" by the organisers, not that he knows much about them.'

'Where's Rosie now?' Marie asked.

'She's gone to borrow some suitably trendy gear from her niece. She'll be back at ten, to wait for the call.' Jackman glanced up at the wall clock. 'It's only six o'clock, so we have plenty of time to go see Toni, and grab some supper and a few hours' rest.' Jackman stood up. 'Ready?'

'Ready.'

\* \* \*

Jackman drove fast through the lonely fenland towards Harlan Marsh. The long reed-fringed drove seemed endless. He slowed down a little. From the day he began driving in this terrain, he'd learned never to underestimate these seemingly benign roads. A change in camber, a hump-back bridge, a sudden and unexpected bend or even simple complacency could have you nose down in a deep ditch in seconds.

Tiredness overwhelmed him as he eased the car around a bend and saw Harlan Marsh town ahead of him. This visit really could have waited until the morning, but then he would need to get the search party out to the old sanatorium.

Neil Clarkson opened the door. He was not exactly welcoming. 'Keep it short, DI Jackman, my daughter is exhausted.'

Maybe so, but she *is* alive, Jackman thought to himself, *and* safe, unlike poor Emily. 'Of course, sir. Just a few minutes with her, and we'll be out of your hair.'

Clarkson frowned. 'Alone?'

'It's better that way, if you have no objection. Youngsters don't like their parents hearing their secrets.'

Clarkson stood back reluctantly and pointed down the long hallway. 'Third door along the right-hand side. Knock loudly, she's probably got her headphones on.'

Toni's room was a real mix of childish and more teenage stuff. Two cuddly teddy bears sat in front of a poster showing some kind of night creatures locked in a bloody, pointed-fanged embrace. Jackman's nephews loved *Twilight*, but this had a more sinister, erotic edge to it. Jackman was pretty sure that her parents were not particularly happy with their daughter's choice of artwork.

'What's the music?' he asked, as Toni took out the earpieces.

'Band called Taking Back Sunday.' She looked at Jackman patiently. 'You won't have heard of them.'

'Oh, I didn't have you down as an Emo.'

For a moment her eyes widened, there was a hint of amusement but she didn't comment. And that was fine, because it was total luck that he'd recently listened to an interview about the Emo subculture on Radio 4.

'I've been thinking about Emily,' said Toni slowly. 'Did I tell you she spoke funny?'

'What, like a speech impediment?' Marie said.

'No, like an accent. I think she's from Eastern Europe.' Toni's fingers idly brushed the screen of her phone and brilliant-coloured pictures flashed across it.

'I'm not sure, but I can remember something about grandparents who wouldn't leave their village, even though it was really gross. You know? Like bombed out?'

Jackman puffed out his cheeks and exhaled slowly. That could be why they had no missing person report. There was a large migrant worker community of EU nationals living in Greenborough, but they stuck together and didn't trust the police.

'And her name's not really Emily.' Toni stared down at a photo of a moody-looking youth with an oily, tanned torso and bleached teeth. 'She said the English couldn't pronounce her real name properly, so she called herself Emily because she liked it.'

Jackman rubbed his forehead and tried to think. This was getting more problematic by the second.

'And that really is all I can remember.' Toni swiped the beautiful boy from her screen and replaced it with a Pokemon character.

'You've done well, Toni.' Marie's voice was soft.

'Do you think she's dead?'

The bluntness of the question made Jackman shudder. 'We are doing our best to get to her before anything like that can happen.'

'I think she's dead. The men at that place . . .' Toni gave an involuntary shiver. 'I saw their eyes. Especially one of them, the one that hurt me. He had horrible eyes.'

'How do you mean?' Marie asked gently.

'Like blank. Like, yeah, he was all excited about the day that she was born and all that, but even then his eyes were still blank. Like in a zombie film, but I've never seen a human being really look that way.'

Jackman felt a chill descend around them when Toni spoke about the man who had taken her. He had really terrified her, and Jackman was sure that it would take more than a little time to make those horrible memories fade.

Marie looked at him, and he knew that she was thinking the same thing.

Marie moved the conversation away from dead eyes. 'Toni, when we spoke to you at the hospital, you said that somebody was singing. Do you remember that? Could you explain what you meant?'

Toni screwed her face up in concentration. 'I'd forgotten that. It seemed so weird! I mean totally creepy. In that stinking cellar with the candles and the wine and funky music playing, this one guy starts to sing, and his voice was . . .' She lifted her hands in a little gesture of amazement. 'Like some choir boy! But better, stronger. I mean, like really powerful, like he had no control over the volume. It was kind of awesome.'

Marie glanced across at Jackman and shrugged.

Jackman frowned. He was certain that this information was hugely significant.

'Thanks for that, Toni. We are going to go now. I think it's time you got some rest, okay?' He took a card from his pocket and handed it to her. 'Maybe you could write down anything else that comes to you. Anything, no matter how small — and ring me?'

The girl took the card, and her cold fingers touched Jackman's as she did so. 'I keep seeing her. I see her face as they dragged her away.'

She placed the card on her bedside cabinet and slowly turned towards them. Tears filled her eyes.

Marie took the girl's hand in hers.

With one hand to her ribs, Toni slipped a thin arm around Marie and held on tightly, burying her head in Marie's chest. 'All because of her birthday,' she sobbed. 'If it had been different, it could have been me they took, couldn't it?'

The gobby little pain in the arse had vanished.

Marie stroked the girl's hair and made soothing noises. 'But it wasn't you was it, sweetheart? You are safe home where you belong. Now all you need to do to help Emily is write down any new memories, anything that comes to you, okay? And then, when we find her, and we *will* find her, Toni, you can put all this behind you and get on with your life.'

The girl cried for a little longer, and Jackman became conscious of her father waiting anxiously outside her door. At least he had the good sense not to enter.

They left some ten minutes later, convinced that there really was another young victim out there somewhere, waiting for them to find her. But would they find her alive?

\* \* \*

As the car sped back towards the station, Jackman said, 'I hope I'm right, but my housekeeper generally leaves me some hot food when we are busy. Want to share?'

Marie had heard about Mrs Maynard's legendary home-cooked dishes, and her stomach grumbled. 'I'd love to, if you're sure.'

'Excellent.' He gave her a little smile, 'Although it'll probably be the first time she's forgotten. But no worry, M&S is lurking in my freezer waiting for emergencies.'

He turned the car off the main road and headed towards Cartoft. 'It will give us a chance to plan tonight and talk over what we've just heard from Toni.'

'And in nicer surroundings than the nick.'

Marie loved Jackman's windmill home, it felt so welcoming. She would give her eye teeth for a place like that. Bill would have loved it. She could imagine him out in the old store, working patiently on some ancient motorcycle engine. She gave an inadvertent sigh.

'You okay? Not worrying about Rosie again, are you?'

'No, just a little nudge from the past. Sometimes things creep up on you when you least expect it.'

'Bill?'

She nodded. 'I know it's pointless, but when someone dies too soon, when they are still young, you can't help wondering how they would have turned out.' She rubbed her hands together thoughtfully. 'I try to imagine what he would have made of things — modern policing, all the new technology, like cars that park themselves and phones that operate your central heating.' She laughed softly. 'He was a bit of a technophobe really. I think that's why he loved old motor bikes so much. He liked things that smelled of oil that you could tinker with and coax back to life. Plugging your car into a computerised diagnostic reader didn't do it for him at all. And I really don't think he would approve of having your parcels delivered by drone.'

Jackman nodded. 'I feel a bit the same. I mean I love how science has given us ways to solve crimes so much quicker, and the advances in medical science are undeniable, but I think my heart is happiest with the simpler things.'

Marie brushed away her thoughts of the past when she realised that they were turning into the lane leading to his home.

'Fingers crossed that Mrs M. has worked some magic in my kitchen.' He grinned at her. 'And I don't think a small restorative glass of wine would go amiss either.'

He pulled up under the car port, turned the engine off and flung open the door. 'Can you smell cooking?'

Marie stepped out and inhaled. 'I'm getting a distinct whiff of curry. Is there an Indian restaurant in Cartoft?'

'There is nothing in Cartoft, and I mean nothing, other than the church and the village hall, so that bodes very well.'

Together they hurried over to the mill.

The smell of aromatic spices greeted them at the door.

'Oh yes!' Jackman's eyes lit up. 'It won't be like anything you'd find in a curry house. Mrs M. doesn't use recipes, she just does her own thing.' He led the way through to the kitchen, picked up a note from the table and read it out.

*"Chicken curry keeping hot in the small oven, and there's some of that foreign bread stuff that you like in a tray under foil. Heat it for a few minutes. Don't forget the gardener's coming on Thursday to do the hedges. Hetty."*

Marie smiled. 'I'd like a Mrs M. Do you rent her out?'

'She's worth her weight in gold, believe me.' Jackman took off his jacket and threw it over the back of a chair. 'Make yourself comfortable. I'll get the wine while the naan bread is warming.' He opened the fridge and took out a bottle of Chardonnay. 'I have no idea why, but for some reason it's perfect with chicken curry.'

'It better not be too nice, or we'll have to call off tonight's sortie.'

'Don't worry. I'm rationing it.' He splashed wine into two glasses, replaced the top and returned the bottle to the fridge.

A few minutes later, he was dishing the food into two large bowls and putting the hot bread on a plate between them. 'Dig in and enjoy.'

As they ate they talked about Toni and the worrying things she had said. If Emily was a migrant worker, tracing her would be difficult given the tight knit community that she would live in. After a while, Marie added, 'I know we have the Windrush search to contend with tomorrow, but we mustn't forget that we have to go and talk to the residents of Allenby Creek.' She finished the last mouthful then said, 'Surely someone must have seen something? It's such an out of the way spot, you'd think a strange car or someone you don't recognise would stand out.'

'Let's hope we find someone who uniform missed on their house-to-house.' Jackman stood up and collected the plates,' Oh dear, how time flies. Thanks, Mrs M. Much appreciated.'

'I'll second that.' Marie smiled at him. 'About tonight, I feel quite . . .' She paused.

'Excited? Apprehensive?'

'Bit of each, I suppose. This mission of Rosie's could provide a lot of information, but at the same time, men who do that sort of thing make me feel almost homicidal, as well as sick to my stomach.' Marie made a disgusted face.

'I empathise with that, believe me. That's why we have to nail them, as soon as we can.'

Marie nodded. 'Yes, I know. I just hope that we are not sending Rosie into a situation that's too dangerous.'

'We'll all be close by. If she has the slightest trouble, that club won't know what hit it.' He narrowed his eyes. 'But I get the feeling that she will just test the waters tonight. She'll gather as much intelligence as she can without blowing her cover, and leave with an option to return, should it be necessary.' He smiled at Marie. 'For once, I don't share your concerns. I think Rosie will be ace at this. She's done undercover before and apparently very well.'

Perhaps it was their two genders that was the cause of this rare difference of opinion between her and Jackman. Marie fervently hoped she was wrong, and it would be Jackman saying, "I told you so!"

'Now, would you like a coffee before we plan tonight's strategy?'

'Perfect, thank you.' Marie took a deep breath and decided that as the evening was going to go ahead anyway, she might as well be prepared. 'Let's get it sorted.'

* * *

As ten o'clock approached, Jackman began to feel the same mix of apprehension and excitement. The arrangement was far from perfect. As they had no idea where they were going, they couldn't plan a suitable recce, or back-up. They were going to have to wing it.

Rosie, wearing an outfit that would have scandalised Jackman on any other occasion, stared unblinking at Chloe's phone, willing it to ring.

Marie paced the CID room, as did Max Cohen. In fact, Jackman thought, Max was even more worried than Marie, which was not like him. Usually he loved this sort of thing.

'Bingo!' whispered Rosie and grabbed the mobile.

Everyone held their collective breaths.

'Jubilee Lane, the old rowing club near the mill.' Rosie snapped the phone shut and jumped up. 'Anyone know it? Because I don't.'

'Relax, flower,' said Max, feeding the data into his computer. 'It's only about twenty minutes away, on the road to Harlan Marsh. I used to go fishing near there with a mate of mine. The mill is derelict and all sealed up. I'm getting a satellite picture of the area now.'

'As far as I remember, the clubhouse is closed too. There was a fire there a few years back and they moved the rowing club to new premises.' Jackman nodded to himself. 'There are no residences in the lane, and everything else is abandoned, so it's the perfect place for a party.' He turned to Gary. 'Go and give uniform the exact location. I want a unit well out of the way, but close enough should we need them. And softly, softly, please. No blues and twos under any circumstances.'

'Here we go.' Max brought up an aerial view of the rundown clubhouse, and scanned the surroundings. 'If we drop Rosie here,' he pointed to a narrow lane, 'she could walk through and tie up with the main path to the venue. I should think most of the partygoers will come from this direction, from the main road.' He traced his finger further along the river edge. 'I think we could find some pretty good cover along the towpath and around the mill. We need to be as close as possible.'

Jackman straightened up. 'I agree. Everyone ready? So let's get out there. Rosie? Still up for it?'

'Am I ever! Bring it on.'

Jackman smiled at those bright intelligent eyes looking out from behind false eyelashes. Rosie's choice of clothing and clever make-up made her look about sixteen. The only one of them who wasn't all revved up was Marie. She had said pretty well nothing since they'd arrived. It worried Jackman, but he knew that she would be behind them all the way if the shit were to hit the fan.

'Check her wire, Max. We can't afford to lose contact.'

'Already done, guv. And it's not standard issue. I've adapted it myself. It's top of the range. She has the best signal and range available.'

Jackman looked around. 'Then let's go, folks. And good luck. We have some seriously bad men to get the dirt on.' He touched Rosie's shoulder. 'Be careful in there,

Rosie. The *slightest* problem and you get out. And I mean it. No heroics, just leg it, fast.'

# CHAPTER FOURTEEN

Rosie slipped in behind a group of four or five youngsters and tried to listen to their conversation. It was clear that they were already pretty pissed, even before they got to the free booze. Rosie felt her anger mount. These silly kids were such easy prey for the perverts. She took a deep breath. She needed to keep her concentration. She couldn't afford to miss a thing.

One the girls ahead of her was hanging onto a skinny, spiky-haired youth, jabbing a finger at him as she lurched unsteadily along beside him. 'And you can keep your leery eyes off that ginger slapper if she turns up again tonight. I saw you, Calvin, with your tongue hanging down to your belly button.'

Calvin shrugged. 'Dunno who you're talking about. Do you, Billy?'

The other boy kicked at an empty drink can as he sauntered along, hands stuffed deep into his jeans pocket. 'Nah. Unless you mean the tart with the tramp stamp?'

Rosie tried to hide a smile. She knew that the boy was referring to a tattoo worn just above the girl's bottom.

The other two girls, arm in arm, tottering along in their high-heeled fashion boots, laughed loudly. 'Yeah! We saw you, Calvin. Couldn't take your eyes off her tits, could you?'

Calvin continued to stroll calmly along. 'Bollocks. You were all too wasted to know what was happening.'

Rosie had been hoping to slip into the venue as part of the group, but as they moved towards the dark hulk of the boathouse, she decided to hang back and go in alone. If there was to be any confrontation, it would be better to be away from other kids.

As it turned out, it was easy.

'I don't know you.' The man who stood just inside the door was slim and well-dressed with a slight northern accent. He took her wrist and held her back.

'I'm a friend of Luke's,' said Rosie with a bored smile. 'He can't make it tonight, but he told me I might enjoy myself.' She looked the man full in the eyes and ran her tongue slowly around her scarlet lips. 'Do *you* think I'd enjoy myself here?'

The man let go of her hand and smirked. 'Oh, I should think you'll have a ball, angel. Maybe several if you're lucky.' He grinned at her. 'And if you *do* have a good time, come and see me before you leave. Maybe I can arrange to make you a regular.'

'Thank you.' Rosie blew him a kiss and disappeared into the boathouse. 'Oh, so easy', she whispered, knowing that Max and Charlie would be somewhere close by, listening to her every word.

Somewhere up ahead, Rosie heard music. She followed some other revellers through a big deserted area lined with metal racks protruding from the walls. She guessed that rowing boats would have been stored here once.

'This way.' A man stood in the shadows, ushering the teenagers into a big, crowded back room. There were a dozen small tables with empty wine bottles holding candles. Considering that it was such a dump, the room had an oddly cosy feel. The techno music was loud and the beat reverberated through her body, making her wonder what effect it would have on her microphone.

'Drink? It's free.' An older man took her arm and drew her towards a table crammed full of beer and cider cans and dozens of plastic glasses of wine. 'You're new, aren't you? And all alone?' He peered at her inquisitively. 'Now would that be gutsy, or foolish, I wonder?'

Rosie took a mental snapshot. The man was around forty, with thin straggly hair, small eyes and a narrow sharp nose. The waistband of his cheap suit fought with his gut. He had very bad taste in clothes.

'I do as I please,' she said disdainfully, picking up a glass of white wine that she had absolutely no intention of drinking. 'I don't need a bodyguard.'

'Well, it gets pretty intense in here as the night goes on. I hope you're up for it.'

*I'm up for seeing you in a holding cell, you scumbag.* Rosie shrugged and said, 'I like intense.'

The man leered at her and she felt his eyes on her short, shiny red miniskirt.

'So how did you find out about us?' he asked, sipping what looked like neat Scotch from a straight-sided glass.

'A friend told me.'

'And who would that friend be?' His piggy eyes never left hers.

'Luke, if it's any of your business.'

'Luke Jones?'

Rosie thought quickly. Luke and Chloe's surname was Perry, but did he use an alias when he came here? 'Luke with black hair and a blonde Mohican stripe, and breath that could unblock drains.'

'Ah.' The man smiled and stepped away from her.

'Well, enjoy yourself, sweetheart. Er, what is your name?'

'Petra,' said Rosie, then remembering why she was there said, 'And yours?'

126

The man's lips tightened and he stared hard at her. Clearly no one had ever asked that question before. 'Harry.'

'Dirty Harry?' She ran her fingers across the lapel of his cheap suit and saw his Adam's apple move up and down. 'Sometimes,' he said in a hoarse whisper.

Rosie took that as her cue to leave. 'Then see you later, Harry . . . maybe.' *Or maybe not, you tosser!*

Rosie moved towards some kids who were swaying around a makeshift dance floor. No one took any notice of her as she danced between them until she spotted a place on the far side of the room where she could get a good look around.

She needed to find a regular, someone that would talk to her. She pretended to sip her wine as she checked out the possible candidates. It would have to be a boy. The girls wouldn't be friendly, they would see her as a threat.

After a while she spotted a slightly older-looking boy, sitting alone with only a can of lager for company. As far as she could tell, there were no girls hanging around him, and he hadn't made any effort to dance, or chat anyone up.

'Moving in for a chat with a local,' she whispered to the invisible Max.

'This chair taken?' Not waiting for a reply, Rosie sat down and crossed her long legs seductively.

'Looks like it is now.' For a moment she thought he was going to get up and move away.

'I don't know anyone here,' she said softly.

'Well, you're not missing much.' He looked around. 'Load of wankers.'

'Oh, I was told these parties are really cool.' She gave him a shy smile. 'My name's Petra.'

The boy ran a hand through his shock of dark hair and looked at her thoughtfully. 'You don't look like the slags this place usually attracts. I'm Will.'

'Why do you come here if it's such a crap place?'

'Good point.' He took a long slug of his lager. 'To keep an eye on someone who shouldn't be here, but who seems to have some kind of death wish.'

'Girlfriend? Sister?'

'Dumb brother, actually.' He rolled his eyes. 'He was such a cute kid, too.'

Will reached down beside his chair, lifted up a second sealed can of lager and passed it to her. 'If you want a drink, Petra, have this. Never touch the wine, or anything anyone offers you that has already been opened.'

Rosie put down the wine on the scarred, damp table and accepted the can. She peeled back the ring pull, allowed the froth to settle, then sipped the drink. 'I should have thought of that. You've actually seen the drinks being spiked?'

'Regularly. It's all part of the fun — so they tell me.'

'And is that too?' She gestured with her head towards a long table cloaked in shadow at the very back of the room.

Three men sat along the far side of the table and watched the teenagers intently, particularly one couple who were frantically groping at each other's writhing bodies. Rosie saw a tiny red light. One of the men was operating a small handheld digital camcorder.

'As I said, they're wankers. There's no such thing as a free lunch or a free drink, Petra.' He sniffed. 'Oh, you'll be alright tonight. They never try anything on your first visit, but after a couple of times they'll want payment, in some form or other. Know what a voyeur is?'

'Better than you think,' she murmured, knowing that he wouldn't hear her above the music. 'If those guys are perverts, why doesn't someone shop them?' She hoped she sounded naïve.

'The men take pictures of everyone, and they warn you off by threatening to send copies to your parents, or whoever they think would scare you the most.' He looked rather sadly across the floor to where a younger boy was being fondled by a drunken girl with a tragic haircut and make-up that would have scared birds.

'And as most of these idiots finish up half-naked and off their heads, it's not something they want to share with Mummy and Daddy.'

Rosie followed his gaze. 'Your brother?'

Will nodded. 'Sean. He's only fourteen, and the way he's going he'll be lucky to make it through the next couple of months without picking up an STD.'

'And he won't listen to you?' Rosie tried hard not to sound too adult, but she had a strong feeling that Will was on the level.

'He's addicted to these parties. Apart from tying him down, the best I can do is just be here and watch out for him.' He frowned. 'I've no proof, but I reckon worse things happen here than just a few sick old blokes jerking off over some horny young girls.'

Rosie swallowed. 'Like what?'

'Don't mean to scare you, and I'm probably wrong, but I think certain girls are "picked out," if you know what I mean, for other things.'

'Dirty bastards! I assume you mean for sex?'

'What else would they want them for?' said Will morosely. 'I've seen those old guys take some of them to one side, then later they've gone, just disappeared.' He turned a serious face to Rosie. 'You don't belong here. Get out while you can — and don't come back.'

'I may just do that, Will. Tell me, have you ever met a girl called Emily while you're here?'

Will shook his head. 'Don't think so. Why?'

'She's a friend of mine,' Rosie lied. 'She went all secretive on me and I haven't seen her for a few days. I wondered if she had been coming here, that's all.' She looked around again. 'But what about you? Surely the men that run these parties notice that you don't, er, join in?'

Will smiled at her. 'Well, I'm not actually dead from the waist down. For the sake of watching out for Sean, I do occasionally find a fit bird and have a quick game of tonsil hockey.'

Rosie laughed. 'I'm afraid I haven't seen too many fit birds here so far.'

'No? I thought I was looking at one right now.'

Rosie stiffened. There was no mistaking the look in Will's eyes. How far would she need to go in order not to blow her cover?

* * *

Charlie Button chuckled softly in the darkness.

They had found a small deserted outbuilding attached to the derelict mill and almost directly behind the boathouse. The signal from Rosie's hidden microphone was strong, and the hi-tech equipment sensitive enough to filter out the background noise, leaving Rosie's speaking voice, even her whispers, coming through crystal clear.

'I do believe that girl is enjoying herself,' he said.

'What the hell do you mean by that, Charlie?' Max said.

Jackman turned his head. Max never spoke like that to Charlie.

'Just that she's getting on with the job rather well.' Charlie sounded nonplussed. 'And she's acting out her part as a teenage raver very convincingly.'

Jackman watched Max struggle to hold his temper.

'She shouldn't be in there.'

Ignoring his colleague, Charlie went back to listening, passing on snippets as they came through. Then he got to his feet. 'She's getting out, sir. She's seen someone she recognises.' He listened again. 'She says to meet her where we dropped her off, in five minutes.'

Max was first out of the old storeroom door and before Jackman could even stand up, he had run out into the night.

As he followed him out, Jackman wondered about Max's behaviour. Could he be . . . ?

It took a little longer than Rosie had said but not long after her message, she came hurrying towards them.

Max had run on ahead. 'Are you okay? Shit! You had us scared.'

Rosie raised her eyebrows. 'I'm fine, absolutely fine, you muppet! It was just that I recognised a man who turned up just then, and I couldn't let him see a cop there, could I?'

'Who was he?' asked Marie, who had materialised at Rosie's side.

Rosie shook her head. 'Even though I have a damned good memory, I just can't place him, Sarge. I recognised him the moment I saw him, but try as I might I can't recall where from.'

Marie put her arm around Rosie. 'Don't worry, it'll come back to you when the adrenalin has worn off. And well done, flower. Let's get back to the station and debrief you.'

As they drove back, Rosie described the man as shabbily dressed in scruffy chinos, a polo shirt and a nylon tracksuit top. He was tall with slicked-back hair and wearing wire-rimmed glasses.

'Probably someone you've helped put away at some time or another,' said Charlie Button. 'Maybe a look through the sex-offender's file might jog your memory.'

'Yeah, that's a good idea.'

'Hope you don't mind me saying so, but it sounded as if you were rather enjoying yourself with your little friend, Will.' Charlie gave her a smirk. 'Things were getting a bit steamy in there, weren't they?'

Rosie cuffed the back of Charlie's head. 'Mind your own business. Will was very helpful. He told me quite a lot, and I have his mobile number if we need to follow anything up.'

'Cradle-snatcher.'

'Eavesdropper.'

'Just shut up, you two,' growled Max. 'This is serious! It's no joking matter.'

'We know that,' murmured Charlie. 'And you need to chill. Rosie is fine, so stop worrying.'

They drove the rest of the way back in silence. Jackman knew he'd been right. Max Cohen had fallen, hook, line and sinker for Rosie McElderry.

# CHAPTER FIFTEEN

The following day Jackman was in his office before seven. He had not slept well and had decided to get up early and get as much office paperwork out of the way as he could. At eight o'clock Marie backed into his office carrying two coffees and a packet of Jammy Dodgers. She pushed his door closed with her hip.

'I saw you were busy, so I left you in peace.'

'Appreciated, Marie, and so is that coffee.'

She sat down opposite him and tipped sugar into her mug. 'I've been thinking about Toni Clarkson. What with last night's caper, I'd pushed her to the back of my mind, but then I woke up at two this morning worried sick about her.'

Jackman put down his files. 'You know, for the first time I caught a glimpse of what young Ethan Barley saw in her. She's devastated by the thought of Emily being taken, isn't she?'

'No wonder. When you think what happened to Shauna Kelly, Toni was lucky to come out alive.' Marie placed her mug on his desk. 'And talking of Shauna, uniform tells me that one of her school friends confirmed that Shauna confessed to attending a "party" in, as she put it, "some filthy hovel filled with gorgeous fit blokes and dirty old men.'"

'So it's as we suspected. Oh, that poor mother.'

Marie shook her head. Then she asked, 'When are we going out to Windrush?'

'We are all organised for eleven this morning.'

'Then if it's all set up, would you mind if I took one of the kids and drove out to Allenby Creek, just to do a quick recce of those houses there? Maybe someone saw something the night Shauna drowned.'

Jackman piled up his files. 'Forget the kids. Finish your drink and I'll come with you. We've plenty of time.'

'Excellent. I'll go grab a pool car.'

* * *

No one they spoke to knew or had seen anything of Shauna Kelly. Jackman was beginning to believe they had wasted their time. The last cottage they tried was a mess of weathered wood, cracked and broken tiles and crumbling brickwork. But smoke was rising from the chimney and a pleasant aroma of baking lingered in the doorway.

A woman answered their knock, calling out for to them to come in. She was around forty, with long hair, already greying and pulled up into an untidy French plait. She had a warm smile.

'Oh yes, those nice officers called the day before yesterday, but,' she shrugged and rubbed a floury hand across her forehead, 'I couldn't help them. I went to the market in the morning, then I never left the cottage again.'

'You live here alone, Miss . . . ?' asked Jackman politely.

'Seale, Megan Seale, Inspector Jackman. And no, this is my father's place. I'm just looking after him for a bit. He's getting on, and he's been proper poorly.'

'Did the police speak to him as well?' asked Marie.

'No, Sergeant. Dad was asleep, and well, I leaves him when he drops off like. He's getting forgetful, and he wanders a bit too. It sounds awful, I know, but when he's asleep I can relax for a while. Get a few chores done.'

Jackman looked around the old kitchen and noticed the cigarette ends nestling in an ashtray close to the fire. 'Does your father sometimes go out at night, Miss Seale?'

The woman dusted flour from her apron. 'Yes, he does, unfortunately. I do my best to stop him, but . . .' She gave a helpless shrug.

'Do you think I could have a quick word with him? I promise not to upset him.' Jackman smiled at her.

'I'm not sure you'll get very far. He came in earlier to tell me that Winston Churchill was about to address the nation, and would I make sure that the wireless was tuned in to the Home Service.'

'Just for a moment or two?' Jackman upped his smile.

'Of course. But don't expect too much. Oh, and if he calls you Gordon, that's his son, my brother. He died ten years ago, but Dad still thinks he's here.'

Jackman's heart went out to the woman. 'I'll not keep him long, I promise.'

'He'll be out back in the lean-to. His name is Stan.'

Leaving Marie to talk to Megan, Jackman walked through the ramshackle cottage and out into a strange narrow room with windows on three sides. It might have passed as a conservatory if properly built, but this wasn't the case. Jackman sincerely hoped it would remain standing just a little longer.

'Stan? Hello there! My name is Jackman. Can I have a word?'

The old man stood staring out of the grimy window towards the marsh. On hearing Jackman's voice he turned and looked at him without curiosity.

'You know this part better than most, I'm told. Lived here a long time, I guess?' began Jackman.

Stan sat heavily back into an ancient armchair, and in a weak ray of watery sunshine, Jackman saw thousands of dust motes rise up around him.

'Have you been out on the strand at darklings?' Jackman tried using his almost forgotten dialect in the hopes of jogging the old man's memory.

'Aye. A few nights back.' The voice had the deep gravelly timbre of the heavy smoker.

'See anything interesting?'

The old man frowned. 'Mayhap, but me mind's a jumblement. I seems to think I saw a pretty lass, and a truck where a truck shouldn't be. Out there in the moonlight, it was. No. Shouldn't be there.'

'What kind of truck, Stan?'

'Big dark thing, all thick wheels, too many lights and growling noise.'

Jackman's brow creased. 'A 4x4? An off-road vehicle?'

'Like as much, I suppose.' Stan wrinkled up his leathery face. 'But the man who drove it were worse. One look at his face and yer'd see 'e's as black as the devil's nuttin' bag! He spoke to the lass and the next thing she was running like a hare.'

'Where to?'

He pointed vaguely towards the sea, then he swung round and stared at Jackman. 'And when are you going to fix that broken gutter pipe, Gordon? That drip, drip, drip keeps me awake at night.'

Jackman looked into the rheumy eyes and saw that his window of opportunity had closed. 'I'll fix it, Dad,' he said softly, and slipped quietly out of the musty-smelling room.

Outside in the car, Marie looked at Jackman eagerly. 'A 4x4, you say?'

'*And* a pretty girl.' Jackman bit his lip. 'But the old guy's mind comes and goes, and he'd probably not be able to tell us much more if we sat with him all day.'

'But she *was* here! This is where they brought her, isn't it?'

'I believe it is, but we can't prove it.' Jackman drummed a tattoo on the steering wheel. 'Damn it! It's almost worse than not knowing at all.'

Marie stared at her watch. 'We should be getting back, sir. I'm sure there will be some loose ends to tie up before we head out to Windrush.'

Jackman grumbled something and pulled the car onto the road.

\* \* \*

At ten o'clock Jackman gathered the team in the CID room.

'Have you organised a warrant to check out Windrush, sir?' asked Charlie Button.

Jackman nodded. 'I know Broome promised cooperation, but I've hedged my bets. I've swung it with upstairs, and a constable has already collected it from the magistrate.'

He looked at Max, and saw that the young man was his old self again. 'I'd like you to have a word with Stefan, our Polish interpreter. See if he's heard anything on the Eastern European grapevine regarding a missing teenager, a girl who calls herself Emily. Tell him we believe she's in grave danger, Max, and make sure he understands this is not just an excuse to harass them, okay?'

Max nodded. 'I'll do it now, before we go.'

There was a knock on the door and they all looked up as PC Andy English entered, carrying a folder of files from the council's planning office, and the signed warrant.

He handed them to Jackman. 'We may need this, sir, if my hunch about the big bloke is correct. Fair gave me the creeps, he did. I'm dead certain he's what my old gran would have called, "lacking up top." And he's built like a brick outhouse. I wouldn't want to upset him.'

'Benedict Broome did say that Mr Lee could get a trifle overprotective of the place. Frankly, I can't wait to meet him. Now, what have you found out about the planning permission?'

'Well, Broome does have permission for a material change of use for the proposed development. It seems that he has requested to modify the old sanatorium, add certain other structures and make it a sanctuary, just as the big guy said. Most of the plans have been accepted. It's just that he seems to have altered the specifications a dozen times.' Andy stared at the paperwork in his hand. 'The man in Planning said he was a nightmare, and even now, when work is almost about to begin, he's not convinced that he won't try to change things again.'

'What do we actually know about Broome?' Jackman asked. Broome, on his own, seemed to be prepared to spend a fortune on the old place. Who, other than major players in the business world, had that kind of money to flash around in this gloomy financial climate? Very odd.

'I checked him out, sir, and he's not known to us. All we know is that he lives with his housekeeper in one of those big houses along the waterway. You know those old three-storey Victorian terraces?'

Jackman recalled the educated speaking voice. 'You mean Admiralty Row? That's one classy address. He must be loaded if he owns that property *and* the Windrush estate.'

Andy nodded. 'Absolutely. You do know the old story, sir, don't you?'

Jackman nodded. 'About how the sanatorium was won in a wager? Is it really true?'

'Oh yes. Broome won the place playing poker.'

Marie grinned at him. 'How come the Lottery only ever gets me a tenner once a year?'

'You and me both, Sarge. Anyway, I've asked Kevin Stoner to keep digging into Broome's history.'

Jackman nodded. 'Okay. So even though it all seems kosher, you still think we should check the place over?'

Andy looked at him. 'Absolutely, sir. Micah Lee definitely steered us away from parts of it. Plus he was really uptight about our being there at all. We need to return and not just go with the scenic tour.'

Jackman nodded. 'Okay, that's good enough for me, Constable. Get your team together. We'll move out at eleven o'clock.'

## CHAPTER SIXTEEN

Across the marsh the morning sky was as blue as the Aegean, but a cloud of foreboding hovered above the officers.

Max and Gary had stayed behind to chase up the interpreter and keep the office running, while the rest of the team headed out to the old house at Roman Creek.

Uniform would carry out the main search but Jackman wanted to see the place for himself.

Charlie stared out of the car window. 'It's strange, isn't it, sir? Although it's close to the marsh, this area is on a rise.'

Jackman looked ahead of them. 'You're right. It's something of an anomaly. It's almost a hill.'

'It was once an island, or so I'm told,' said Marie. 'When the land was reclaimed and drained, this place, now called Roman Bank, was then called Romsey. I think it means, *island,* or *dry ground in marsh belonging to a man called Rum,* same as the one in Hampshire.'

Jackman gazed at her in admiration. 'You never cease to amaze me, Marie. Let's hope your interest in these old places proves useful.'

Marie smiled, but as the car drew closer to Windrush, Jackman noticed that she was looking increasingly anxious.

'What's the matter?' he asked.

'It's changed so much since I was here last,' she said, 'and I get the feeling it's not for the better.' She looked out of the window at the rambling and desolate old sanatorium. 'I can't believe how different this place feels now from when I came here on that health and safety course.'

'That was decades ago, wasn't it, Sarge?' Rosie laughed. She nudged her younger colleague. 'Charlie here was probably still in nappies.'

Uniform were already out of their vehicles, and Andy English stood waiting for Jackman to give the go-ahead.

Jackman took the search warrant from his pocket and nodded at him. English returned the nod, and he and some of the other men went quickly up the steps to the front entrance of the old building.

The team hung back with the rest of the group at the bottom of the stone steps, all waiting for their first glimpse of the man who had made such a strong impression on PCs English and Stoner.

It didn't take long for him to open the door.

'My God! Conan the Barbarian lives,' whispered Rosie, eyes wide.

Micah Lee was a beast of a man. He had a thick mop of dark hair and a face that looked as if it had been crudely chiselled out of a rough hunk of granite. His eyes were deep set, under heavy overhanging brows. He was tall and powerful, although not in an athletic way. His strength seemed more inherently Neanderthal than developed through exercise. Jackman found it impossible to judge his age. But what struck him most was the almost tangible sense of resentment at their presence. Lee's lips were tight with anger.

'Sensible of you to organise that warrant,' Marie said quietly 'I have a strong feeling we'll need it.'

Jackman stared openly at the Goliath of Windrush. For one awful moment he thought that Micah Lee would have to be physically restrained. And he wasn't sure how many officers it would take.

PC English bravely approached the man, told him that they had Mr Broome's full approval for a detailed search, and mentioned that they also had a warrant.

Lee seemed to crumble. Jackman saw a wave of emotion wash across his craggy face. His intense anger subsided, replaced with trepidation and an almost childlike fear.

Fear of what? Jackman wondered.

'Just do it,' Micah said suddenly. Then he turned on his heels and marched back through the front doors.

Jackman watched him disappear inside, then called out to Andy and his colleagues to go in. 'Top to toe. Pay extra attention to anything underground — cellars and the like. Anywhere that could conceal a missing girl. Call me if you find anything, okay?'

A tall, bald-headed sergeant immediately took over, and soon men and women were heading off in pairs to check out the big old house, the numerous outbuildings and the surrounding grounds.

'Sir!' The sergeant called over to him. 'Would you like to help or stay with Mr Lee?'

'We'll join you, Sergeant.' Jackman had no wish to play nanny to a giant, volatile baby. 'Which area shall we cover?'

'According to my aerial map, there's a ward block around the back, sir. It doesn't seem to have been prepared for renovation yet, so watch your step. It could be dangerous.' The sergeant placed a tick on his list and turned away.

They made their way around to the back of the building towards the single storey building that housed the additional wards. The exterior had once been white but now great patches of rendering had crumbled away, leaving the brickwork exposed and decaying.

'This could take some time,' said Rosie, picking her way over some fallen debris. 'This place is bigger than it looks.'

Marie nodded. 'It's a rambling old pile and it's a sin to have let it fall into ruin like this. When I was here it was rundown, but at least it was still usable.'

Jackman pushed a door open and they all peered inside.

The ward had been long and wide, with one side opening out through a series of French doors onto concrete terraces. Jackman reminded himself that it had once been a TB sanatorium, and in those days they pushed bed and patient outside to get the benefit of the fresh air.

Now the windows were cracked and broken, and plaster and rotten woodwork lay scattered across the floor. A thick haze of dust motes swam in the shafts of sunlight that penetrated what remained of the glass. In one corner a pile of old metal-framed institutional beds had been heaped together, in another a stack of broken bedside cupboards and rusting skeletons of chairs. Jackman saw something move, and a rat broke cover and ran for a dim, gaping hole in the wooden floor.

Marie sighed. 'Maybe we should stick together. We can't afford any broken ankles or cuts and bruises from all this leftover junk.'

'Shame big Micah never got this far with his clean-up,' grumbled Charlie Button. 'He's done a great job on the front and the sides of the house.'

'I think this part is going to be demolished,' Jackman said. 'I glanced briefly at some of the plans that Andy showed me, and as far as I can remember the back of the building is destined to become some kind of sheltered garden with seats and water features. Not that my imagination is capable of seeing it right now.' He took a deep breath and stepped inside. Marie, Rosie and Charlie followed and they began their sweep.

They searched every room, each cupboard and corridor. There were five wards, identical in their design. As they reached the final ward Jackman called out, 'I think we can declare this area clear. Agreed?'

Rosie and Charlie agreed immediately, but Marie seemed lost in thought.

'Marie?'

'I'm thinking we need old plans, old maps of the area. Ones that go way back to when the original house was built.' She looked at Jackman, a light glinting in her eyes. 'When I was here last, there were all sorts of stories flying around about the history of this place. I read a bit about the general history, just because it interested me, but there were other stories.'

'Like what?' asked Rosie.

'Like ghost stories?' said Charlie excitedly.

'More like legends and folklore. One was about wreckers.'

Jackman brushed unsuccessfully at some plaster dust on his jacket. 'Did we have wreckers along this coast? I thought that was Cornwall.'

'We had some alright. It's documented that Mablethorpe had its share, and if the old stories have a grain of truth in them, it looks like this area tried their hand at it too.'

Jackman stared out towards the marsh. 'Well, the Wash is just beyond this marsh, and then it's the North Sea. It's possible, but it's a very long way to drag their illicit cargo. How did they get it here, I wonder?'

Marie rubbed her chin. 'That's why I want to see some old maps, because I'm thinking tunnels and old storerooms.'

'Then maybe uniform will find something. They are checking for cellars, aren't they?' said Rosie.

Jackman nodded. 'Maybe, but if Marie is right and this house was used by wreckers for hiding their illegal haul, then the entrances would be concealed. We do need old plans.'

Rosie squatted down on her haunches, 'Maybe Fred Flintstone in there has some, if he's been doing all this work.'

Somehow Jackman did not think that Micah Lee would have the plans. Benedict Broome would be the one to contact for those. But, before they went down that route, there was another way. Jackman took out his phone and keyed in Max's number. It took only seconds to relay what they needed, and then he shut his phone and looked at Marie. 'He's sourcing them now, and if he finds anything useful, he'll ring back and Gary will drive out with them. If Max hits a brick wall, we'll go to Broome for help. Although I'm sure Max's IT skills will access everything we need in less time than it would take to get Benedict Broome to open his front door.'

Marie straightened up. 'I think we should see how the others are doing. These wards are holding no secrets. Shall we go find the sergeant?'

\* \* \*

'Anything so far?'

The sergeant in charge shook his head. 'Nothing substantial, sir. Some of the rooms have been used recently, but it's probably just Micah Lee staying over. He seems pretty attached to this place, considering he doesn't own it. And he's obviously working his fingers to the bone.' He passed a broad-knuckled hand over his shaven head. 'But regarding the search, there are no signs of anyone having been held here at any time, but this is a big area to cover. We've hardly scratched the surface yet.'

'Well, the ward block at the back is clear, so you can tick that off your list. Oh, and I've requested any architects' plans on the original building and any old maps, just in case there may be rooms or cellars that were sealed up in later years,' Jackman added.

'Good idea. For all we know, this place could be a rabbit warren of underground tunnels.'

Marie started. 'What made you say that, Sergeant?'

'Well, it may have nothing to do with it, but see that stretch of marsh over there?' He pointed across the fields to a broad stretch of wetland. 'It used to be called Chapel Marsh. They reckon that back in historical times there was an old Abbey out there, the coastline being different back then. Anyway, the sea took it when they flooded this part of the land, and all that was left was a tiny chapel, and that got used by smugglers right up until the time of the Second World War, when that got washed away too.'

Marie's eyes lit up. 'I've heard of that. But you mentioned tunnels?'

'Yes, apparently the smugglers used a system of tunnels to bring their contraband inland. Of course a lot of them could have caved in or collapsed with the high tides and the bad weather, but they say that one or two were really well constructed. The locals, and my old grandmother is one of them, reckon they still exist somewhere around here, maybe underneath the Roman Creek sea-bank. You've probably noticed it's a very unusual piece of higher ground, so tunnels could be possible. Just sit in one of the local pubs and you'll hear a load of old wives' tales about them.'

Marie felt a tingle of excitement. 'Did any of these tunnels connect with the house here?'

The sergeant raised his shoulders. 'No idea, Sergeant Evans. They may not even exist. It might all be just superstition and folklore. You never can tell, can you?'

Marie grinned. 'Oh, they exist. I'll stake my new Suzuki on it. Thank you, Sergeant.' She turned to Jackman. 'So, what next?'

'I suggest we let these guys here continue and get back to base and see what Max has dug up. This search will take until the light goes, so we'd be better off doing a different kind of groundwork, using a computer instead of a shovel.'

# CHAPTER SEVENTEEN

The CID room resembled a Second World War chart room. Max had pushed several tables together, and they were covered in neat piles of maps, diagrams and plans.

'Oh my! Who's been a busy boy, then?' Rosie laughed.

Marie glanced at him. Had Max blushed?

Max pushed his rolled-up sleeves further up his arms. 'I was just getting ready to pack Gary off to meet you. We've managed to get our hands on quite a lot of useful stuff.'

'I can see,' said Jackman. He clapped a hand on Max's shoulder. 'Well done! We knew we could count on your computer skills.'

The young cockney looked proud. 'Thank you, sir. I've found maps, plans, deeds, building permission applications, geophysical surveys and related data, and even aerial cartographical views of Windrush and the surrounding landscape.'

'We've tried to arrange them chronologically,' said Gary. 'Oldest at the top, and working down to present day. These are particularly interesting.' Gary held up a batch of geophysical printouts. 'They were taken a few years back when an archaeological dig was planned for the Roman

Bank, but they couldn't get permission to bring in the diggers. They show the ground right up to and including the edge of the Windrush estate.'

Marie stared at the papers. 'I'm not sure what I'm looking at.'

'They are high resolution images that show subsoil structures or traces of human activity.'

Gary seemed to know his stuff. Marie was impressed.

He pointed to a shadowy dark square and a series of grey circles and lines. 'This is what they were after. The archaeologists believed that there was an ancient Roman villa on the spot, and this data supports their theory. They then widened the geophys to see what else might be there, but someone pulled the plug on them, and it never happened.'

Marie felt a surge of excitement. 'And their data actually covered part of Windrush?'

Gary picked up a batch of paperwork. 'Yes, right up to the walls of the house on the marsh side.'

Jackman looked over Marie's shoulder. He frowned and jabbed a finger onto one of the maps. 'What's this area here?'

'Is that one of the areas that is being redeveloped?' asked Rosie.

Jackman unfolded the plans Andy had given him. 'No. All the renovation and new building will take place immediately in and around the house itself. The old stores and the barn area that you are looking at are bordered on this plan by a thick green line.' He squinted at the legend in the bottom right-hand corner of the map. 'Green box indicates Stage Three Development. Work proposed. See attached addendum.' He unfolded the rest of the papers. 'And no attached addendum.'

Marie drew in a breath. 'That probably means there are no plans for that spot for the foreseeable future.'

'Then it could be a pretty good place to hide someone,' Jackman said. He turned to Gary. 'Can you actually read those geo-fizzy things?'

'Not with any accuracy, sir. We could easily be looking at the foundations of earlier structures on that site, a barn or something like that.'

'Then we need an expert.'

'And I believe I can help you there, dear friend.'

They all turned around. Rory Wilkinson was standing in the doorway.

'Sorry. I've been earwigging on your fascinating conversation. It just so happens that I've an old friend at the university that knows a lot about all this. He is an archaeology student, but don't be fooled by the "student." He's been on digs all over the world, and he's doing a paper on the use of various non-invasive technologies in archaeology. His name is Ted Watchman. You'll like him.' Rory pulled out his phone. 'And it will be my great pleasure to secure his services for you.'

Jackman nodded briskly. 'Brilliant! Ask for his help and, Rory, do stress the importance. This girl is still missing, but she might just be alive.'

'Consider it done.' Rory talked for a few minutes, then turned to Jackman. 'Should he meet you here, or at the site?'

'Tell him to go directly to Windrush. We'll meet him there.'

\* \* \*

Jackman and his team arrived at the old sanatorium before their new recruit.

With a shiver, Jackman hurried back into the foyer and saw the dark figure of Micah Lee watching them from his tiny porter's room. He seemed to be concentrating on Marie in particular, and the look on his face was one of utter hatred.

Halfway across the hall, Jackman turned and stared back at Lee. It took considerable resolve to hold a gaze of such intense loathing. Eventually Lee broke off and looked away.

Max's phone rang as Jackman hurried over to rejoin the team. He listened and pulled a face. 'The fire chief is trying to locate a heat-seeking camera. They share one with several other stations but it's not on base at present. Same old story, no bloody money for anything these days. He said he'll ring me when he finds one.'

He put away his phone. 'Sir, with all this going on, I forgot to tell you that I contacted Stefan, the interpreter. There is one possible missing woman. Her name is Aija, Aija Ozolini. She's not Polish, she's Latvian, and she definitely uses a different name when she's around English-speaking people. He's still trying to find out what that is.'

Jackman's heart beat faster. 'Has she been missing long?'

'She's not been officially reported missing at all, but her community is definitely worried about her. And the timing fits like a glove.'

\* \* \*

They wandered over to the place where the maps showed unidentified marks beneath the ground.

The area behind the storehouses consisted of flat concrete and scrubby, tired grass, surrounded by wind-blasted shrubs, brambles and weeds. Even the old barn and storerooms seemed lacking in character compared with the house, which although decrepit, was impressive in an aging Victorian Gothic style.

'This is definitely a spot worth checking out when the prof's mate gets here.' Gary stared down at the geophysical map. 'Nothing to show on the surface, though.'

They all looked around.

'Nothing at all,' said Rosie, sounding disappointed.

Max kicked impatiently at some loose shingle. 'This place is bleeding miserable.'

Marie sat on a low stone wall, a little apart from the others, and stared out across the wetlands. How different the place felt from when she had been there as a young copper! There had always been an air of mystery to it, but it was a very old property, where many people had died over the course of the years. It had been a hospital too, after all. Stories about the place had been passed on, changing and being embellished, until they became part of folklore. When she was on her course, Marie had revelled in these stories, but today the place had a different feel to it. Marie was a down to earth, no-nonsense woman, but even she felt as if something dark and unwholesome had draped itself over the old building and all the land around it.

A skein of greylags flew across the marsh. They wheeled and landed neatly on a lime-green patch of sedge close to the water. Their harsh, honking calls blended perfectly into the dreary landscape.

Marie felt a hand gently rest on her shoulder.

'Does this place give you the creeps?' asked Rosie softly. 'Because it definitely does me.'

'Me too,' added Gary. They both sat down beside her on the wall and Gary stared at the dust that clung to his polished black boots. 'My sister hated this stretch of the marshes.'

Jackman ambled towards them. 'Your sister died, didn't she?'

Gary nodded. 'Not long ago.'

'Is that why you wanted a change of scenery?' Jackman said gently.

'It was partly the case, but working at Harlan Marsh nick was . . .' Gary sighed.

'Did you come here a lot? You and your sister?' asked Marie.

'Only when we were bringing one of the animals to see the vet.' He pointed across to the other side of the Roman Bank where a small farmhouse nestled in a clump of trees. 'Our vet lived over there. He used to do consultations from his front room. Still lives there, I believe, although now he has a modern surgery in Harlan Marsh town. Nice bloke, great with our dogs. Even so, Anne hated coming out here.'

Rosie tilted her head. 'Why?'

Gary smiled sadly, took out his warrant card holder and removed a small colour photo. 'My sister, Anne.'

Marie hid a smile. They looked like twins.

'Right from when she was a little kid, she would do anything rather than go across Hobs End Marsh.' Gary pointed to the area immediately in front of them. 'That stretch over there. Years ago it was called Chapel Marsh, but the name changed during the war. It has always had a bad reputation, and most of the older locals still refuse go out there.'

Jackman gave a little sigh. Every local knew some weird and wonderful story, and it certainly got in the way of their investigations. He had little time for mumbo-jumbo.

'So what superstitious crap keeps them away?' he asked. 'This part of the coast is one of the richest areas for collecting samphire, it should be a little goldmine. So what are they scared of? Jack-o'-lanterns or boggarts? The green mist? Or perhaps it's the Black Dog!'

Gary smiled and raised his hands. 'I know, I know. Superstition is alive and well and living in Lincolnshire.' His smile faded. 'But even I don't like this part, and I really don't believe in boggarts.'

'But your sister did?' Rosie handed him the photo.

'Oh no. Anne didn't believe in all that stuff. I think all those stories she heard as a kid affected her, and she did have some sort of odd sensitivity to atmosphere. It's difficult to explain, but there were certain places that upset her quite badly.' He looked out over the sedge and reeds of the watery marsh. 'And this was one of them.'

Gary took the picture back, stared at it for a moment and then carefully returned it to his warrant card holder. 'Frankly, although I think Anne was right about the place, there might have been other reasons for the locals keeping away. People say they've seen someone in dark clothes walking around at night. They say only a devil would walk those paths in darkness.' He held up his hands and grinned. 'But I say that a smuggler would certainly walk here. This marsh meets the Wash, and the Wash meets the North Sea.' He raised an eyebrow.

'And the North Sea meets boats stuffed with illegal incoming drugs.' Jackman nodded. 'We've already talked about this, but in more historical terms.'

'We've got rid of most of the trade in this area, but you'll never stamp it out completely. There's always some silly sod ready to take on the marsh and the killer tides,' added Gary.

'So what was the original folklore story about this spot? And why was your sister so affected by it?' Rosie leaned forward, her elbows resting on her knees.

'I forget the whole story, but it is supposed to be one of those places where weird natural phenomena occur when the weather is just right. And you can imagine what the old web-foots make of them! Mind you, although all marshes have their ghost lights, it's the sheer abundance and regularity of the marsh lights here that make it different. That and the strange noises. A whole plethora of weird sounds come from Hobs End, something to do with movement in the boggy soil I think. Anyway, one day when we were walking our dogs up to the Wash bank, Anne said she heard whisperings, voices, saying things she didn't want to listen to. It scared her half to death. Then a few years back, my old dog did a runner after a visit to the vet's, and we came down here looking for him. Anne heard things then too.'

154

'The same sort of whisperings?' Rosie was beginning to sound like a schoolgirl in the dorm at midnight.

'No, she said it was more like church music, chanting or singing. It had her in pieces. She fair ran off the marsh, she did.'

'A boggart that sings! That's a new one for the old crones to pass around when they've finished reading the tea-leaves.' Jackman shook his head. 'Where the hell is our archaeologist? We are sitting around telling bloody stories while Emily could be breathing her last.'

'I'll go back to the house and look out for him, sir.' Rosie brushed dried grass off her trousers.

Max stood up immediately. 'I'll go with you.'

Marie watched them walk away and then turned to look back over the lonely stretch of marsh. She wanted terribly to be gone from here.

Gary pointed back to the house. 'Looks like our man is here, Sarge. Rosie is waving to us. Shall we go?'

* * *

A white van, dirty, dented and half dead, groaned to a halt behind their police car. Ted Watchman, the young man who got out could be nothing other than an archaeology student. His wavy hair was unfashionably long. He wore round wire-rimmed glasses and mismatched clothes.

'The fire chief sent you this little beauty, sir. Lovely bit of kit!' the uniformed sergeant said, looking at the thermal-imaging camera with undisguised longing before passing it to Jackman. 'I hope you know how it works.'

'If you're stuck, Inspector, I do. Hey, that's not your average handheld job either! That's a state-of-the-art industrial model.' Ted smiled.

'As long as it works, I don't care what it is,' Jackman mumbled. 'So where did the Fire Service get it from, if it's not standard issue?'

The sergeant smiled grimly. 'I've been told to tell you to guard it with your life. It's on loan from a Search and Rescue Team, and apparently it's worth a couple of grand more than my car.'

Hastily, Jackman passed it to Ted. 'I'll leave it to the expert, thank you. But, as a civilian I need to explain the risks involved should you need to accompany us anywhere of possible danger.'

'As I think I'm the only person here who can operate this camera, and because I've been in some very dangerous places before, sir...' Ted grinned, 'I'm game if you are?'

'That's not the kind of risk assessment that I was thinking of, Mr Watchman, but we seriously need your help.'

Gary handed Ted the geophysical surveys. 'This is the area that interests us, sir.'

He circled his finger around the storerooms and the barn, and his voice was grave. 'We are looking for anywhere that may conceal a missing girl. Time is of the essence.'

'Call me Ted, and Rory told me what you're looking for.' He took the plans and stared at them 'Hey! This was the Roman villa dig, wasn't it?' He flopped down on the ground and spread the sheets around him.

'Apparently,' Jackman said.

'I've seen some of these before. It was an absolute travesty that this dig was aborted. The university was certain they could have made a monumental find here.' He bent closer to the printouts and let out a low whistle. 'Whoa! There's a lot going on here.' He looked up at Jackman. 'Can I see the actual area, please?'

'Sure. Come on.'

Ted strode alongside Jackman. 'I've got some equipment in my van. I brought everything I could think of that might be useful.'

'Good, but I cannot stress enough how quickly we need to move.'

'Okay, we'll check out what we've got first, and then take it from there. That camera you've borrowed could save us hours.'

Jackman's heart sank. 'We don't have hours, Ted. This is not archaeology. If there's a girl down there, she might be dying. It's crucial that we find her.'

For the next fifteen minutes, Ted paced, measured, consulted his surveys and muttered to himself. Then he began drawing in a large plain A4 notebook.

Jackman felt like shaking him.

Ted let out a long noisy breath. 'Right, well, normally at this point I'd do checks of my own, use an EM conductivity instrument, maybe even run a ground-penetrating radar check to confirm my initial interpretation, but if time really is so important . . .'

'Believe me, Ted, it is,' growled Marie.

'Then this is what I consider to be beneath this area, given all I have are old geophys surveys.' He thrust the drawing at them. 'There was another building here. Looks like a large, long structure. Its foundations can clearly be seen and they extend beyond the present storerooms and the barn.' He blinked at Jackman and pushed a lock of hair from his eyes. 'My guess is that it was a much earlier storehouse of some kind, with an extensive cellar system of its own. The upper part was demolished and the present barn, stores and yard erected over the top of it.'

Jackman looked carefully at his sketch. 'And these?' He pointed to a network of double lines.

Ted's eyes glinted. 'Tunnels, Detective Inspector. Probably six or more. Some going under the main house, some extending towards the highway and some leading right out onto Hobs End Marsh.'

# CHAPTER EIGHTEEN

Jackman had no proof that Emily was being held in the tunnels beneath Windrush.

He had no proof that the tunnels were even accessible.

He had coerced a small army of uniformed officers into searching a dangerous wreck of a building with little or no justification, and he had got one of his detectives to sweet-talk the Fire Department into loaning him equipment that was worth a small fortune. Even the university had sent one of their finest, complete with enough technology to unearth a lost city.

And now he had requested and received reinforcements, in order to find the entrances to six underground tunnels that might not even exist.

He was beginning to doubt his sanity, until the team gathered in a circle on the foyer floor and held a discussion, and Jackman found that they all agreed with him.

Rosie's expression was eager. 'It all follows, sir. Small things, I know, but they add up. You told us Toni Clarkson heard something like a chorister. Gary's sister heard some kind of choral church music. And from these maps, and Gary's description of where she was, they were right over one of the tunnels.'

'And Micah Lee,' Charlie Button whispered, 'is definitely hiding something.'

'Whatever, even if all this turns out to be a crock of shit,' Max added, 'There *are* underground rooms and tunnels beneath this dump, so our girl could be being hid in one of them. End of. Let's search the place.'

Marie patted Max on the back. 'Can't argue with that, can we, sir?'

It made sense. A university expert had pointed to underground structures that could easily be used as places of concealment for an abducted girl. And Jackman was convinced that Emily was somewhere very close by. It was time to bite the bullet.

*If I've got this wrong, the super will crucify me — publicly.*

Jackman watched the preparations for the search and considered his position. He came to the conclusion that he was skating on thin ice.

Three o'clock came and went, and the search parties determined that four of the six tunnels were either collapsed or inaccessible. But Jackman still believed that they would find her down there.

\* \* \*

The call came just before the purple evening shadows began to spread across the marsh.

'We've found an entrance, sir!' The policewoman was red-faced and sweating. 'It's the marsh tunnel, and it runs for about a quarter of a mile out into Hobs End.'

Jackman saw a flush of excitement darken Marie's pale face.

'Where is it?' he asked.

'There's an old building there, sir, little more than lumps of concrete and partially collapsed walls. I suppose it was an old cottage that was abandoned because of the danger of flooding. It's a little way above sea level, and there's a hatch that leads into some kind of cellar, and then a door into the tunnel itself.' She wiped her forearm across her brow. 'We've been down as far as the door. It's locked, so we'd like permission to break it down. We can't just bust in without authority, can we, sir?'

'In order to protect a life you can, and I believe that someone is in mortal danger. As soon as the rest of the team arrive, we'll follow you, Constable. And we'll go in.'

The marsh path was narrow and uneven. They ran, slipping and tripping, until they reached the derelict building.

As he paused to get his breath back, Jackman saw Marie looking thoughtfully at the moss-covered piles of masonry and ancient brickwork. He thought she was also sure they were in the right place. One by one they eased through the old hatch and found themselves in a tiny cellar. The stench of damp, mildew and rotting plant-life made them gag.

Unlike the cellar, the door to the tunnel was new.

Jackman stared at it. The wood looked strong, and the heavy-duty lock had fresh oil glistening around it.

A police constable stood waiting, a weighty metal enforcer under his muscled arm. 'Sir?' He looked at Jackman and swung the piece of equipment upwards in readiness.

This was it. Jackman's heart raced. He looked around at his team and knew that they all felt the same.

Even Ted Watchman, gently cradling the precious thermal camera like a new-born baby, looked as though he had been wired to a socket and was waiting for the switch to be thrown.

It took half a dozen blows to shatter the lock. Then they moved forward.

Jackman began to run.

The light from their torches bounced off the walls and made intricate patterns on the roof of the tunnels. Jackman wondered where they were heading.

Ted puffed along beside him. 'We must be getting close to Windrush house now, Inspector. According to the survey, the tunnel should be finishing soon.'

'There's a door up ahead, boss!' called back Rosie, who had sprinted ahead. 'We're going to need that enforcer again.'

Jackman raised a hand. 'Wait, all of you, and keep the voices down for a moment.'

They had no idea what they would find in there. For all they knew, their abductor could be waiting with a knife to Emily's throat, or she could be sitting on a homemade bomb. Or it could be an empty room.

'Okay, Ted, this is your moment,' Jackman said grimly. 'I need to know if there's anything alive behind that door.'

He heard the young archaeologist exhale nervously, and move closer to the heavy wooden door. He carefully unfolded the camera's display screen and pressed a series of buttons. The screen came alive, and he moved it from left to right.

The whole search team was holding their breaths.

Ted remained silent, angling the camera this way and that, and then he gave a little sigh. Jackman's heart sank.

Then Ted whispered, 'Yes. There's a heat source. It's faint, very faint, but it's there.'

'Just one?'

'Just one, I'm certain of it.' Ted stepped back. 'Inspector, it seems to be a very big area in there. In fact, it's massive.'

'Constable! Break it down.'

They all stood back to give the big policeman room to swing the enforcer. Jackman felt sick with apprehension. It might be Emily. Or it might be a stray cat.

If Emily was there, what state would she be in? And if it was a cat? Jackman thought about the massive search party and everything it entailed, and imagined the ice cracking beneath his feet.

# CHAPTER NINETEEN

As the enforcer crashed into the door, Marie began to ready herself. She had no idea what lay on the other side, and she suspected that it might haunt her for some time to come.

She looked around at her colleagues and saw that they were all becoming increasingly uncomfortable. Right now they didn't need time to think, they needed action. It was taking too long to break down that door.

At last the door began to give way. A few seconds more and they would be in. Marie moved from foot to foot impatiently, and then looked up. Above the door hung a carefully painted sign. It read: CHILDREN'S WARD.

'We're through!' The call echoed down the tunnel, and Marie's heart lurched. She moved to Jackman's side and steeled herself.

* * *

In the flickering shadows of their torches, nothing seemed real, and Jackman felt as if he had been thrust into some freakish nightmare.

He had been prepared to find either a girl's body or a terrified teenager, possibly injured, but certainly tied up and gagged.

But it was nothing like that.

The Children's Ward was big, some seventy feet long. Along the entire length of the far wall stretched a row of metal-framed hospital beds, all with pillows.

Covers.

Occupants.

Jackman clapped a hand over his mouth. His wide eyes travelled slowly down the row. How many were there, for God's sake? The silver beam of his Maglite caught the pillows and revealed decaying flesh and skulls.

There were shocked murmurs and someone retched.

'Stay where you are! Keep back, all of you. I want no one contaminating this scene,' he said steadily.

'There's a light bulb!' A torch beam pointed upwards and someone called out, 'My God, there's electricity down here!'

'There's a switch here.' Jackman recognised Gary's voice. 'DI Jackman? Shall I?'

Jackman noted Gary Pritchard's thoughtfulness. He had known what the shock of illuminating the scene without warning might have done to his colleagues.

Jackman's voice betrayed no hint of emotion. 'Do it, Gary. We're ready. Just think about Emily. We have to find her as quickly as we can.'

Gary flicked the switch. Thankfully the light was dim. A string of low wattage lamps swung from the ceiling, although they did little to soften the horror that surrounded them.

'Get that bloody camera working, Mr Watchman!' Jackman called out. 'We need to locate her without contaminating the whole place. If you can bear to, just find out which one is still alive, and if you haven't the stomach, give the camera to me.'

As Ted lifted the camera, Jackman called Marie to his side, and together they appraised the scene.

All the beds except one held a body. Beside each bed was a small cabinet, with a small glass vase of freshly picked flowers. The "patients" lay silently, some younger, some older. Their hands were folded over the top of the sheets, and their heads rested on faded dusty pillows. Marie counted out loud. There were thirteen of them.

Some were like sleeping dolls, some nothing but bare bones and fleshless skulls. Some had the translucent parchment skin of a mummy, while others were still putrefying, which accounted for the sickening stench.

Suddenly Ted called out. 'I've picked her up! She's in the third bed from the end!'

'Get the medics! Marie! With me.'

Jackman ran down the row until he saw rich dark hair cascading over a fresh pillowslip.

'Oh, Emily,' he breathed. 'We've got you. We've got you now.' He took the girl's hand in his and looked up at Marie. 'It's cold, but not deathly cold.'

He called out to Ted. 'Could you face checking the other beds with the camera? Most of them are all long gone, but maybe . . .'

'Is she . . . ?' Ted called back. 'I mean, I saw heat still in her. She can't be . . . ?'

'I have no idea, Ted.' Jackman touched Emily's neck, desperately feeling for a pulse, but he felt nothing. 'She might be alive, but I think she's been heavily drugged. She needs medical attention, and fast.'

The heavy camera shook in his hands as Ted swept the room. 'She's the only one, I'm afraid.'

'Okay. I didn't expect anything else, but we needed to check. Thank you, Ted.'

'Not quite the kind of discovery I'm used to unearthing,' said the young man shakily. 'Thank God.'

Jackman stood up. 'Marie, check whether there is another way in or out. The rest of you, get back down the tunnel. Tell the sergeant that this whole area, house and grounds, are to be sealed off. No one in and, apart from the medics and an escort, *no one* out.'

He looked at his team, all of them poised, ready for instruction.

'Rosie, we need the pathologist. Speak to Rory Wilkinson, and tell him to muster as many scene-of-crime officers as he can. He'll have to ask other districts for help. In order to avoid cross-contamination there has to be one SOCO for each victim, so he's going to need a truck-load. Somehow we have to get Emily to safety and still try to preserve the integrity of this scene for forensics.'

He glanced down at the recumbent figure on the bed.

'Gary, I want Benedict Broome and Micah Lee picked up immediately. Arrest them on suspicion of murder and abduction. We can't have them talking to each other, so I suggest you take Broome to Saltern where I can interview him, and send Lee to Harlan Marsh. They still have a custody suite, don't they, Gary?'

'Yes, sir.'

'Then do that.' He turned to the waiting uniforms. 'The sergeant and I will stay with Emily. Everyone else should get out. And not a word to anyone, especially the suspects, understand? I need to debrief you all before this gets out. We do not know what we are dealing with here.'

'Other than a murdering, son-of-a-bitch monster,' muttered a shaky voice.

'Exactly. So talk to no one. Understand? Not a soul.'

As the echoes of their footsteps died away, Jackman and Marie went to Emily's bedside and stared down at her pale face. Marie gently touched her cheek with the back of her finger.

'You were right, Toni *was* telling the truth. Emily does exist.'

Jackman still held Emily's hand in his. 'Let's pray that the paramedics shift their arses, because I'm really not sure that she'll make it. Poor kid, what she's suffered. I can't even begin to imagine it.'

Marie continued to gaze down at her. 'Thankfully, it hasn't been long since she was abducted. She's pretty bruised, but she seems to be relatively unharmed . . . well, on the surface at least.' Marie turned to look at all the other beds.

'My God, sir, what on earth has gone on here?'

He looked down the row of beds. 'God knows, Marie. The things the human mind can dream up are beyond belief.'

'Human? Are you sure about that?'

Jackman waved his hand. 'Look around you, Marie. Their beds are neat and tidy. Their hair, what's left of it, is brushed. There are flowers beside their beds, and the lockers look clean enough to feature in a sodding Flash advert. He's taken more care of these poor souls than some people do their sick relatives.'

'Just a shame he had to kill them first,' growled Marie. 'It's too twisted to get your head around.'

'You're not kidding.' After a while Marie added, 'Do you think there is any chance that we will find Kenya Black here?'

It had been one of the first things Jackman had thought of when he saw the bodies. 'I don't think so. There are no really small children that I can see.'

'But what if she had been kept incarcerated for years, then . . . disposed of?' Marie shivered and glanced towards the doorway. 'Where's that sodding ambulance crew?'

'I know it's a crime scene and we have to process it, but they don't pay us enough to have to cope with a nightmare like this one,' Jackman said.

'I'm not sure that finding the Lost Kingdom of the Dead is dealt with in the guidelines for police procedure and crime scene management, do you?'

'Maybe I'll write an addendum when I have a moment.' He let out a sigh of relief, 'I hear footsteps.'

Two green-clad paramedics, led by a uniformed constable, entered the room.

'Oh sweet Jesus!' The first man bundled his equipment bag under one arm and crossed himself.

'Over here!' Jackman called out. 'She's in a bad way.'

The two paramedics hurried towards them, the second man pulling a trolley behind him and looking from side to side with a horrified expression.

'Look, just forget what's surrounding you, and do your best for this girl, okay?' Marie stared down at her. 'Her name is Emily and we have reason to believe that she's been heavily sedated.'

With an effort, the medic gathered himself. 'If you'd just stand back, we've got her now. Do we know what she's been given?'

Jackman shook his head. 'Another girl who was with her recently was given some sort of benzodiazepine. A new kind of roofie, possible street name "Ooblie," if that helps?'

'Oh, that lethal bloody stuff. It's possible, and her symptoms seem to match, but I'm pretty sure that's not all she's had. Well, we'll do what we can here and then get her in an ambulance.'

It took ten minutes to get a line in, some fluids going and a heart monitor in place, and then Emily was carefully secured to the stretcher, and wheeled away from hell.

As he left, the paramedic gave them the thumbs-up.

The silence fell like a thick cloak around them and Jackman decided they should wait outside for the pathologist.

There was no one left for them to help.

Jackman took one last look around at the line of dead youngsters sleeping peacefully in their neat beds, when suddenly it hit him. 'Why the hell didn't I notice that before?'

Marie halted in the doorway. 'Notice what?'

'There are names over the beds. Look! Little plaques, with a single name on them.' He began to walk down the long line of hospital beds. 'Corrie, Tessa, Annie, Lucy . . . Shit! The killer has left us their names! I've been so involved with getting Emily to safety that I've forgotten my basic scene-of-crime protocol. We must check each bed. And we need to look for Kenya.'

Jackman stopped at one of the much older beds and peered at the label. 'Damn it, most of them have faded with age. We'll need the lab after all.' He let out a long sigh.

'Come on. Let's get out of here.'

* * *

As they emerged from the tunnel into the warm evening, Marie felt tears slowly trickle down her cheeks. During her time in the force she had seen many terrible things — the massacred farm workers at Red House Farm, the bodies in Dovegate Lane, Simeon Mulberry and his wife, Charlotte. But today? What she had seen today was beyond all imagining.

She had to ring her mother. She needed to tell her mum that she loved her.

She dialled, glad, for once, that her mum lived far away in Wales. If her mother knew what her daughter had to confront every day of her working life, she would probably never sleep again.

'Mum?' Marie pressed the phone closer to her ear and smiled. 'Hi, you, and yes, we are up to our necks as usual.'

'You've had a very bad day?'

'The worst, Mum.'

'Can I help?'

'You already have. Tell me about something normal that happened today, something ordinary.'

'The dog was sick on my best mat.'

Marie laughed. 'That's exactly what I wanted to hear.'

'There's better to come. Maeve Henshaw's shed blew down in the wind last night and the entire Boy Scout troop turned out to save all her mushrooms.'

Her mother's lilting voice was the perfect antidote. By the time she ended the call she was herself again, DS Marie Evans, a damned good detective. One who was about to put away an evil killer of young women and children.

She pushed her phone back into her bag and inhaled deeply. Whatever was coming next, Marie was ready.

# CHAPTER TWENTY

Even Rory Wilkinson was silent when he saw what awaited him in the underground room. He turned to Jackman and simply said, 'If I were you, I would accept any offers they make regarding counselling.'

'I'm okay, Rory. I hear what you're saying though, and maybe I'll have a chat with someone when I've caught the man who did this.'

'You think it's a man?' asked Rory.

Jackman didn't answer. A woman? Surely a woman couldn't . . .

'I only say that because of the nice touches.' Rory looked around. 'The flower vases and the neat way the victims' clothes are hung up.'

Jackman looked nonplussed. 'Clothes?'

'Look, over to the far wall. See that row of metal lockers? The victims' clothes are all neatly hung up and labelled. Our killer couldn't have been more helpful. Not only do we have first names, we have the clothes these poor souls were wearing when they went missing. Some are very fragile, little more than rags, but others are almost new.' Rory looked around the underground room. 'The atmosphere and the low temperatures down here have slowed deterioration considerably, but it will take a while to get answers to all your questions, Inspector.'

Jackman nodded. 'I know. But the man — or woman — who did this was probably in this very room as recently as this morning. Now they are out there, somewhere close, and because of what they have just lost, I don't have to tell you how dangerous they are.' Jackman stared at him. 'I don't have long, and if Emily doesn't recover, I only have you to help me.'

'And I will. One thing I do know, one of the victims is very much older than the others.'

'What is the significance of that, I wonder?'

'I'm not sure, but one of these corpses is twenty to thirty years old. I'll give you a much closer estimation after we've carried out a post-mortem, but that one is definitely the oldest, so maybe she was the cause of all this.' Rory adjusted his glasses and looked around. 'I keep thinking I've wandered into one of those weird modern art exhibits. You couldn't stage anything more grotesque if you tried.'

'Can I take a look in those lockers?' Jackman raised his gloved hands.

'Of course you can, but you will notice that although there are thirteen victims, including your one survivor, there are only ten sets of clothing.'

'It's still a fantastic piece of luck, Rory. It will help with identification.'

Rory nodded. 'There's one thing that I don't like about this place, apart from the blindingly obvious. What do you smell, apart from the stench of decay?'

'Antiseptic? Bleach? Some sort of industrial cleaning fluid?'

'Exactly. And look at the floor. There's no dirt, no fluff, no cobwebs. I've got more dust-bunnies floating round my lounge.' Rory gave a little shrug. 'I'd say this place is as close to sterile as he or she could get it.'

'Which will play havoc with your search for evidence?'

'I'm not saying that. Our methods are far more sophisticated these days. It's almost impossible not to leave some traces. We'll just have to work a little harder than normal. And on that note, I think I'm ready for my team to come in now, so if you have no objection?'

Jackman walked towards the door. 'Whatever you need, Rory, just ask. Additional lighting, manpower, extra vehicles, anything. No one will dare scream, "Budget!" on this occasion.'

Rory nodded. 'I'll be in touch as soon as we find anything that will be of use to you.'

Jackman raised his hand in thanks, and stood back as the first wave of blue-suited, hooded figures carried their equipment into the underground room.

As he walked back along the tunnel he could hear Rory's voice. 'Oh no! Not like that, dear heart! Please! Think egg-shells and butterfly wings, not bloody great sides of beef!'

Jackman smiled to himself. He was mighty glad that Rory Wilkinson was heading up this forensics operation. If there were answers waiting in that chamber of horrors, Rory Wilkinson would unearth them.

* * *

On his return to Saltern-le-Fen, Marie met him in the front office. 'Gary's brought Benedict Broome in as instructed. But there was something of a problem, I'm afraid.'

'Why, what happened?'

'Oh, it's nothing to do with Broome himself, sir. It was his housekeeper, a woman called Elizabeth Sewell. She collapsed and she's now being checked out in A&E. It happened when she saw the uniforms marching up the garden path. Benedict told Gary that she's of a "nervous disposition." He said she's a patient at the psychiatric out-patients department at Saltern General. We decided to get her thoroughly checked out, just to be on the safe side,

especially as we'll most likely be wanting to interview her.'
Marie sniffed. 'And don't worry, we have two officers with
her until we can bring her in and neither will ask her about
the case, so the clock won't start ticking until she's released
from hospital care.'

Rory's question sprung to Jackman's mind. *"Are you
sure it's a man?"*

'And Micah Lee?'

'He's safe at Harlan Marsh.'

Jackman checked his watch. They would be able to
detain Broome and Lee without charge for thirty-six hours,
twenty-four on his authority, and then a further twelve on
that of the super. From what they had found at Windrush,
he had no qualms at all about arresting them, but he
needed to find evidence to tie them to the crime. And
given the amount of forensic work involved, they hadn't a
hope in hell of getting answers before the time limitations
expired. Every second counted, but they needed a bucket-
load of luck too.

'Can I have a quiet word before the debriefing, sir?'

'Of course. We'll use my office.'

Marie followed him in, closed the door and sat down.

Jackman leaned back in his chair. 'Fire away.'

'When you went back underground with Rory, I
walked out over the marsh for a while, trying to clear my
head. I hadn't gone more than a couple of hundred yards
when I heard whispering. In the shadows of evening and
after seeing what we'd just seen, it was seriously weird.'

Jackman looked at her. 'The ghosts of Hobs End
Marsh?'

'No, it was you.'

'Me?' Jackman exclaimed.

'It took a while to realise that you and Rory Wilkinson
were right beneath my feet in the tunnel to the Children's
Ward. There must be air ducts or shafts or something, but
they distort the sound and it's *really* strange! Now I know
why the marsh has such a reputation, and why Gary's sister

173

heard voices but he didn't. It would depend where you were standing.'

'So she was hearing real people underground! Gary will be pleased to hear that.'

'And we should be too, because it could answer the question of the singing.'

He nodded slowly as the frightening picture became clear. 'The killer actually sang as he walked the tunnels to the Children's Ward?'

'Well, we know he's been coming here for years, and smugglers before him, so that might explain the superstitions.'

'The lights on the marsh at night could be connected too. If there are shafts coming up from the tunnel, and we already know that he ran power from the barn down to the subterranean room, maybe there were points of light up on the surface sometimes? If the shafts can conduct sound, why not light?' Jackman grinned at her. 'Well done, Detective! You've just scuppered the Ghostly Legend of Hobs End Marsh!'

'And I feel very good about it. All this talk of creepy goings-on was freaking me out. I like facts.'

'Okay, well our next job is entirely about facts. It's time for the debriefing. Is everyone here?'

'Yes, sir. They are all in the murder room waiting for you.'

'Right, I'll be there as soon as I've reported to Superintendent Crooke. And after the debrief we can interview Broome.' Jackman felt a slight thrill pass through him. 'And, Marie? Great work.'

* * *

Ruth Crooke looked even more haggard than last time Jackman had seen her. 'Was it as bad as they tell me?'

'Probably, ma'am. Maybe worse. I don't know what they said.'

174

'Whatever, I'm sorry you had to be the one to walk in on such a terrible thing, Jackman.'

He shrugged. 'Better me than a family man with young girls of his own.'

'And you have Broome and his caretaker in custody?'

'Yes, I'll be interviewing them as soon as I've debriefed the team. Do you want to be present for that, ma'am?'

'No, you go ahead. I've got the assistant chief constable hanging around my neck, and then there's the media to sort out.'

Jackman gasped. 'Surely we're not going public this soon? Hell, I really need a bit of space before the frenzy begins.'

She gave him a tired half-smile. 'Cool down, Detective. I'll hold it off for as long as I possibly can. I just need to be ready to jump in before someone leaks it. You know I can't keep the lid on something of this magnitude for long. We've got half the Fenland Constabulary out on Hobbs End Marsh, and whereas it's hardly a bustling metropolis, people do notice. They talk, *and* they ask questions, *and* if we don't give them something to satisfy them, they put two and two together and come up with bloody five.'

She was right. For all Jackman knew, some web-foot had already seen pretty blue lights out on the fen and rung the local rag. 'Sorry, ma'am. Please buy me whatever time you can. Just enough to get the owner of Windrush interviewed and either held or released.'

Ruth Crooke nodded. 'I'll do that. Oh, and I've asked the other CID officers to reorganise their workloads and offer you whatever support you need, especially with the identification process. Just liaise with them directly. They are all yours.' She straightened up, and something of the brusque old super returned. 'Now go and sort out your debriefing, and don't forget the new directive on psychological trauma. There's confidential screening and a counselling service available, and it's down to you to actively encourage anyone who is affected by this to talk to the shrink as soon as possible.'

*Right, blow everything out of proportion, and make the ones who have got it all sorted out in their heads feel guilty because they're not basket cases.* 'I'll make sure they know their options, ma'am.' Jackman turned to make his escape.

'Just keep me abreast of every new development, Rowan. Everything. As it occurs.'

'Wilco, ma'am.'

＊ ＊ ＊

The debriefing took considerably less time than he had thought it would. Jackman was something of an expert on body language and he felt relieved that none of his officers seemed to be unduly disturbed. He was, after all, dealing with seasoned police men and women, not a bunch of impressionable schoolkids.

He had asked Marie to keep an eye open for anyone she considered to be struggling, but she agreed with him. It was just another job to most of them, only a bit more gruesome. Already the grim jokes had started to do the rounds and under the circumstances, he took that to be a good thing.

'Who is at the hospital with Emily?' he asked.

'A uniformed WPC and one of DI Osborne's detective constables. Oh, and Stefan found us a Latvian interpreter, just in case she turns out to be the missing EU national from Greenborough. They have instructions to ring you directly there's any news,' said Marie. 'The last report was that she's still in the resuscitation room, and they have no idea if she'll pull through.'

Jackman prayed that she would recover. Just a few words, just one name, or a description, and they could nail the bastard that had done this.

The room slowly emptied, until Jackman was left with Marie and Rosie. He glanced at the clock. It was just after nine. 'It's too late to do a house-to-house tonight, Rosie, but I want you to organise one for first thing tomorrow. Get a couple of uniforms to go out to Roman Creek and call at all the properties in the surrounding area. There aren't many, but they need to check them thoroughly, okay?'

Rosie nodded. 'Will do, boss.'

'Tell them to be careful. There's nothing to say this *is* the work of Broome or Lee. It could be anyone at all. So they should tread carefully and report anything unusual.' He turned to Marie.

'The custody sergeant has agreed that we can talk to Broome, as long as we keep it short. He has his codes of practice to consider.' He pulled a face. 'Damned PACE, yet again.'

'So we'd better get to it.'

# CHAPTER TWENTY-ONE

Jackman and Marie sat outside the interview room and waited for Benedict Broome to be brought up from the custody suite.

'Before we go in, Marie, maybe we should just cram what little information we have on Broome. What do we know?'

Marie opened a thin file. 'This is what Andy English and Kevin Stoner came up with. It's not much.' She stared at the notes. 'Benedict owns that expensive place on the waterway. He's been there for over ten years. His housekeeper has a small annexe. She's been with him from the beginning, apparently, looks after the house, cooks and so on. Other than a gardener who comes in twice a week, that's it.'

'What does Benedict Broome do for a living?'

'It doesn't say. There's no mention of any job.' She read on. 'There's a note from PC Goode regarding Broome's parentage. He says that he's hit a brick wall trying to trace them.'

'Sounds like a task for our Max, doesn't it? Assuming that Broome gives us any satisfactory answers. I just wish Toni Clarkson had not been so heavily drugged. She might have been able to pick either him or Micah Lee out in an identity parade. As it is, all she can recall is that he had weird eyes.'

'And the word of a kid who had just been fed a bag of "Ooblie" wouldn't exactly hold water anyway.' She looked up. 'Ah, good, it looks like we're on. The sergeant is beckoning to us.'

'Right, let's go see what Mr Benedict Broome can tell us.'

\* \* \*

Benedict Broome was led into the interview room, but before the custody sergeant handed over to Jackman and Marie, he stepped back outside and said in a low voice, 'Keep it brief. It's getting late for a full interview, and I ought to tell you that he's waived his right to have a solicitor present.'

Marie shrugged. 'Well, that is his prerogative, but not advisable under the circumstances.' As they entered the room, she wondered what kind of man they would find.

For the purposes of the tape, Jackman introduced himself, asked Marie and Broome to do the same, and explained the use of the tape recorder. Then he made quite sure that Broome understood the severity of his position.

'I really must advise you to have a solicitor present, Mr Broome, considering the seriousness of your situation and the nature of the discovery beneath your property, namely, Windrush, at Roman Creek.'

Broome looked straight at him. 'Detective Chief Inspector, I am more than willing to answer your questions. What you have discovered is horrible, absolutely devastating. I am as shocked and overwhelmed as you, maybe more, because that place was intended as a sanctuary, a place of peace and tranquillity.' He gave a bitter laugh. 'What chance of peace now, when I know that some evil person has used it to commit such terrible deeds?'

Benedict Broome was well-built, in that good food and fine wine kind of way. He wore expensive clothes, and he had the confident air of a successful businessman.

'And of course I don't want to hold things up for you or myself. Frankly, whether a solicitor is present or not, I can only tell you what I know, and be assured that I will not hold back, and it will be the truth.'

He sat back in his chair, hands folded in his lap. Jackman took his time to reply.

Marie watched them both carefully. Broome was erudite, obviously had a clear understanding of the law, and was very different to most of the "clients" that passed through this room. Jackman was clearly taking all that into consideration.

'Very well, sir. May I ask you whether it has been explained to you clearly why you are here today?'

Broome confirmed that he was fully aware that an abducted young woman and a number of bodies had been discovered beneath one of the outbuilding and yard areas of Windrush. As the owner of the property, he and the people who worked for him would naturally have to be questioned.

'Were you aware of the tunnels beneath your property, sir?' asked Marie.

'Only by way of historical legend. All old houses like Windrush have secrets, don't they? Priest holes, secret rooms and passages, sometimes cellars and yes, quite possibly tunnels. Although it has to be said that there are very few in the fenland, since it is reclaimed land. Windrush is built on a small rocky outcrop, supposedly once an island. That is what makes it so unusual.' He scratched his chin thoughtfully. 'There is most certainly a sealed door from the main cellar, but that was cemented up long before I took possession. Given the age of the building, I'm sure it isn't the only one.'

Marie frowned. 'But surely you had extensive surveys done when the plans were drawn up for your rebuilding work?'

'Yes, DS Evans, I did. But as I understand it, the underground room that contains the bodies is not part of my present programme. If everything went well and finances allowed, then I intended to go ahead with two more stages. That area would have been Stage Three, and no plans or surveys have been undertaken yet.' He let out a long sigh. 'And now they never will.'

'What is your occupation, sir?' Jackman asked abruptly.

'I'm in the financial world. I trade the markets.'

'So you have considerable funds at your disposal?'

'I'm comfortable, although there's never enough, DI Jackman.' Broome gave a slight smile. 'Especially with a money-pit the size of Windrush.'

'And you really won it in a wager?' asked Marie.

'I really did.'

'So you're a gambler?'

'I've already said that I trade the markets. That certainly makes me a risk-taker, you can call it gambling if you like.'

Marie looked at him with interest. He sounded cultured and self-assured.

'Were you born around here, sir?' Jackman asked.

'No, I'm not Fenland born and bred. I was born in the West Country and my family later settled in Cambridgeshire.'

'And your parents?' Marie asked, noticing that Jackman was watching Broome intently.

'Long dead,' he said, with no emotion in his voice. 'They died when I was in my late teens.'

'So who looked after you?'

'I had help from those around me, and luckily there was money. But to a point, I looked after myself.' He sat forward, elbows resting casually on the table between them. 'Things happen. You just have to get on and deal with them, don't you? I survived, that's what counts.'

'So what brought you to the Fens?'

'My solicitors and I spent years trying to unravel the complexities of my family's estate, and some while back I discovered that I owned the property in Admiralty Row. I saw it, liked it, and that was that. I re-housed the tenants and moved in.'

He sounded so plausible. Marie wished she had Rosie's ability to read people.

There was silence as the two police officers wondered how to proceed.

Marie looked at her notes. Should she throw in a question about the singing? She decided against it. It would be too easy for Broome to lie, and she wasn't quite ready to play that card just yet.

Jackman looked fixedly at Broome. 'Your man out at Windrush, Micah Lee. He seemed rather edgy when we spoke to him. Would you know why?'

'Apparently Micah Lee had an accident when he was small, and it left him with learning difficulties. He is a good, strong, manual worker, but doesn't have much in the way of academic ability. I felt sorry for him, and the job out at my property has given him something to focus on. And he's extremely loyal.'

'Where does he live, sir?'

'He lodges at a farm out in Fendyke Village. It's owned by a potato farmer called Tanner. Micah does some seasonal work for him and I understand that he helps out around the place when he's not at Windrush.'

'Mr Broome, we need to ascertain your movements around the time when the young woman was abducted,' Marie said. 'Where were you on Friday last?'

Broome was silent for a moment. 'In the morning I was in my office at home. I do most of my business dealings by phone and internet. And in the afternoon I took my housekeeper to the hospital for an out-patient's appointment. I dined alone that night as far as I can remember, then I probably made some more phone calls and retired at,' he rubbed at his clean-shaven chin, 'around eleven, I should think. All rather vague, I realise, but in general my life is not an exciting one.'

'And Elizabeth Sewell? Has she been with you long?'

'She came to me a week or so after I moved in. She suffers with her nerves. She's very delicate, but the solitary nature of the job suits her. Plus, she's an excellent cook.'

Broome's responses had been so mundane that, apart from his gambling, he might have been the most humdrum mortal on the planet. But there was something else there.

Jackman glanced at his watch and brought the interview to a close. 'It is time for you to get some sleep now, sir, but there will be more questions.'

'Of course, DI Jackman.' He raised his hands. 'I am entirely at your disposal.'

\* \* \*

'Emily has been identified!' Max almost vaulted over his desk to get to them. 'She *is* the Latvian girl, Aija Ozolini. The Latvian interpreter, Janis, took her uncle to the hospital, and he gave us a positive.'

'How's she doing?' asked Jackman.

'Not good, boss. Touch and go. She's still on a ventilator.'

'Well, at least she's out of that goddamned hellhole.' Jackman reminded himself to tell young Toni Clarkson about Emily's rescue.

'And Prof Wilkinson has been on the blower asking you to ring him on his mobile as soon as you can.'

Max returned to his desk and added, 'This trace on Broome's background is driving me mad. Whatever way I approach it, I get a big fat zero. You'd think he was found under a gooseberry bush. It's like he doesn't exist!'

'Maybe he doesn't.' Marie perched on the corner of Max's desk. 'I'm picking up something very odd about that man, and if I were you I'd broaden out your next search.'

'Like how?' Max asked.

Marie shrugged and yawned. 'I don't know. I just can't believe he's the boring well-off man he professes to be.'

Jackman couldn't help yawning too. 'I agree. He's just too good to be true.' He looked at his watch. 'Damn! It's much too late to go see Micah Lee now. We'll have to ring Harlan Marsh and set something up for early tomorrow. He might need to have an appropriate adult with him to safeguard his interests. After what Broome told us, I'm not too sure about that man's mental condition. He could be disabled, and I don't want to find any of our interviews considered inadmissible.'

'Dead right,' muttered Marie. 'I'll ring Harlan Marsh now and get it sorted.'

'And I'll ring Rory.' Jackman picked up his phone and keyed in the pathologist's number.

'I'll go above ground and ring you back!' yelled Rory over a crackling line. 'We need to talk.'

Rory sounded out of breath when he called again.

'So what have you got for me?'

'Well, first — and you really don't need me to tell you this, I'm sure — the length of time between each murder shows the increasing assurance of a serial killer. It seems that his kills were quite rare ten years ago, but now he's starting to kill more frequently.'

'So hopefully we've stopped him before he goes on a spree.'

'Possibly. But don't forget that you've destroyed his precious lair. You won't exactly be his favourite person. In fact, my friend, he'll hate you for it, and he could lose control and kill again just to spite you.'

'Unless I can put him away before he has the chance,' muttered Jackman. 'So what else have you got?'

Rory sniffed. 'It's a small and very annoying thing. When we documented the clothing, we found that your lone survivor had the wrong shoes. They wouldn't fit her in a month of Sundays, and they don't belong to any of the other victims either.'

Jackman told him they had seen exactly the same thing with Toni Clarkson.

'Ah, my hero! That solves it. I really hate those irritating details. Now for something of much greater significance.' Rory paused, most likely for dramatic effect. 'One of my scene-of-crime officers remarked on the amount of equipment in the underground room, and how it would have been impossible to drag it all across the marsh and down the tunnel. I'm suspecting that the owner of Windrush will use the fact that the entrance to the underground burial chamber is on the marsh, which is common land, and hence could have been used by absolutely anyone. Am I right?'

Jackman told him the point had already been made.

'I thought so. For that reason, I did a close examination of the room, and the wall in particular. It is almost impossible to see with the naked eye, but one wall isn't plastered quite like the others, and under close scrutiny the faintest outline of a doorway is just visible.'

Jackman felt a thrill of excitement. 'So the beds, and everything else were brought in from an entrance located somewhere on the Windrush property itself?'

'Oh I think so. I suggest that the room was all set up, and then the entrance was sealed, either to stop anyone from Windrush stumbling upon it, or else to make it look as though it has nothing to do with the owner. The beds are almost certainly a legacy from the time when the house was used as a sanatorium.' Rory took a breath. 'When we hand the scene back to you, I suggest you consult my dear little friend Ted again. Perhaps he could use some of his wonderful equipment and investigate what is on the other side of the wall?'

'I'll do that, Rory. Believe it or not, he's still here. He and one of our IT lads are busy transposing all the underground tunnels and old structures into some sort of computerised map of the estate.'

'Excellent! He always liked a challenge. And while you are talking to him, do you think you could you ask him if he knows of a locally-based forensic anthropologist who would be prepared to give us a hand with the oldest skeleton? I've got my hands full and I'm pretty sure that lady holds some big secrets.'

'I'll ask him. And what do you mean, "big secrets?"'

'Well, I can tell you that this is not the first place where that girl was laid to rest.'

Jackman's brow drew together. 'Exhumed? Dug up? Can you expand on that? My mind is throwing up some rather bizarre scenarios right now.'

'Probably no more outlandish than the truth. This lass was most definitely brought here sometime after her original passing. Don't ask me how I know, my report will fill you in on that.'

Jackman let out a long breath. 'I'll definitely ask Ted about finding someone to help you with her. As you said, she could be the key to what happened.'

'Well, I'd better get back to my private Hades. I cannot tell you how much work we have to do tonight.'

'How are you going to cope, Rory? There are so many bodies. The morgue is not geared for it, plus your everyday stuff.'

Rory laughed. 'I'll share a secret with you. There is a special facility down in the bowels of the hospital. It's not widely known about, but it was set up yonks ago to enable the Home Office to handle a major epidemic or a natural disaster. It hasn't been used for years, not since that heatwave that took so many of our old people. Right now, I've got some of my technicians down there getting it powered up and ready to roll. So don't worry, dear heart, there's plenty of room for all. Now I must go. We'll talk later.'

Jackman ended the call and wondered about that first girl. Had the killer murdered her, buried her, then returned much later and exhumed her body in order to place her in a hospital bed with pretty flowers on the locker? Jackman gave a snort of disbelief, and went in search of Ted Watchman.

He found the young archaeologist still poring over ancient maps and computer printouts. On hearing about the wall and a possible door in the underground chamber, Ted's eyes lit up and he said he'd love to investigate it. He told Jackman that one of the university faculty members, Professor Jan Wallace, was a brilliant forensic anthropologist, and he'd ring her first thing in the morning.

Jackman ordered him to go get some sleep, and then went to look for Marie.

'Harlan Marsh were not particularly helpful,' she muttered. 'But hopefully everything will be in place for the morning. They reckon Micah Lee is pretty flaky.'

'Tell us something new.' Jackman frowned. 'I really wanted to talk to him tonight, but the bloody Police and Criminal Evidence Act won't allow it. A load of wrist-binding red tape that we are stuck with.'

'Don't worry, we'll see him first thing.' Marie stifled a yawn.

Jackman didn't hide his own yawn. 'Let's hope he's a little more amenable then.'

Marie grimaced. 'You'd think he owned the place. I've never seen such an angry man.'

'Maybe a night in the cells might make him a tad more helpful.' Jackman let out a sigh. 'Let's go find the others, then get home. What a bloody awful day!'

They found the whole team gathered in the CID room, all looking grey with fatigue.

'Okay, guys, pack up whatever you're doing. Our suspects have been tucked up for the night by their custody sergeants, so we can do no more. Go home, all of you.'

Marie turned to Gary. 'Ready, flatmate? My guest room awaits you, and so do the meagre contents of the fridge, unless you fancy picking up a microwave meal on our way home?'

'I've got some food in a freezer bag in my car, Sarge. I can rustle us up something in half the time it would take to get through the supermarket, even at this time of night.'

Marie licked her lips. 'How long did you say you were staying?' She turned to Jackman. 'Night, sir. See you in a few hours.'

He lifted his hand to them, and then made his way slowly to his office. He desperately wanted to get back to his comforting home in the windmill, warm himself beside the Aga and snuggle down in his cosy bed. But he knew he should use the comparative quiet of the night in the police station to think through everything that had happened.

He closed the door. The air conditioning hummed softly, and distant voices called out from different parts of the building. Compared to the day-time, the office was as peaceful as an empty chapel.

He sat at his desk, elbows on the polished wood surface, and placed his chin in his cupped hands. He closed his eyes, which stung with tiredness, as if he'd rubbed sand into them. Behind his sore, closed lids he saw the lockers with their little vases of flowers.

Why had a cold-blooded psycho-killer made time for a gesture so tender? So loving?

Jackman had a feeling that if he knew the answer to that, he would be right at the heart of what had happened at Windrush.

He wished they had a profiler. Jackman needed someone to talk to about the killer's motives, his psyche.

But after a bad experience in the past, the super was dead set against psychological profiling.

Jackman leaned back in his chair and stared at the ceiling. He was getting nowhere. If all he could come up with was vases of flowers, it was time to pull the plug and go home.

# CHAPTER TWENTY-TWO

'Sorry, sir. I've hit a problem.' Gary entered Jackman's office, his expression anxious. 'You asked me to check the last of those CCTV pictures of Nick Barley with those guys from the drinking club.'

Jackman looked at him. 'What did you find?'

'I found nothing, because they've disappeared.' Gary shifted uncomfortably. 'Well, not exactly. They have been appropriated by Chief Superintendent Cade. When I asked why, I was told that his CID office "*had cleared their backlog and were eager to help you out*". It was also made clear to me that as the original girl was probably abducted from the Harlan Marsh area, they'd be more likely than us to recognise any of the men seen talking to young Barley.'

Jackman's teeth clamped. Cade had absolutely no right to do that. Not without his say-so. There was now a positive connection between the underage drinking club, the abduction of the girls, and a serial killer, so what the hell was Cade up to?

'Curiouser and curiouser,' breathed Marie softly, swinging the pool car keys on her finger.

'The bastard!' Jackman whispered. 'Hang on here, Marie. I'm going to see the super.'

Jackman stormed into Ruth Crooke's office and blurted out the news about Cade taking the CCTV footage.

'I know,' said the superintendent quietly. 'And you should calm down, Rowan, because he's quite right. They've been after this gang for months. They have a much better chance than you of identifying them.' She indicated a chair, but Jackman ignored her and continued to pace the floor.

'There are the correct channels and there is common decency, ma'am. And he's used neither.'

'Chief Superintendent Cade is only helping you out. He said that he's very grateful for your assistance, so now you are so busy, he's returning the favour.' The super's eyes narrowed. 'Now I suggest you accept it as such. You have plenty on your plate right now with twelve young bodies to find identities for, not to mention a killer probably loose in the Fens.'

'Don't remind me.' Jackman flopped into the chair and was about to say more when the superintendent's phone rang. Ruth passed it across the desk to Jackman.

'I'm sorry, Rowan. Aija Ozolini, known as Emily, died a few minutes ago. The officer at the hospital would like to talk to you.'

Jackman was devastated. After all that Emily had suffered, then to be rescued, only to die anyway. He gritted his teeth to hold back howls of frustration.

'DI Jackman here.'

'Sir, I wanted you to know that Emily did regain consciousness, just for a brief time, but the doctor said that the drugs had done irreparable damage. She had a massive heart attack, and there was no bringing her back.'

'Did she say anything about her captor, Officer?'

'She was speaking in her language, sir, but Janis the interpreter was with us. He said that she was mostly fretting about her family, but she did say something about someone singing to her. Then she got really panicked and started screaming something about eyes. I wrote down exactly what Janis said, sir. It was, "Dead eyes! Oh my God! Get away from me! Please! Don't look at me!" She didn't say anything else. Janis did his best to get some sort of description from her, but not long after that her heart gave in.'

Jackman thanked the constable and passed the phone back to Ruth Crooke. His sadness was already giving way to rage. 'I have to go. I need to tell the troops, even if it's not the news they wanted to hear.'

'Well, remember, Rowan, you already have two suspects in custody, and one under supervision at the hospital. It's a better start than we normally get.'

'And my only eye witness has just died. And if our suspects turn out to be innocent, there is a psychopath out there somewhere.'

\* \* \*

Jackman gave the team the news of Emily's death. Their faces fell. They had pinned all their hopes on her.

'What's your gut feeling about the two suspects, boss?' asked Charlie.

'None as yet. We've only spoken to Broome so far. Micah will need very careful handling.'

'I'm afraid we won't be talking to him just yet,' added Marie. 'I've had a message from Harlan Marsh. The FMO has seen him and said that he's not fit to interview, with or without a responsible adult. They are going to let us know when we can see him.'

Jackman swore. Today was turning into a nightmare. 'Then there's nothing we can do about it. We can try this farmer that Lee lodges with. Tanner, I think his name is.'

'Maybe I could help uniform out with the house-to-house at Roman Creek?' asked Rosie. 'They are pretty stretched, and there are more properties out there than I thought.'

'Good idea. Right. This is how things stand so far. Ted Watchman has gone over to Windrush to check out a possible sealed entrance to the underground room. The crime scene isn't released to us yet. Micah Lee is unfit to interview, and our CCTV footage on the drinking club has been hijacked. Not a great start, but we've plenty to get on with.'

He looked at the team. 'I suggest that Charlie goes with you, Rosie, to pitch in with the house-to-house, and Marie comes with me. Max? I'd like you to go to Broome's town residence. Take a couple of uniforms and see what you can find out about the man. Don't ransack the place, but take a careful look around.' The memory of all those flowers on the dead girls' lockers came back to him. 'And don't forget to check the annexe where Elizabeth Sewell lives. Oh, and while you're there, find out who the gardener is.'

Jackman turned to Gary. 'You come with us to Mr Lee's lodgings. We'll see what Mr Tanner thinks about him.' Then he remembered something. He called across to Clive, the office manager. 'I'd like you to be at your diplomatic best, and phone Grace Black.' He pulled a face. 'She needs to be assured that we are not forgetting our responsibility to Kenya. Tell her that this case has escalated, and that I will be in touch personally very soon, okay?'

Clive gave him the thumbs-up. 'Don't you worry, sir. I'll be discreet, polite, sensitive, tactf—'

'Okay. I get the picture.'

\* \* \*

As they drove out of town, Jackman looked at Gary. He seemed quieter than usual. 'Is it Emily?' he asked. 'I know how disappointed we all are, all hoping she would point us to the killer.'

Gary shook his head. 'That's true, but no, something else is bothering me.' He screwed his face up and then it came out in a rush. 'Thing is, I was really concerned about Chief Superintendent Cade taking those CCTV tapes, sir, so I had a word with a mate of mine at Harlan Marsh.' He turned to Jackman. 'He's straight as a die, my friend, and I know he won't mention this.'

Jackman slipped the car into fifth gear and listened.

'Apparently, as soon as he heard that you were up to your neck in bodies out at Roman Creek, Cade hared over to Saltern like a greyhound out of a trap. He asked the super how your enquiries regarding the drinking club were going — and the rest is history.'

'What do you make of that?' asked Marie from the back seat.

'That he knows someone involved in this illegal club and wants to protect them.'

'Another of his buddies up to his armpits in the brown and sticky stuff!' Marie snorted. 'So why ask us to investigate in the first place? If he has friends up to no good, you don't invite a crack team to start poking around.'

'Frankly, Sarge . . .' Gary nibbled on his bottom lip. 'I'd bet a fiver on the fact that he really believed that Toni had done one of her usual running-away tricks, and he was just showing off to Neil Clarkson by getting you to look for her.' His eyes narrowed, 'I'd put nothing past that man. And looking back on it, our hunt for the club has been dogged by bad luck from the day we started. I've been thinking for a while now that someone was tipping them off.' His face was set. 'I've seen evidence disappear, witnesses suddenly drop charges, and all manner of dodgy goings on in my time at that station.'

Jackman swung the car off the main road and onto a long straight drove. He stared out across the fallow fields, and said. 'Would your mate make a few more discreet enquiries for you?'

Gary nodded. 'He owes me one so I'll call in the debt. Mind you, if he thought he was helping to upset Cade's applecart, he'd do it for love.'

'Then ask him to keep an eye on Cade's "helpful investigation" into the club.'

Gary pulled out his phone and called his friend. 'Sorted.' He smiled grimly. 'He's a good lad. He'll ring me when he knows something.'

For a few minutes they all contemplated the sunshine glinting on the silver-grey waters of the wide drain running alongside the farm drove. 'This is a very beautiful county,' said Gary quietly. 'How can the people in it do so much evil?'

The house where Lee lived was a typical fenland farmhouse. With its chimney stacks at either end of the steep slate roof, central porch and front door, and bay windows either side, it looked to Jackman like a child's drawing.

The barns that were set around were neat and tidy, and oddly silent.

No one answered the door. Jackman was just beginning to think that they'd had a wasted journey when a tall, muscular man, wearing dusty jeans and a shabby wax jacket, appeared from one of the larger storerooms.

Gary waved, and the man strode over to them.

Gary showed him his ID. 'We're looking for Mr Tanner. I'm PC Pritchard and this is DI Jackman and DS Evans.'

They offered their warrant cards and the man glanced at them.

'I'm Bill Hickey, the farm manager. I'm sorry, but Mr Tanner is away for a couple of days. Is this about Micah?'

Jackman nodded. 'You know him, obviously.'

'Yes, I've been looking after the farm here for five years now, and Micah was here before I came. Funny bloke, not too much up top, but he's solid. Damned hard worker too. He helps us with the potato grading after the harvest. Never complains, just gets on with it.'

'Is he a friend of Mr Tanner, or just a lodger?' asked Gary.

'Guess they are friends of a sort, although not particularly close. They are both bachelors, and quite private men, so I suppose the situation suits them. Micah has his own sitting room and bedroom and shares the farmhouse kitchen.' Hickey plunged his hands deep into his pockets. 'Your guys came out here last night. They looked in his rooms, but they wouldn't say what had happened.'

'Sorry, sir, but we can't either, not yet.' Marie looked at the manager with interest. 'Where is Mr Tanner?'

'He's in Germany, visiting one of the big agricultural machinery manufacturers.'

'When did he go?'

'Night before last. He'll be back tomorrow.' Hickey looked from one to the other. 'Is Micah all right? I mean, he hasn't had an accident, has he?'

'He's safe, sir,' said Jackman warily.

'But he's in trouble.' Hickey gave a slight grin. 'That man's temper is awesome. I'd not be surprised if he's given someone a good thrashing.'

Jackman shook his head. 'He's helping us with our enquiries, Mr Hickey, but he hasn't been in a fight. Do you have a key for the house? We'd like to see Mr Lee's rooms.'

Hickey nodded and took out a large bunch of keys from his jacket pocket. 'I'm not sure Mr Tanner would like this, but I guess it won't hurt. Mind if I come with you?'

'Lead the way.'

The house was clean and bare, with no ornaments, houseplants, photos, TV or computer. No life, thought Jackman.

Micah's room was the same. Every object was purely utilitarian. Jackman gave Marie a helpless glance. 'I don't think it'll make the cover of *Hello*, do you?'

'And it doesn't tell us anything about what kind of person he is.' Marie turned to Hickey. 'What's Micah Lee like? Where is he from?'

The farm manager puffed out his cheeks. 'I don't think I'm the one to ask, Sergeant. He does have his problems, but I don't know what caused them. He keeps himself to himself, although I seem to recall him saying he'd lived in Derbyshire when he was younger, somewhere near that plague village in the centre of the Peak District. Eyam, I think it's called.'

'How about friends?'

'He doesn't have any that I know of, and anyway, he has been spending so much time on that job of his out at Roman Creek that I don't really see him at all.'

Jackman shrugged and took one last look at the bare walls. 'I've seen enough. Thank you, Mr Hickey.'

'You really should speak to Toby Tanner about Micah, Detective. I'm sure he knows him better than anyone. I'll get him to call you as soon as he gets back.'

As they got back to the car, Jackman muttered, 'I hope Charlie and Rosie are doing better than we are. What an odd place. No home comforts at all.'

Gary agreed. 'I suppose that can happen when there is no woman and no love in a home.'

Jackman wasn't so sure of that. After all, he had no partner to share his life with, but he still felt that his house was a home. But whatever the reason, the place was strange.

* * *

Rosie and Charlie's morning had been considerably more successful. They had met an old couple whose parents had worked at Windrush when soldiers were billeted there in the last world war. They had supplied a wealth of trivia about the place, and some pretty good tea and biscuits too. The husband, Ernie, was a fount of local folklore. In a hushed voice he'd told them that while walking their two dogs along the sea-bank path, he had heard a strange and eerie voice singing mournfully in the twilight.

Their second call was also quite informative. The cottage owner, a short, stocky, heavily-bearded man called Ralph Jenkins, was the local RSPB representative, and spent a lot of time out on the marsh cataloguing waders, waterfowl and migrant visitors. He admitted having seen someone out on the marsh at night in all weathers. 'The fool! I'm a yellowbelly, born and bred, Detectives, and I know better than to do that.'

Their last call was to Gary's vet's house. Luckily they had chosen his one day off.

'Come on in. Want a cuppa?'

Philip Groves, dressed in old corduroy chinos and a check shirt, led them into a welcoming, cosy sitting room. Nearly every seat held some sort of animal. Rosie counted six dogs of varying breeds and at least three sleeping cats.

'Standing room only, by the look of it.' Groves smiled, then addressed two Jack Russells. 'Come on, lads! Jacko! Willoughby! Shift yourselves! Give the lady a seat!'

Rosie sat, and Willoughby leapt straight onto her lap.

'Oh dear, I hope you like dogs, miss.'

'Love 'em,' said Rosie, tickling the little animal's ears.

Charlie turfed a fat fluffy cat from a small armchair, sat down and explained their visit.

'Has something serious happened out at Windrush?' asked Groves.

'Yes, sir, although we are not at liberty to give any details, I'm afraid.'

'Has that big guy who is working there had an accident?' Groves' face grew serious. 'I've seen him alone out there at all hours. Damned dangerous, I reckon.'

'No, he's okay, Mr Groves,' said Rosie. 'But have you seen anyone other than Mr Lee, he's the big guy you mentioned, out at Windrush or on the marsh close by?'

Philip Groves shrugged. 'Well, I don't think I've ever actually met the owner, but other than Mr Lee, there's my neighbour, Jenkins, our bird man. He's always out there on the marsh paths. And Ernie Coulter walks his dogs along the sea-bank pretty regular-like, and you get the odd rambler.' He wrinkled his brow. 'Come to think of it, I saw someone a week or two ago, in the evening, way out in the bleakest part of the marsh. And that's not a sensible thing to do at all, unless you know the tides and the weather really well.'

'So it must have been a local?' asked Charlie.

'I'd hope so. It's a dangerous spot for an incomer. This is a very small community, Detective, but it was no one I recognised.'

'Do you live here alone, Mr Groves?' asked Rosie.

'Apart from this lot.' He pointed to his pets. 'I started with one dog, an old lurcher, and one cat. Somehow the others have gradually found their way to me over the years, and look at us now.'

'Have you ever heard singing, sir? Out on the marsh?' Rosie asked.

Groves stopped smiling, and she saw a strange look cross his face.

'Didn't think you'd be interested in all that superstitious stuff, officers.'

'It may not be superstition, sir. If you have heard anything, there may be a very valid reason for it.'

'I've heard nothing other than old wives' tales,' Groves said shortly. 'But I'd be interested to know what you mean.'

'We'll be glad to explain, sir, but not just yet I'm afraid.' Charlie stood up. 'Thank you for your time.' He handed Groves a card. 'If you think of anything else about either the old house, or the marsh, give us a ring.'

As they left the room, Charlie turned back. 'Oh, I nearly forgot! A colleague of ours wished to be remembered to you, sir. PC Gary Pritchard?'

'Gary! Of course! He and his lovely sister used to come here with their dogs before I opened the practice in the town. Really nice man, Gary, salt of the earth. Loved his dogs to distraction. Give him my best, won't you?' He glanced at Rosie, who had Willoughby still in her arms. 'And speaking of which, I'm afraid the dog has to stay here, DC McElderry. But my surgery has a small rescue centre attached. It's run by volunteers and a few of my vet nurses, so come and see us if you can give a dog or a cat a good home.'

'Not working the hours I do, Mr Groves. It wouldn't be fair.' Rosie placed the little dog on the ground with a sigh.

# CHAPTER TWENTY-THREE

Back at the station, Clive handed Jackman a memo. 'This is from the pathologist, and just to let you know that I spoke to Grace Black. She was most understanding. She said that she realised a lot was going on at present but she would appreciate an update from you when you have the time.'

'Fair enough,' said Jackman. He skimmed the memo, then turned to Marie. 'The crime scene isn't ready to be released yet, but Rory has said that you and I can take another look around. And Ted Watchman has confirmed that a large entrance in one of the walls of the chamber has been very professionally sealed up. Ted has also ascertained that the work was done from a tunnel on the house side of the area. That means the beds and all the other stuff were brought in from Windrush.'

'Which ties it even tighter to Broome,' Marie said eagerly.

'Or to the man who has spent a very long time working there.'

'Mr Micah Lee.'

'Exactly. God, we desperately need to talk to that man! I'm just about to ring Harlan Marsh and try to lean on the medical officer. Go and see if Rosie and Max are back yet, then we'll get ourselves back to Windrush.'

* * *

An exhausted-looking Rory Wilkinson beckoned them over and pointed to one of the small labels that hung above each bed.

'As you were thoughtful enough not to contaminate my crime scene, you would not have handled these cards, and hence not noticed what is written on the back.' With gloved fingers, Rory turned the card over and showed them a line of small, faded handwriting.

'Dates of birth?' Jackman thought immediately of Toni and the man who had demanded to know exactly when she was born.

'*Partial* dates of birth, on each card. All have the day of the week, some the month and others the year, and some have faded completely. But observe, on every card, the weekday is underlined.'

Marie looked closer. 'They are all born on a Wednesday?'

'Well, we can't be certain about the older ones until we do lab tests, but all the ones that are legible are exactly the same.'

"Monday's child is fair of face, Tuesday's child is full of grace . . ." Jackman looked at Marie for help.

'Wednesday's child is full of woe!' Marie shook her head.

'I'm sure a good shrink would find it very interesting indeed,' said Rory, carefully replacing the card.

'If we had one,' grumbled Jackman.

Rory looked at him over the top of his glasses. 'Well, I do have a friend. He's a simply brilliant forensic psychologist, *and* he's retired, so he might be prepared to give you the benefit of his expertise. I can ring him, if you like?'

Jackman thought of the super's aversion to profiling and the trouble that the last one had caused, then said, 'Yes, please do. I would love to run quite a few things past him.'

'Good. I'm certain he'll be a great help.' Rory's face broke into a broad smile, 'And he's simply gorgeous! Mature, yes, but my! If I wasn't spoken for, well . . . but I'm getting carried away. Now, before I forget, I have to say thank you for organising such a lovely forensic anthropologist for us. I'll introduce you in a moment, but my, what that woman doesn't know about bones isn't worth knowing.'

Rory turned back to the cards. 'There is one more thing about these cards, well, about the handwriting actually.' He bit on his lip. 'This is by no means conclusive, but the technician who has been cataloguing the cards is a graphologist, and he's sure that a woman wrote them.'

Jackman looked at Marie and knew she was thinking the same as him. Did those vases of flowers, and the neatly hung clothes, all carefully labelled, mean that Rory had been right all along? But what about the man with the strange eyes? The chorister? Could he be an accomplice?

'Do you have any female suspects in the frame, Jackman?' Rory asked.

'Sort of. We have a woman named Elizabeth Sewell,' Jackman whispered. 'She's in Saltern General Hospital at present, unfit for interview.'

'Well, I'd keep a very close eye on her if I were you. I suggest that she knows rather a lot about our Children's Ward.' He lifted an eyebrow. 'But come and meet the oldest resident, and Professor Wallace. Everything that we can do in situ has now been done, so she's packing up our girl for transit.'

Rory stopped and made his introductions from a distance, warning them not to get too close for fear of cross-contamination.

Jackman looked at this expert on death, and was immediately reminded of his Aunt Hilda. The woman that looked out from the face mask was short, stocky and bright-eyed. She obviously had trouble keeping her wild mane of greying hair inside the hood of her protective suit, which created the illusion of an enormous head.

Jackman fought back the impulse to call her Auntie, and asked instead why the skeleton's leg seemed so deformed.

'I will be able to tell you more when I examine the remains under controlled conditions, but I believe that she had an ankle fracture in early childhood. It must have been so severe that it sheared off the end of the tibia. Even now I can see distortion and fracture-related bony callus. I would say that it never healed correctly and she was either not treated properly, or suffered another later injury to the same weakened site. Come and see me tomorrow at the morgue and I'll tell you more.'

'Do you have an approximate age for her, Professor?' asked Marie.

'I'd rather not guess, but if it's important, I'd estimate that she was in her mid-teens. Tests will help get that estimate closer to the truth.'

'Professor? Rory Wilkinson says that she was killed much longer ago than the other victims. Would you be able to give us a vague idea of when she died?'

Almost tenderly, "Auntie" laid a creamy-brown long bone into a box, and stared at it thoughtfully. 'As a rough estimate, twenty years, maybe more.'

Jackman wondered who on earth this girl was, and why she had been important enough to risk exhuming her from her legitimate grave to bring her here. It was bizarre.

Rory handed Jackman a sheet of paper. 'I've had one of my techies prepare this for you, rather than wait for the full report. I thought you might be able to get on and make some preliminary searches.' He pointed to the list. On it were all the details from the cards, and a clear description of the clothes that had been so lovingly stored. Jackman knew that those clothes would be vital for final identification. It was not just the trace evidence that would no doubt still be present. Everyone remembered exactly what a child was wearing when they went missing.

'Thanks, Rory. I really appreciate that.' Jackman placed it carefully in his pocket.

'No problem. And I should think you will be able to have your scene back by tonight, as long as logistics can work out a way of transporting my patients off this marsh. They are talking about a fleet of all-terrain vehicles getting as close as they dare, and the bodies being ferried by stretcher bearers from the tunnels to the vehicles. It sounds like the evacuation of the WWI trenches! Anyway, it has all been photographed, documented, swept and dusted, and everything of importance bagged and tagged. Hopefully, the residents themselves will be transferred into my tender care at the hospital by tonight, and then our real work can begin.' He stood back. 'Now, dear friends, I must ask you most respectfully, to bugger off and let me get on.'

Jackman grinned, thanked him again, and they began the long trek back through the tunnel.

* * *

As soon as Gary saw Jackman and Marie arrive, he jumped up, followed them into the office and closed the door. 'Sorry, sir, but I think there is something very unpleasant going on over at Harlan Marsh.'

'It involves Cade?' Marie almost spat the name out.

Gary sat down heavily opposite his new boss. 'He has taken personal command of the drinking club investigation, and he's keeping things very close to his chest. My mate has been drafted into his team to help them.'

'Does he think Cade is protecting someone?' asked Jackman.

205

'He thought so to begin with, but now he's really worried. Take a look at this. It's a scan of one of the pictures that Cade commandeered. My friend emailed it to me.' He took a sheet of paper from his inside pocket, unfolded it and passed it across the desk. 'Do you remember it? It's where young Nick Barley is talking to two men.'

'The one where you and Marie both thought you recognised one of them?'

Gary nodded. 'Look closely, sir. This man is obscured by the shadow from the building, but I don't think it's one of Cade's buddies at all. I think it is Cade himself.'

Gary lowered his voice. 'And guess what? Shortly after my friend got hold of it, the original disappeared. *And* the CCTV tape met with an unfortunate accident.' He pointed to the picture. 'No one knows about this and now, sir, it's the only copy.'

Jackman snatched the picture up and peered at it. 'My God! It's not clear enough to challenge him on, but I'd say you are right!'

Marie leaned over and took it from him. 'So that's who it reminded me of,' she whispered. 'The bastard!' She looked up. 'Boss, I've heard that there's software now available that can compare the shape and dimensions of the man in that picture. It doesn't have to be perfect, just as long as part of it is complete. The program just fills in the gaps. All we need is another photo of Cade for comparison, and we could identify him.'

'And do we have that kind of technology?'

'We don't, but the university does. Ted was telling me they use a similar package in his department.'

Jackman frowned. 'We'd be operating well outside the regulations if we did that. We'd have to be extremely careful. Can you imagine the furore if it got out? And supposing we'd got it wrong? We'd all lose our jobs for starters.'

'The words "shit" and "fan" spring to mind. But if a senior officer is bent, we *have* to know.' Marie looked at Gary. 'You've worked for him. We all know he's a slimeball, but do you think it's possible he's mixed up in something as serious as this?'

Gary did not hesitate. 'Yes, Sarge, I do. I'd stake my pension on it.'

Jackman looked as though he was sucking a lemon. 'So the next question is, just how involved is he? Is he at the margin, just getting his rocks off watching some dirty sex, or is he in deeper? Although I doubt he had anything to do with the actual abductions. Surely even Cade wouldn't sink that low?'

'Young Toni said she'd been to these gatherings several times, but she'd never seen the man who took her to the bogus "party" before.' Gary raised his eyebrows. 'This is just a thought, but would Toni recognise Cade if we showed her his photo?'

'We can't do that, Gary,' said Marie. 'If anyone found out, they'd throw the book at us. They would say we were putting ideas into her head. And she'd recognise him anyway. Don't forget he's a friend of her father.'

'But I'm willing to bet that Cade is only pals with Neil Clarkson because of the money he donates to police coffers. Somehow I don't think they socialise outside Lodge meetings. They couldn't be more different.' Jackman gave a humourless laugh.

'So are you suggesting that we show her his photo, sir?' Marie asked.

'It's very risky, and we certainly couldn't do it with her parents around. With all these deaths, we really don't have time for this, but,' Jackman shrugged, 'I do believe we ought to do it.'

He looked at Gary.

'This will be totally off the record, and you don't have to be part of it. Your job will be in jeopardy if you're caught.'

Gary took a deep breath and straightened up. 'I'll risk it, sir. I know things about Cade that only a man who'd worked with him would. I'm ready to go out on a limb.'

'If you're absolutely sure? Toni really liked you. In the hospital she trusted you more than anyone. Okay, you talk to her, and in private.' Jackman paused. 'And I don't think it's the right time to tell her about Emily, unless she asks straight out. I'll leave that up to you.'

Gary gave a nod. 'I'll play it by ear. But could I say something before I go?'

'Of course.'

Gary took a deep breath. 'All this photo stuff is fine. Of course we must follow it up, and I'm certain we could prove it is Cade. But I know him, and he'll wriggle out of it somehow. I think the only way is to catch him red-handed. We need to go back undercover, to another one of those illegal parties, and arrest him in situ.'

There was a silence. Then Jackman drew in a long breath. 'Get Rosie and Max in here.'

'But, sir?' Marie half stood, and then sat down again.

'I know you don't like this, Marie, and neither will Max, I'm sure, but Gary is right. We need to go back in.'

\* \* \*

Max, as expected, was not happy, but Rosie was immediately on the phone to her new clubbing buddy, Will, and arranging to meet him.

'He loves his brother, and he'll be just as glad as us to see the drinking club closed down.' She looked at Jackman. 'I trust him, he's a nice kid, and I think he'll forgive me for lying to him. I'm sure he'll help us.'

'Since there's no way to stop this happening, I'll go with Rosie this time,' said Max. 'And don't worry, I'll make a real effort with my appearance to blend in.'

'Then we watch for the texts. It won't be for a few days, but as soon as we get the message, we'll go in.'

'And if Cade's there, we hit the place with every officer we can spare,' added Marie grimly. 'In the meantime, I'll organise the photo evidence with Ted.'

'This sounds more like the sergeant we all know and love,' said Jackman.

'Frankly, sir, if we do take Cade down, I'll be dressing up and dancing on the table.'

\* \* \*

As he closed the door behind him, Gary suddenly realised just how much he hated Chief Superintendent Cade. The man had been around for so long he'd learned to live with him, like a disability or a terrible illness. Cade's rank and the powerful men that he mixed with, made him seem untouchable. Gary had thought things would never change. But now they had the chance to finally bring him down.

Gary went to his desk and switched on the computer. If he got this right — and he knew exactly how to go about it — he could right an awful lot of wrongs.

A determined smile spread across his face. He was very glad he'd come to work with DI Jackman in Saltern-le-Fen.

\* \* \*

Jackman hoped he was doing the right thing. Risking his own job was one thing, but allowing others to do the same was quite another. He looked anxiously at Marie. 'Do you trust Ted Watchman?'

Marie nodded vigorously. 'I do.'

'Then go find him. See what is needed for that photo comparison, and tell him we need total discretion. This *cannot* get back to anyone, here or anywhere else. Okay?'

Marie nodded again and left the room.

Jackman turned to Max and Charlie. 'Could you two gather up as many free hands as you can from CID? We need to compare this list against missing persons and unsolved cases.' He handed Max the paper Rory Wilkinson had given him. 'We have clothing, first names and partial dates of birth, so we need to start identifying the victims as quickly as possible. Tell them I want their findings as soon as they have them. And, Max, you are to concentrate on a young woman who had a severely deformed lower leg and foot. We believe she was the first to die, maybe twenty years ago.' He paused for breath.

'And, Charlie, please ask Clive to contact whoever is on duty at Benedict Broome's house to find me a sample of Elizabeth Sewell's handwriting. Now I have the unenviable task of grovelling to the super about using that psychologist. And I think she'll like that idea about as much as an ice-water enema.'

As Jackman walked to the lifts he glanced at his watch. The FMO at Harlan Marsh had promised to ring as soon as Micah Lee was fit for interview, and he hadn't. Knowing what he now knew, Jackman wondered if the hold-up had something to do with Cade. He still found it hard to understand why he would risk so much — a high-powered job with untold fringe benefits and a bloody good pension — just to watch a few teenagers groping each other in the dark. It was all too much to take on board, especially when he had a psychopathic killer, thirteen murder victims, as well as suspects to interview. Suddenly Jackman stopped short.

Christ! Had he sent Micah Lee to Harlan Marsh, right into the tender care of a man who knew all about him?

With a dry mouth he hurried towards the super's office. This case was taking them into very dangerous waters indeed, and it was up to him to steer them through to safety. He just hoped he was up to it.

# CHAPTER TWENTY-FOUR

Gary had a satisfied smile on his lips. With no hesitation, Toni had picked out Cade from the ten mugshots he showed her. As Gary walked back towards his old Suzuki, another car was drawing up at the Clarksons' house.

'Ethan Barley! What brings you to this young lady's door?' Gary greeted the young man.

Ethan grinned broadly. 'Got back together with Toni.'

'Yuk!' From the passenger seat, Nick Barley was pulling a face at his brother.

'Don't you approve?' Gary asked with a smile.

'Ah, it's okay I suppose. Maybe it'll keep him off my back.'

Ethan told his brother to stay put, he'd only be a few minutes, then he loped up the path towards the house. Gary took a long look at Nick and decided to take a gamble. 'Do me a favour, son?'

Nick looked suspicious.

'I just wondered if you recognised anyone on this.'

Gary had been very careful. He had reproduced a close-up picture of James Cade from a police magazine. He had copied it and cropped out all trace of a uniform, so that Cade looked like any other civilian. Then he had taken nine photos of random individuals from old cases, added them to the "rogue's gallery" and produced a perfect ID sheet.

'Anyone you know?'

Nick looked closely. 'Just one. That git there. But he never looked that tidy.'

Gary's heart jumped. The boy had fingered Cade!

Nick Barley handed the paper back. 'He was often hanging around with the bloke who got me to copy the keys, and he was at the party in the crypt.'

'So how does he dress?'

'Always the same. Greased back hair, glasses, scruffy black chinos, a dark polo shirt and a black nylon tracksuit top.'

Gary felt sick. That was the description Rosie had given of the man she recognised, but couldn't place. She had actually seen Cade at a party! And hopefully Cade hadn't recognised Rosie.

'Dirty bastard,' grunted Nick. 'Is he the one that spiked Ethan's bird's drink?'

'Could be, Nicholas. And maybe he's done far worse than that.' Gary paused for a moment, then added, 'Would you testify?'

'What? Go to court? Fucking hell!' The boy's eyes widened.

'It could do you a lot of good, son. Our boss would be extremely pleased with you, and she's got a *lot* of influence. And if she's pleased, I'm sure she could make things considerably easier with your father.'

The boy sniffed. Shrugged. 'I dunno. I suppose, well, I could, but . . .'

Gary smiled at him. 'Good lad! I knew you had it in you.'

As he walked away, Nick called him back. 'There was another girl, wasn't there? Emily?'

'I'd rather we kept this to ourselves, Nick. I don't want Toni hearing about it yet.' Gary paused. 'Emily's dead.'

Nicholas's pasty face turned whiter still. 'Dead? What? Murdered?'

'Abducted from one of those parties, Nicholas. Drugged, imprisoned, probably raped, made to suffer terribly, and left to die. I'd say that was murder, wouldn't you?'

Nick breathed deeply for a minute, evidently near to tears. Then quietly, firmly, he said, 'I'll testify.'

\* \* \*

Marie was pacing in the foyer. It was after six and the university had rung half an hour ago to say they were couriering Ted Watchman's information to her. Then she spotted the leather-clad motorcyclist peeling off his helmet and ringing the bell. She met him at the door, signed for the packet, admired his big Yamaha and gave him a fiver.

She pulled open the large manila envelope and stared at the contents. She didn't dare remove them as there were other officers around, but she could see the series of face recognition photos. Marie withdrew the short explanatory note, scanned it, and let out a soft whoop of delight.

She'd been pretty certain, but as the hours had passed she had begun to doubt her own convictions. Now she held a positive match in her hand.

She thought of Valerie, her dearest friend and first crewmate. She'd had a cheeky smile and blonde hair that swept her shoulders, striking green eyes and beautiful skin. She saw Valerie eagerly jumping behind her onto her motorcycle and daring her to break the speed limit. In their time off they often went up the coast and walked along the beach. It had been a happy time in those early days — the days before Cade.

Marie's eyes narrowed as she looked at the photographs. 'Your time is up, bastard,' she whispered to herself, then gathered the documents together and hurried from the foyer.

She almost fell into Jackman's office.

'From the look on your face, I don't need to ask, do I?' said Jackman slowly.

'It's the result we hoped for.'

Jackman slid the report and the photos halfway out, glanced at them, then returned them to the envelope and locked it in his desk drawer. 'This stays here until we need it.' He clipped the small key onto the ring with the other keys, and pushed them deep into his pocket. 'Insurance. We are going to need every bit of evidence we can get if we want to nail Cade.'

Marie yawned. 'It's half six. Shall I send out for some food?'

Jackman nodded. 'In a while. There are a few things I need to catch up on first. Could you ask Clive if he's heard from the lab regarding those handwriting comparisons?'

Marie caught Clive tidying up his desk and shutting down his computer.

'I'm off home, Sarge.' He handed her a sheaf of papers. 'All these are for the DI. The phone has been red hot in the last half hour. They are mainly non-urgent, with the exception of the pathology report on the top.' Clive switched off his printer and locked his desk drawer. 'See you in the morning, Sarge.'

Marie murmured good night, picked up the report and went back to Jackman's office.

'Look, sir! The handwriting on the cards over the beds is an exact match with the samples that Max took from Elizabeth Sewell's annexe.'

Jackman read the report and groaned loudly. 'This is lunacy! It doesn't make sense. How can a weak and sensitive woman, someone known to be both physically and mentally delicate, possibly be involved in murder on this scale?'

'Because she wrote them for her beloved employer, Benedict Broome. What else could it mean?' Marie frowned. 'But whatever it means, we now have a direct link between her and the scene of the crime. We are going to have to get her moved to a secure unit, aren't we?'

Jackman picked up the phone. 'Damned right, we are. I'll get an order to have her moved from the general hospital to Saltern Hall Psychiatric Hospital pending evaluation. And we need to speak to Benedict Broome again.'

While Jackman arranged for Elizabeth Sewell's transfer, Marie went out into the main office to fetch them some strong coffee.

Max was lifting a pile of printer paper from his desk. 'Sarge, have you got a moment? Things are looking good here. The forensic team have done some work on the name card for the oldest body. It's Fleur. They are still working on the others but they are hopeful they'll have some more names very soon. And the other CID teams have been hard at it with the IDs. We have a girl called Hebe Brock, a Scottish traveller who went missing five years ago. Date of birth tallies and she was reported as having had the top of one finger amputated in an accident. Our victim had an identical bone injury. Plus there is a fifteen-year-old serial runaway from Calne in Wiltshire. Her name is Sophie Berry, and she's been missing for seven years. The date of birth, Christian name, a red jacket and a charm bracelet all match. Another girl is named Tessa Avery. It was assumed that she had run off with her boyfriend to Spain, but her parents never heard from her again. She's been missing for three years and came from Surrey.'

'Interesting, isn't it? So far, none of them are high-profile cases or local mispers.'

'Emily was local,' said Max. 'So obviously the killer was getting more confident.'

'Then, thank God we found his lair when we did. Good work, Max.' Marie patted him on the shoulder. 'Anything more in the pipeline?'

'Well, everything we have is now on the Police National Computer, so they could get more hits at any moment.'

'Then maybe you should take the opportunity to get home?'

'I'm trying to find out more about Fleur, our really old skeleton, Sarge, the one with the badly broken ankle. Because of her age I'm certainly not having as much luck as the others, but I'd like to keep at it for a while longer.' Max typed in another search. 'Plus I'd quite like to see if the PNC coughs up anything interesting over the next hour or so. We've sent out some pretty motivating enquiries.'

'Okay, but don't stay all night, kiddo.'

As Marie went to the coffee machine she wondered about Max's social life. Did he even have one? Despite his striking good looks, Marie got the impression that Max's ideal night in would consist of a takeaway, a pot of coffee, and fast broadband.

Carefully balancing three hot polystyrene beakers, Marie placed one next to Max, and took the other two back to Jackman's office.

Jackman was just replacing the phone as she went in. He seemed edgy all of a sudden. 'Something wrong?'

'Everything.' On his face was a mixture of anger and mystification. 'Elizabeth Sewell is being transferred, but I've just been speaking to the FMO out at Harlan Marsh, and told him it's imperative that we interview Micah Lee. He says the man's mind is in a state of flux. One minute he's lucid and reasonable, the next he's climbing the walls.' Jackman glowered at the phone. 'I don't have the time to go there and sodding well sit around waiting for one of his "reasonable" moments.'

'Couldn't an officer from Harlan Marsh do it for you? Someone who is on hand to monitor Lee's moods?'

'What, you'd actually trust someone from Cade's manor, would you?' Jackman barked.

'I trust Gary,' she said quietly. 'So I'd trust anyone Gary vouched for. They can't all be bent, can they? One rotten apple won't have contaminated the whole barrel.'

Jackman put his head in his hands. 'You're right. Sorry, Marie. Ask Gary to come in, would you?' He sat up straight. 'In fact, get the whole team together in the CID room. We need to talk.'

* * *

Jackman perched on the edge of a desk in front of one of the white-boards. Down one side of the board was a list of the victims. Full names, photographs and the places where they disappeared were being added minute by minute. Already they had photos of Tessa Avery, Sophie Berry, Hebe Brock, and just a few seconds ago, Annie Crane and Lucy O'Connell had been added.

At the top of the board was the name Windrush, and below that, Benedict Broome, Elizabeth Sewell and Micah Lee.

Jackman stood up and pointed to the name Elizabeth. 'This woman is a direct link to the Children's Ward. However, we already know from Rory that some of the dead girls had been seriously assaulted using a great deal of force, and possibly raped, so that means that either she had an accomplice, or her involvement is in some way,' he shrugged, 'accidental.'

'But she *is* connected to Broome, and to Lee, by virtue of his being employed by Broome.' Marie pursed her lips. 'So what if her employer asked her to print out some labels? She'd do it, wouldn't she? And she'd not necessarily be aware of what they were?'

'That,' said Jackman, 'is what I mean by accidental. And maybe she'd do it for a friend too. We need to talk to her as soon as she's been assessed at Saltern Hall. Meanwhile, Gary, I need to find a trustworthy senior detective at Harlan Marsh, someone who would interview Lee for us, and preferably without Chief Superintendent Cade knowing. Is there such an officer?'

'Only one that I know of, sir. DI Jim Salmon.'

'Jim Salmon? The same guy who used to be our dog handler years back? He's a detective now?' Jackman's eyes widened. 'Perfect, I'll ring him as soon as we've finished.'

He turned back to the board. 'So who else have we spoken to?'

'Broome's gardener, boss. Bloke named Len Curtis.' Max looked at his notebook. 'Funny sort. It was hard to get him to string two words together. But he has been out to Windrush a few times, with messages or deliveries for Micah Lee, and he only lives a couple of miles from Roman Creek.'

Jackman wrote the name on the board. 'Who else?'

'Philip Groves, the vet who lives a short way from Windrush, on the edge of the marsh. And two other neighbours, a bird-watcher called Ralph Jenkins, and a couple called Ernie and Betty Coulter,' said Rosie.

'And we spoke to Bill Hickey, the farm manager where Micah Lee lodges.'

Jackman paused. 'But the farmer was away. What was his name, Gary?'

'Toby Tanner, sir. He's expected back from Germany tomorrow, according to Hickey.'

'Is that it?'

'No, sir,' said Charlie. 'There were several other people living in the Roman Creek area that uniform saw, but most were elderly women, apart from a couple who have a holiday let a bit further up the coast road. No one they'd pay a second visit to, and all the so-called "neighbours" are well scattered over a very large area. Windrush is quite remote.'

Marie raised her hand. 'Maybe we should include Asher Leyton in the list of people we've spoken to. It's a very vague connection, but he did know of Shauna Kelly and she has definitely been placed at one of those parties. Plus we also know he has a penchant for talking to street girls.'

Jackman added Asher Leyton's name.

'Okay, so we go back and talk to Benedict Broome, Elizabeth Sewell and Micah Lee. And on a different tack we hit the drinking club again.'

As there were other officers in the room, he kept strictly to the abducted girls, Toni and Emily, and the victims of the Children's Ward. 'The organisers may have nothing directly to do with the abductions, but we need them brought in, questioned, and those damned parties brought to an end.'

He looked around at the tired faces staring back at him. 'Now, all of you who can, get yourselves home and get some rest. We start again tomorrow.'

* * *

'That guy is one serious fruitcake,' said the Harlan Marsh custody officer as he closed the door of the interview room. 'Well, he's all yours, and the best of British in trying to get any sense out of him.'

DI Jim Salmon wondered if he had been a little too quick to agree to help out DI Jackman. He'd already heard that Chief Superintendent Cade had tried to interview Mad Micah, and had had to abort the attempt almost immediately. He just prayed that Cade wouldn't get to hear about this particular effort. At least the chief was off duty until the morning.

Along with his sergeant, DS Terry Langer, and a social worker hastily acquired from the duty roster to safeguard the prisoner's interests, Jim reluctantly entered the small room.

Micah Lee sat bolt upright, his eyes wide and staring, and his nostrils flaring with anger.

Jim Salmon looked at Micah and decided that Jackman owed him bigtime.

With a deep sigh, he switched on the tape and made the introductions.

'Mr Lee, we need to talk to you about an underground room beneath the property called Windrush at Roman Creek. That is the property belonging to Mr Benedict Broome, and where you have been working for some time.' Jim kept his voice even and quiet. He knew that Micah would react badly to any show of assertiveness.

'We are interviewing you because of your knowledge of the layout of Windrush, Mr Lee. Having worked on it for so long, we feel that you may be able to help us.'

'What room? I don't know about any underground room!' boomed Micah.

Jim saw a vein pulsing in the side of Micah's head.

'Surely you know that there is a tunnel leading from the back of the main house out towards the old barn and the storeroom, and that there is an underground room beneath them?'

The big man looked like a caged animal. He chewed furiously on his bottom lip, and drummed his fingers frantically on the table top. 'I don't know of any tunnel. No, no tunnel.'

Jim attempted a smile. 'Okay, but do you know—?'

A keening howl suddenly erupted from Micah's lips and reverberated around the tiny room. They all leapt up, Jim's chair fell backwards, and the social worker uttered a little scream.

Then, before anyone could move, Micah took a series of ragged, gasping breaths and pitched forward onto the floor.

Jim hit the panic button. 'Get help!' he yelled, and threw himself to his knees beside the unconscious Micah. 'We need an ambulance.'

'The duty doctor is in the building,' called Langer. 'He was dealing with a junkie as we came in.' He ran for the door. 'I'll get him.'

The doctor was at Micah's side in minutes.

'It's probably some kind of panic attack. He's sweaty and tachycardic. He may well have hyperventilated, causing him to faint, but,' the doctor checked Micah's pulse again, 'we need to get him to the hospital to be checked out properly. I'm not just covering our backs, Detective Inspector Salmon, I'm not at all happy with his condition. There could well be a neurological reason for this and we can't risk leaving it.'

'Ambulance is on its way, boss.' The sergeant leant around the door. 'And uniform are organising an escort.' He stared down at Micah. 'I can't say I'll be sad to see that one go. He's one scary guy!'

As the stretcher was hoisted into the back of the ambulance, Jim wondered how he was going to tell DI Jackman that he'd inadvertently hospitalised his prisoner. And even worse, how would Chief Cade react when he found out?

* * *

It was very late by the time Jackman and Marie concluded Benedict Broome's second interview. He had politely but vehemently denied any knowledge of work ever having been carried out from an underground tunnel. He told them he knew nothing of any such tunnel. He also denied any knowledge of the name cards allegedly written by his housekeeper.

In the end, they called it a day. Jackman had decided to keep quiet about the killer's singing. He agreed with Marie that it would be best to keep that piece of information to themselves until they could use it more effectively.

'I wonder if Broome was a choirboy,' mused Marie as they left the interview room. 'But he didn't grow up around here, so it would be hard to find out.'

'Worth a try though.' Jackman punched in the security number and flung the door open. 'But right now, we all need sleep. Go check the team, Marie, and pack whoever is left off to their homes and their beds. Then I suggest you gather up your new lodger and get home yourself.' He smiled at her. 'And how is your new role as landlady going?'

'Brilliantly! Gary actually does a cooked breakfast before he goes to work! He's perfectly house-trained, a wizard in the kitchen, and frankly I'm thinking of keeping him on.'

'Ah, then my Mrs M. had better watch out. Even I don't get breakfasts.'

Marie grinned, and was about to say more when Jackman's mobile sounded.

'Ah, Jim! What have you got for me?'

Marie saw Jackman's expression drop.

'Shit! How the hell . . . ? Oh well, not your fault, Jim. I'm just sorry to have put you through it. They've taken him to the Pilgrim Hospital in Boston? Yeah, but make sure he's watched twenty-four/seven, and two officers at all times. Have you got the manpower for that, or shall I get you some back-up? Right, well, thanks for trying. Night, Jim. Oh, and any aggro from your chief, refer him to me, okay?'

He closed the phone and stared grimly at Marie. 'Micah Lee categorically denied knowing about any tunnels or underground rooms, and then he collapsed. He's been taken in for neurological evaluation. That puts two of our three suspects out of our direct supervision, and I don't like that one bit.'

Marie agreed, but right now, she could barely think straight. She was exhausted. 'I'll go sort out the others, then I'll see you in the morning, sir. Let's see what tomorrow brings, shall we?'

'And speaking of the morning, Benedict Broome is supposed to either be released or charged at eight a.m., so I'd better get someone round the magistrate for an extension. And considering what's beneath that man's property, I'll go on getting bloody extensions until we have the truth.'

## CHAPTER TWENTY-FIVE

After a restless night, Jackman rose early and, taking a leaf out of Gary's book, cooked himself a proper breakfast. He was locking the door to Mill Corner when his mobile rang.

'Marie? Surely you're not at work already?'

'I am. I'm sorry to start your day like this, but we've got a problem.'

'What's wrong now?'

'Micah Lee has done a runner from the hospital.'

'What! How the hell did that happen?'

'It was no one's fault really, sir, apart perhaps from underestimating his strength.'

Jackman jumped into his car and slammed the door. It was *always* someone's fault when a prisoner got away. It didn't happen often, but when it did, it was after they'd got themselves into hospital. 'Okay, tell me. Just don't say someone left their post to go to the sodding toilet or blood may flow.'

'No, nothing like that. They thought he was unconscious when they took him down to radiology for a scan. There were two constables and two nurses with him, but as he came out of the scanner and they went to replace the restraints, he went ballistic. He's badly hurt one of the

Boston men, concussed the other, and laid out both nurses.'

'No!' Jackman's anger turned to concern. 'How badly hurt?'

'Suspected fractured skull, sir. Apparently he smashed their heads together. PC Bladon came off worst. PC Smythe is mildly concussed.'

'And the hospital staff?'

'Shaken up and bruised, but no serious injury.'

'So where did he go? Was CCTV operational?'

'Yes. He was seen at the rear of the hospital where he accosted a porter, took his clothes and his wallet, then went over the hospital wall and made off through residential gardens and fields towards the West Fen Catchwater Drain.'

'So we've lost him?'

Jackman heard an intake of breath, then a sigh. 'We lost him.'

'Okay, I'll be there in fifteen. Get me a very strong black coffee and we'll re-group.'

Jackman hung up and gave a bitter laugh. For a while there, he'd actually been thinking today might go better!

* * *

When Jackman reached the murder room, his anger had dissipated, and he was left with a feeling of things slipping away from him.

Marie was the only person in the big room, and she looked about as cheerful as he felt.

She held out a coffee and said, 'Max left a note to say that two more victims have been unofficially identified via the PNC. We need the lab results to be certain, but their first names and DOBs match. One is a youngster from Bristol called Corrie Anderson, and the other girl, Charlotte King, is from Hull.'

'And neither rings a bell. Our killer always took low-profile missing persons from different locations, didn't he?

No one who was ever plastered across the tabloids or made the media in a big way.'

'Jackman,' Marie stared at him with a perplexed expression. 'I'm thinking about those dates of birth. What *is* it about being born on a Wednesday that made them a candidate for death?'

Jackman's head shook slowly from side to side. 'We'll only know that when the case is over. And right now, I think we'd better concentrate on trying to capture Mad Micah, don't you?' He drew in a deep breath. 'And while we wait for the others to get in, will you ring the psychiatric hospital for me and see if Elizabeth is fit enough to interview?'

Marie went to get the number. As she flicked through her file, she said, 'So where do you think Micah will have gone?'

The million-dollar question. 'If Benedict Broome were free, I would have laid good money on Micah going to him, but . . .'

'Would he go home, do you think? If he's mentally unstable maybe he needs a familiar place?'

'But surely he knows we'll be watching? There are already uniformed officers at the farm. And Windrush is crawling with police and forensics.'

Jackman could still see the anger in Micah's craggy, ugly face when they arrived to search Windrush. Maybe his anguish had been because he had known, even then, that it was the beginning of the end for the Children's Ward.

Marie hung up. 'You have a green light, sir. They are a bit iffy, but it's okay as long as her doctor sits in, and we keep the interview short.'

Jackman thought for a moment. 'I'm wondering if it might be prudent if you went, and took Rosie with you. If this woman is so fragile, perhaps having a man asking the questions is not the best strategy.'

'You could be right, sir, and as I just saw Rosie coming in, we'll get off before the doctors change their minds.'

* * *

Marie and Rosie hurried from the car park and up to the heavy glass doors of Saltern Hall Psychiatric Hospital. Marie pushed the intercom button and announced their names. The door hummed and the catch released.

There were no rattling key chains, metal locks or clanging iron doors, just pass cards and security number pads.

'Dr Mason is expecting you. I'll escort you down to his wing.' The receptionist was a smartly uniformed man of around thirty. He was short-haired, tall and muscular. Not the sort you'd willingly mess with.

Elizabeth was in a private room, with two constables stationed outside. Dr Leonard Mason and a male nurse were waiting with her, and let them into the room. It was spotlessly clean, and although rather Spartan, seemed comfortable enough.

Marie had been warned that Elizabeth would be under mild sedation. She was perfectly lucid but fragile, and her psychiatrist and another medic would remain with them throughout the interview.

Marie had already decided to keep the questions to essentials only, just in case the doctors pulled the plug on them.

They introduced themselves to this possible accomplice to multiple murder in the gentlest voices they could muster.

Elizabeth looked at them with very little expression on her face, until her eyes fell on Rosie. 'What a pretty girl,' she said, a strange smile twisting her lips. 'You remind me of . . . no, she was much blonder.' The smile remained, although Elizabeth's eyes were the saddest Marie had ever seen. She wondered who Elizabeth was thinking of.

'Elizabeth, your employer, Benedict Broome, sends his best wishes. He said to tell you that he is fine and that you are not to worry about anything. He said that you can talk to us quite candidly. We are only here to find the truth. Do you understand?'

Again the head tilted. 'Ah yes, Mr Broome. Benedict.' Elizabeth tugged at her sleeves, pulling them down over her thin fingers.

Rosie added. 'Is he a good employer? Does he treat you well?'

'Oh yes! I couldn't wish for better. He's very kind. I don't know what I'd do without him.' They could see her hands, the fingers just protruding from her sleeves, twisting constantly. 'But what do you want with me? Why am I here?'

'We have something here that we'd like you to see. We were wondering if you recognise it.' Marie placed a clear plastic evidence bag in front of her. Inside was one of the name cards from the underground chamber. Even through the film, Marie could clearly see the name, "Lucy," written on it. 'Is this your writing?'

'I think so.' She squinted as she tried to make out the neat print through the plastic. 'I'm sure I wrote that.'

Marie heard Rosie take a breath. 'What is it, Elizabeth? What was it for?'

There was no reply, and Marie managed to quash her overwhelming desire to lean forward and shake her. 'Is it yours, or did someone ask you to do it for them?'

The fingers twisted. 'Not mine.' She frowned. 'But, who . . . ?'

'Mr Broome, maybe?' Rosie maintained a calm, even tone.

'It must have been, mustn't it?' She pushed it back towards them.

'Or a friend, maybe?' Marie asked.

'I . . . I'm not sure.'

Marie bit her lip, and saw the doctor's sharp eyes on her.

'Careful,' mouthed Mason. 'Don't push her.'

She looked at the mousy woman more closely. She wasn't nearly as old as she looked. She was very thin, fine-boned, with almost porcelain-like skin, but there was something about those sad eyes that said she was not as fragile as she made out. Suddenly Marie decided on a different tack.

'Micah Lee is missing, Miss Sewell. He's disappeared.'

The fluttering hands flew to her mouth. She gave a little gasp, and Dr Mason found his voice. 'DS Evans, can I have a word, please? Outside.'

Exactly what Marie had hoped for. As Marie stood up and accompanied the doctor outside, Rosie remained quietly seated with Elizabeth. She would get the chance to observe Elizabeth's honest reaction to Marie's statement.

Marie listened to the doctor admonishing her, but watched through the window from the corner of her eye. She saw Rosie's lips move, smile. Marie could also see that she was indeed getting a response. With only the nurse and the "pretty girl" in attendance, Elizabeth Sewell obviously felt less threatened. Marie decided to dispute the doctor's objection to her tone and extend her expulsion from the room a little longer.

She drew out their "chat" for five minutes, until the doctor gave her permission to go back in for a short while longer. Marie asked about the tunnels. But this time she saw no comprehension at all. Elizabeth said that she had never heard Mr Broome speak of tunnels or underground rooms at Windrush. She'd been there several times with him, but never alone.

Marie placed the evidence bag back on Elizabeth's lap, and raised her eyebrows. 'Any more thoughts on this?'

'Philip!' she said suddenly. 'They were for the cages for some of the animals at his veterinary surgery — the unlucky ones.'

Marie's head spun. Philip? Philip Groves? 'How do you know Philip the vet?'

'I work for him.' For the first time she really smiled. 'Only as a volunteer, of course. I love animals. I've been helping out there in my spare time for years.'

'And you wrote these for Philip Groves?' Marie pointed to the cards.

'I'm not sure,' she murmured. 'I thought *his* labels had names like Fluffy, and Rocky on them. And little pictures of bones and paw prints? Oh dear, maybe I'm getting confused.' Her hands began to twist again.

'I think that's enough now.' Dr Mason stood up. Marie felt like screaming with frustration.

The two detectives thanked Elizabeth and they left.

As they waited for their escort, Rosie said softly, 'Guess who I remind her of?'

Marie raised an eyebrow. 'Buffy the Vampire Slayer?'

'Very droll, Sarge. No, I remind her of someone called Fleur.'

'The oldest victim!' Marie breathed. 'So what's the connection between the first girl to die and Elizabeth Sewell?'

'I'm not sure, but she was pretty annoyed with herself for having told me. I asked her who Fleur was and she clammed up, went on to talk about Micah.'

'What did she say about him?'

'She's desperate we find him. And she said something rather odd.' Rosie frowned. 'She said that you and I should leave him to the men to sort out.'

'Meaning what, I wonder?'

'Well, I reckon she's meaning he is a danger to women.'

'That's not exactly news. I should think Micah is a danger to anyone.'

Rosie lowered her voice as the escort arrived. 'I don't think that's what she meant. I'm certain she was warning me.'

Outside in the fresh air, Marie unlocked the car and flung her handbag onto the back seat. 'Right, back to the station, Rosie, and your first job is to check Philip Groves' vet practice. See if the "unlucky ones" get nice little name cards with paw prints on them, courtesy of kindly voluntary worker, Elizabeth Sewell.'

'Will do, Sarge. And what then?'

'I'm even more anxious to discover all we can about Fleur. Her connection to Elizabeth puzzles me, and it could be a major lead if we can identify her. Pitch in with Max on that one.'

As they crawled slowly through the town-centre traffic, Marie asked Rosie what she thought about Elizabeth.

'I get the impression that she's genuinely confused, which bothers her. Her confusion is probably caused by all the drugs she's on, but I cannot see her being involved in anything as hideous as the killings. I'm also certain that she'd remain loyal to Benedict Broome with her dying breath, if necessary. She might be a fruit loop, but I swear she's not deliberately lying.'

This was pretty much what Marie had thought. But the urgent need to find the killer left her with little patience for playing guessing games. 'If she needs interviewing again, Rosie, I suggest you go alone. I think you'll get more from her.'

The young woman smiled. 'I think your rank put her off, Sarge. I noticed that she didn't like the doctor either, although she was fine with the nurse and me. I would say she has a problem with authority figures.'

'I wonder what her problem is? Why is she such a nervous wreck?' Marie turned into a side road and doubled back to the station. 'Maybe I'll ask Broome. If he's been spending his precious time taking her for out-patient appointments, I'm willing to bet he knows exactly what is wrong with her.'

\* \* \*

As they stepped through the doors into the station foyer, Marie heard someone call out her name. Jackman was beckoning her over to where Superintendent Ruth Crooke was talking animatedly with a tall, slim man with a neatly trimmed beard and dark-rimmed glasses.

'Ah good, Sergeant Evans, just in time to meet Professor Henry O'Byrne. He's the friend of Professor Rory Wilkinson that you were expecting.'

Marie did a double take, giving Jackman a sideways glance. The super was actually smiling at the man, and in an uncharacteristically warm manner.

'Coincidentally, he's an old acquaintance. Henry is a respected psychologist, an expert in the area of serious child abuse.' She gave him an admiring smile. 'He has worked on some of this county's most difficult cases, and now he's all yours, because I'm afraid I have a meeting.' She looked at Jackman. 'The press have cottoned on to the activity around the hospital morgue. I have to give them something, but I'll do my best to say as little as I can.' She shook her head then hurried away calling out, 'But it won't be long before the balloon goes up, so be prepared.'

It had to happen. It always did.

Marie shook the professor's hand. His smile was warm and engaging. Jackman had told her that Rory had called him *"gorgeous, in a mature way."* Marie could see what he meant.

'Let's go up to my office, Professor,' said Jackman. 'It's quieter there, and the coffee is better.'

First they took him to the murder room, and as he appraised the photographs, they gave him a brief summary of what had happened.

For what seemed like an age, Henry O'Byrne walked up and down, staring at details and then standing back to take in the whole picture. Finally he followed them into Jackman's office.

'I know it's asking a lot, sir, but could you give us some kind of profile on the sort of person who could do something like this?' Marie didn't know how much time this man was prepared to give, but the question was worth asking.

'Well, much as I enjoy the TV crime series, I have to tell you that I don't believe offender profiling actually works in real life. It is not truly reliable and it can be quite dangerous if interpreted incorrectly. I know the FBI Behavioural Science Unit in their bunker down below Quantico would disagree, but the percentages are on my side. No matter what the dramatists tell you, there is only a small chance of getting an arrest through profiling. In some cases you might just as well draw the names out of a hat.'

He looked at them apologetically. 'I can see that you are disappointed, but you'd be better getting your man, or woman, with good solid police work and the support of a good pathologist and his laboratory.' He peered at them over the top of his glasses. 'But what I *can* do is advise you using straightforward psychology, the science of mind and behaviour. And that can be very informative indeed.'

'Great!' Jackman's face lit up. 'I can live with that, and to be truthful, I totally agree.'

And if it was okay with Jackman, it was fine by her. Marie nodded and her mood lightened considerably.

'So what would you like to know?' asked Jackman.

'Might I see the crime scene? I need to be there, to breathe the air and see everything that the killer would have seen.'

'You sound like Rory. He likes to be first on scene and have some time alone with the corpses. He says they often share their secrets with him.'

'I totally understand that. But then we do share a lot of similar traits.' The professor grinned at them.

It's always the nice good-looking men, isn't it! Marie thought.

'I'll take you out to the scene as soon as I've checked on my team.' Jackman stood up. 'Are you up for a ride into the misty marshes?'

Henry beamed at Jackman. 'Oh yes!'

Rosie was just hanging up the phone as Marie approached her desk. 'Philip Groves' veterinary nurse says that several of the animals in their rescue centre do have name cards on their cages. Elizabeth Sewell does spend time there on a voluntary basis helping with the rescued animals, and it was Elizabeth who wrote the name plaques.'

'Mmm. Doesn't sound like the sort of thing a killer would be interested in, does it?'

'I'm certain she's not involved, Sarge. She's done them for someone else, and I'll bet she has no idea what they were for.'

'That may be the case, but it would be helpful if she could remember who the hell asked her to do them. And sweetly barking as she may be, don't rule her out yet, okay?'

'Shall I try her again?'

'Not just yet. Help Max try to get a handle on Fleur first. She's a vital link.'

'Will do, Sarge.'

'We are just taking the psychologist, Professor O'Byrne, out to see Windrush, but ring my mobile if anything interesting shows up.'

'Okay, but one thing before you go.' She handed Marie a brown envelope. 'This came for DI Jackman, it's from forensics.'

Marie took it over to where Jackman was deep in conversation with Charlie Button.

'Open it, would you, Marie? I'm almost finished here.'

She skimmed though the memo and felt a surge of frustration. It was a short report on the findings from the drinking club venue at the old chapel. None of the dozens of samples taken had matched any known offenders. Well, at least they had new samples on file, and could use them to tie in any suspects — including one of their own.

'We are ready when you are!' Jackman called out to the professor. 'Get ready for your trip to the nastiest Children's Ward you'll ever see.'

# CHAPTER TWENTY-SIX

As they drove out towards Roman Creek, Jackman and Henry O'Byrne talked about murderers, and what might bring someone to the point where they took another person's life. Jackman mostly listened.

Approaching the lane that led to Windrush, Henry said, 'I don't believe that anyone is born evil. I do think that some people lack the capacity to understand the consequences of their actions. If they are exposed to cruelty at an early, impressionable age, and then continue to suffer violence, neglect or abuse as they grow, then they become desensitised. They become conditioned to believe that violence is an acceptable way to express their pent-up anger.'

'Do you think our killer is someone like that?' Jackman asked.

The professor shook his head. 'Oh I'm just generalising. I need to see a lot more before I start making any judgements.'

They were waved through the gate.

Marie was pensive. 'Even after years in this job, and having seen some terrible things, I'm still amazed at what people are capable of doing to one another.'

The professor turned and looked at her with an expression of great sadness. 'Sergeant Evans, when a person lacks empathy, and sees others as objects rather than human beings, they are capable of *anything* and will experience no remorse whatsoever.'

Jackman gazed out of the windscreen. What complicated animals humans were! 'In our job,' he said, 'we deal with simple criminal activity, but you have to contend with people in confused mental states. How do you cope, Professor?'

Henry O'Byrne smiled. 'The same way you do. It's a job. It pays the mortgage, clothes and feeds us. We may be passionate about what we do, but it is not our whole life. I'm betting that you have friends and family, and love nothing better than spending time with them.' His smile broadened. 'And it helps that we know the difference between right and wrong, as do most people. I like to believe that most people are pretty decent, all things considered, and we happen to deal with a very small minority.'

Jackman opened his door and got out. 'It's nice to meet an optimist. It's quite refreshing. Believe me, optimists are all too rare in the police force!'

Inside the house, the professor looked around him. 'I bet this was quite something once. Such a shame it's been so neglected.'

Jackman's phone rang.

'Jackman? It's Rory Wilkinson. Are you free? I have something that you should know about.'

'Fire away. Your friend Henry O'Byrne and I are out at the scene.'

Rory sounded excited. 'Jackman, I'm almost certain that none of our victims were actually killed in that underground room. They were all killed elsewhere and brought down the tunnel to the ward, using the old trolley that we found close to the door. There were tiny particles of cloth and fabric caught on splinters in the rough wooden base of the thing.'

'So we are looking for another site where the actual killings took place?'

'I'm afraid so.'

Jackman asked the question he'd been dreading. 'Do you know if the victims were sexually assaulted?'

'With the older bodies it is impossible to tell yet, although Jan Wallace has compiled a very detailed report on the first girl, the one we know as Fleur. She's a completely different story and I'll leave Jan to talk to you about her. Some of the more recent ones had certainly suffered sexual assault and possibly rape, although not all of them. The younger ones seemed to have escaped that fate.'

'I wonder why Emily wasn't already dead? She was drugged, and had certainly put up a fight at some point, from the state of her feet and her torn clothing, but she was still alive.'

'I guess the murderer thought he'd killed her. You said yourself that her signs were very weak.'

That was true. Jackman had felt nothing in the way of a pulse.

'Jan Wallace says she will be calling you, if that's alright?'

'Just in case we are still down in the chamber, get her to ring the CID room. They'll take the details. And, Rory, we've had a lot of response from other forces regarding the girls' identities, but we can't say that any of them are hundred per cent positive until we get the DNA results. Any idea when that's likely to be?'

'It is not a straightforward, simple process. But because of the number of victims, I'm using the university and a private lab run by a colleague of mine. They deal mainly with paternity testing, but have volunteered to chip in. I can't tell you exactly when they'll be back — hopefully not long, but I'll fast-track anything of real urgency.'

'Make Fleur the number one priority, will you?'

'She already is. You'll realise why when you speak to Jan Wallace.'

Jackman ended the call and was suddenly overcome by a feeling of unease.

'Right, Henry. First stop, the crime scene.'

The professor doffed an imaginary cap. 'Lead on.'

They spent almost an hour underground, and the psychologist was silent for most of the drive back to the station.

'Such method!' he said suddenly. 'Everything planned and laid out so perfectly. A tidy, methodical mind. Even the beds are exactly the same distance apart. I'm certain that if you measured those gaps they would be perfectly equal.'

'What does that tell us?' asked Jackman.

Henry O'Byrne took a deep breath. 'A lot. The whole setting spoke volumes.' He turned in his seat and faced Marie, his eyes shining with excitement. 'I think I can show you more about the man who engineered all that than you would ever hope to get from one of your profilers. I never imagined that we'd find such a beautiful blueprint of the mind.'

'You said 'he.' You're certain it's a male?' asked Jackman.

'Without a doubt.' And Henry lapsed back into silence for the rest of the journey.

* * *

When they returned to the CID room, Max told them that "the archaeologist woman" had phoned. Marie rang back immediately.

'I know you're busy, Detective,' said Jan Wallace, 'but I was wondering if you could come over to the mortuary. I've got a lot of information regarding your earliest victim, Fleur. Some of it is quite complicated and needs explaining in person.'

Marie winced. 'I'll try, but could you give me the basic details now, and I'll get there as soon as I can. We're up to our necks here.'

There was a pause. 'I understand, but you should know that I counted twenty-seven different bone injuries on that young woman. After studying the pathology of her bones, I found them to be severely lacking in minerals, and as the analysis showed malnutrition and anaemia, I believe she starved to death.'

Marie hadn't expected that.

'I can also confirm that she was indeed disinterred. However, and this is quite remarkable, most of the skeleton is still present, just some of the very smallest bones are missing. She was fifteen when she died, which is what the name plaque says. There is quite a lot more, Sergeant, when you have the time, although nothing as important as what I have just told you.'

'Look, I really appreciate your help, Professor Wallace, and I'll get over to see you just as soon as I've tied up a few things here, okay?'

She replaced the phone, her brain running riot. 'Starved to death?' she whispered to herself. 'And exhumed after burial? What was going on?'

Rosie sat down next to her. 'You look a trifle perplexed.'

'And so will you, flower. Listen to this.' She called to Max and Charlie, and relayed Jan Wallace's information.

'Bloody hell,' said Max. 'I know I'm supposed to be the detective, but what the hell is this all about?'

No one answered.

\* \* \*

As soon as Jackman emerged from his office, Marie brought him up to date on what Jan Wallace had found.

'Get some refreshments organised for the professor, Marie, and tell the team to come to my office. The prof is going to give us his thoughts, and then you really should go and talk to Jan Wallace.'

A few moments later they had all gathered in Jackman's office. The professor began.

'Earlier, DI Jackman asked what the murderer's very particular attention to detail meant. Well, there is an enormous difference between an organised killer and a disorganised one. The organised killer is usually of average or above average intelligence, forensically aware and careful to select a location in which he feels comfortable. He chooses his times carefully, is well prepared, and likes to feel that he is in control. The disorganised killer, on the other hand, is often of lower intelligence, acts spontaneously, and uses whatever comes to hand, so the scene that he leaves behind him can often reflect his disorganised state.

'So our man is organised?' said Marie.

The professor tilted his head to one side. 'Obsessively. He had taken great care of his victims. There were no instruments of torture, no restraints, nothing to scare or threaten. Everything was clean and tidy, down to the flowers and neatly stored clothes. According to the photographs, the bodies were undisturbed and made to appear comfortable and peaceful.'

'That ties in with what the pathologist has told me. Forensics found nothing to show that they had been killed there,' said Jackman.

'Everything in that chamber contradicts the fact that the girls were drugged, abducted, beaten, possibly sexually assaulted or raped, and then murdered.'

'Could he have some kind of split personality?' asked Charlie.

The professor nodded. 'Multiple personality disorders are very rare, but it's a possibility. He would have different characteristics and skills, and the two personalities would most likely not be aware of each other.'

Jackman rubbed at his temple thoughtfully. 'What would trigger the transition from one state to the other?'

'Generally trauma of some kind.'

'That would fit,' Jackman said. 'After he's murdered his victim, the trauma of what he's done causes the second, nurturing personality to take over.'

'It would be very, very unusual, but not impossible.'

'So where would he initially take his victims after he'd drugged them?'

'I would suspect somewhere close by, but not the house. There was too much going on there with all the building work, and he could have been seen. And we know that he used the tunnel from the marsh to access the room, so I'd say look within a mile or so of the tunnel entrance.'

'And if our murderer is Micah Lee, that is where he could be hiding,' added Marie.

'I can't believe that he'd go back there, with half the police force out looking for him, but we can't take the risk. We'd better get a search party out to the marsh and the surrounding fields before darkness falls.' Jackman glanced at his watch. 'And we don't have long.'

Max jumped up. 'I'll go and alert uniform.'

'Just make sure that Windrush remains under careful guard, Max. I want new officers brought in. We can't afford to leave Windrush unprotected.'

'Wilco, sir.'

Marie looked at Jackman. 'And Jan Wallace?'

'Better hold off until we get this search underway.'

Max hurried from the room and Jackman turned back to the professor. 'Do you really think we are dealing with a man with two personalities, Henry?'

'It would answer a lot of questions. I'd like to know how this progressed, so we have to know everything we can possibly discover about that first body, the one you call Fleur. Especially if she wasn't murdered.' He drew in a breath. 'And, DI Jackman, regarding what you said earlier about not going back to Windrush? Not only is it well

242

documented that killers like to return to the scene of their crime, you ought to know that as an organised criminal comes to the end of his career, he often descends into chaos. His mind cannot go on being calculating and clever forever. He is under constant pressure, and begins to break down. That's when he makes mistakes and gets caught.'

'So you think it's possible that he will find his way back if he can?'

'He is by now in turmoil. His mind will be a vortex of anger, hate and confusion. The world has turned on him, and he knows there will be no happy ending. He'll go back because he has nowhere else to go. And even if he is breaking down, there's a very good chance that he'll think he is clever enough to take on the entire police force.'

As he began to digest this information, Jackman heard Rosie's phone ring. She walked quickly over to him.

'That was Gary, sir. Apparently Ethan Barley has been dragging his brother Nick round all the sleazy bars and low spots in the area in an attempt to find the man who paid him to copy the chapel key.'

'And they got lucky?' Jackman felt a surge of excitement.

'They did, sir! He rang Gary from a grotty dive on East Street, in Harlan Marsh. Gary's tailing the man now. He can't afford to bring him in because it would mean the next party would be cancelled, and then we might lose our chance to take Cade down. Gary's going to keep tailing him and find out who he is and where he lives.'

'Excellent, but we need to be very, very careful. *Nothing* about this must reach Cade's ears, or we're snookered. And that *cannot* be allowed to happen.'

Jackman looked across to see Marie staring at him. She desperately wanted Cade to pay for something he had done in the past. Jackman just wished he knew what it was.

## CHAPTER TWENTY-SEVEN

A team of uniformed officers were now scouting the area around Roman Creek, so Jackman and the team pressed on in the CID room.

'Should we bring in that vet for questioning?' asked Max, munching thoughtfully on a sandwich. 'We've decided that Elizabeth Sewell couldn't be our killer, yet she knows someone called Fleur, *her* cards are in that hellhole, and she's written almost identical cards for the animal cages at Philip Groves' veterinary practice.'

'He's got a point, sir,' said Rosie. 'Even though I cannot see that man being a cold-blooded killer.'

Jackman stared at his sandwich and put it down. 'Maybe we should. He does live close to the marsh, and if we are looking at a split personality, then who knows? How would we know what to look for?' He looked across the room to where Marie sat a little apart from them, deep in thought. 'Penny for them?'

She looked up. 'Not worth it. My thoughts are about as clear as sump oil.' She leaned back in her chair, stretched, and said. 'Okay. Twelve dead girls, all born on a Wednesday. In the same room, another dead girl, but she died of starvation. One girl, Toni, abducted and lives. One other girl, Shauna, abducted and dies, but in a totally different place. Two out of three spoke of a man with dead eyes. Have any of us seen anyone with "dead" eyes? No, we haven't. Micah Lee has a horrible face, but his eyes are deep and very expressive. Benedict Broome has perfectly normal eyes. Elizabeth Sewell is a woman. And not *one* of the people that we've interviewed, and we've spoken to quite a few, had weird eyes.' She groaned loudly. 'And who the hell is Fleur?'

'It all comes back to her, doesn't it?' Jackman said.

'There is absolutely nothing on record of anyone by that name going missing,' added Max miserably.

'What am I missing?' Gary breezed in with a smile on his lips. He looked around and the smile faded. 'Well, I see things are not too good here, but at least I have a name and an address for one of the drinking club organisers. It's Brendan Keefe, and he lives on the outskirts of Harlan Marsh town. He's ours for the taking, when we are ready.'

'Good work, Gary. I suppose he didn't have strange eyes, did he?' asked Jackman hopefully.

'Shifty, sneaky, piggy, but strange, no.'

'Pity. Sit down.' He pushed across his untouched sandwich and said. 'We are still trying to fathom out who Fleur might be.'

Gary picked up the sandwich. 'Ah.' He bit into it gratefully, chewed and then said, 'Not a very common name, although—'

A civilian entered the room.

'Sorry to bother you, DI Jackman, but the duty sergeant thought you should know that the body of a white male has been found out on the edge of the marsh. It seems that it's a hanging, but because of its location he thought it might be of interest to you.'

Jackman sat bolt upright. 'Where exactly is the location, Constable?'

'The old mill at Goshawk End.'

Gary said, 'I know it! It's between Roman Creek and Hurn Point, and right inside the area we're searching for Micah Lee.'

Jackman was already halfway to the door. 'Then you come with me, Gary, and you too, Max. It'll do you good to get some fresh fenland air. Once in a while you need to break that chain that attaches you to your computer.' He smiled at Marie. 'And you can have a break from dead people. You and Rosie keep chasing Fleur. Have another word with Jan Wallace. There might be something new from the forensic point of view.'

'I wonder if it's Micah who has killed himself?' said Marie, almost to herself.

'It could well be. Don't worry, I'll ring in and let you know.'

\* \* \*

There wasn't much to see at the old mill. But what they did see was surprising.

The body wasn't swinging slowly on a creaking rope. It was lying in a crumpled heap on the dirty floor, surrounded by broken vegetable crates.

'One body, life undeniably extinct, with rope still attached, and it's not Micah Lee,' murmured Jackman.

'Some sort of fight took place by the look of all this mess,' said Max.

Gary shook his head. 'Don't think so. It looks to me as if he climbed up these boxes . . . No, that's not right. They are too far away from the body.'

'And how did the rope become detached from the timber spar?' Max stared up to the heavy beam. 'It seems sturdy, and it doesn't slope downward.'

Jackman stared at the dead man. He looked at the twisted body, thankful that the face was turned slightly away. 'I think the question we should be asking is how did a dead man loosen the rope from his own broken neck?'

'Ah, right. So who was here with him?' asked Max.

'If they tried to save him, then it had to be someone who cared.' Jackman looked at the configuration of the old vegetable boxes, the timber beam, and the man's body. 'I'd say someone came in and found him, and then climbed up the pile of boxes and pulled the rope free of the beam. And because no one phoned this in or called an ambulance, I would guess it was someone who wanted nothing to do with the police.'

'Since the body isn't Micah Lee, could it have been Micah Lee that found him?' said Gary. 'I wonder how long ago all this happened? I'll get a shout put out that Lee may be somewhere in the area and on his toes. There are only so many places he can get to from here.' Gary moved towards the door.

'Could he get to Windrush on foot?' asked Jackman.

'He could. But it would mean crossing a pretty bad stretch of wetland, best not attempted unless you know the paths well.'

'But he worked close to here, didn't he?' ventured Max.

'And if he knew the marsh that well, then maybe he knew about the tunnels,' Jackman mused. 'Right now we should get back. There's nothing we can do here. Uniform will keep this place sewn up until our overstretched forensics department can sort that poor sod out and work the scene. We don't even know who he is. There is no ID on him.'

As they walked back to the car he wondered why the man had chosen to take his own life. The word that kept coming up was "guilt." Guilt or desperation. Surely it was no coincidence that a man should kill himself in such close proximity to the crime scene? There had to be a connection. Perhaps he had done it out of despair at losing his precious girls?

'I suppose it *is* suicide?' said Max softly. 'He could have been assisted.'

'I don't think so. Looking at the inverted V-shaped furrow in the victim's neck left by that rough rope, I'd say it was definitely a deliberate, and in his case successful, suicide.'

Jackman glanced back at the derelict old mill. All that was left of it was a shell of old bricks and a weather-beaten wooden door. It must have had sails at one time, but they had long gone. And luckily it was nothing like his lovely home at Mill Corner.

* * *

'There's someone asking for you, Marie.' The desk sergeant pointed to a young woman sitting in the foyer.

Marie was about to tell him to get someone else to deal with her, when she recognised Asher Leyton's fiancée, Lynda Cowley.

Marie went over and sat next to her in the almost empty foyer. 'Miss Cowley, isn't it?'

The girl nodded. 'I'm so sorry to bother you, Sergeant Evans, but he's disappeared.' She tried to hold back her tears. 'Asher didn't come home last night, and he's not been at work today.' She dabbed at the perfect make-up around her eyes. 'It's not like him, he's so thoughtful. He'd never go off without telling me. Something has happened to him, I know it.'

Marie thought quickly. Asher Leyton had talked to the dead girl, Shauna Kelly, on more than one occasion. *And* he had been warned about curb-crawling. They had talked to him about Shauna's death, and now he had gone missing.

'When did you see or speak to him last?'

'Lunchtime yesterday. He rang to say he had a late appointment, but he'd be home for supper.' She began to wail. 'But I went to bed really late, and he never came home.'

248

Marie promised to make some enquiries. 'I'll do what I can, but he's a responsible adult, so you do understand that I can't register him as missing?'

Lynda nodded and left the station, still crying.

Marie walked over to the desk. 'Danny, get one of your crews to go have a word with the old toms down on Dock Lane, would you? See what they can tell you about a man named Asher Leyton. And maybe put an alert out on him. I'd like to have a quiet word with that young man.' She gave the sergeant a description of Asher and made her way towards the lifts.

Things were speeding up. In fact the flood of new developments was threatening to drown them. Time to find Jackman and tell him about this latest worrying event.

\* \* \*

As evening approached, another call came in.

Gary's voice was sombre. 'Uniform may have found your second crime scene, sir. It's an old caravan on a piece of land attached to the Windrush estate. The problem is they only found it because it was on fire. There are men down there and a fire chief in attendance, but there's no way they can get an appliance out there. It's just mud and cabbages all the way to the marsh.'

'Who does it belong to?'

'The land belongs to a tenant farmer called Smith, but he says the old van was there long before he took it over.'

'Was anyone in it?'

'They don't think so, although it's impossible to say for sure until they can get inside. The farmer is trying to get a tractor and irrigation hose down there, but it's taking time.'

Jackman saw their crime scene going up in smoke. 'Come on, Gary. Even if it is burnt to the ground, we need to see this.'

'Okay, boss. I'll let them know we are on our way.'

\* \* \*

249

As Gary drove, he had the feeling he had forgotten something important. The others talked and tossed theories around, but Gary remained silent. Things were racing away from him, and he was getting left behind.

They parked and trudged over the ploughed field. There was little left to see other than a charred wreck of twisted metal and warped panels.

The fire officer who met them looked grim. 'I'm afraid it's not good, sir.'

'Someone died in there?' Jackman asked.

'No, no bodies. But I did find blood evidence, and from the assortment of paraphernalia inside, it looks like you have a particularly nasty crime scene here.' He grimaced. 'What's left of it.'

'What kind of paraphernalia?' Marie asked.

'Well, it's all badly burnt, but there are the remains of leather restraints, and other leather items, a black full-head mask and some other weird stuff. There are chains with ankle and wrist cuffs, all bolted to the base of the caravan. More is showing up all the time, but it's still smouldering and it's too dangerous to stay inside for long.'

'I assume that it was started deliberately?' asked Jackman, his voice slightly shaky.

'Oh yes. We found the remains of a LPG gas bottle with the valve open, and we could tell that an accelerant was used in the bedroom area.'

So, thought Gary, someone has done a clean-up job. Getting rid of the evidence, and covering up for themselves, or someone else. He stared at the smouldering ashes and smelled the acrid stink of burning rubber.

'It all fits, doesn't it?' said Marie. 'He takes them to the caravan, does whatever he does, then kills them.' Her face was taut with anger. 'And then the bastard takes the bodies over the lower marsh path to the entrance to the tunnel, loads them onto the trolley and wheels them down to the Children's Ward.'

'To sleep forever,' whispered Gary. 'Or so he thought.'

'You know what I find worrying?' said Jackman quietly. 'That the beast who did all this could be watching, as the last flame consumes his torture chamber.'

They turned from the burnt-out caravan and walked back to the car. 'I think we should go up to Windrush and get a report from uniform. We no longer need men combing the area for the second crime scene, so it may be wise to get some extra manpower around the house and the tunnels. Just in case the killer does what the psychologist said, and returns to his lair.'

## CHAPTER TWENTY-EIGHT

Marie had always loved the marsh evenings. The sky was a breathtaking display of colours and the misty shadows that spread across the water were otherworldly. Even the sounds were peaceful. Bird calls, the rustling of small animals in the undergrowth, and the wind making the tall reeds sway and dance.

But tonight was different. Every shadow concealed a hidden threat, and Marie sensed something dark and menacing drawing closer in the wind off the sea.

Jackman and Gary were busy checking the security status with the uniformed sergeant, and Rosie and Max were speaking to some of the foot-soldiers.

Marie walked across to a low wall that edged the garden. It looked over the wetlands and out to where the marsh met the Wash. She could see dozens of lights and a multitude of police officers silhouetted against the evening sky, all returning from their hunt for the murderer's killing ground.

She sat down in the shadow of one of the huge old oak trees that formed a barrier between the garden and the countryside beyond, and wished that this awful case would end.

More than anything she wished they could identify Fleur.

Her phone started to play its lilting ringtone. It sounded like falling rain, reminding her of the Welsh hills.

'I just needed to know that you are safe.'

Her mother's voice made her smile. 'Yes, your daughter is safe and well.'

'And I'd like you to stay that way, sweetheart. Is it a bad time to call?'

'It's fine. There's no one I'd rather have a call from, believe me.'

'I got the feeling that your difficult case had turned into a nightmare. Am I right?'

'Spot on, Mum. This is one I really need to see the back of.'

'Well, I know you can't talk about it, but I'm wondering if you'd like me to come and stay for a few days?'

'There is nothing I'd like more, but I'm going to say no, Mum. We are so busy that I'd never see you.'

'Then take great care, and remember that I love you.'

'Don't I always?' Marie said. 'And I love you too.' She smiled and hung up.

Marie had very good instincts, good peripheral vision, pretty fair hand-eye coordination, and the ability to make an instant evaluation of a situation and act accordingly. In other words, she was a copper and a motorcyclist. So, when she saw the slightest flash of a reflection in the screen of her mobile as she hung up, she knew that all was not well.

Jackman was some way away talking to the uniforms, and Gary was leaning on a car and speaking into his mobile. Rosie and Max were over by the house, so she was alone. Or should have been.

Marie made a sideways dive, hopefully away from whoever was behind her.

He cannoned into her with all the force of a charging rhino. Her swift movement had unbalanced him, and they both found themselves on the ground at the base of the wall.

Micah was first up, with surprising speed, and he flung himself back at her, hands outstretched towards her throat.

She twisted away and rolled onto her side, but he grabbed and held onto her wrist. The grip was a vice locked shut.

Marie let out a cry, but his other hand went across her mouth and cut it off. She felt her teeth slice into the soft flesh inside her lips and cheek.

'You bitch! You destroyed everything! Now let's see how your family likes being torn apart.'

Marie was hardly able to breathe. So I'm going to die, she thought, just like that.

Then the grip slackened, gradually. The blood rushing through her veins made a roaring sound in her ears. The hand across her mouth began to shake and loosen, and she gasped.

She choked, fell away from her attacker, and looked up to see Gary wrestling him to the ground and snapping cuffs around his wrists. Micah's face was a mask of pain and confusion. He rocked backwards and forward and moaned as if in terrible anguish.

As far as the cuffs would allow, Micah curled up into a tight ball. He dribbled and sobbed, and repeated over and over, 'Oh no! Please, please, no!'

Gary hauled him to his feet and called to Jackman to help him. Micah was frog-marched away from her, pushed into the back of a police car and driven away. Jackman insisted that this time he would not go to Harlan Marsh Police Station.

Marie sat for a moment, getting her breath back, mopping at her bloody mouth with a handkerchief, and trying to make sense of what had just happened. Micah had been intent on killing her, but when Gary had got hold of him he'd dissolved into childlike tears. Hardly the reaction she would have expected.

'Jesus! I think we know who our killer is, don't you?' said Jackman. He knelt down beside her and put an arm around her shoulder. 'Oh, Marie, I'm so sorry. I should have stayed closer. We knew he could be out there somewhere. Are you alright?'

'My fault,' she croaked. 'I asked for it. I wandered off.' She coughed, and it felt like she had hot coals in her gullet.

Jackman gently helped her up. 'I'll take you straight to A&E.'

'No hospital.'

'You really should get checked over by a medic.'

'Forget it, sir, you are wasting your breath.' She gave him a pained smile, 'And believe me, I've just realised how precious breath is!'

'You have a lip that makes you look like you've overdosed on Botox. You may need stitches in that.'

'I don't have time, sir. There's something about all this that isn't right. All I need is to get back to the CID room where someone can make me a very strong coffee with enough sugar in it to rot every tooth in my head.'

'Has anyone ever told you that you are the most stubborn and obstinate woman . . . ?'

'Yes, sir, you did, last week, and then again a few days before . . .'

'Shut up, Marie, or I'll get someone to stitch your mouth shut!'

\* \* \*

Bill Hickey was behind with his work. With the boss away, things had backed up, especially the paperwork. He had a small office area in a converted store attached to one of the barns, and although it was late, he decided to stay on and check the invoices. Bill was a methodical man, and the heap of unopened mail was bothering him.

Just as he was throwing the last torn envelope into the bin, he glanced out of the window, and saw a light inside the farmhouse.

The police had left some while ago, telling him that Micah Lee had been apprehended again. Mr Tanner wasn't home yet, so who the hell . . . ? Bill jumped up, grabbed his keys from the desk, and ran around the barn and across to the house.

The front door was unlocked. Bill had checked it himself after the police left, and it had been properly secured then. He frowned, took a deep breath and slipped inside.

He stood just inside the door and heard sounds coming from the upper floor. It sounded as if the intruder was in Tanner's room.

For a moment Bill was undecided what to do. He knew he should call the police, but he was curious to see who it was in the boss's bedroom. He wasn't afraid. Bill had done a stint in the army and he still kept himself in good shape. As he moved towards the stairs, he decided to call the police — after he'd got the burglar by the scruff of the neck.

Bill moved carefully along the landing. He had been right about where the thief was. Tanner's door stood open, and Bill could see a hunched figure directing a torch beam at a large wooden desk in the far corner of the room.

Bill was across the floor and had the man in an arm lock before the intruder even realised what was happening.

He screamed and tried to wriggle away, but he was no match for Bill, who dragged him up and across to the doorway, where he switched on the light.

'What the hell do you think you're doing?' Bill growled.

He was staring at the terrified face of a young man.

'I . . . I . . .' His mouth began to tremble.

Bill frowned. This wasn't exactly your usual type of robber. He loosened his grip a little. 'Okay, what were you after? Money?' He pointed with his free hand towards the jumble of papers and items on the desk. 'Because clearly you were looking for something.'

Again he received no answer. The young man seemed to be fighting back tears.

Bill's frown deepened. The intruder had no bag with him, had nothing stuffed into the pockets of his old check jacket, and seemed totally unequipped for a burglary. Then Bill remembered the front door. Unlocked, but not forced.

He thrust a hand into the jacket pockets, and pulled out an old-style door key. Exactly the same design as the one on his own keyring.

'Who the hell are you?' asked Bill, pushing his captive ahead of him towards the desk. 'Why have you got a key? And what were you doing with the boss's things?' He stopped talking as his eyes fell on the items lying on the desk.

Credit cards, an open wallet, a Filofax, a signet ring. And a passport?

As soon as he saw the name "Tanner," Bill tightened his hold on his captive and picked up the telephone.

* * *

'It's Bill Hickey, sir, he's asking for you.'

Jackman listened to the hurried message, then said, 'Stay there. I'll get some officers over to you straightaway.' He hung up and looked at the others. 'That's the farm manager at Micah's lodgings. He's caught an intruder.' He downed his coffee and grabbed his jacket. 'Gary, ask uniform if they could get a car over there. But from what Hickey just told me, I think our presence is required as well. Are you up to this, Marie?'

'Two more Paracetamol and I'm good to go,' Marie rasped.

* * *

The intruder sat on the end of the bed with his head bowed. They recognised him immediately.

'Asher Leyton?' Jackman said incredulously. 'I think you have a lot of explaining to do, don't you?'

Asher slowly looked up at him. His face was a sickly white, his hair unkempt and his eyes red and sore. 'I've nothing to say,' he whispered.

'Well, I think you have,' said Jackman. 'What is your connection with Mr Toby Tanner? And what were you doing with his belongings? Particularly with his passport.'

Asher shook his head and remained silent.

'Sir?' Marie was checking the items on the desk with gloved fingers. She lifted up the Filofax and turned the pages. 'There's no entry in his diary about travelling abroad, and no mention of tickets or boarding cards or flight information either.'

Jackman's gaze travelled from Asher Leyton to Bill Hickey. 'You said he went to Germany?'

The big man shrugged and looked puzzled. 'That's what he told me. He always made his own arrangements for things like that, so . . . I don't understand.'

'Perhaps *you* could explain, Mr Leyton?' asked Jackman icily. 'Oh yes, and your lovely fiancée has been to see us. She spoke to Sergeant Evans here. The poor girl is worried sick. I'm sure she'll be pleased to know that you're safe.' He paused, 'Although I'm not sure she'll be quite so pleased about the house-breaking charge.'

Asher sank lower into the chair and stared at his hands, clasped tightly together in his lap. 'I've nothing to say.'

As Jackman tried to coax him into talking, Marie checked Tanner's belongings again. There was nothing at all to indicate that he'd gone abroad. She carefully replaced everything in its original position, ready for the SOCOs to bag and tag it, then picked up the gold signet ring. It looked well-worn, so why leave it behind if you were going away? In fact, why take it off at all?'

'Marie?'

'Sorry, sir,' she muttered, placing the ring back on the desk.

Jackman beckoned to two uniformed constables who were waiting by the door. 'Take Mr Leyton to the station, please.' He shot Asher a cold stare. 'He might feel more like talking when he sees the accommodation we have on offer. Not exactly Granary Court.' Jackman turned to Bill Hickey.

'We'll be closing this room up, and I'll need you to call at the station to make a statement, sir.'

Hickey nodded and accompanied the two policemen and Asher Leyton down the stairs.

Jackman frowned at Marie, then down at the passport. 'Tanner never went abroad, did he?'

'No. And he disappeared just around the time we made the discovery at Windrush. I think Mr Toby Tanner and Micah Lee were in this together.'

Jackman looked at her. 'But what on earth has our little curb-crawler got to do with it?'

Marie suddenly blinked. 'Hey! What if they are all members of the drinking club?'

'They could be, couldn't they?' Jackman's eyes widened. 'And one of the prostitutes down at Dock Street confirmed that Leyton was a regular. Maybe life with his beautiful young WAG isn't fulfilling enough for our Mr Leyton?'

'So he gets his jollies with old toms and at illegal sex parties.' Marie smiled, then winced as her split lip opened up again. She dabbed at the bleeding but couldn't stop the smile.

'And Tanner?' Jackman looked down at the signet ring, his eyes narrowing in thought. 'I wonder . . .' He looked at Marie and the light dawned. 'The dead man. That hanged man was dressed in tough, outdoor clothing, strong boots, had no ID on him and no jewellery. But I did see a pale line around his little finger.' He pointed to the signet ring. 'A pinkie ring, maybe?'

Marie exhaled. 'Tanner didn't go to Germany, he bloody killed himself! Either because he couldn't live with the shame, or . . .'

'Or because he knew what was hidden under Windrush!' Jackman exclaimed. 'Time to get back to the station, my friend, but before we go . . .' He walked to the bedside table, picked up a small alarm clock and dropped it into an evidence bag. 'I'll get Rory to cross-check the prints on this with those of the hanged man.' He looked at Marie. 'If we get a match, then I'm willing to bet that Tanner contacted his little friend, Asher Leyton, and let it slip that he was planning on topping himself. God knows how Asher knew he'd be at the mill, but I'm sure he'll tell us in the fullness of time.'

Marie took one last look around the room. 'Asher took Tanner's ID to slow down the identification process. Naming a John Doe can take forever, so I kind of understand that, but why bring them back here?'

Jackman shrugged. 'Are we sure he was bringing them back? He might have been looking for something else, and planned on taking everything with him when he left.' He followed Marie to the door.

'We'll have this place taken apart if we have to.'

# CHAPTER TWENTY-NINE

The CID room was emptying out as more officers went home. But Rosie, Max, Charlie and Gary worked on.

Rosie hung up the phone. 'The boss's on his way back. I'll order the pizzas now, shall I?'

'May as well,' said Max. 'Extra cheese and no anchovies for me, please.' He turned to Gary, 'How about you, Gazza?'

'Er, yes, whatever you're having is fine.'

'You're quiet tonight, Gary. Wishing you were back at Harlan Marsh?' Max smiled at him.

Gary leaned back in his chair and stretched out his arms in front of him. 'No bloody fear! But I am missing something, lad, and it's driving me nuts.' He looked around the office. 'Why would you dig up a body and move it somewhere else?'

'Because I didn't want her found,' said Max immediately.

'But that girl Fleur died of malnutrition.'

Rosie replaced the handset. 'So he starved her to death. That's murder too.'

Gary drew in a deep breath. 'Mmm, I suppose so.'

'Or . . .' said Charlie, scrolling up and down on his computer, 'He *had* to dig her up.'

Gary blinked. 'For what reason?'

Charlie looked thoughtful. 'I was thinking of my mate's dog, actually. He'd buried the dog's ashes in the garden, and then his mum and dad decided to move. He was gutted about leaving the dog behind, so he dug the casket up and took it with him.'

Rosie chewed on a thumbnail. 'That's quite possible. He could have dug her up because something was going to happen to the place where she was buried.'

Gary stood up and paced around the office, stopping at the evidence boards. 'Yes. That is a very good point indeed.'

The phone shrilled out, and Rosie picked it up. 'It's the lab.' She put her hand over the mouthpiece. 'Rory Wilkinson has an urgent message for Jacko.'

'Then I'd better take it, hadn't I?' said Jackman, as he and Marie walked into the room.

'Sorry, sir.' A red-faced Rosie handed him the phone.

'DI Jackman here.'

They all watched him speak, and when he hung up, five sets of eyes were staring at him expectantly.

'Rory has isolated two identical, and viable, prints from the Children's Ward. There is no match on our database, but from their position, they almost certainly belong to our killer.'

'Where were they?' asked Marie.

'One on the underside of one of the hospital beds, and the other on a clothes rail.' Jackman pulled out a chair and sat down. 'And as Marie and I have just sent him some dabs from Toby Tanner's house, we might have answers very soon.' He looked at Marie. 'I'd get you to tell everyone about our adventures down on the farm, but from the look of your face, I guess it really hurts to talk.'

Marie raised her eyebrows and dabbed at her lip. 'You are not bloody kidding, sir!'

While Gary half listened to Jackman, something still niggled away in the back of his mind. It had almost come to him, and then the DI and the sarge had arrived, and his train of thought had evaporated.

'So does this mean we have to let Benedict Broome go?' asked Max. 'We took his prints when we brought him in.'

'Not yet. Just because his prints aren't in the Children's Ward doesn't mean he's not involved, and we still have to wait for forensics to tell us what happened in that caravan.' Jackman shuddered. 'That's one report I'm not looking forward to reading.'

* * *

The pizza arrived and they ate at their desks. The initial excitement of the news about the prints had worn off. They had yet to find a suspect to tie them to. And Marie was beginning to feel the effects of having been bulldozed to the ground by the mammoth Micah Lee.

It was almost too painful to eat, but she needed food. As Marie tried to force down a small piece of pizza, she pondered what Jan Wallace had told her about Fleur's multiple injuries. They were almost certainly the result of serious abuse, but where did you start to look when the girl had been dead for two decades?

She managed some gooey pizza topping, washed down with coffee, and gave up on the crispy base. She couldn't get Micah's words out of her head. "You have destroyed everything." And he had also said, "Let's see how *your* family likes being torn apart." What family? Was he referring to the dead girls?

'You really should go home.'

She had been so deep in thought that she hadn't noticed Jackman watching her. 'It's easing, sir, and there is no way I'm walking out of here before you.'

'Remember what I said about being stubborn?'

'Vaguely.'

There was a shout from the CID room. Marie looked through the open door and saw Gary jump from his chair. Marie pushed the picked-at pizza aside and she and Jackman went out to see what was happening.

Gary let out a shaky breath. 'Sorry, sir, and Sarge, but I've come to a terrible, a really *awful* conclusion.' He swallowed. As the team watched him open-mouthed, he said, 'It's about Fleur, and Charlie's mate's dog — and a new onion processing plant.'

Jackman blinked several times. 'Are you sure you're alright, Gary? That didn't make a whole lot of sense.'

Gary flopped back into his chair. 'We were talking about reasons why you'd dig up a body, hence Charlie's mate's dog. Then Rosie said what if something was happening to the place where the body was originally buried, and I've been racking my brains to think what has had to be pulled down to make way for something new — and that's where the onion processing plant comes in. It's a long shot, but the old house that stood on the site of the new plant had a small family graveyard.'

'They planned to build the plant on the Hurn Point road, didn't they?' said a perplexed Rosie.

'Yes. The ground has been razed but the plans have been put on hold, right?'

Rosie nodded. 'That's right. The residents of the area lodged an objection because of the smell. It's been pending for ages apparently.'

Gary scratched his head. 'Well, it's only just come back to me what used to be on that land.'

Rosie frowned. 'It wasn't a house, was it? It was a riding stable, and it went bankrupt. How does that fit in?'

'I've been trying to remember what was there *before*. There was a big old house on the adjoining plot of land. It's long gone, but it was called Alderfield.'

Marie stiffened and looked across to Jackman. The name was horribly familiar.

Gary continued, his voice hollow. 'Alderfield was the home of Simeon and Charlotte Mulberry. Simeon killed his wife, then shot himself in front of his children.'

Silence filled the big room. Marie's brain danced with confusing thoughts and suppositions.

Suddenly Jackman found his voice. 'Were you on that investigation, Gary?'

'Not exactly, boss. I was at Harlan Marsh when it occurred, but it was such a sensitive case that most of us lower ranks were kept in the dark about the full details.'

'We are going to have to uncover every damned thing we can about that case, especially where that young girl fits in.' Jackman looked at Gary. 'Do you know anyone who'd help us? Anyone who was involved in the original enquiry?'

'Maybe, although whether he'll talk is another matter.' Gary bit his lip. 'It was a bad business, sir. Harlan Marsh dealt with it, well, as far as they were allowed to. Then one evening a special unit arrived, and everything was spirited away. They took evidence boxes, reports, statements, everything, including the DI that was heading up the enquiry. He was moved elsewhere overnight, and a month later, it was like it had never happened.'

'Why?' asked Jackman.

'We never asked, boss. It was made very clear at the time that it was better for us to let it lie.' He shrugged. 'We knew they weren't messing around when the DI, the only man to ask questions, found he'd been posted a very long way away.'

'Do you know where he is now?'

'He retired years ago, but he came back to this area last autumn. He lives at Fosdyke, got a little place on the river towpath.'

'What made it so sensitive?' asked Max.

'The children, Max. They saw Simeon blast their mother across the room, then do the same to himself. It was done to protect the children.'

Rosie frowned. 'Surely there had to be more to it than that? Evidence and investigating officers don't usually get spirited away unless there's either an in-house investigation, or someone's really blundered.'

'Maybe we'd better ask your old colleague, Gary. What's his name?'

'Duncan Hewitt, sir.' Gary ran a hand through his hair. 'But don't hang by your eyelashes. That case was bad news for DI Hewitt, and last I heard he was still bitter as aloes about it.'

Marie began collecting the leftover pizza boxes and throwing them in the bin. 'If we are to find out if Fleur was connected to the Mulberry family and Alderfield, we are going to *have* to get him to talk to us, aren't we?'

'Tomorrow,' Jackman said. 'We've done enough today. We will go and see him in the morning. After we've sorted out interviews with Asher Leyton, Benedict Broome and Micah Lee, if he's not still away with the fairies.'

'Can I make a suggestion, sir?' Gary asked Jackman. 'It might be a good idea not to mention anything about Alderfield, the Mulberry deaths, or ex-DI Hewitt to Superintendent Crooke just yet.'

Jackman's eyes narrowed. 'Don't worry, I wasn't going to. Explaining the simple stuff is hard enough, but telling her that we are sniffing around a closed and highly controversial case? Despite what people may tell you, I really don't have a death wish.'

# CHAPTER THIRTY

A green-gold sunrise lit the fields with a warm glow. Jackman had decided to send Gary and Marie to talk to the retired policeman — Gary, because he had a kind face that the man would recognise, and Marie was a damned good, honest detective. Hopefully Hewitt would recognise that.

They left her car in a small parking area just off the A17, and continued on foot down the towpath. The River Welland was wide and fast-flowing at this point. Years ago there had been rickety old wooden moorings along the bank, but they had been taken down since Marie had last walked this way.

'I used to love walking the dog here when my dad was alive,' she said softly.

'Better way than usual to start the day,' said Gary, swatting at a small fly. 'I assume the interviews threw up nothing?'

'Asher Leyton is staying silent. Micah Lee has been arrested for assaulting me. He's been seen by the doctor, and although he's calmer now, we decided to give him a little longer before interviewing him.' Marie touched her bruised face. 'And Benedict Broome, well, I'm not sure about Benedict. He was very upset when he heard that

Micah had attacked me, but he seemed even more disturbed by the fact that his housekeeper was being questioned.'

'Do you think Broome is connected to the drinking clubs, Sarge?'

Marie kicked at a stone. 'I can't see it.'

Gary watched a cormorant fly slowly downriver, throwing a dark shadow onto the greenish water. 'My mate at Harlan Marsh said that Cade has been "busy with other matters." It seems that his enthusiasm to help you out has waned.' He gave a little snort. 'He was pretty pissed off to hear that Jim Salmon had tried to interview Micah Lee, but interestingly enough, he let it go when he learned that Salmon had got nothing from the man.'

'Surprise, surprise.' Marie looked along the path to where a small cottage sat between two big rectangular fields. 'Is that it?'

Gary nodded. 'Now we just need to get him to talk.'

Duncan Hewitt opened the door, and Marie knew instantly that she was going to need every ounce of persuasiveness that she could muster.

Hewitt was tall, a little overweight, and the red across his nose suggested that he liked his drink. He had retained a full head of hair, and he wore "outdoor" clothes — dark green cargo trousers, a check shirt, and a worn khaki gilet chequered with bulging pockets. He made it quite clear that they weren't welcome.

At first Marie wasn't certain how to tackle him. If she was too nice he would think her patronising, and she was also certain that if she mirrored his belligerent attitude, he'd slam the door in their faces.

She finally decided on a detective to detective approach, throwing him enough tempting little tasters to make his natural copper's curiosity kick in.

And somehow it worked. Ten minutes later, she and Gary were sitting in cane armchairs and sipping strong tea in a neat little hexagonal conservatory.

'I swore I'd never talk about it again,' said Hewitt. 'But,' he gave a gruff sigh, 'The damned memories never leave me be, so what the hell?'

'Our own case is harrowing,' said Marie with feeling. 'A body count of thirteen young women.'

Duncan Hewitt whistled through his front teeth. 'That is bad. So, what can I tell you?'

'What really happened in Alderfield, sir?' Gary spoke softly.

Hewitt gave a snort. 'I'd love to know!' He placed his mug on the cane table and sat back. 'I'll tell you what we saw, *and* what I suspect, and what you do with the information is up to you — except,' and he stared at Marie, 'it never came from me. Is that understood?'

Marie and Gary nodded.

'Alderfield was a good-sized country house with quite a few acres of land. When we got the call, we weren't sure what we'd find, because it was one of the children who dialled 999.' Hewitt swallowed. 'We found Simeon Mulberry in the entrance hall, a double-barrelled shotgun beside him. His wife, Charlotte, was lying at the bottom of the stairs. They had both been shot in the head. The gun had discharged both barrels, and two shell cases were found close by.'

'And the children?' asked Marie, not sure if she really wanted to hear the answer.

'They were all there. Silent as the grave. White faces, and terror in their eyes. Some had blood on them.' Hewitt looked into the distance, as if he were back in that old house and seeing it all afresh. 'It freaked us out, Sergeant Evans. Totally freaked us out.'

'How many were there?'

'Six children — five boys and a girl. The oldest was in their late teens, and the youngest little more than a toddler.'

'So does anyone know what caused Simeon to snap and murder his wife?'

'Maybe I should tell you about that man before we go on.' Hewitt's eyes darkened. 'To the outside world, Simeon Mulberry was an astute businessman with the Midas touch, and he was clever enough to make friends with a lot of important people. But in truth, he was a perverted sadist who hid his vile activities behind an elaborate façade.' Hewitt stared at them. 'Simeon was the most evil man I've ever had the misfortune to meet.'

'You actually met him?' Gary sounded shocked.

'Oh yes, at some of the formal functions we have to attend as part of the job. He was handsome as a movie star and could charm the birds from the trees, but he had a heart as dark and cold as a frozen cesspit. I'm just sorry that he never came to court, or went to prison, because in prison he would have been justly punished for his actions. The other inmates would have seen to that.'

Marie suddenly had a vision of blood-spattered children. 'What kind of sadist?'

Hewitt's face was full of disgust. 'The worst kind. Beneath the house was a basement room with bars at the small high windows, and locks on the door that would have withstood a mad bull. We found a row of purpose built cages, Sergeant.'

Marie felt sick. This was like listening to a synopsis of some ghastly horror film. But Hewitt had more to say.

'The children themselves never spoke about the abuse that they suffered, but their scarred bodies said it all. At the hands of their own father they had suffered every kind of mistreatment in the book. It was hard to assess the depth of their trauma. On the surface they were remarkably well-adjusted and very intelligent, with the exception of one boy, who had sustained a head injury in early childhood, probably at his father's hand.'

'What happened to them?' asked Gary. 'We were never told anything.'

'They were taken away and protected for a time, then given new identities and new lives. I'm told that they had psychiatric monitoring and support for years, but eventually they went on to lead their own lives.'

Marie stared out of the window, across the acres of farmland. This was not the end of it.

Duncan Hewitt gave her a knowing smile. 'You're waiting for the next instalment?'

Marie nodded. 'You should never have been railroaded out of the county, just for doing your job, so it makes me think it has something to do with all those "important" people that you mentioned? The ones that Simeon cultivated.'

'Well done, well done! Oh yes, there were politicians, councillors, barristers, financiers, *and* policemen. Simeon had sucked them all in. And exposing him as a monster would have been horribly embarrassing, and very dangerous, for some people in important positions.' His voice was bitter. 'I have to say, the cover-up was a masterpiece of skilful manoeuvring. I believed then, and I still do, that I was close to uncovering a connection between Simeon Mulberry and one of our own top brass.' He looked at Marie grimly. 'There was something rotten within our ranks, and my keen nose was getting a little too close to the source of the stink.' Hewitt pulled a face. 'So I was got rid of. But that was not the whole reason. I was the only one to voice an opinion to my commanding officer that Simeon's "suicide" was nothing of the sort. He was "helped," as sure as we are sitting here.'

'Helped?' Marie's eyes widened.

Hewitt looked tired. '*You* know what a copper's instincts are like, Sergeant Evans, you get a feel for something. And there was something not right when we walked into Alderfield that day.' He heaved a sigh. 'Not that I could ever prove it, but everything was wrong. The bodies, the children, the gun. It was all there, just as you'd expect, but . . .' He gave a shrug. 'I wasn't the only one to think this, I was just the only one stupid enough to *say* it.'

'Say what?' asked Gary slowly.

'Some of us believed that the children, having witnessed their mother's death, might have been instrumental in killing their father.'

'The children?' Marie felt slightly dizzy.

'Who else? And could you blame them? That monster had six children, and he abused every single one of them.' Duncan suddenly stood up. 'I've got something, if you'd like it? I call it my memory box.'

In the sunny conservatory Marie felt a chill seep through her body. She hadn't imagined this. Worse still, she had no idea what any of it meant in relation to Fleur, or to the deaths at Windrush.

Lost in thought, she hardly noticed Hewitt return. He handed her a large cardboard box. 'Here you are. It's all yours, Sergeant. My diaries, my notes, a few illicit mementos, all those interesting little things I just couldn't throw away.' He drew in a long breath. 'I hope they help you, but be warned, they do not make good bedtime reading. Oh, and I don't want them back. I was going to burn them, and if you don't take them, I still will.' He looked at her solemnly.

'And I'd rather you didn't come back, because with that box gone, I intend to put the Mulberrys behind me, forever.'

Clutching the box, Marie stood up. 'The senior police officer involved with Mulberry, who was he?'

Hewitt swung the door open. 'I value the few years of life that I still have left to me. And as his seed still flourishes within this fertile land, I won't be sharing that information. Goodbye, Detective Sergeant Marie Evans, and good luck.'

* * *

Jackman called the team together in his office and Marie told them what Hewitt had said.

None of them spoke immediately. Then Rosie said, 'James Cade comes from a family of police officers, doesn't he?'

'Maybe that's not an avenue we should be pursuing. Let's work on what's at hand, that can wait until the time is right.' Jackman sounded serious. 'Now, forensics stated that Fleur had been terribly abused, and because of the close proximity of the disused graveyard at Alderfield, one would assume that she was the Mulberry girl.'

Gary flipped through DI Hewitt's notebook, 'But that's not possible. The only girl was taken into care, and her age is wrong.'

'What were their names?' asked Rosie.

Gary shook his head. 'We only knew of them as Child 1, Child 2 etc. Unless Duncan knew differently?' He took another notepad from the box, and opened it.

'I can find out,' said Max eagerly. 'Can I use your computer, sir?'

Jackman stood up. 'Help yourself.'

Max dropped into Jackman's chair, and they all watched his fingers fly across the keyboard.

'Weird.' He glared at the screen, and typed in more commands. After a few moments he grunted, 'This isn't right, boss. "Access Denied," on a simple birth registration? Why?'

'Because I fear we have wandered into dangerous territory. Max, close the computer down. Where the Mulberry case is concerned, I think we need to be canny from now on.'

'No problem, sir. There are other ways, now I know to tread carefully.'

Gary looked at Max with interest. 'That sounds promising.'

Max grinned. 'I love a challenge.'

'His hacking skills are legendary,' added Rosie. 'But don't tell a soul, or he's stuffed, as far as his job is concerned.'

'I always knew this team was different,' said Gary. 'In fact—'

There was a loud knock.

'DI Jackman!' Clive leaned around the door. His words tumbled out. 'Sir, the duty sergeant says could you go downstairs immediately. Someone has just come in and he says he's responsible for the findings beneath Windrush.'

\* \* \*

Jackman and Marie went immediately to the custody sergeant, who told them that the man had been cautioned and arrested, and they could see him as soon as they wanted.

Jackman paused for a second before entering the interview room. He turned to Marie and said, 'Watch him carefully. See what you can pick up from his body language.'

Marie nodded. She opened the door and they went inside the gloomy room.

Jackman made the introductions for the tape.

Philip Groves was dressed in neat, casual country clothes. 'I would have come sooner,' he said. 'Only I had to make arrangements for my animals. I know I won't be going home again.' His voice was soft and cultured.

'Mr Groves, you have stated that you are responsible for . . . for what exactly?'

'The Children's Ward is mine.'

Jackman swallowed hard. Other than the police and forensics, no one had been informed of what lay beneath Windrush. He asked Groves to tell them what he knew about it.

'It lies beneath the ground and is approached from an old Victorian tunnel from the marsh. There was no one else out on the fen at night, as I told your detectives, and I'm sorry I lied to them. I was the one out there.'

Jackman looked at Philip Groves and tried to find one thing that told him he was sitting opposite a ruthless killer. There was nothing.

'I took the girls along the passage on a trolley, then into the ward, and so to bed.'

Jackman saw the confusion on Marie's face. 'Did you . . . did you sing as you went?'

'Sometimes. I prepared the place years ago. Windrush was empty for some time before it was won in that wager. I used to wander around there a lot. That was when I found the tunnel from the house, and I found all those old beds and lockers too. They were ready to be dumped, so I took them down the tunnel and set up the ward. Sadly I had to seal it up when it was finished, in case the new owner stumbled across it.'

Jackman glanced at Marie. Groves knew far too much. So why did he not feel elated at this confession? The murderer had just walked in through the front doors and practically prostrated himself before them.

'We need to take your fingerprints, Mr Groves, and a sample of DNA, if you agree?'

'I have no objection.'

'You also have the right to a solicitor. You can either request your own, or we can get the duty solicitor.'

Groves stared down at the table. 'I don't need one, Detective Inspector.'

'It's your choice, sir, but I really would advise it.' Jackman looked at Groves, and although he still could not see the murderer, he *could* see the man who had placed those vases of flowers beside the beds. 'What was on the bedside lockers, Mr Groves?' he asked casually.

Groves gave a little sigh and looked at Jackman with the saddest of grey eyes. 'I know what you are talking about. Yes, I took them fresh flowers. Check my garden, Detective. The plants will match the ones in the little vases.'

'One last question. The first victim. Her name was Fleur. What can you tell us about her?'

Philip Groves sat a little straighter in his chair. 'I'm sorry, but I don't wish to say any more.'

# CHAPTER THIRTY-ONE

'No, no, no, no! This isn't right!' Jackman paced his office.

Professor Henry O'Byrne followed him with his eyes. 'But what about his statement? It's utterly damning.'

Jackman knew that, but still the alarm bells jangled in his head. 'He knew all about the underground chamber, yes. He'd obviously been in it, yes. I can't argue with that because his prints match the ones that Rory found. But Philip Groves never drugged, assaulted and brutally murdered those girls. He's protecting someone.'

'Maybe, or maybe your young detective's theory of a multiple personality is right, and he's protecting his other self.' The professor scratched his head. 'At least he's agreed to let me sit in on the next interview. Maybe I can shed a little light on this.'

Marie leaned against the wall, apparently lost in thought. Then she said, 'Jan Wallace, the forensic archaeologist, said that whoever placed Fleur's skeleton on that hospital bed had an expert knowledge of anatomy.'

'Like a veterinary surgeon,' Henry O'Byrne murmured.

'Exactly. Like a vet.'

Jackman threw up his hands. 'Maybe it was him! But it doesn't mean he killed her.' He resumed his pacing. Could Groves have killed them? The question wove itself around his mind like a cat's cradle.

'You're thinking that a man who heals tiny kittens and sick puppies couldn't kill, aren't you?' said the professor.

'Maybe.'

'Just remember that he also sticks needles full of lethal drugs into them and watches them die.' The professor's eyes never left Jackman. 'He slides cold steel beneath their soft furry skin and sees their warm blood flow. Don't underestimate Philip Groves, DI Jackman. It might be a big mistake.'

Jackman heaved a loud sigh. 'I know, I know. I just wish I could get my head round all this. And I still believe that Fleur is the key, if only we could identify her.'

'I totally agree,' said Marie, leaning over Jackman's desk and taking a sheet of blank paper from his printer tray. She pulled a pen from her pocket and wrote Fleur's name in the centre of the paper.

'Brainstorming,' said the professor. 'Good idea.'

'I was just thinking about direct connections.' Marie drew an arrow from Fleur to the name Elizabeth Sewell. 'She said Rosie reminded her of Fleur.' Marie wrote the name Philip Groves, and connected him to both Fleur and Elizabeth. The name Benedict Broome followed, then Micah Lee. And then Toby Tanner, and Asher Leyton. Soon the paper was full of names and interconnecting lines.

'And this is helpful?' asked Jackman acidly.

Marie pushed the paper away from her. 'Probably not. I'm going to find Max and Rosie. See if they've had any luck.'

As Marie left, the psychologist pulled the scribbled sheet towards him and slowly ran his finger over the maze of lines. 'Oh, what a tangled web we weave . . .' He tilted his head. 'I wonder what Sir Walter Scott would have made of this little tangle. None of them, and yet *all* of them, woven together.'

* * *

Max was using his own laptop for his unauthorised excursion into restricted territory. A constant stream of numbers, codes and letters flashed up and disappeared on his screen.

Every now and again he looked over to where Rosie sat working. He wished this horrible case was over, because the more he saw of Rosie McElderry, the more he understood where his feelings were heading. But right now, he had serious work to do.

Rosie called across to Marie. 'That was forensics, Sarge. The hanged man is Toby Tanner. The fingerprints are an exact match. They've done DNA testing too, and there's no doubt. And that's not all. As soon as they ran the prints, they hit another match, lifted from the nasty party in Fendyke Chapel.' Her voice dropped to a whisper. 'Respected gentleman farmer Toby Tanner has been slumming it with Cade and his pervy friends.'

Max punched the air and grinned at Rosie. 'So we were right! He was connected to the parties.'

Rosie grinned back. 'That's probably why he topped himself.'

'Did Asher Leyton's prints show up too?' asked Marie.

'No. Just Tanner's, so maybe Asher didn't go to the chapel that night.'

Marie was just about to reply, when Max looked at his screen. 'Sarge! I've done it! Look!' He waved a printout at her. 'You are *so* not going to believe this!'

Marie took the sheet from him and, passing over the "restricted" header, read down the list of names and dates. 'What? Jesus! The boss needs to see this! Come on, you two.'

* * *

Marie's voice crackled with excitement. 'The Mulberry children were called — wait for it — Benedict, Tobias, Micah, Philip, Elizabeth and Asher!' She handed Jackman the report. 'They were all given new families and new lives but for some reason, they all came back here.'

'Because they had to,' the psychologist said softly. 'Those poor fledglings *had* to return to the nest, to find somewhere where they could be together again. They had no choice. Despite the good intentions of the social workers and the courts, they had to find each other again, like moths drawn to a flame.'

Jackman exhaled. 'We need to talk to Benedict. No wonder he was so worried about Elizabeth! She's his sister.'

'And Asher!' Rosie looked aghast. 'It was his *brother* that he found hanging in the old mill! That explains why he is in such a state.'

'And of *course* he had a key to the farmhouse,' added Marie, 'because his two brothers lived there. I'm betting he went there to see if there was anything in Toby's home that might link them to the Mulberry family.'

'Siblings, all of them,' whispered Jackman. He looked at the psychologist. 'Just how damaged could this family be? I mean, looking at Benedict and Philip, they seem to have integrated perfectly into society. One is in finance, and the other is a respected veterinary surgeon.'

The professor shrugged. 'Irrelevant. They will *all* be damaged by what happened to them. Some more than others, but I guarantee that not one of them is normal. I would be willing to stake a large amount of money on the fact that every single one of Simeon Mulberry's children has been traumatised and affected in some manner.' He leant back in his chair. 'You know that the abused can become the abuser. In your job you've seen it a thousand times.'

Jackman had. 'One of them, Asher, has a strong sexual compulsion. Is that the sort of thing you mean?'

'Absolutely. And depending on his mind-set, the opportunities open to him, and the extent of the original damage, that sort of thing can escalate over time.'

'To rape?'

'Usually to sexual harassment, then rape, and finally even to murder.'

Jackman rubbed his eyes. 'Hearing that makes me wonder if the Children's Ward is some kind of twisted family business.' He looked around. 'Where is Max?'

Marie looked out the door. 'He's still on his computer.' She called across to him. 'Max? Is there more?'

'Give me one minute, Sarge.'

Everyone was silent. Henry O'Byrne picked up Marie's graffiti-covered sheet of paper and waved it. 'Tangled webs and deception. It was all here.'

'Except for Fleur.' Rosie's voice was sombre.

'Maybe not, flower.' Max walked in and handed Jackman another document.

'A birth certificate?'

'Wasn't easy, because there was an error in her birth date, but I've located the only girl in this area registered with the name of Fleur, and guess who Mummy and Daddy are?'

Jackman read out the names. 'Simeon and Charlotte Mulberry, of Alderfield House, Hurn Point. My God! She's their sister! There were seven Mulberry children!' He looked at Max. 'Would you check for a death certificate?'

'I'm ahead of you there, boss, but there's nothing. There is no official record of her death.'

Jackman stood up. 'Okay, Max, you've done some totally brilliant work today. Well done.' He beckoned to Marie. 'Prepare yourself, Sergeant. It's time to pay a visit to Mr Benedict *Mulberry*.'

# CHAPTER THIRTY-TWO

'Sir, we know about you and your family's tragic past. Your real family, that is. I have no problem with the fact that you chose not to tell us. You all have new lives with new identities. But now, I'm afraid, the circumstances have changed. Your family history is an integral part of this murder enquiry.' Jackman paused. 'Are you Benedict Mulberry, eldest son of the late Simeon and Charlotte Mulberry of Alderfield House, Hurn Point, Harlan Marsh?'

Marie watched him closely. Benedict's face remained impassive until Jackman mentioned his father by name. She saw a nerve jump beneath his right eye.

There followed a long silence. Marie wondered what thoughts were going through Benedict's mind. His memories must be the stuff of nightmares.

Finally he spoke, and his voice was steady. 'Yes, I was Benedict Mulberry. But I'd appreciate your being so kind as to continue to refer to me as Benedict Broome.'

Jackman nodded. 'I can do that.'

'You know about the others?' asked Benedict.

'Yes, sir,' said Jackman. 'But we felt it only right to discuss it with you first.'

'That's good, that's good.' Benedict sounded infinitely weary. He seemed to have aged since they entered the room. 'You can talk to Philip, and probably Asher, about this. Tell them that you know about us, and I have said it's alright to be honest. They will understand that we have no choice, but if there is any way you can avoid it, please don't confront Micah or our sister, not yet. Elizabeth couldn't cope, and Micah, well, Micah is volatile. As I'm sure you already realise.'

They nodded.

'And Toby. Although he may appear to be tough as old boots, he is as fragile as a butterfly. I would ask you to be especially compassionate when you talk to Toby, Inspector. He may look like a sturdy farmer, but beneath that weathered skin he is still a frightened child.'

Jackman gave Marie a swift look. He had no choice but to tell Benedict what had happened to his brother.

'Benedict, I'm afraid I have some bad news. A man's body was found today, out at the old mill close to your old home at Alderfield. I'm very sorry, but we have reason to believe that the man is your brother, Toby.'

Benedict closed his eyes and clasped his hands together as if in prayer. His voice was soft. 'Oh no. Poor Toby. I always thought he would be the first to go, unless of course Micah lost his temper once too often and got himself killed in a fight.' He sighed. 'Can I see him?'

'Not just yet, sir,' said Jackman. 'I'm sure you'll appreciate that there are procedures to follow. And he will need to be formally identified.'

'How did he kill himself? A shotgun, I suppose. He had two at the farm.'

'He hanged himself.'

'Oh. I'd have thought he would have used the gun.'

Like his father did, thought Marie.

'I'm glad he chose the mill,' said Benedict. 'It was our quiet place. Somewhere we went when things got bad. If I were going to kill myself, I'd go to the mill too.'

'I'm afraid it was Asher who found him. We wondered how he knew where to go.'

Benedict sighed again. 'Poor child.'

Marie thought of the man who slipped away from his pretty fiancé and into the arms of a prostitute.

'What happened to Fleur?'

Jackman's question took even Marie by surprise.

Benedict just sat, white faced, and said, 'She died. She got sick, and died. Why on earth do you want to know about Fleur?'

'Because we found her body in the chamber below Windrush.'

'What? Our father told us she had been cremated!' Benedict Broome pushed back his chair and stared at them.

'Fleur was one of the thirteen young women found there, Benedict,' said Jackman.

Benedict put his hands to his mouth. 'That's impossible!'

'I think you should tell us about Windrush.' Jackman was unrelenting. 'It wasn't really going to be some swanky retreat, was it?'

'Oh, but it was, although not for everyone. It was for us.' Benedict's voice was low and husky. '*Our* retreat! Our home. Somewhere we could be together again, where we belonged.'

'And the bodies? All those dead girls, Benedict? Where did they fit in?'

'I know nothing about them, I swear.'

'Your brother Philip has been arrested for their murder. Did he forget to mention what he was up to beneath your precious retreat?'

'Philip? Oh come now. Forgive me, but you are very wrong there.' Benedict began to laugh. 'DI Jackman, Philip is the gentlest man I've ever known.'

'He has confessed.'

Benedict shook his head. 'I think you need to speak to him again. I can't tell you why he's done such a stupid thing, but believe me, Philip is not your killer.'

\* \* \*

'We are going to have to move our suspects to different stations, now we know they are related.' Jackman rubbed at an aching shoulder. 'But from past experience, and knowing what we know *unofficially*, I'm loathe to let them out of my sight for five minutes.' He frowned. 'We will have to let Asher go. We have nothing to hold him on now we know he had the key to Toby Tanner's place legitimately.'

He and Marie were waiting for Philip Groves to be brought to an interview room.

Marie kept her voice low. 'No one other than the team and the professor knows anything yet. Let's hang fire until we've spoken to Philip again.'

'Ah good, I'm in time.' Professor O'Byrne hurried towards them along the corridor.

'May I still sit in? We have permission from Mr Groves, I mean Mulberry.'

Jackman lifted a finger to his lips. 'It's Groves, okay? And yes, we'd be grateful for your opinion. I'll just ask you to keep quiet and observe, that's all.'

\* \* \*

Philip Groves — Marie still found it hard to think of him as Mulberry — sat across the table from them. He looked hollow, as if all the life had been drained out of him.

Jackman told him what they knew of his past, and about his brother Toby's death.

Finally he said, 'You are right, I didn't kill the girls. I found their bodies and took them to a place of safety.' His voice was soft, gentle, and terribly tired. 'That's all I ever did. I took them from a world of hurt, where people didn't treat them right. I looked after them.'

'They had families, Philip, people who loved and missed them.' Marie spoke softly.

'No they didn't, Sergeant.' He spoke calmly. 'If they had cared so much, their children would not have run away or been left so vulnerable that some man could take them, defile them and kill them. I was their real family. I loved them, and in the end, I was all they needed.'

'How did you find them, Philip?' Jackman asked. 'You don't just *find* dead bodies.'

'Whoever killed them left them in the old ruin on the marsh. In the small cellar room that leads to my tunnel.'

'Who was it? You must have seen him leave the bodies. And *he* must have known what you were doing, mustn't he? He dumps a dead body, then when he returns a few months later with the next one, lo and behold, it's gone!'

Philip shook his head. 'I never saw him, and I have no idea what he thought about the girls disappearing, if indeed he even realised. You saw that derelict building, Sergeant. As far as I could tell, he just opened the door and pushed them through into the darkness.'

'I'm sorry, Philip, but I suggest that you *did* know who it was. You may not have seen him, but from the things he did to those girls, you knew.'

Philip stared down at the table.

'Come on. You are an educated man, Philip. You and your brothers and sisters suffered terrible, terrible hurt at the hands of your parents. You knew that one of your brothers was so damaged that he had the capacity to kill. Didn't you?'

'You were just cleaning up after him, weren't you? Protecting him, like you and Benedict have always done,' Marie added.

'I didn't know who killed my lovely girls, and I didn't want to know. I simply took them home and gave them back their dignity.'

'And is that what you did to Fleur? You took her home?'

Philip's eyes flew wide open and his head came up sharply.

After a moment he said, 'I saw him. I saw our father digging the hole in the family graveyard. He was digging it where we used to bury the animals.'

'You saw him bury your sister?'

Groves nodded. 'As soon as he had finished filling in the grave, I promised Fleur that I would take her home one day. I told her that she'd sleep in soft sheets, in a proper bed, with sweet-smelling flowers at her side. She would never spend another night on the cold floor of a stinking cage.'

Jackman glanced at Marie. She was forcing back tears.

Why would you dig up a body? Gary had asked. Now he knew.

'And you did go back for her, when you knew that Alderfield was about to be bulldozed?'

'I went back as soon as Benedict acquired Windrush. I was going to do it earlier, but I had nowhere to take her that was safe and permanent.'

'You did it alone?'

Philip mumbled, 'Yes, alone. I never told the others about her grave.'

'Why not? You were all so close, surely they would have understood,' said Marie.

'I couldn't add to their distress. How could I give them even more heartbreak to bear? They had been told she was ill and had died. That was enough, especially for the little ones. Only I knew that she had died at our father's hand. It was one burden I had to carry alone.' Philip looked at Marie. 'We have secrets, Sergeant. Each one of us is troubled. We are different from other people and always will be. That is why we needed to have a place of our own. A place where no matter what we did, we would not be judged. The world would be safe from us, and we would be safe from a world that could never understand what our parents had turned us into. Windrush was to be that sanctuary.'

There were things Jackman did not understand. 'But, Philip, you went through university! You are a veterinary surgeon. That takes a lot of doing, many years of study. You are a professional, intelligent, full of compassion and . . .' He ran out of words.

'I'm not an evil man, Inspector, but I grew up in a house of evil. I am a freak.'

'If you didn't kill those girls, what about the name tags over the beds? How did you know their names and their dates of birth? How did you know they were all born on a Wednesday?' Marie spoke so coldly that even Jackman was taken aback.

Philip swallowed. 'I . . .'

'I'll fill in the gaps, shall I?' Marie leaned forward. 'You are the mender, aren't you? You are the healer. You know everything there is to know about your brothers. You knew exactly which one of them had lost control, and you knew why. But this time you couldn't fix him. As he grew up, he became more and more dangerous, didn't he?' Marie's eyes bored into Philip's. 'And he was fixated by girls, little ones *and* older ones, as long as they were born on a Wednesday, like him and his sister. Fleur.'

Jackman looked at her with astonishment.

'Toby killed them, didn't he? He wasn't fragile, as Benedict would have us believe, he was psychotic and an incredibly dangerous predator.'

Philip heaved a sigh and Marie sensed relief in it. 'You have to understand that Toby suffered more than any of us, other than Fleur. I knew that he would never be able to integrate back into society. Benedict and I worked ceaselessly to keep him out of harm's way. Micah lived at the farm in order to watch out for him, but we needed to get him to Windrush. And we were almost there.'

He looked at Marie, tears in his eyes. 'Now he's dead, and it's the answer to a prayer. I'd like to believe that he is up in heaven singing for his Maker, but I doubt that very much. You asked me before if I sing, and I do, we all could, but Toby had a voice that would make angels weep. Sadly, that was the only beautiful thing about Toby. I should have put him out of his misery years ago. After all, I have the knowledge and the wherewithal, but I couldn't bring myself to do it.'

Marie thought about the flowers. She could believe that.

\* \* \*

Marie left to get Philip some water, and Jackman asked him about Asher and his perfect fiancée.

'Asher? He's not a bad boy really. Somehow he managed to come out of our personal hell with a sort of mixed-up, old-fashioned moral code, even if he does have a problem with sex. He adores his girlfriend and respects her wishes, but because of his obsession with sex, he regularly visits prostitutes.'

'And goes to sex clubs?'

Philip shook his head. 'No. Not Asher. The clubs were Toby's hunting ground.'

'Can you tell us anything about them, Philip?' Jackman asked. For the sake of the recording, he added that DS Evans had just come back into the room.

'Not really, other than a few old locations. I tried to stop him, but he was too secretive. He would get a text or a call, and disappear.' Philip sighed. 'I just prayed that none of the girls he met were born on a Wednesday.'

Jackman decided to bring the interview to a close. He told Philip that whatever he was charged with, it wouldn't be murder.

Philip didn't seem to care. He was a husk, emptied out. As they stood up to leave, he said, 'What will they do with my sister?'

'Fleur? When it's over, she will be buried properly, and with dignity.'

'That's good. And, Inspector, my other sister, Elizabeth. Is she safe?'

'She's in a psychiatric hospital. Yes, she's safe.'

'She self-harms. That's her problem. But Benedict looks after her.'

Of course, thought Marie. Those long sleeves pulled tightly down over her hands. That full-length skirt, down to her ankles, even in the stifling heat of the hospital room. She should have known.

Jackman had his finger on the recorder button. 'Philip? How much did the others know? Especially Benedict.'

Philip looked up. 'About?'

'The Children's Ward? The abductions? The drugging of Wednesday's Children? And what Toby did to them in that caravan out on the marsh?'

'Nothing, Inspector. They knew nothing. Ben's whole life was devoted to keeping Elizabeth safe and working on ways to finance the rebuilding of Windrush.' Philip gave a little shrug. 'Although I'm sure he won't be surprised when you tell him what happened.' He let out a long sigh. 'It would have been kinder to put us down when they found us, like a litter of kittens. They should have known that we would never survive in the world. Especially when some of them began to suspect what might really have happened at Alderfield.'

'To your parents?' Jackman asked.

Philip nodded.

'The police believed that you were responsible for both your parents' deaths?' added Marie.

'After what my father *and* my mother put us through, we were no longer responsible for anything.' Philip gave a humourless laugh. 'But yes, they suspected as much. The problem was, the police saw things that no one should. The horror of what they found in that house clouded their judgement. We were damaged then, Detectives, and it was too late to do anything about it. They should have locked us away and allowed us to rot. Then twelve girls would not have had to die.'

One small detail still bothered Marie. 'Can I ask one last question, Philip? We never found any photographs of Toby. Not at the farmhouse or anywhere. Why was that?'

Philip gave a small smile. 'There were very few pictures ever taken of any of us, Sergeant, but Toby had strange eyes. They were so pale that in some lights he looked as if he had no pupils, and the camera always picked that up. He looked either blind or dead.'

Dead eyes.

As Jackman and Marie walked away, from behind the locked door came the sound of the purest voice singing a lullaby. This time it didn't turn their blood to ice, it melted their hearts with sadness.

# CHAPTER THIRTY-THREE

'It's tonight! Ten thirty, location to be advised.' Rosie snapped the phone shut. 'We're on!'

\* \* \*

Rosie and Max slipped out of their car and moved away into the darkness of the tree-lined lane. As she watched them go, Marie felt a surge of emotion. Two of their own were walking into a very dangerous situation, but another woman she cared about might finally be about to get some justice.

Jackman was fastening his stab-proof vest. 'Ready?'

'Everyone is in position.'

'You seem much more relaxed about this now, Marie'.

'I'm fine. Sometimes you need to take extreme measures, especially when you are dealing with someone who thinks they are above the law. If Rosie and Max are up for this, then so am I.'

'Me too.' Jackman moved away from their vehicle and towards the ramshackle collection of huts and outbuildings that were scattered around the old grain store.

Marie came up beside him. 'Max has produced some very tasty spyware for this operation,' she whispered.

'That lad has left nothing to chance. Those designer glasses have a camera embedded in one of the arms, and everything he sees is relayed to the lads in the van. They have an HD digital video recorder and everything is being backed up, along with anything we hear on Rosie's wire.'

'Well, we've sent in the bait. We just have to hope that the big fish will swim in the pool tonight.'

* * *

The grain store had been abandoned years before, and Rosie guessed that it had been chosen because there were no neighbours for miles around.

She smiled lasciviously at the man on the door, and whispered, 'I said, I'd be back, didn't I?'

He nodded and openly stared at her cleavage.

'Hope you don't mind, I brought my boyfriend.' She nodded at Max, who was staring with apparent disinterest at the weird surroundings. 'It seems to me you get more fun here if you have someone to play with.'

'You should have come and found me, sweetie.' He ran a finger down her bare arm. '*We* could have had some fun.'

'You were far too busy, handsome.' She leaned closer to the doorman and whispered, 'Should I leave him behind next time, what do you think?'

'I think that's a really good idea, babe.'

'Petra,' she said.

'Nice name. I'm Lenny.'

'I'll remember that.' Rosie blew him a kiss, draping her arm over Max's shoulder.

After half an hour of drinking and trance music, the partygoers were beginning to loosen up. Max had found what he decided was the optimum spot for people watching, especially the older men that were collecting in the shadows.

'Sorry, Detective, but we need to either dance or snog, unless you want people to notice.' Rosie put her arm around his waist and pulled him towards her. 'You choose.'

'No offence, flower, but dancing will give me more chance to see who's coming and going through that back door.'

'None taken. Groove away.'

'Shit, was it like this last time?' asked Max, watching a couple of kids who looked about twelve, getting busy on a wooden bench.

'You've seen nothing yet, Maxie-boy,' Rosie took a sip from her can of lager. 'Just like I've seen nothing of our bloody target.'

'Maybe he won't show. He knows Toby Tanner is dead, and that he was linked to the parties.'

Rosie leaned over his shoulder. 'No, he'll be relieved that Tanner's out of the picture. Harlan Marsh is under his thumb, and he thinks *we* are far too busy tidying up Windrush to worry about anything else.'

Rosie moved to the thumping beat. 'He won't be able to stay away from his dirty little enterprise.'

Another twenty minutes went by, and Rosie began to wonder what they could do that wouldn't be the talk of the mess room for the next five years.

'Jackpot.' Max moved closer to her, turning her slightly, as if in an embrace. Two men were standing just inside the back door.

'Cade,' muttered Max. 'And bang in my sights. Hope you're seeing this, guys?'

Rosie wound herself around to Max's side. She recognised him immediately. The greased back hair and the glasses were no disguise at all. 'All we need now is to get something on him that he can't wriggle out of.'

The music pulsed and the ravers gyrated around them. 'Rosie! Watch him!'

Rosie leant down, ostensibly to pick up a can from the floor. She knelt for a moment, her eyes trained on Cade, seeing him take a roll of notes from the other man and push them into his pocket.

Rosie saw Cade beckon to a dancing teenager, talk to her for a few moments, and then gently push her towards the man beside him. The girl, with the older man's hand on her shoulder, left through the back door.

'Do we go now?' asked Max edgily.

'Hang fire.' Rosie had seen two girls, who looked totally wrecked, approaching Cade.

'Oh lovely! Keep it up, kids, let's see what he does. Have you got him lined up, Max?'

'Centre stage. This couldn't have gone better if we'd set it up.'

As they watched, the two teenagers flirted with the older man, and to Rosie's delight, he began to reciprocate. First, a kiss, then a hand on a buttock. The hand slid around the girl's tight miniskirt and began to slide beneath the shiny material.

'Gotcha, slimeball! Time to go! All units!'

Rosie and Max threw their beer cans to the ground and, side-stepping the dancers, hurried forward directly towards Cade.

'Perhaps you'd like to come with us, sir.'

Without waiting for an answer, they bundled him backwards through the door and into the back room. 'James Cade, I'm arresting you—'

'Like hell you are!' Cade swung around like a man possessed, and flung Rosie backwards into the wall. The air rushed from her lungs and she doubled over in pain.

'Max! Don't let him get away,' she breathed, clasping her ribs. Max hesitated, staring at her with a horrified look on his face. 'Leave me, you idiot! I'm just winded. Nail that bastard!'

\* \* \*

It was a scene of utter chaos. Blue lights flashed. Men and kids were running in all directions, and the squeal of tyres and engines joined in with the techno music that still throbbed in the old silo. Cade ran out and across the concrete back yard towards his hidden car. Max raced after him. He was fitter and faster, but he didn't have Cade's desperation.

Suddenly Cade stopped, picked up a length of wooden fence post from a pile of rubbish, and swung it straight into Max's midriff.

Max went down like a wounded animal, and Cade ran on, straight into the path of Sergeant Marie Evans.

Marie charged at him, taking him clear off his feet in a perfect rugby tackle.

Cade hit the deck. He scrabbled desperately to get free of Marie's weight. Marie moved back slightly, just enough to allow him to make another attempt to run. Then she hit him.

She felt the impact all the way from her knuckles to her shoulder, and she was glad of it. She rubbed her clenched fist and stared down at the unconscious figure. 'It's not much, Val,' she muttered, as she took her cuffs from her pocket. 'But I hope it makes you feel better. It certainly makes me feel good.'

As she leant over Cade and snapped the cuffs into place, she felt the dark cloud finally lift. Until now she had believed that Cade would never pay for the terrible things he'd done while wearing a police officer's badge. Marie stared coldly down at him. 'Let's see you try to wriggle out of this one, *Chief* Superintendent.'

Gary was at her side. 'I hope you're right, Sarge, but I'll only believe it when I see a new name on his office door.'

Still out of breath, Rosie approached, supporting the winded Max. 'Where the hell did you learn to hit like that?'

'Anger Management Classes, would you believe. Works a treat!' Marie looked at her colleagues. 'And well done to you two! Great job.'

Max grimaced. 'Our pleasure! I reckon it was worth a couple of cracked ribs just to see that haymaker, Sarge.' He grinned admiringly at Marie. 'Just remind me never to upset you!'

'I'll second that!' Jackman stood looking at her in amazement. 'They don't call you Super Mario for nothing, do they?'

'I had something of an incentive.'

'Let's clear up this mess and go home, shall we? And maybe you can tell me what that particular incentive was?'

Marie smiled at him. 'I can now.'

\* \* \*

Marie sat opposite Jackman in his office, a half-bottle of Scotch and two glasses between them.

'I never drink on duty, but in Cade's case I am making an exception.' Jackman poured the whisky.

He sat back and savoured the first sip, then let out a long sigh of relief. 'Talk to me, Marie. You told me that Cade blighted your friend's career, but what did he actually do?'

Marie held onto her glass and stared into it. 'He pestered her, harassed her, belittled her, ruined every chance that came her way and finally broke her spirit. All because she rejected his vile advances.' She took a long swallow and winced as the alcohol touched her split lip. 'Valerie was one of the brightest recruits, full of optimism and hope that she could make a difference. She was intelligent and good-looking, but Cade wore her down. Like a lot of coppers, she would go home and have a drink after a shift, sometimes two or three. And it gradually took hold of her. Everything started to go wrong, and she knew she couldn't hack the job anymore. In the end she threw in the towel and moved away.'

'Marie, I'm so sorry. I had no idea it was that bad.'

'She was my dearest friend. She was to have been my bridesmaid. She got on like a house on fire with Bill, and she was so happy for me when Bill and I got engaged. I missed her then, and I still miss her.'

'Couldn't you get in touch with her? Go visit her, maybe?'

She shook her head slowly. 'It's too late, Jackman. She got drunk one night. Several witnesses saw her stagger out into the road. Ironically, she was hit by a police traffic car on its way to an RTC. She died before she got to hospital.' A tear formed in Marie's eye. 'And although Cade didn't physically kill her, he caused her death as surely as if he had wrapped his fingers around her throat and squeezed.'

'Oh Lord! That's terrible! No wonder you hit the bastard so hard.'

Marie stared at her bruised knuckles. 'Most satisfying thing I've ever done.'

'I'm sure the memory of it will live with him for years to come.'

'Oh, I *do* hope so.'

Clive put his head around the door. 'DI Jackman, I'm sorry to interrupt, but the super wanted you to know that she needs to hold a press conference. She wondered if you would go and prepare Grace Black before this hits the media.'

Jackman stretched and groaned. 'Oh dear! Yes, of course, I will.'

'I'll go with you,' said Marie. 'I just wish we had something to tell the poor woman, but the bodies have all been named now, and there was no Kenya amongst them.'

'At least we can tell her that we will now be concentrating on her girl's case.' He picked up the phone. 'I'll give her a ring and tell her we are on our way.'

When she picked up, Jackman asked if it was convenient to call on her.

'You're a bit late, Inspector. I already know there have been what I believe you call *significant finds*.' She gave a tired laugh. 'I still have my sources.'

'I'm sorry that is the case. We didn't want you to hear it from others first, Mrs Black.'

'I also realise that whatever you have found, it does not involve my Kenya, or you would have been knocking on my door long before this.'

'That is true, Mrs Black, but Kenya will now be our number one priority.'

'Then you call on me when your investigation gets under way. I'm fully prepared for whatever the papers and the television are about to throw at us.'

'I wish I was,' said Jackman sombrely. 'I'd avoid watching the news for a while if I was you.'

'If they were talking about my child it would be different. As it is, I still have hope.'

Jackman thanked her and rang off. 'I think the poor woman is desensitised after so long.'

Before Marie could answer, Gary knocked on the door and walked in, closely followed by Ted Watchman.'

'Good Lord, are you still with us? With everything that you have witnessed recently, I thought you would have high-tailed it back to your university long before this.'

Ted brushed a lock of hair off of his face. 'You can't get rid of me that easily, especially not when there is a mystery still to solve. I've been going over the maps and the underground surveys of Windrush, and I'm worried that we have missed something.'

Jackman glanced at Marie. 'I'm not sure if I can take too many more surprises.' He looked back at Ted. 'I'm not going to like what you are about to say, am I?'

Ted shrugged. 'Probably not, but I'm going to tell you anyway.'

Jackman felt exhaustion creep over him. 'Okay, tell us the worst.'

'It's the gatehouse lodge, at the entrance to Windrush.'

Marie tilted her head to one side. 'But that was checked and double-checked by uniform in the initial search for Micah. All it contains is a bit of old furniture left from previous tenants, and little else. There is no cellar, and apparently the attic has several decades' worth of rubbish in it, but no signs of entry for years, going by the undisturbed dust and cobwebs.'

'Sorry, Sergeant Evans, but I beg to differ. My geophys reports distinctly showed something below that building. I did mention it, although I thought it was a simple cellar. I thought it would have been checked as a matter of course in the police search.'

'It was. I spoke to the officers myself.' Marie looked puzzled.

'Can we check it out ourselves?' asked Ted. 'Only, careful examination of the survey shows what appears to be a short tunnel terminating there. I could be wrong, but I think it was a spur from the tunnel that the old-time wreckers used.'

Jackman exhaled. 'It is almost one in the morning. We can't do anything until tomorrow. But if you think we need to look at this place, Ted, then we'll be guided by you. But until then, everyone home, and for heaven's sake try to get some sleep.'

As they slowly packed up their things and left, Jackman decided that sleep would probably be quite hard to come by. He, for one, was still fired with adrenalin.

# CHAPTER THIRTY-FOUR

'I wish we still had that heat-seeking camera,' muttered Max.

'Bit too pricey to have hanging around, I'm afraid,' Gary said. 'We'll just have to use our eyeballs.'

Officers were slipping silently through the trees and bushes, and taking up their positions around the gatehouse. Jackman had decided that if they were to find more nasty surprises, this time they would be well-equipped to deal with them.

He spoke quietly to Ruth Crooke, who had insisted on joining them to direct the operation. 'Ted Watchman has isolated another underground area. It's much smaller, but considering the terrible things that have been going on here, there is a good chance there may be more bodies.'

'How is it accessed?' she asked.

'From a tunnel that joins the original marsh tunnel. An armed response vehicle arrived a short while ago, and a small tactical firearms unit is already in place at the entrance, just in case.'

The uniformed sergeant in charge walked up to them and addressed the superintendent. 'We are confident that the rest of Windrush is now clear, ma'am. As far as we can tell there are no more accessible concealed places, either above or below ground. The Lodge *had* been searched, but we think that the entrance to the cellar must have been very cleverly hidden.'

'There have been officers in and out of that gatehouse for days now. Do you really think we missed something?'

Jackman looked at her. 'Ted is certain, and that is good enough for me. The lad knows his stuff.'

'After finding what you did in the Children's Ward . . .' The superintendent swallowed. 'Well, we know that the killer is dead and we have two more of the Mulberry family safely locked up, but there is no knowing what might be down there, is there? Take care, won't you?'

'I will be careful, I have two armed officers, and I'll make sure that my team are safe.'

'Good luck, Rowan.'

'We're all ready, ma'am. Everything is in place, not even a starving cat could slide out of that place without us seeing it. We are just waiting for your orders to go in, ma'am.'

'Then get to it, Inspector.'

* * *

Jackman went in first with Marie, Max, and Charlie. They moved around the ground floor as quietly as they possibly could. Their objective was simply to identify the position of the entrance to the cellar. They would not attempt to open it, and there would be no crashing and banging about. The most effective tool they had was their eyes. This time they had the advantage of *knowing* that there was a cellar. They just needed to spot the anomaly that would give the secret door away.

When they finally located it, Jackman at once forgave the first search team for their oversight.

It was in the hallway, a dingy and badly-lit vestibule that reeked of age and neglect. Two walls were panelled in dark wood, and the rest had a thick, badly dented dado rail, with wood panels below and damp-stained wallpaper above. There were coat hooks on one of the full panels, and a tarnished gilt-framed mirror on the other.

Much to everyone's surprise, it was Charlie Button who found it.

They were on their second recce of the place, when Charlie stopped by one of the tall panels looking puzzled. Then he lightly touched the panel with the coat hooks attached, and turned to Jackman, excitement sparkling in his pale eyes. 'Different texture wood and it's fractionally proud of the wall level, sir. I think it's on a pressure spring. Push it firmly and it will spring outwards and slide along.'

His voice was low and Jackman could barely hear him, but when he touched the wall himself he understood exactly what Charlie meant.

Jackman signalled to the others and they melted back through the open front door and into the overgrown garden.

While Charlie explained the precise position of the secret entrance to the sergeant and discussed how best to execute a successful entry, Jackman wondered what might lie beneath their feet.

He remembered the gruesome items that had been found in the burnt-out caravan. Wrist and leg restraints, leather masks . . . He stopped himself.

In a minute or two he would have to be one of the first down into that cellar, and he needed to be ready to cope with absolutely anything. He took some deep breaths, drew himself up and took a step forward.

\* \* \*

The operation was smooth, understated, and very effective.

The door opened onto a narrow staircase. It went straight down, parallel to the hall and ended in a small basement with a low ceiling. They saw rickety shelves with rusted paint cans, mouldering sacks and cardboard boxes eaten away by mildew and the teeth of small rodents. The floor was littered with rubbish, and the smell of decay was overpowering.

On the far wall was another door. It looked ordinary enough, with chipped paintwork and a single lock.

'Take it down.'

Once again the metal enforcer was swung slowly back and forth, and the two armed officers waited to move forward.

And then they were through, and they all halted abruptly.

The room was clean. Spotlessly so. Curtains with a pretty floral pattern hung from a white curtain rod, in front of a trompe l'oeil window. There was a bed with a chintzy tapestry throw over it, and a small writing desk, littered with pens, pencils and paper. Shelves full of books lined one wall, a collection of teddy bears sat on top of a white-painted tallboy, and a stack of colourful jigsaw puzzles stood in one corner.

Over the bed there was a picture of tiger cubs at play. A wooden frame, with a string of pink fairy lights hung from it, forming a bright arch of twinkling ruby lanterns above the pink, padded bed-head.

It was the last thing Jackman had expected.

As he moved slowly around, trying to make sense of it, Marie touched his shoulder and nodded silently towards the far side of the room.

A narrow door, in concertina folds, was moving, very slightly.

The two AFO's, bulked out with body-armour and carrying automatic weapons, moved fast.

For a long moment neither Jackman nor Marie dared to breathe, and then they heard a young voice call out, 'Don't hurt me! Please don't hurt me.'

The firearms officers closed in and one of them ripped back the door.

They saw a bathroom, neat and compact, with a proper toilet, and an old short bath with a modern shower unit over it. Huddled almost underneath the bath itself, was a young girl. She sat on the pink bath-mat hugging her knees, and looked up at them from eyes wide with terror.

Jackman found it hard to stop himself from rushing forward and gathering the child up in his arms.

Marie asked the question for him. 'Kenya?'

'Asher! I want Asher.' The shaky voice was growing stronger. 'Please! Find me Asher! I want Asher!'

* * *

There were procedures to follow, and they were very strict. Jackman knew that he could not just remove the girl from her "home." The regulations dictated that he immediately request a specially trained child victim support unit to assess the situation.

He thought all of this, but what really worried him was why the child was calling for Asher Leyton.

'Door at the back of the linen cupboard, sir! It's still open. It leads to the tunnel! We can hear noises and we're in pursuit.'

The two officers crashed through the small aperture and disappeared. The girl began to scream, 'Asher! Don't hurt him! Please don't hurt him!'

Marie dropped to her knees a few paces from the hysterical girl. 'It's alright. Honestly, it's alright. We just need to talk to him. We won't hurt him.' She took out her warrant card and held it up for the girl to see. 'You understand that we are the police, don't you? We are here to help you, that's all. My name's Marie, and this is Jackman — and you are Kenya Black, aren't you?' She smiled warmly at the child. 'I cannot tell you how pleased we are to meet you.'

The girl rocked backwards and forward, avoiding eye contact, but Jackman saw her nod, very slightly.

Jackman couldn't believe it. She was alive! Kenya Black was alive! After how many years? Eight? Almost a decade, and she was alive and safe.

Jackman stared at her, dumbfounded. She was slim and pretty, dressed in skinny jeans and a T-shirt, and apparently unharmed.

Then his elation faded. He thought of the Mulberry children.

He stared at Kenya, cowering on the floor and rocking backwards and forward. He knew he was out of his depth. It was time to get help.

\* \* \*

Jackman ran back up to the stairs and into the hallway, shouting for a WPC to go down and assist Marie.

His superintendent stood open-mouthed. Jackman knew she was as stupefied as he by what they had found in that strange little boudoir below ground.

'And you say she looks to be in good physical health?' asked the super for the second time.

'As I said, skinny and pale, but I've seen far worse going through Saltern's school gates. God knows what state her mind is in, but physically I'd say she's been looked after very well.'

The superintendent let out a long breathy whistle. 'This takes some getting your head round. I'll have to make an emergency call, Rowan. I'll get some professionals out here immediately. And well done to you and your team. This is not the kind of result anyone ever dared to even dream about.'

*Grace Black did. She never gave up hope,* thought Jackman. Then before he could speak, he heard noises coming from the stairs, a muffled crashing, and shouting.

Marie had told Kenya that they wouldn't hurt Asher, but Jackman had a bad feeling that they might have done just that.

He waited, dumbly, gnawing on the side of his forefinger. He really didn't want to go back down to the cellar. If Asher had been hurt, then he didn't want Kenya to know about it, not yet. The poor kid had had enough shocks.

'Sir?' Gary hurried in through the front door of the lodge. His ashen face told Jackman everything.

'They've shot him, haven't they?'

'He's in a bad way, boss.' He shook his head. 'I was there. It was horrible. He just ran. They gave him all the warnings, but he still ran.'

'But he wasn't armed, was he?'

'No. He did have something in his hand, although it didn't turn out to be a gun. For a moment I thought he would just give up, he seemed so . . . so lost, and so desperate. Then he just ran headlong at our armed officers.' Gary swallowed hard. 'Even then they tried to apprehend him, but a warning shot ricocheted off the wall and hit him in the head. I thought it was game over, but the medics say he's hanging on by a thread.'

Jackman groaned, thinking of the impact this would have on Kenya Black. They didn't know the exact situation yet, but everything indicated that Asher Leyton had been the only living person Kenya had had contact with for almost a decade.

Then *they* show up — and shoot him!

Jackman closed his eyes and fervently wished things had turned out differently. He knew a little about the strange bond that could form between hostage and captor.

Gary was looking at him. 'They say you've found a girl alive, sir. Is that true?'

Despite the way things had turned out, Jackman couldn't hold back his smile. 'Yes, it's true, Gary, and believe it or not, the girl is Kenya Black.'

Tears welled up in Gary's blue-grey eyes and he wiped them with his sleeve. 'Well I'm damned! After all this time.

I just can't believe it.' He looked at Jackman. 'And is she . . . ?'

'Amazingly, she seems fit and well. When they've brought her out, go down and see her room, and where she's been living for the past ten years. You'll be as utterly gobsmacked as I was.'

'It's going to be a while before we piece it all together, isn't it? I mean, everything that happened to her.'

'Let's hope Asher pulls through. The biggest question is, why is she not dead? I cannot understand why she was not lying in a bed in the Children's Ward, along with the others. What made her different?' Jackman shrugged. 'I'd better get back down there and see how Marie is coping. Gary? Would you go to the hospital and keep a close watch on Asher Leyton? If he wakes, and let's pray that he does, ring me immediately, and then write down every word he utters, got it?'

'On my way, boss.'

As he left, Jackman called after Gary. 'You said that Asher had something in his hand? What was it?'

'A child's toy, sir. A little teddy bear.'

Jackman breathed in slowly. When Kenya went missing, she'd had a teddy bear with her. A jointed one, with arms and legs that moved. So it had stayed with her throughout her captivity. A comfort. Something she loved.

And Asher had taken it with him when he tried to get away. A memento?

## CHAPTER THIRTY-FIVE

Jackman read the memo that the super passed across her desk.

> *Kenya Black has been taken to a safe place. She will be cared for while slowly preparing her to be debriefed about her life at the hands of her abductor. It is imperative that she be able to contextualise her experience, for her own sanity and for the sake of others. All relevant information will be available to you, as and when it becomes available to us.*

He didn't recognise the signature.

'Rowan, you are something of a hero to Grace Black.'

'I'm no hero. My team just did their job, that's all.'

'I don't think that's how she sees it. There have been a lot of empty promises made to that woman over the years. Between you and me, I believe that we let her down badly. She told me that you and your sergeant, Marie, were the first police officers that she actually trusted. She felt certain that you would be the ones to give her closure. The fact that you have given her back her daughter has exceeded her wildest dreams.'

'I just wish I knew how much is left of her daughter after all that time in captivity.'

'Early indications are good, Rowan. That is the main reason I asked you up here now.' Ruth gave a rare smile, 'Considering Asher Leyton's psychological problems, in other words his sex addiction, it will probably come as a pleasant surprise to hear that Kenya Black suffered no sexual abuse during her confinement. The medical examination confirms that he never touched her, not once. She's still a virgin.'

Jackman thought about the room in which Kenya had been held. He certainly didn't understand it, but he believed what Ruth Crooke had told him.

For a while neither of them spoke. In their job they were always prepared to expect the very worst, and something as astonishing as this was hard to comprehend.

'And the psychologists are not attributing her affection for Asher to Stockholm Syndrome either. She says that he has been kind to her. And, abductor or not, he has been her whole world for most of her life.' Ruth raised her eyebrows. 'She says he rescued her. We don't know any more than that — after all, it is very early days — but it seems that, considering everything that has happened to her, Kenya is incredibly well-adjusted.'

'So, did he rescue her from Toby Tanner, I wonder?'

'That is one of the first questions she will be asked. We need to piece together some sort of sequence of events. It does not look as though Asher Leyton abducted her for his own ends. He certainly incarcerated her for almost a decade, but for what reason? We now know that she was not a sex toy, and on examining her clothing, we suspect that he took her outside to play. There are traces of soil and plant material in the grooves of her trainers, and our officers discovered newish Wellington boots and a rain jacket in a closet.'

'Kenya is alive, and twelve others are dead. Why?' Jackman mused.

'Bizarre, isn't it? Kenya obviously never entered that nightmare of a caravan. And Philip never took her on that awful last trip down the tunnel to the Children's Ward.'

'Maybe I need to speak to Philip again, ma'am. He could know something about this, although I'm pretty certain that Asher was the only person who knew that the little girl was there.'

'I agree, but go ahead and talk to him if you want.'

'It's Asher I'd really like to talk to.'

'Wouldn't we all, but he's still hanging between life and death. I'm afraid it will have to be Kenya herself who tells us her story.'

'Which will take time,' added Jackman.

Ruth Crooke tilted her head. 'I'm not so sure. She's already talking, something nobody expected. She's confused and fragile, but she's is not in serious traumatic shock, as she would have been if she had been regularly assaulted. It's almost as though she believes she has led a perfectly normal life, and only now has found out that it was quite different to that of other children.'

'He did keep her mind stimulated. You could tell from the things in that room. Games, toys, puzzles, and books by the score.' Jackman drew in a deep breath, and let it out very slowly. 'I'm still having trouble getting my head around the fact that she is actually alive. Her case has been in the background for a decade. Most of us believed that her mutilated body would turn up one day simply by chance. No one imagined that she would one day walk unaided out of her own little underground world!'

'When I asked you to tie this case up once and for all, never in a month of Sundays did I think that it would end like this!'

311

As Jackman reached for the door handle, Ruth Crooke added, 'I forgot to mention, Chief Superintendent Cade is moving to another county, somewhere out near the Welsh borders, I believe.'

Jackman froze, his hand still gripping the cold brass handle. 'He's getting out of it! The bastard!'

'I never heard that, Rowan. But it's the best we could hope for.'

It wasn't the best that he could have hoped for. Jackman had hoped that the evil sod would be hung out as food for the vultures. 'How did he manage that?' he asked through gritted teeth.

'He declared to the investigating officers that he had deliberately infiltrated the club in the hopes of bringing in the men at the top. He said that you and your team ruined his undercover operation.'

Jackman swallowed hard and felt his cheeks grow hot. 'But there was hard evidence! Forensic evidence. Photographs, witnesses.'

'Nothing that would hold up in court. And some of the things that you mentioned don't seem to exist anymore.' Ruth seemed to deflate as he watched. 'He is a powerful man, and a dangerous one, Rowan. As I said, the outcome is the best that we could hope for, and I suggest you leave well alone.'

Jackman thought about how devastated Marie would be at the news. He quietly said, 'So some other poor innocents in a different area get the benefit of his filthy attentions?'

'Maybe not.' The super smiled like the Mona Lisa. 'He's not the only one with friends in high — and low — places.' The smile broadened. 'I have taken it upon myself to put a few influential people *in the know*, so to speak. If you check the *Police Gazette*, I would be expecting to see news of an early retirement in the next few weeks. It's not the result you would have liked, Rowan, I know. And it's far from what he deserves, but at least it will remove him from a position of influence on the force. It's the most I can achieve without opening Pandora's Box.'

Jackman relaxed his grip on the door handle. He knew how things worked. 'Thank you, ma'am.'

'My pleasure, believe me.'

* * *

Marie listened to what Jackman had to say, then gave him a resigned smile. 'I should have known that whatever I did it wouldn't be enough. Not with a snake like that.'

'If Ruth Crooke is true to her word, and I believe she will be, that man will not be able to glance out of a window without spotting someone from Vice looking back at him.'

'I hope he burns in hell.'

'Ditto,' said Jackman, picking up his phone. 'Gary? Yes . . . yes . . . Right! Excellent, we'll see you in ten.'

He stood up. 'Asher has regained consciousness and he wants to see us.'

They ran down to the yard, and in less than ten minutes were looking down at the sleeping form of Asher Leyton.

'The doctors say he is very lucky,' Gary whispered. 'The damage was not as severe as first thought, and since he woke up all he has done is ask about his sister.'

'Which one? Elizabeth or Fleur?' asked Marie.

'Kenya. He says that she is his baby sister.'

They sat at the bedside, waiting for Asher to wake up.

Jackman grinned at Gary. 'We've been told that Harlan Marsh Police Station has hung out the bunting and is planning a massive party now that Cade has gone. But I was rather hoping that you might like to stay on here in Saltern-le-Fen?'

Gary broke into a smile. 'Really?'

'There is a place for you in our team, if you'd like it?'

Before Gary could answer, Asher moaned and opened his eyes.

'She is safe, Asher,' Jackman said softly. 'Kenya is being cared for, and she's perfectly safe now.'

Tears fell from the young man's eyes. 'That's good, that's good.'

'She says you saved her. Is that right?'

Asher gave an almost imperceptible nod.

'From Toby?'

'He found her playing on a beach. He brought her back to Windrush, but I saw him.' Asher swallowed loudly.

'So you took her and hid her away?'

'My sister Fleur died, and I missed her so much. I was only a baby but I remembered her and I always loved her. She had such a terrible life. I thought that the same was going to happen to Kenya, and I couldn't let that happen, could I?'

Tears flooded down his cheeks. One of the nurses bustled in, declaring that her patient should rest.

Jackman stood up. 'We've heard enough.'

'I'm so tired,' yawned Marie.

'I'm exhausted,' Gary added.

'Is it any wonder?' Jackman shook his head. 'Who in their right mind would choose to do this job?'

'We would!' said Marie and Gary in unison.

Jackman just nodded.

# EPILOGUE

Jackman and Marie walked across the marsh at Roman Creek. Apart from the wind rustling the reeds and the cries of the seabirds, all was quiet. No one sang beneath the ground, and no one ever would again. The tunnel had been sealed, closed up forever by experts using a very large amount of hardcore, best-quality cement.

'I cannot believe that a year has gone by, can you?' Marie pushed a hand through her thick chestnut, windblown hair.

'I don't know about that. All I know is that I'm still wading through the sodding paperwork.' Jackman looked back to where the brooding old Victorian Gothic house called Windrush had once looked out over the marsh towards the Wash.

Jackman leant back against an old weather-worn cattle trough and gazed out to where the horizon met the sky. 'Speaking about reports, Ruth Crooke heard from CID at Harlan Marsh just before we came out. One of their crews had a shout to a small fire in a deserted old public house on the edge of the marsh. When they broke in, guess what they found?'

'Go on, surprise me.'

Jackman smiled. 'Let me just say that the beer cellar had been used for other purposes.' He gave a little nod of satisfaction. 'The last missing link, I believe. It completely ties in with Toni Clarkson's description of the place she and Emily were abducted from. Forensics will confirm, but it's almost certainly the missing drinking club venue.'

Marie grinned. 'I knew we'd find it one day! Well, it's taken a while, but now that whole nasty episode is finally sewn up.'

Jackman smiled grimly. 'And about time too.' His eyes widened. 'But hey! Have you seen the memo regarding Asher Leyton?'

Marie puffed out her cheeks, 'Now if ever there was an argument for karma, that's it. A man with a serious addiction to risky sex takes a bullet in the head, against all the odds he survives, only to find that he has totally lost his libido! If he wasn't partially paralysed and spending a very long time in a secure psychiatric hospital, it would be really funny.'

'Something the report didn't mention was the fact that Kenya was encouraged to write to him. Grace Black told me. It was decided that if all ties were severed, she would have to go through a full-blown grieving process, and on top of everything else, it could have been the straw that broke the camel's back. So she writes.'

'Well, she's confirmed what he told us about saving her from his psychopath brother, Toby. Asher seemed to lose touch with reality at that stage. If he'd gone to the police, he'd have been a hero.'

'And his brother would have been locked up in a tiny space, just like when he was a child. Asher couldn't let that happen again, and although I'm sure he'll never tell us, I think he saw an opportunity to try to recreate the perfect childhood with Kenya, something he never had with his real brothers and sisters. Grace says she signs her letters, "Little Sis," and I think he honestly wanted for them both to be happy, to be a proper little family. I believe that is why he never touched her.'

'Sounds about right, as long as he got his jollies elsewhere. The evidence that was taken from her room showed lots of children's games for two, all well-worn and apparently well-loved. He taught her to read, for heaven's sake! And from the waste left there, it looks as if he even tried to make sure she ate well.'

'And they did go outside sometimes, Kenya confirmed that. It must have been when Micah was not working on Windrush, and when Asher knew that Toby was busy on his farm.'

'Sounds almost idyllic, if you ignore the fact that Grace Black and her family were torn to shreds by his actions. Her marriage failed and she lived in purgatory for all those years. He saved Kenya, and condemned her mother to hell on earth.'

'Which is why he is in secure psychiatric care.' Jackman frowned, 'It's a wonder that Philip never saw them. He said that he went out to Windrush every single day.'

'He spent his time below ground, and you wouldn't see the lodge house from the tunnel entrance. Asher would have been very careful indeed with his "little sister."'

Marie looked back towards the end of the marsh path. 'We've got visitors.'

Four figures were making their way towards them. 'I thought the team should all be together out here for one last look around.'

Marie looked at him. 'Why?'

'Wait for the others and I'll tell you.'

He watched as a black and white oyster-catcher winged its way low over the lagoons.

Marie waved at Max, Rosie, Charlie and Gary, trudging along the uneven path. Jackman and Marie noticed that Rosie and Max were holding hands.

'So where's the picnic?' asked Max. 'Boiled eggs and pork pies. Love them.'

'Sorry, guys, the pork pies are off. Will this do?' Jackman leaned down and took a bottle of champagne from a bag at his feet. He pulled out six clear plastic glasses and offered the bottle to Marie. 'You do the honours, Sergeant.'

When everyone had a drink in their hand, he raised his in a toast. 'To you all. I can't begin to thank you for all the work you've put in over the last twelve months.'

As the salty sea breeze caressed their faces, they touched glasses and drank.

'Why here, sir?' asked Rosie. 'I like fresh air and all that, but this usually happens in the CID room.'

'Because in a few months' time this area will be gone. This part of Roman Marsh is to become a marina. The old sanatorium site is to be razed to the ground, and Hobs End Marsh will be flooded to give waterway access to the new moorings and boatyard.'

'Best thing ever!' Gary exclaimed. 'This marsh has been a place of fear and death for far too long. My sister would have been thrilled.'

Suddenly Marie's eyes narrowed. 'Then someone has made a killing, so to speak, selling off all that land. Can I guess who it is?'

'You won't need a second guess. Benedict Broome is a very wealthy man.'

'Jammy git,' muttered Max. 'Still, you have to hand it to anyone who can come through something like that more or less unscathed.'

Unscathed? Jackman looked across the marsh and followed the flight path of some pink-footed geese. He remembered Philip Groves saying, "We are all damaged. We all have secrets, each one of us."

As they walked in comfortable silence back to the sea-bank, Jackman wondered about the "capable" Benedict Broome.

Philip had been their physician and their healer, but Benedict had been the one they turned to for answers. Benedict sorted the problems. Benedict found ways to provide for them, protect them, and bring them back to the fold.

So Benedict was the fixer. Which left only one mystery unsolved, as far as Jackman could make out. The murder of Charlotte and Simeon Mulberry. Had Benedict fixed that too?

Jackman breathed in the salty, ozone-laden air and shook his head. Maybe it was finally time to close the book, and let sleeping dogs lie.


## THE END

Thank you for reading this book. If you enjoyed it please leave feedback on Amazon or Goodreads, and if there is anything we missed or you have a question about then please get in touch. The author and publishing team appreciate your feedback and time reading this book.

Our email is office@joffebooks.com


www.joffebooks.com